THE IRISH WITCH

What could be the trouble that had caused
Georgina to send for Roger Brook so urgently?
Into whose hands had Susan and Charles
fallen? At first, the coupling of their names had
puzzled him, because he had believed Charles
to be with Wellington's army somewhere in
south-western France. But only through Charles
could Georgina have learned that from the
Pyrenees he had returned to Paris . . . Charles
could have sent her that information in a letter,
but it seemed more probable that, for some
reason, he had gone to England. But why
should the two people be in peril? And from
whom, or what?

BY DENNIS WHEATLEY

NOVELS

The Launching of Roger Brook
The Shadow of Tyburn Tree
The Rising Storm
The Man Who Killed the King
The Dark Secret of Josephine
The Rape of Venice
The Sultan's Daughter
The Wanton Princess
Evil in a Mask
The Ravishing of Lady
  Mary Ware

The Scarlet Impostor
Faked Passports
The Black Baroness
V for Vengeance
Come Into My Parlour
Traitors' Gate
They Used Dark Forces

The Prisoner in the Mask
The Second Seal
Vendetta in Spain
Three Inquisitive People
The Forbidden Territory
The Devil Rides Out
The Golden Spaniard
Strange Conflict
Codeword—Golden Fleece
Dangerous Inheritance
Gateway to Hell

The Quest of Julian Day
The Sword of Fate
Bill for the Use of a Body

Black August
Contraband
The Island Where Time Stands
  Still
The White Witch of the South
  Seas

To the Devil—a Daughter
The Satanist

The Eunuch of Stamboul
The Secret War
The Fabulous Valley
Sixty Days to Live
Such Power is Dangerous
Uncharted Seas
The Man Who Missed the War
The Haunting of Toby Jugg
Star of Ill-Omen
They Found Atlantis
The Ka of Gifford Hillary
Curtain of Fear
Mayhem in Greece
Unholy Crusade
The Strange Story of Linda Lee
The Irish Witch

SHORT STORIES

Mediterranean Nights   Gunmen, Gallants and Ghosts

HISTORICAL

A Private Life of Charles II (*Illustrated by Frank C. Papé*)
Red Eagle (*The Story of the Russian Revolution*)

AUTOBIOGRAPHICAL

Stranger than Fiction (*War Papers for the Joint Planning Staff*)
Saturdays with Bricks

SATANISM

The Devil and all his Works (*Illustrated in colour*)

Dennis Wheatley

THE IRISH WITCH

ARROW BOOKS

ARROW BOOKS LTD
3 Fitzroy Square, London W1

An imprint of the Hutchinson Publishing Group

London Melbourne Sydney Auckland
Wellington Johannesburg and agencies
throughout the world

First published by Hutchinson & Co (*Publishers*) Ltd 1973
Arrow edition 1975
Second impression 1975

© Dennis Wheatley Limited 1973

Made and printed in Great Britain
by The Anchor Press Ltd
Tiptree, Essex

ISBN 0 09 910440 7

For
PAT AND MARISE DERWENT
A small appreciation of their
many kindnesses to Joan,
myself and the children

Contents

1

Only a Few Days from Home

On the last morning of the year 1812, in the chapel of the
Royal Castle, Stockholm, Roger Brook married a girl
he had first met nearly two years earlier. She had then
been Lady Mary Ware.

When Roger had first become acquainted with his new
wife she had been staying at the British Legation in Lisbon as the guest of the Minister's niece, who had been
one of her friends at school. Lady Mary was an orphan
with no close relatives, and very little money; for her
father had been far from rich, and the greater part of his
income was entailed so had gone with the Earldom to
a distant cousin. Although no great beauty, little Mary had
a piquant charm, and Roger had found her both intelligent and amusing. But he had not had the faintest intention of marrying her.

That was not because she lacked fortune and influence,
as he had ample of both himself; and, when, having fallen
desperately in love with him, she had plucked up the
courage to ask him to make her his wife, he had told her
gently that it would be disastrous for them to marry,
because, for one thing, he was of an incurably roving disposition and, for another, as she was then only eighteen
and he was just over forty, he was much too old for her.

But he had come to Portugal only to collect a legacy

and, in fact, when he got home, intended to settle down
for good; for he had high hopes of at last within a few
years, marrying his adored Georgina, with whom he had
been in love all his life. She had returned his love, ever
since their teens; but a great part of his life, as Mr. Pitt's
most resourceful secret agent, had had to be spent abroad,
and it was not until the death of her last husband, the
Baron von Haugwitz, that she had been free to agree to
marry him.

Yet. alas, things had gone woefully wrong. In his
second identity as *Colonel Comte de Breuc*, one of Napoleon's A.D.C.s, he had again got caught up in the Emperor's affairs and sent to Germany. In Berlin he had
been falsely accused of the murder of Von Haugwitz, and
condemned to death. A reprieve had led instead to
several months in prison, but meanwhile Georgina had
had seemingly incontestable evidence that he had been
executed. Desperately distressed, and no longer caring
what became of her, the beautiful Georgina had agreed
to gratify the vanity of the old Duke of Kew by becoming
his Duchess.

On Roger's escape and return to England, grieved
beyond measure as the two life-long lovers were by this
situation, they at least had the consolation that the Duke
was in his mid-seventies and an habitually heavy drinker,
which made it highly probable that, within two or three
years at most, Georgina would again be a widow.

Alas for their hopes! When Roger got back from
Portugal, he learned that the old Duke had had a stroke.
Copious bleedings by his doctors had failed to revive or
kill him, and his consumption of alcohol was now strictly
limited. So the final opinion of the doctors was that he
might, as a paralysed vegetable, live on into his nineties.

Faced now with the possibility that, for years to come,

the lovers would be able to enjoy each other's company only when Georgina came up to London for the season, and for a few odd nights during the rest of the year, Georgina had urged Roger to marry again. He had been averse to doing so, but after a few months living on his own at Thatched House Lodge in Richmond Park—a grace and favour residence of which Mr. Pitt had given him a life tenancy—he had become so bored that he had agreed to go on a secret mission to the Crown Prince Bernadotte of Sweden. Bernadotte had persuaded him to go on as his emissary to the Czar, and that had led to his once more becoming involved with Napoleon, then in Moscow.

It was in October 1812 that, to Roger's amazement, he had again run into Mary, in St. Petersburg. On her return to London from Lisbon having no social background and very little money; she had married a merchant in the Baltic Trade, named Wicklow, and went to live in the City with him. Napoleon's Continental System had damaged British trade with Russia so severely that Mr. Wicklow was one of many who got into financial difficulties. As a last resort he had sold his house and possessions in London and, taking Mary with him, sailed on a final venture with goods for St. Petersburg. In the Gulf of Helsingfors his ship had been wrecked and he lost everything. After living on his wits for a while in the Russian capital, he had committed suicide, leaving poor Mary friendless and deeply in debt.

She was in such dire straits that Roger had not had the heart to leave her there; so resorted to the desperate expedient of taking her back to Moscow with him, in boy's clothes and in the rôle of his soldier servant. There had followed the terrible retreat in which Napoleon left half a million men behind him to die in the snow.

During those many ghastly weeks, Mary shared with
Roger every type of danger and privation. Her unfailing
fortitude and good humour had turned his affection for
her into a much deeper feeling; so when at last they
escaped into Sweden, he decided that, since he could not
marry Georgina, he would never find a more loving wife
than little Mary.

His abiding love for Georgina remained unaltered.
Over the long years the unity of their hearts had impelled
them to disregard the marriages that both had made, and
between his long absences from England as a secret agent
they had always renewed their passionate attachment.

That this would be so again he was well aware but, in
spite of it, he was confident that he could make Mary
happy. The dangerous life he had led ever since his youth
had made him a past master of dissimulation. He would
see to it that she never knew of the occasional nights of
sweet delirium that he spent with Georgina and, for the
first time in the seventeen years since he had lost his wife
Amanda, his charming grace and favour residence,
Thatched House Lodge, would again become a true home
for him. Mary had been there once, loved it, and was
eagerly looking forward to becoming its mistress.

He felt certain, too, that she would also delight in the
children when they came to stay—although they were no
longer children. When he had last seen his daughter,
Susan, she had been sixteen and rapidly becoming a lovely
young woman; while Charles, Earl of St. Ermins, Georgina's son, must by now have left Eton and be a handsome young buck about town.

On arriving in Stockholm after their escape from
Russia. Roger had learned one piece of news that filled
him with considerable anxiety. Although, under pressure
from Napoleon, Sweden was officially at war with Britain,

by mutual consent no hostilities were taking place. Commerce between the two countries was at a standstill but the ships of the United States were filling the gap by carrying goods between them, and Roger had supposed that he and Mary would have no difficulty in securing passages in one of them to an English port.

To his dismay he was told that America was now also at war with Britain. Although war had been declared by the United States as long ago as June 18th, when news of it reached Russia it had been regarded as so relatively unimportant compared to the great war on the Continent that few people, either in St. Petersburg or with Napoleon's army, knew about it; so Roger had not even heard a rumour of what afterwards became known as 'The War of 1812'.

At first this new situation caused him considerable worry about how he and Mary were to get home. But when he consulted the Crown Prince Bernadotte, the latter swiftly reassured him by saying, 'Be not the least concerned, my friend. The British need our goods as much as we do theirs; so they turn a blind eye to American ships entering their ports, and you will find plenty of skippers in Gothenburg willing to run you over.'

It was in this happy frame of mind that, on January 5th, Roger left Stockholm with Mary. It was just a year since he had arrived there on his secret mission to the Crown Prince. But his status was now very different. He had come there in his rôle of *Colonel Comte de Breuc,* giving out that he had recently escaped from a prisoner-of-war camp in England. To make his story credible he had had with him only the clothes he stood up in, and travelled the two hundred and fifty miles from Gothenburg to Stockholm in a stuffy diligence. Now he left with a charming wife and an ample wardrobe, as Britain's unofficial Ambassador and the honoured friend of the Crown Prince, who had placed one of the Royal sledges at their disposal.

With frequent relays of horses, the drive along the well-kept highway, the snow on which was regularly cleared into lofty banks on either side, naturally made the journey much quicker, so they arrived in Gothenburg on the 7th. There were several American traders in the harbour. Learning that one, the *Cape Cod,* was due to sail for Hull in two days' time, Roger went aboard to interview her master, Captain Absolom.

He proved to be a stocky, fair-haired New Englander, abrupt of speech but not discourteous, and readily agreed a price to take Roger and Mary across the North Sea.

Roger was much relieved at this, as he had needed no telling about the cause of the war, since the Americans had been threatening hostilities for several years past, and he feared that he might meet with a certain amount of hostility.

The trouble arose from what was known as the British 'Navigation System'. This had been initiated as far back as Stuart times, the policy on which the System was based being that, as Britain was vulnerable to invasion only from the sea, her shipping must greatly exceed that of any other nation—not for commercial reasons, but so that, in the event of war, great numbers of seamen should be available for drafting into the Royal Navy.

As a result of this policy Britain had secured the great bulk of the carrying trade of the world. As far back as 1728, of the four thousand two hundred-odd ships arriving in her principal ports of London, Liverpool and Bristol, fewer than four hundred and forty had been under foreign flags; and in 1792, when the present war against France had started, there were eighty thousand trained seamen in

British ships. By lowering the percentage of Britons legally required to serve in merchant ships to one in four, fifty thousand more had become available to man warships.

Another principle of British maritime policy was that it was forbidden to import any goods into her Colonies except in British-built ships. And even when, after the war in the 1770s, the United States had gained their independence, British control over their shipping had remained indistinguishable in practice from what it had been in Colonial days.

However, the Americans being mainly of British stock, large numbers of them had the sea in their blood. Moreover, they had better timber for building ships than even that to be procured in England. In the forty years following Independence, this had resulted in their creating a merchant marine second in size only to that of Britain.

Between 1792 and 1805 this had proved to the advantage of both Britain and France, as both countries had had to reduce their merchant fleets in order to increase their navies, and American merchantmen had filled the gap by carrying much-needed supplies, mostly from the Caribbean. It had also, of course, greatly increased the wealth of the United States.

The first cause for complaint by the United States had arisen in May 1805 when, in the test case of the ship *Essex,* it had been ruled by a British Court that American ships should not be allowed to carry goods from the West Indies to a country at war with Britain, unless they had been 'neutralised' by first landing their cargo in a United Kingdom port—and unloading, warehousing and reloading caused most annoying delays and loss of profit to American merchants.

But the real trouble was started by Napoleon's Berlin Decree of 1806, reinforced by his Decree of Milan in 1807, whereby he established his Continental System, the object of which was to ruin British commerce by closing to British goods the ports of all the countries he controlled. That did not seriously affect the Americans, but what followed did.

In retaliation, in the winter of 1806-1807, the British issued Orders in Council, decreeing a blockade of the ports of France and her allies and forbidding neutral vessels to enter such ports unless they had first called at British ports and paid British dues on their cargo.

As the United States could not conform to both the French and British decrees, their ships henceforth risked confiscation by one or the other; but, having no Navy capable of protecting their shipping, all they could do was angrily to declare the decrees of both countries contrary to International Law.

Another matter to which the Americans took extreme umbrage was the treatment of the seamen in their ships by the Royal Navy. A high proportion of the men in the Navy were normally fishermen and others from the seaport towns who had been seized by the press gangs and forced to serve in warships. Understandably, many of them deeply resented this, and took the first opportunity to desert in neutral ports or those of the West Indies. To earn a living, they then signed on as seamen in American traders. As a means of countering this very serious drain on naval manpower, the Admiralty had issued orders that His Majesty's ships encountering United States merchantmen at sea should halt, board them, have their crews paraded and take off any men of British nationality.

To carry out this order justly proved no easy matter, for on reaching America, many deserters had secured forged papers, alleging them to be United States citizens. On close questioning by British Captains it frequently emerged that the men concerned were really British. But, in numerous cases, men who were in fact Americans had been called liars and taken off to serve in British warships. Of the six thousand two hundred and fifty-seven men so removed from United States ships, between 1801 and 1812, it cannot be doubted that at least several hundreds had been illegally impressed, and this had led to ever-increasing antagonism to Britain. The practice had aroused a crisis of indignation when, in June 1807, the British frigate *Leopard* had actually fired on the American frigate *Chesapeake,* forced her to surrender and removed four of her sailors.

But from 1801 to 1809 Thomas Jefferson, who had played a leading part in securing American Independence, had been President of the United States, and he was a man of peace. He was strongly opposed to further federalization of the States of the Union, so was averse to forming a national Army and Navy, and was determined at all costs to preserve neutrality. In consequence, the only action Jefferson took was to instruct Monroe, then United States Ambassador in London, to inform the British Government that all British armed vessels in United States ports were to be recalled at once and would in future be prohibited from entering them.

In 1809, James Madison—another founding-father of the Republic, and responsible more than any other man for the framing of the Constitution—had succeeded Jefferson as President. Unlike his predecessor, Madison was a strong Federalist but, even so, he did little to unite or increase the Militia of the several states or to strengthen their Naval forces. In fact in January 1812 a Bill put forward in favour of declaring war on Britain, for the provision of more frigates and the creation of a dockyard, was actually defeated.

In May 1812, the British Prime Minister, Perceval, was assassinated, and succeeded by Lord Liverpool. Castlereagh remained Foreign Secretary and continued his policy of politely ignoring American complaints, as neither he nor his colleagues could believe that the United States would go to the length of declaring war and that, even if they did, the five thousand or so troops stationed in Canada would be amply sufficient to protect that country from invasion.

In consequence, Roger had been very surprised to learn from Bernadotte that, after so many years of resentful inactivity, the United States had actually opened hostilities the previous summer. He had also immediately assumed that this would make it very much more difficult for Mary and himself to get back to England. But Bernadotte had at once reassured him by saying :

'The United States Navy is so insignificant that, according to my latest information, the British have so far virtually ignored it; and at sea the situation is little different from what it was a year ago. The only difference the state of war has made is that, on such voyages, the American merchant ships now sail under flags of neutral countries. I feel sure you will meet with no difficulty in finding a Captain who will give you and your lady passage.'

And so it had proved. On January 9th Roger and Mary went aboard the *Cape Cod,* which sailed a few hours later, flying the flag of Mexico, carrying a cargo of iron ore, of which Britain was in constant need for the manufacture of cannon and cannon-balls.

The two-bunk cabin they were given was small but clean and, for times when the weather was too inclement for them to sit up on deck, they had the use of the Captain's more roomy day-cabin in the stern of the ship.

Fond as Roger was of Mary, he had not been altogether

happy about her while in Stockholm and Gothenburg. Apart from her schooling at an Academy for Young Ladies, she had few of the graces that went normally with the status of her birth. That was hardly surprising, as her brief married life with Mr. Wicklow had accustomed her to the habits and outlook of well-to-do traders which, in those days, were very different from the attitudes of the aristocracy. In company also he found her to be somewhat gauche, but he hoped that this awkwardness and lack of sophisticated humour would soon wear off when he had introduced her to London society. Moreover, while he could not help feeling flattered by her absorption in himself, he felt her tendency to show resentment, if left on her own, even for an hour, distinctly irritating, as he did her scarcely-hidden jealousy if he showed the least interest in any other woman. But he made allowances for the fact that while in Russia she had had him entirely to herself for so long, and felt reasonably confident that her jealous possessiveness would wear off after they had been mixing with his friends in London for a few weeks; and he was so looking forward to being home again at last that he gave little thought to Mary's passionate obsession with him. Once home he would at long last be able to settle down, and enjoy a life of leisure, free from danger.

2

A Bitter Blow

On their first evening at sea, when they went down to Captain Absolom's state cabin for dinner, they found that he had one other passenger, who was introduced as Mr. Silas van Wyck. He was a fine-looking, ruddy-faced, middle-aged American of Dutch descent, well-dressed and with pleasant manners. They soon learned that he was a merchant and that his family had traded in woollen goods with England for several generations, so he had excellent business connections in Yorkshire and intended to pick up a cargo of woollen goods in Hull for the return voyage to Sweden.

As Roger had heard so little about this new war in which Britain was engaged, he was eager to learn from the Americans how it was progressing. Captain Absolom's natural interest in the effect of the war at sea led him to reply to Roger's questions.

'We folks are in such a poor way for naval craft that there's little we can do against you English. When trouble started, way back in '07, we had only twelve frigates. Mr. Jefferson did nothin' to better matters. He even allowed three of those to rot at their moorings. We've not a single ship-o'-the-line, and last year there were built only two eighteen-gun sloops and two sixteen-gun brigs.'

'Nevertheless,' put in Mr. van Wyck, 'we're a thorn in

the side of the British. Seven years have passed since Trafalgar and in that time Boney's many naval yards from Copenhagen round to Venice have been far from idle. He has again a powerful fleet at his disposal, and Britain needs all the ships she has to keep his squadrons in their ports. Every sail she despatches across the Atlantic to blockade us renders her more vulnerable to her great enemy.'

'Aye,' agreed the Captain. 'Yer right in that, Sir. And to blockade us effectively she'd need to send many more ships than she dare afford. In the Indies and along our southern coast where clement weather mostly prevails she can bottle us up in our ports. But not in the north. No, Sir! The New England coast has rugged shores and is subject to tempestuous weather. The elements there are our friends and render it impossible for British squadrons to keep station. From Boston, Narragansett and New York our frigates be free to come an' go much as they will, and have roved far out into the ocean, even as far as Madeira and the English Channel. On these voyages our principal Captains: Decatur, Bainbridge and John Rogers, have had good success interfeerin' with British commerce. There have, too, been several actions by our ships against vessels of the Royal Navy.'

'How did they fare in these encounters?' Roger enquired with interest.

'Toward the end of August Captain Isaac Hull, in *Constitution*, come up with the British frigate *Guerrière*, and give her a rare pasting. Dismasted her and holed her with thirty shot below the water line. She hauled down her flag and was so bad damaged that come mornin' they had to take off the prisoners and sink her.'

'To be fair,' remarked van Wyck, 'it should be stated that, although 'tis said Captain Hull handled *Constitution* in a most creditable manner, she had a broadside weighing seven hundred and thirty-six pounds against the *Guerrière's* five hundred and seventy; so an advantage of thirty per cent over the British ship.'

"Tis true; but our sloop *Wasp* had no such advantage in her fight with the brig *Frolic*. They bombarded each other till both were near wrecks, yet 'twas the American who boarded the Britisher an' forced her to surrender. That *Wasp* was later robbed of her prize and taken herself by a British ship-o'-the-line coming on the scene was just durned bad luck. In October, too, Captain Decatur's *United States* bashed and captured the *Macedonian,* although there agin I'll admit that the American was much the more powerful o' the two.'

'It seems then,' Mary smiled, 'that although we lost both the *Guerrière* and *Macedonian*, the honours due to Captains and crews were not uneven.'

'What of the war on land?' Roger asked.

Van Wyck shook his head, 'There again we are paying the price of our lack of preparation. When Mr. Madison succeeded Jefferson as President, our army numbered fewer than seven thousand, and Madison was shockingly tardy in making our country ready for war. 'Twas not until last January a Bill was passed authorising an increase up to thirty-five thousand. When last I heard, not half that number had been raised, and our forces must still consist mainly of raw recruits. There are also other factors that render it anything but formidable. Close on forty years have elapsed since our War of Independence, so very few of our troops have had any experience of war. Again, owing to Jefferson's intense antipathy to closer Federation, the Militia in one State is not compelled to serve in any other. By now the law may have been altered, but to begin with it made the concentration of any considerable force on the Canadian frontier out of the question.'

'How have matters so far gone there?'

'Badly for my country, Mr. Brook. As I just now re-marked, it is over half a life time since American soldiers were called on to fight a more capable enemy than tribes of Indians. For senior officers who had any experience of a white man's war we could call only on men who were no more than youngsters during our War of Independence and are now in their sixties. The command of the north-eastern front, from Niagara to Boston, was given to Major General Henry Dearborn, and the north-western, consist-ing mainly of the isthmus between Lakes Erie and Huron, to Brigadier William Hull, uncle to Captain Hull of the *Constitution*.

'These two greyheads—one might say amateurs at war—were pitted against a most redoubtable opponent, the Lieutenant-General of Upper Canada, Isaac Brock, with his British regulars. General Brock is only forty-two and a master of his trade. He at once seized the initiative.

'Realising the importance of gaining allies among the Indian tribes by persuading them that they would be on the winning side, he at once despatched a detachment of two hundred troops and four hundred Indians to the nar-rows between Lakes Huron and Michigan. They took our garrison there at Fort Mackinac by surprise, captured it and so secured Brock's western flank.

'Our first attack was launched in the Niagara area which lies between Lake Ontario and Lake Erie. It seems that Brock foresaw that would be so and, as the British had a strong superiority of armed vessels on both lakes, felt confident that he could hold it. So he sent his main force down to the western end of Lake Erie and strongly reinforced the garrisons at Fort Malden and Amhurst-burg.

'Meanwhile, Hull had brought his force up the Maumee river to Frenchtown on the shore of the lake. From there, intending to reinforce Detroit, he rashly sent ahead of him a ship carrying his baggage and papers. The British captured it, and sent the papers to Brock. Undeterred by this calamity, Hull, still more rashly, crossed into Canada and based himself on Sandwich with the intention of laying siege to Fort Malden.

'All this happened in mid-July, but it was well into August before he could get his artillery into position and begin the siege. By then Brock who, incidentally, had served under Wellington at Copenhagen, had arrived on the scene, and soon forced Hull to retreat on Detroit. By the 16th of the month Brock had surrounded that important town and forced Hull to capitulate with his whole army of two thousand five hundred men.'

Although it was a British victory, Mary could not forbear to exclaim sympathetically, 'Oh, how terrible for the poor man!'

'It was, indeed,' van Wyck agreed. 'But it was due to his own folly and over-confidence. That same month, too, our attempts to invade Canada on the Niagara front and north from Lake Champlain both failed.'

' 'Tis true our armies took a beating,' put in Captain Absolom, 'but our seamen on the lakes showed better mettle.'

Van Wyck nodded. 'Yes, in their encounters they have shown themselves the equals of the British; although at first it went hard with them. Captain Chauncy was given command of our few ships on the lakes and planned to build others. He sent a hundred and forty shipwrights and over a hundred cannon up to Sacketts Harbour, which lies at no great distance from our side of the entrance to the St. Lawrence river. Unfortunately, his choice of place was too close. Opposite it lies the considerable town of Kingston. Ships from there were able to fire upon the building yard, so drove the shipwrights to abandon their work.'

'Aye, Sir,' put in Absolom, 'but Lieutenant Elliot proved a wiser man in choosing Squaw Island. Behind it he built two three-hundred-tonners, then proved himself a real hero.'

With a smile van Wyck turned to Roger. 'Captain Absolom is right in that. We may well be proud of young Elliot. Early in October two British armed brigs crossed the lake from Fort Malden and anchored off Fort Erie. At one o'clock in the morning of the 9th, Elliot took a hundred seamen in two longboats. At 3 a.m. he brought them alongside the brigs and boarded them, capturing both with hardly a shot fired.'

Roger returned the smile and, as a courtesy, raised his glass. 'That was the real Nelson touch. Here's a health to him.'

When they had drunk he said, 'I take it that by then winter was closing in, so put an end to the campaigning season?'

After a moment van Wyck admitted, a shade reluctantly, 'There was one more major engagement. At dawn on October 13th a large force under General Van Reusselaer attempted to seize the heights of Kingston, at the head of Lake Ontario. Six hundred regular troops took the heights, then General Brock arrived with reinforcements from Fort George, but was killed in the first charge he led. Such a disaster for the British should have given us a certain victory. We were robbed of it by the cowardice of our own people. The regiments of unseasoned recruits who should have supported the attack refused to cross the river. In consequence, Van Reusselaer and the brave men with him were driven from the cliff down to the river, and there compelled to surrender.'

'A sad business,' Roger commented. 'And, although your force lost the battle, from all you have told me the loss of such a brilliant Commander may well prove an even more serious blow to us.'

By this time the *Cape Cod* had passed the point of Denmark and entered the Skagerrak, so she was pitching in a medium rough sea. Roger, who had always been a bad sailor, had already begun to feel queasy, so he excused himself and went with Mary to their cabin.

He managed to keep down his dinner and got through the night, but by midday next day the weather had worsened and he suffered his first bout of sea-sickness in the *Cape Cod*. Fortunately, Mary proved to be a good sailor, so was able to look after and comfort him as best she could by telling him that Captain Absolom had said that, if the present favourable wind held, they would reach Hull within two or, at the most, three more days.

It was on the following afternoon that the *Cape Cod* met with another American merchantman, and the two Captains exchanged news through loud-hailers. At the time Roger was still in his cabin but feeling better; so, half-an-hour later, he went up on deck to get some fresh air.

While leaning over the gunwale on the poop with Mary, he noticed that below them, amidships, Captain Absolom was conferring with a group of men which included his two mates, Silas van Wyck, the bosun and the supercargo. A few minutes later the group broke up, the Captain came up on to the poop and shouted several orders. These resulted in the ship changing course from southwest to north.

Van Wyck had followed the Captain up on to the

poop. Looking far from happy, he walked over to the Brooks, and Roger asked, 'What means it that the ship has been put about?'

'It means bad news for you both,' the American replied, 'and for myself, as I'll incur a serious financial loss. So, too, will many British merchants. The ship Captain Absolom spoke with a while back gave us most unwelcome tidings. The British Government recently decided to cut off their noses to spite their faces. They have now decreed a complete blockade against all United States ships, under whatever flag they may be flying. Do we enter Hull, or any other English port, the *Cape Cod* will be impounded and her crew become prisoners of war.'

'Surely you do not mean . . .' Roger gasped.

'I do, and can only condole with you. At the meeting amidships just held, Captain Absolom spoke with the senior members of his crew. They were of the unanimous opinion that even to lie off some small port and unload our cargo by lighter would now be too great a risk. So the *Cape Cod* will keep to the open ocean and head for her home port, New York.'

3

A Lovers' Quarrel

A LITTLE before midday on the day when Roger and
Mary were married in Stockholm, a handsome young
man was sitting on the side of the bed of a very pretty
girl, who was staying at his town mansion in Berkeley
Square.

The girl had auburn hair and fine blue eyes. Her name
was Susan, and she was Roger Brook's daughter. She had
been presented at Court the previous season and was just
over seventeen.

Her companion was Charles, Earl of St. Ermins. He
had inherited the tall figure and dark good looks of his
ancestor, King Charles II, and was some six months older
than the girl. His mother was Georgina, now, by a later
marriage, Duchess of Kew.

Georgina and Roger had been life-long lovers; but,
as a secret agent, he had spent much the greater part of
the past twenty years abroad. In consequence, as Roger's
wife Amanda had died when giving birth to Susan,
Georgina had played the part of a mother to her. She had
shared a nursery with little Charles and they had been
brought up as brother and sister, sharing every joy,
anxiety, distress and naughty prank.

Both had long held the opinion that neither could be
equalled by any contemporary of the other sex and, at the

age of twelve, they had secretly and solemnly become engaged. Neither of them had ever referred since to the matter, but both took it for granted that in due course they would marry and, after greeting Susan in her bedroom that morning, Charles had given her, if not a lover's kiss, something very near it.

That night Georgina was giving a New Year's Eve ball for them. For a few minutes they talked of a new dress that Susan meant to wear, then Charles said, a shade nervously :

'M'dear. I hate to break it to you, but you will have to choose another partner for the supper dance tonight.'

Susan's blue eyes opened wide and she exclaimed, 'What mean you? I fail to understand. We always have the supper dance together.'

'I know it and am much distressed.'

'Oh, come, Charles ! We agreed long since that both of us should amuse ourselves with such flirts as we wished. And you've made no secret of it that your latest is that Irish wench, Lady Luggala's daughter—what is her name?—yes, Jemima. Surely you do not intend to break our custom on her account ?'

'No, no !' He shook his head. 'I find Jemima most amusing company, for she is witty and no prude. But I'd not cut a supper dance with you for any woman. 'Tis that after we have seen the New Year in I have another party that I have promised to attend.'

Susan frowned. 'A party of what kind?'

'It is with friends I made whilst in London during the autumn. It is a very special occasion for them, otherwise I would not desert you.'

'Dam'me, I don't believe you.' Her voice rose angrily. 'Naught but a woman could induce you to throw me over in this way.'

'Nay, you are wrong in that. There will be women there, of course, but no-one to whom I am especially attracted. It is, in fact, just a club that provides unusual diversions in which I have become interested.'

'A club indeed! What sort of club? Charles, be honest. Is it that, now we are again in London, you mean to explore the pleasures of a brothel?'

He bridled. 'No. This is no brothel. Though had I no prospect of relieving the emotions you arouse in me with some attractive woman, I'd not hesitate to go to one. Anyone of my age needs such an outlet from time to time. I told you last summer how I had first achieved man's estate with Mama's maid Harriet, and before she married our coachman last month enjoyed her a number of times. I told you, too, how I paid a midnight visit to Lady Wessex's bedroom while she was staying with us at Stillwaters over Christmas. In neither case did you show any undue perturbation, so why question my actions now?'

This was true enough. Susan had accepted the canons of her day and age that, from their late teens men were entitled to seek sexual satisfaction where they would, whereas girls of good family were required to remain chaste until they married. Then, if it was a love match, a wife could expect her husband to remain faithful to her, at least for a few years. Later perhaps both might seek pastures new, but in all other ways remain loyal to each other. Knowing that she aroused Charles's desires, she had felt it would be unreasonable to object to his satisfying his physical passions with other women; but only with the proviso that she retained his love.

And now that was the crux of the matter. For Charles to be slipping away from a ball given in his own house seemed to her a certain indication that he had started an affair with some woman, and had become so enamoured that he could not bring himself to refuse her demand to celebrate the New Year by sleeping with her. To probe the matter further, she asked :

'This club you speak of, with its unusual diversions. What form do they take ?'

'That I cannot tell you,' he replied. 'I have been sworn to secrecy.'

Tears started to her eyes. 'Charles, you're lying to cover up an intrigue. Are we now, after all these years, to start having secrets from each other ?'

'That is the last thing I would wish,' he protested, then tried to take her hand. But she snatched it from him.

Hesitantly he said, 'I pray you bear with me in this. Although I am bound to secrecy about what takes place, I can at least give you some idea of the type of gathering I mean to attend. Have you ever heard of the Hell Fire Club ?'

She nodded. 'I've heard vague talk of it. Back in the last century, statesmen and other prominent men used to meet on an island up the Thames. There was a ruined abbey there, in which they performed strange rites and copulated with women whom they imported for that purpose.'

'You are right. And it is to a revival of the Hell Fire Club that I belong. I find the secrets of the occult that are disclosed to me there most fascinating.'

'And, no doubt, the woman you are taking with you.'

'I am taking no-one. We draw lots for the women who are to partner us in the rituals.'

Forcing back her tears, Susan cried angrily, 'Charles, I do not believe you ! For you to have bedded pretty Harriet and Lady Wessex was no shame. But to pleasure any slut that is thrust upon you is a very different matter. I do not believe that you would so demean yourself. All this is a tissue of lies designed to cover the fact that you love me no longer and have become besotted by some woman who insists that you sleep with her tonight. Very well then, do so. But what is sauce for the goose is sauce for the gander.'

Charles came to his feet with a jerk and stared down at her in horror. 'Susan! Susan, you cannot possibly mean. . . .'

'Why not?' she retorted sharply. 'Surely you are aware that on reaching their teens girls are subject to the same urges as young men? Since I came out last season, half a dozen handsome beaux have implored me to give them a rendezvous. For your sake I have kept my virginity, but I'll admit that their petting has oft excited me. Why should I now deny myself the delights which several of my young married friends unashamedly extol?'

'But, Susan! You are a girl of good family. How can you possibly contemplate lowering yourself by taking a lover?'

'Lowering myself, fiddlesticks! What of your Mama? Other mothers are oft stupid enough to keep their daughters in ignorance of such matters, but from the time I started to become a woman she has always talked to me frankly about the mating of the sexes. All the town knows that, whenever he is in England, my father is her lover; and, despite her marriages, has been for many years. Once when I pressed her, she confided to me that he first had her when they were both no more than fifteen.'

'I know it, for it was a revelation that you in turn confided to me. But, as you are well aware, my mother has gipsy blood, so she is an exception to the rule.'

'Rule be demned! Well-born girls are no less passionate than those of the lower orders. Why should we suppress our desires? Go, have your new love if you will tonight, but in future, should I feel inclined I too will indulge myself with any man who takes my fancy.'

Charles was appalled. He argued vehemently, and pleaded with her to change her mind, but in vain. At length, as she remained adamant, he said :

'Since you have now revealed to me that you crave physical love, why should we not get married this coming Spring?'

She shook her auburn curls. 'I would like to, but I am convinced that we should rue it later.'

'Why so?'

'Because, Charles, you are still too young. I will now admit that the thought of your embracing Harriet with some frequency and then that older woman, pained me sorely, but I had good reason to conceal my feelings. Among other things your mother told me was that a wedding night can prove an unpleasant experience for the bride if she be still a virgin and, should the husband be a virgin too, the night may prove a disaster for them both. On the other hand, the more experienced the man, the sooner he will bring his bride to reciprocate his pleasure. You can as yet be only an amateur at this game, and must learn much from going to bed with a variety of women. I am resigned to that, and prepared to wait.'

'You are wrong about me, Susan. Harriet had had half a dozen lovers before me, so taught me much. And with Maria Wessex I did it no fewer than five times in a night. She complimented me upon having become as able a gallant as any woman could desire. That is proof that I've had experience enough. Now will you marry me?'

Again Susan shook her head. 'No, for there is another reason why I will not. I have always accounted fools girls who marry at sixteen or seventeen. By burdening themselves with the cares of a household and bearing children when so young, they deprive themselves of what should be some of the most pleasant years of their lives. I've long decided that nineteen, or eighteen at the earliest, is the age at which a girl should marry. I intend to enjoy at least one more London season free of all responsibility.'

Charles thoughtfully stroked his black side whiskers for a few moments. He had never allowed himself to take a liberty with Susan; but, now she had suddenly disclosed to him that her flesh and blood were just as warm as his own, he looked at her with new eyes. A trifle hesitantly he said :

'I'll agree there's sense in what you say about not saddling yourself for another year or two with the duties of a wife. But now that you have told me you feel an urge to take a lover, can we not come to a new arrangement? I would gladly give up the Hell Fire Club and vow absolute fidelity to you if you, for your part, would make me that most fortunate of men.'

She smiled at him. 'I've oft thought on that, and what bliss I would experience in your arms. But, alas, dear Charles, it cannot be. For one thing I could not bring myself to deceive your dear mother by having a hole-in-the-corner affair with you. For another it would spoil for us the joyous anticipation of becoming man and wife and of your possessing me for the first time as your bride. 'Tis better by far that you should get out of your system the craving I am convinced you have for some woman with whom you intend to sleep tonight, then amuse yourself with others for the next year or two. And that, while you are doing so, I should follow my own inclinations.'

He scowled. 'God dam'me! The thought of you being possessed by some other man would drive me crazy.'

'Charles, you are being foolish and making a mountain out of a molehill. Surely you must realise that love and passion are two entirely different things? The fact that you have become irresistibly attracted to some other woman does not mean that you love me, in the true meaning of the word, any the less. And, should I give myself to another man, that will not lessen in the least my enduring love for you. For both of us it will mean no more than the enjoyment of a delicious fruit, or the joy of outriding a companion whom one believed to be better mounted than oneself—a most pleasurable experience at the time, but forgotten in a week.'

Reluctantly he nodded. ' 'Tis an argument difficult to refute. I'll admit that since Harriet left us to marry, I have hardly given her a thought.'

'It will prove so, too, with your present infatuation and with other women whose bodies attract you for a while. Such physical contacts are of no real moment in one's life. What matters is the unity of minds, and that we have. The years we have spent together have forged between us an indestructible bond. 'Tis that, not casual fornication, that constitutes true love.'

He continued to frown. 'About the difference between love and passion you are unquestionably right. You are right, too, in maintaining that physically a girl of breeding must be subject to the same urges as a low-born wench. But, for the most part, the latter give themselves while still unmarried, either from lack of principles instilled when young, or to escape from poverty. You can plead neither excuse and, I repeat, the thought of you playing the wanton is positive torture to me.'

Susan shrugged. 'Do I decide to do so, you will have brought it on yourself. About you sowing your wild oats I make no complaint; but for you to have become a slave to some other woman—that I will not tolerate.'

'Dam'me! There is no other woman!'

'Prove it then by not leaving the house tonight.'

For a long moment Charles considered, then he said, 'No. This meeting is of great importance to me. Should I not attend it, I'd forfeit my membership of the club.'

'Go to it then, or rather her. And in future I'll do as I list. Now leave me, for I am overlate in beginning to make my *toilette*.'

'As you wish. But should I hear your name coupled with that of a gallant, I'll call him out and kill him.' Pale with anger, Charles turned away.

4

The New Hell Fire Club

SUSAN's revelation about her maturity gave Charles good cause for feeling both miserable and apprehensive. The Duke of Kew was his mother's fifth husband, and he had learnt from Harriet that, apart from her life-long affair with Roger his mother had taken many other lovers during the long periods Roger had been out of England. So, with his passionate half-gipsy blood on one side and that from the Merry Monarch on the other, he had accepted it as natural that his thoughts turned frequently to satisfying his amorous inclinations.

That auburn-haired Susan shared his disquieting cravings had never occurred to him. But thinking it over, he recalled what pretty Harriet had told him about Roger and his mother. She had a gift for painting and owned a studio out on the hill above Kensington village; but she used it also as a *petite maison* in which to spend nights of love-making with Roger. Both of them trusted Harriet and never bothered to stop talking when she was within earshot. Several times she had heard snatches of conversation when Roger was gaily describing affairs he had had while on the Continent. Harriet had concluded from this that he was 'the very devil with the women'. Should that be so, it could well account for his daughter Susan also being hot-blooded.

It was now clear to Charles beyond all doubt that he and Susan shared the same outlook about uninhibited immorality; but, while he had never questioned his own inclinations, he found it hard to reconcile himself to her giving free rein to hers. Even so, since she refused to marry him for at least a year, or become his mistress, he saw that he had no option but to accept her declaration that 'what was sauce for the goose was sauce for the gander'. No other course being open to him, he decided that he could only pray that she would not, after all, allow one of her beaux to seduce her; and, hard as it might be, do his utmost to put such a possibility out of his mind by keeping it occupied with his own diversions.

He had not lied to her when he had declared that he had not become temporarily bewitched by some other woman, and that it was a meeting of the re-created Hell Fire Club to which he was going that night.

For several generations past the occult had provided one of the principal interests of a large part of high society, in all the capitals of Europe. Such men as the Comte de St. German—who asserted that he possessed the secret of the Elixir of Life—Cagliostro and Casanova, had all intrigued many royalties and wealthy members of the nobility by holding seances and performing mystical rites. Where trickery ended and the application of unrecognised scientific laws began, no-one could say but, shortly before the French Revolution, Dr. Anton Mesmer had undoubtedly effected many cures by means of his magic tub.

In the previous October Charles had been in London for a week, to be measured and fitted by his tailor for some new clothes. It was then that a friend of his had introduced him at the revived Hell Fire Club. On that first visit he had been allowed only to witness the opening of a fascinating occult ceremony, and had his fortune told by a lovely woman who played the rôle of High Priestess.

Having then eagerly expressed his wish to be made a member, in mid-November he had thought of an excuse to go again to London, and had been duly initiated, the ceremony ending by his possessing the beautiful priestess-witch.

His lovely initiator then told him that he was now entitled to attend any of the meetings which were held once a week, and that there were five when attendance was obligatory: New Year's Eve, Lammas in February, May Day's Eve, Beltane in August and All Hallow's Eve. Failure to be present, unless a valid excuse could be given, meant expulsion from the club.

Charles had replied that he might have to remain in the country until after Christmas, but he would greatly look forward to New Year's Eve. He had not known then that his mother intended to give a ball that night. Her first mention of it, a few days later, had greatly perturbed him; but the knowledge that he would be debarred from the club for good if he did not attend the New Year ceremony had determined him to do so, even at the cost of upsetting Susan.

In consequence, at the ball he booked no dances for after midnight and, having drunk the usual toasts, slipped away unobserved to collect his cloak, then left the house by the back door which gave on to a mews.

It had been raining hard, but now the rain had lessened to a drizzle. He had his own coach, which his mother had given him as a seventeenth birthday present, and earlier in the day he had ordered it to be waiting for him in Bruton Street. It was standing near the mews entrance, and some thirty feet beyond it stood another coach with a man and woman nearby.

By the light of the flambeaux in the sconces fixed to the railings on either side of the front door of the house opposite, Charles saw the man hand the woman into the coach. As he did so the light glinted on the auburn ringlets that dangled from beneath a scarf his companion was wearing over her head. Instantly Charles realised that she was Susan.

Running forward, he pushed aside the man, thrust his head into the coach and cried, 'Susan, what is the meaning of this?'

She started back, then replied quickly, 'Captain Hawksbury is taking me on to another party for an hour or two.'

'He'll do no such thing!' retorted Charles hotly. 'You know well enough that you are not allowed out unaccompanied by a chaperone.'

'I am of an age to please myself,' Susan snapped back. 'And I will go escorted by whom I choose.'

Captain Hawksbury was a notorious roué, and Charles had disliked Susan's welcoming his attentions in London the previous summer; but at that time it had not even entered his head that she might possibly allow him to seduce her. Now, since their conversation of that morning, he was seized with sudden apprehension that she might. Fear for her, mingled with furious jealousy, welled up in him, and his voice became sharp with anger.

' 'Tis unthinkable that you should go off alone with a man in the middle of the night. I'll not allow it!'

The Captain was a well-built man, and half a head taller than Charles, who had not yet grown to his full height. Laying a hand on Charles's shoulder, he said in a quiet, amused voice, 'Pray calm yourself, my young lord. Miss Brook has done me the honour to agree to accompany me to a pleasant party, where I will take good care of her. 'Tis no business of yours where she goes.'

'By God, it is!' thundered Charles. 'And I'll not let her. She shall return with me to the house this instant.'

As he spoke, he put one foot on the step of the coach and stretched out a hand to grab Susan's arm. Hawksbury's voice suddenly changed to an angry rasp.

'Damn you, boy! I'll not brook your interference.' His hand tightened on Charles's shoulder, and he gave a shove that had all a strong man's strength behind it. Charles, having one foot on the coach step, overbalanced and fell full length into the gutter, which was full of muddy water from the recent downpour.

Livid with rage he shouted at Hawksbury, 'By God, you shall pay for this! I'll call you out and see the colour of your blood!'

Hawksbury gave a bellow of laughter, 'What? Fight a duel with a stripling like you? Is it likely? You'd be lucky if you got away with a swordthrust through the arm. Aye, and within the first minute of the encounter.' Turning contemptuously away, he got into the coach and slammed the door behind him.

As Charles picked himself up, he cried, 'Don't be so certain! Age and height count for little in a duel, and I was taught to use a rapier by no less a champion than Miss Brook's father. I vow I'll prove your equal, if not your better.'

Thrusting his head through the open window of the coach, Hawksbury flung at Charles the taunt, 'Then, being so fine a swordsman, my little cockscomb, why do you skulk here in England? Have you not heard that we are at war with that brigand, Bonaparte? Get you to the Peninsula and slay a few frog-eaters. Do that, and I'll meet you in a duel, but not before.'

Leaving Charles seething with impotent fury, the coach drove off.

Having fallen in the gutter, Charles's white satin breeches and silk stockings were soaking wet and smeared with mud. It was impossible for him to present himself at the club in that condition. For a few minutes his mind was so filled with anxiety about Susan that he no longer felt any inclination to go there. But to return to the ball, where he would have to pretend to be gay and carefree, was out of the question. The only other alternative was to go up to his room and sit there, brooding miserably. It then crossed his mind that if he did not go to the club, he would forfeit his membership. Moreover, there he would at least find distraction that for the next few hours would divert his mind from tormenting apprehensions about what Susan might be letting Hawksbury do to her.

Turning, he hurried into the house, ran up the back stairs to his room and quickly changed his clothes. Ten minutes later he left again, got into his coach, put on a mask that hid the upper part of his face and told his coachman to drive him to an address in Islington.

At that date Islington was a fashionable suburb and many of the quality had fine houses there. A little before one o'clock Charles's coach set him down in front of one in a handsome terrace. Further along it several other coaches that had brought members to the club were standing. Telling his man to join them and wait for him, Charles ran up the steps of the house and gave a tug at the iron bell pull.

The bell was still clanging when a grille in the front door was opened and a pair of eyes peered out at him. From a pocket in his long waistcoat Charles produced the symbol of his membership. It was a brooch having a stone known as a 'cat's eye'. He held it up so that the person behind the grille could see it. The door swung open on well-oiled hinges. The liveried footman who had let him

in closed the door behind him and bowed him towards a
room on the right of the pillared hall. On entering it he
took off his blue satin tail coat, his waistcoat and breeches
and hung them on pegs among a row holding a number of
similar garments. Then, from another row of pegs he took
one of several grey robes with hoods, such as are worn
by monks, and put it on. Having tied the cord round his
waist, he pinned the cat's eye brooch over his heart.

He was now garbed in the traditional costume worn
by the members of the original Hell Fire Club, which
had been founded some fifty years earlier by Sir Francis
Dashwood, Chancellor of the Exchequer and, later, Lord
le Despenser.

Dashwood had founded the Order of St. Francis of
Wycombe, the inner circle of which included the Earl of
Sandwich, First Lord of the Admiralty, Thomas Potter,
Paymaster General, and other distinguished men who,
together with Dashwood himself, formed a coven of
thirteen. There were also associate members to this society
of rakes, among them Lord Holland, the Earls of Oxford
and Westmoreland, the Marquis of Granby, the Duke of
Kingston and the notorious John Wilkes.

The meetings of these gentry were held in the Abbey
on Medmenham Island in the Thames, and consisted
of blasphemous rituals followed by orgies. In order the
better to parody their mockery of Christian rites, the men
all wore the robes of monks and the women they brought
with them from London—the majority of whom were
among the most beautiful *demi-mondaines* of the day, but
also some society women who concealed their identities
with masks—wore the costume of nuns.

Leaving the cloakroom, Charles went up a staircase in
the middle of the hall, leading to a large salon on the first
floor. Some thirty to forty ladies and gentlemen were

assembled there, enjoying a buffet supper, some standing at a long table carrying an excellent cold collation, others sitting at small tables to which they had carried plates and glasses.

All the men except one were clad similarly to Charles, in grey monks' robes with hoods that hid the colour of their hair, and were masked. The exception was a tall, gaunt, hook-nosed, elderly man known as the Abbot. He wore a mitre on his head, in the centre of which there was a large cat's eye, a robe of mauve silk and, dangling from his neck on a gold chain, there was, instead of a crucifix, a diamond-studded *crux ansata*, the Egyptian symbol of immortality.

Beside him at the top of the stairs, receiving the guests, stood the Abbess, whose name was Katie O'Brien; a woman who, both in face and figure, had a loveliness that would have drawn the eyes of many men in a large gathering immediately towards her.

In striking contrast to the angelic beauty of the Abbess, the features of the tall Abbot were of a special ugliness that might have been designed in hell. His great hooked nose above a receding chin gave the impression of a bird of prey, the high cheekbones of his thin face were pitted with the scars of smallpox and his hooded eyes seemed to gleam with evil. His mouth was loose, his teeth uneven and yellow. His hypnotic glance radiated strength and power; and Charles, having on the night of his initiation seen this Priest of Satan avidly possess several women one after another, knew that his lust was insatiable.

It could be only this last characteristic, Charles decided, that made these lecherous women give themselves to the hideous Abbot so eagerly. It then occurred to him how fortunate he was to be a man, so had been initiated by the beautiful witch; whereas the women members had all had to submit to being initiated by the Abbot and, however licentious by nature, must have felt an almost overwhelming horror at having, for the first time, to give themselves to this repulsive representative of the dark powers.

The women were also masked but wore the black gowns of nuns, and white, banded coifs across their foreheads, from which black weeds concealed their hair and the sides of their faces.

In their case there were three exceptions. Two were clad in the white costumes of novices and, in addition to masks, wore veils that entirely obscured their features. The third was the Abbess, who was wearing a mauve silk robe and, on her bosom, a huge cat's eye, surrounded by emeralds. She was Irish and had achieved a considerable reputation in occult circles in Dublin for her prophetic gifts. A few years earlier she had come to London armed with introductions from several of the Irish nobility to friends in England also interested in the occult. Some while after Lord le Despenser's death, the original Hell Fire Club had disintegrated, but memories of it had lingered on, and she had had the clever idea of resurrecting it as a means of attracting wealthy patrons.

She was a tall woman and, alone among the ladies, wore no mask. Her face was very pale and, although she was in her early forties, not a wrinkle marred the perfection of her magnolia skin. Two features made her strikingly beautiful : a very full-lipped mouth, which she painted scarlet, and a pair of magnificent dark-blue eyes, such as are rarely seen outside Ireland. Above them black eyebrows curved down to meet across the bridge of a Roman nose, giving her an imperious expression.

Some of the members of the club were old acquaintances, and did not seek to hide their identities from one another, while others preferred to remain incognito; but

the Abbess could have put a name to any of them, and at
once recognised Charles.

From the beginning she had been particular about
whom she admitted to her Order and she had accepted
Charles, in spite of his youth, only because he had special
qualifications. Not only was he an Earl with a fine town
mansion and White Knights Park, a great property in
Northamptonshire, but she had special designs concerning his future. Since she had personally initiated him the
previous November, she had not seen him and, for the past
quarter of an hour, had feared he did not mean to come
that night.

Moving forward to meet him, she gave him a charming
smile, extended her left hand for him to kiss and said in a
husky voice with a slight Irish lilt :

'It is late you come, little Brother, but are nonetheless
welcome.'

As he took her hand, his own trembled slightly from
the memory of the pleasure she had afforded him at his
initiation. Bowing, he murmured, 'I pray your pardon,
Reverend Mother. I was detained by an unfortunate
accident.'

'It is no matter.' She waved her hand, on which there
was another big cat's eye in a ring, toward the buffet. 'You
still have time to fortify yourself with a glass or two of wine
before our ceremony, and you are called on to make libation to Lilith-Venus in the person of one of my lovely
daughters.'

Walking over to the buffet, Charles was handed a
goblet of champagne by one of the footmen. A minute or
so later he found the Abbess beside him. Holding out a
small, black velvet bag, she said :

'As you are late in arriving, there is only one number
left, but your chance of drawing a partner who will de-

mand as much as you are capable of giving is not lessened by that.'

Charles put his hand in the bag and drew out an ivory plaque on which was the number 6 and was attached to a piece of magenta ribbon. Having bowed her away, he tied the plaque on to his cat's eye brooch and, now filled with excited anticipation, began to look quickly about the room.

The friend who had introduced Charles to the club had told him that the majority of the female members were married women who had elderly or unsatisfactory husbands, and found this way of satisfying their pent-up desires greatly preferable to taking a regular lover; as, by concealing their identities, they were spared the anxiety of clandestine meetings and any possibility of becoming involved in a scandal. This applied also to the unmarried girls who had been introduced by cynical roués, after finding that they delighted in lechery and had a taste for variety. All of them came from the higher strata of society, as the Abbess had no mind to dispense to professional courtesans any part of the twenty guineas she charged her male members for each attendance.

Owing to their masks, coifs and nun's robes, all the women present, apart from height, appeared almost identical, and Charles had to spend several minutes mingling with the crowd before he found the nun with a plaque numbered 6 suspended from her cat's eye brooch.

That she wore this number was, in fact, no matter of blind chance. She was an Irish widow named Lady Luggala, and an old crony of the Abbess's, who had slipped her the plaque while Charles was standing at the buffet with his back to them. It was part of a plan they had made that Charles should partner the widow that night, and she had been impatiently awaiting his arrival.

She was seated at a small table, with a monk wearing plaque number 18. He at once stood up, kissed her hand and said, 'Sister, at our next meeting I pray that it may be my good fortune to draw the same number as you as, from your voice, I know 'twas my luck on a previous occasion.' Then he bowed to Charles and moved away.

Greeting her politely, Charles took the vacant chair and smilingly scrutinised her. She was tall, and her movements were graceful. Her cheeks were a little heavily rouged and faint lines showed at the corners of her mouth, telling him that she must be considerably older than himself. Her firm chin and good teeth were vaguely familiar to him, so he felt fairly certain that they had met before in society, but he could not even make a guess at her identity. In any case, the fact that the man who had just left them had evidently desired to partner her again seemed to Charles a good indication that he had drawn a lucky number. After a moment he said :

'It seems, Sister, that you are not a newcomer to these gatherings. Have you attended many of them?'

She smiled. 'Yes, I was an early member of the Order and come here regularly whenever I am in London. I find our meetings most stimulating, mentally as well as physically, and always eagerly await the next. What of yourself?'

'I humbly confess that this is my first attendance, as I was not initiated until last November, and have since perforce been living in the country. I can only hope that I shall not disappoint you.'

At that she laughed. 'You would not be here unless our Abbess had proved you to be virile. In fact, if I am not mistaken, it was you whom I saw initiated in November, and with our beautiful Reverend Mother you gave a creditable performance. You are, I feel certain, still very

young, so must lack experience in the more subtle ways of
pleasing women. But it will lie with me to ensure the best
results, and I do not doubt that we shall enjoy our amorous
encounter.'

Before Charles had time to reply a silver bell jingled.
Immediately silence fell and the Reverend Abbess
announced in her deep, husky voice, 'My children! The
hour has come. Let us proceed to the Temple of Delights.'
On the arm of the gaunt Abbot she then led the way downstairs, followed by the pairs of men and women, the two
white-clad novices and their escorts bringing up the rear.

Behind the main staircase another, narrower one led
down to the basement. It was one large room, the full
length and breadth of the house, the upper floors being
supported by two rows of arches on carved stone pillars.
A thick black carpet covered the whole floor, but it was
visible only in a three-foot-wide central aisle running
from one end of the great room to the other. The whole
of the rest of it was covered with scores of many-coloured
silk cushions piled one upon another. Along the aisle the
signs of the Zodiac had been embroidered into the black
carpet with gold thread.

The temple was dimly lit, the only light coming from
the far end where two seven-branched candelabra, holding black candles, stood on an altar and, in front of it,
two four-foot-high pedestals holding chafing dishes, from
the centre of which rose slightly flickering oil flares.

A few feet before the altar stood a curiously-shaped
piece of padded furniture resembling a stool, but the left
half of it curved downward, while the right half rose in a
hump, so it appeared impossible to sit on it in comfort.
Two black curtains, forming an angle to the altar, were
suspended on rods from its sides to the pillars of the
nearest arches. On one was embroidered the *yang* and on

the other the *yin*—the ancient symbols for the male and female. On the wall behind the altar hung a rich scarlet banner with a black cross upside-down. Beneath it, centrally between the two seven-branched candelabra, stood a strange idol which no newcomer to the place could easily have identified.

But Charles, on first being taken down to the temple, had realised what it was. From his childhood he had been loved and spoiled by Roger's greatest friend, Lord Edward Fitz-Deverel—known to his intimates as 'Droopy Ned'. One of 'Uncle' Ned's hobbies was the study of ancient religions. He had often told Charles about Egypt in the distant past, and shown him pictures of the strange gods the Egyptians worshipped. Among them had been the cat god, Bast. So Charles had recognised the idol on the altar as a mummified sacred cat, which must have been brought from Egypt by some traveller.

The Abbess and the Abbot halted before the altar. Both made obeisance to the idol, then turned about to face the congregation. They, in turn, made obeisance, then the couples settled themselves comfortably among the sea of cushions. Only the two novices and their escorts remained standing. They had halted at the rear of the temple, and as Charles's partner had seated herself on the first cushions she came to, the novices were only a few feet behind them.

In a loud voice the Abbess cried, 'He who on joining our Order was re-christened Abadon shall now bring forward the seeker after truth whom he has brought to us.'

The man addressed led his white-robed novice up the aisle, then stood aside. The Abbot threw some herbs on the chafing dishes and they went up in clouds of aromatic smoke. The Abbess took both the novice's hands in hers, held them in silence for a full minute, then said in a toneless voice that was barely audible to the congregation :

'My child, you are in grave trouble. Your family is noble, but now poor. They are in very serious financial difficulties. Owing to this they wish you to restore their fortune by marrying you to a rich merchant.'

The girl gave an audible gasp of surprise, then the Abbess went on, 'You are already engaged to this man. He is much older than you, and you hate him. You are in love with a younger man—a soldier. Normally events would take their course, and a life of misery as the wife of this man you hate be yours. But your good angel has brought you here so that you may be offered a way to save yourself. Our Order has been granted power to alter the course of human lives. If you desire to join it, you must first submit to an ordeal which may seem repugnant to you. But it is of brief duration and, once initiated, we can assure you a happy future. Think well on this, my child, and let me know your decision through him we call here Abadon.'

Releasing the girl's hands, the Abbess signed to her to go and, turning about, she was escorted by Abadon back to the rear of the temple. As they halted there, the Abbess cried in a loud voice as before :

'He who on joining our Order was re-christened Nebiros shall now bring forward the seeker after truth that he has brought to us.'

The other couple advanced up the aisle. Again the man stood aside and the Abbot threw herbs on the chafing dishes. The Abbess took the novice's hands, remained in deep thought for a moment, then said :

'My child, you are fortunate. You are surrounded by love and wealth. No-one will force you to do anything against your wishes. But I see sorrow ahead for you. It arises from a breach which has very recently occurred between you and a young man who loves you and whom you love dearly. The Powers tell me that separation from him threatens you, a separation that may last for years. It may even be permanent. Our Order can call upon forces that will alter the course of events. They could protect you from this grievous loss if you are willing to submit to an ordeal you may think unpleasant. By no means every novice finds the initiation ceremony hard to bear, but should you do so, a period of distress soon over is no great price to pay in order to prevent the man you love being taken from you by circumstances over which you have, at present, no control. Think well on this, my child, and let me know your decision through him whom we here call Nebiros.'

While the second novice and her escort returned to their place at the back of the temple, the Abbot disappeared behind the curtain on the left of the altar, to re-emerge a moment later carrying a great two-handled urn. At the same moment a huge negro, wearing only a loin cloth, came out from behind the right-hand curtain carrying a similar urn.

As though at a signal, the whole congregation came to its feet and, in pairs, forming a long queue, walked up the aisle. From his initiation ceremony Charles knew that the urn held by the negro was empty. Into it every Brother would drop a purse holding twenty guineas, and members of both sexes who wished to secure information about the future would drop notes asking their questions. The notes were signed with the names by which they had been re-christened on initiation, but the Abbot and Abbess knew their real names and, in a few days' time, they would receive written answers. The urn held by the Abbot contained wine, heavily loaded with a powerful aphrodisiac, a few sips of which were enough to double the potency of those who drank it.

The only future matter about which Charles would have liked to know was whether Susan would carry out her threat to take a lover, or if, on second thoughts, restrain herself out of love for him. But he had not dared put his question on paper and bring it, for fear that the answer would be the one he dreaded, and so add to his torment on every occasion when she had the opportunity to be alone with one of her beaux. When the Abbot presented the Hell-broth loving cup to him, he took only a single sip for form's sake, because the thought of what was soon to come had already aroused his passions to fever pitch.

While the proceedings with the urns were taking place, the Abbess threw more handfuls of herbs on the chafing dishes. The flaming oil that rose from the centre of the dishes swiftly turned the herbs into clouds of pungent smoke, filling the temple with the scent of musk and incense, calculated further to excite the lust of the monks and nuns.

As they returned to their places among the cushions, they began to embrace, kiss and fondle one another. With the impatience of youth, the moment Lady Luggala re-seated herself, Charles threw his arms about her and pressed his mouth to hers. She opened it readily and sucked in his tongue. Next moment he had pushed her over on to her back and, despite her mock chiding, thrust one of his hands up beneath her robe. Under it she had on only a silk shift and his eager fingers slid swiftly up between her thighs. Closing her legs tightly, she pushed him back and said with a low laugh :

'You wicked boy. If you go too fast you will spoil things for us later. Desist now, I beg. We must wait until the Reverend Mother has performed her ritual. Then we'll be free to rid ourselves of all our clothes and I'll let you do what you will with me.'

As Charles withdrew his hand, a bell tinkled, the Abbot and the negro disappeared with their urns behind the curtains either side of the altar, the company fell silent, ceased embracing and all eyes became fixed on the Abbess. With a swift gesture she plucked her coif from her head and threw it aside. A mass of dark, curling hair fell to her shoulders. With equal swiftness she pulled undone a silk bow beneath her chin. Her robe slid down onto the floor and she stepped out of it stark naked.

Holding her arms aloft, she stood motionless for a moment, her eyes wide, staring straight in front of her. Although the majority of those present had seen her naked before, a little gasp of admiration paid tribute to her beauty. Her figure formed a perfect adjunct to her lovely face. She was close on six feet in height. Her shoulders were broad, her breasts stood out round and firm, with no sign of the sagging usual in women over forty. Her waist was slender and her hips curved out from it down to powerful thighs. The whiteness of her skin was accentuated by big, brown circles surrounding her red nipples, and the Vee of dark, crisp curls that covered her strongly-developed *mons veneris.*

Having allowed her congregation to gaze their full, she turned about to face the altar. Raising her arms again, she cried in a loud voice :

'Oh, mighty Bast, sister of Set and daughter of Lucifer, we pray thee intercede with him—the most beautiful and most gifted of all the Archangels : the Sun of the Morning, the Lord of This World, the Giver of all Power, Wealth and Joy here in the Principality bestowed upon him by the Almighty—that he may grant our desires. In devotion to you, dear Bast, and to Him, I will now receive into myself two libations of the essence that creates flesh.'

Turning about, she clapped her hands three times, then

threw herself face down on the curiously-shaped padded
stool. Her full breasts fitted into the downward curve on
the left side and her buttocks were raised up over the hump
on the right. In response to her claps, the curtains bearing the *Yang* and the *Yin* again parted. From the left the
Abbot emerged and from the right the huge, coal-black
negro. Both were now stark naked and erect. Stretching
out a hand the Abbess grasped the member of the Abbot
and drew him toward her. The negro flung himself upon
her from behind.

The silence was suddenly broken by a girl's voice gasping, 'Take me away.'

It came from one of the white-clad novices. Charles
swivelled round on his cushions to stare at her. The mask
and veil entirely hid her face and hair, but he could have
sworn that the voice was Susan's.

Her escort whispered angrily, 'Be silent!'

Again the girl's voice came, louder this time. 'Take me
away at once! I refuse to witness this disgusting spectacle.'

As she spoke she had turned towards the stairs. The
man grasped her arm to pull her back. In a low, harsh
voice he said, 'Shut your eyes if you will. But you must
remain till the ceremony is completed.'

When the girl had spoken the second time, Charles
could no longer doubt that she really was Susan, and now
he recognised the man's voice as that of Captain Hawksbury. Jumping to his feet, he covered in a matter of
seconds the short distance that separated him from the
arguing couple. Addressing Hawksbury, he whispered
fiercely :

'Unhand this lady! I intend to take her out.'

'Hell's bells! What has this to do with you?' Hawksbury exclaimed in surprise.

'No matter,' Charles snarled. 'She is coming with me.'

Hawksbury had let go Susan's arm and turned to face him. Cockfighting and contests between pugilists were the favourite sports of the day, and many a young man of gentle birth prided himself on his performance in the ring. When at Eton Charles had learned to box and had proved himself a formidable opponent against others of his weight. Now, with the precision of a professional, he lashed out and landed a terrific punch under the side of Hawksbury's jaw. The Captain went over backwards, landing with a heavy thud at full length on the floor of the aisle.

All this had happened very quickly, but those nearby among the congregation had heard the fierce whispering and several had called, 'Hush! Hush!' or 'Be quiet there!' in low, angry voices.

As Hawksbury was bowled over, Susan let out a scream. Within a minute everyone present sprang to their feet. The nearest men scrambled over the cushions and ran at Charles. He turned to defend himself and knocked down the first to come within striking distance. The next landed a blow on his ear. A third struck him hard in the stomach, momentarily winding him. Others seized his arms and, strive as he did to free himself, he was soon overpowered.

His mind was in a whirl. What they would do to him he had no idea, but he felt certain that they would regard as an appalling sacrilege his violent interruption of their satanic ceremony at its highest point. It was possible that they might content themselves with expelling him from their Order. But, if the Abbess proved vindictive, she might put some terrible curse on him, perhaps even render him impotent. Between the faces staring at him he glimpsed her now. She had risen from the stool and was standing, still in her splendid nakedness, between the Abbot and the negro. Her dark eyebrows, which met over the bridge of her imperious nose, were drawn down in a ferocious frown, and her mouth was set in grim lines that showed her to be in a most evil temper. Scowling, she began to walk forward.

Charles's mind flashed to Susan. It was she who had been the cause of the ugly scene that had ruined the tribute to the dark gods. He was now powerless to get her away from this company of rakes and licentious women into which, all too late, he now realised he had allowed himself to be drawn by fascination with the occult and his urge to satisfy his lust in exciting surroundings.

Had he been brought up to be religious, he would never have done so, but neither his mother nor 'Uncle' Roger, for whom he had an unbounded admiration, ever went to church. Both of them had told him that they believed every person to have many lives, and that the original teaching of Jesus Christ had been perverted almost from the beginning by the fanatical St. Paul, followed in the early centuries by ignorant and often evil priests.

Susan, he knew, had absorbed the same ideas : a belief that no man could absolve another from his sins, and that the only sin one could commit was deliberately to cause others to be unhappy. Such a belief could explain why she had allowed herself to be brought here, but she could have had no idea of the rituals performed at Satanic ceremonies, otherwise she would not have attempted to leave the temple.

Yet the fact remained that it was her attempt to do so which had led to this abrupt disruption of the night's proceedings; so Charles was filled with fear that the Abbess would regard Susan as the principal offender and vent her wrath even more severely on her than on himself.

He was now powerless to protect her, and it was certain that no-one else there would. She was helpless in

their hands, and was incapable of resisting anything they
decided to do to her. They were gathered there to slake
their lusts on one another. The Abbess's ritual was to have
been followed by an orgy. They would not be content to
go home without it taking place. The Abbess might decree
that Susan was to be stripped, and that any number of
men who liked should possess her forcibly. At the awful
picture this possibility conjured up, sweat broke out on
Charles's forehead.

Suddenly a tall man near the altar cried in a loud voice,
'Unhand that young fellow and let him take the novice
hence. 'Tis not fitting that anyone should be brought here
who is not a willing participant in our revels.'

'Aye, aye!' several other voices supported him, and a
woman's treble called out, 'We want no squeamish young
prudes in our joyous company.'

But the majority of those present howled down the pro-
testors, and one man shouted above the rest, 'She'd not be
out with our Brother who brought her at this hour of
night if she were all that innocent. She'll make good sport
for us. Strip her and let's see if she is a virgin.'

'Well said,' yelled another. 'And if she is, let Aboe make
a woman of her on the altar.'

Charles's heart lurched in horror. Aboe was the giant
negro.

During this altercation the two men holding Charles
had released their grip on him. With a sudden plunge
forward he broke free. For him to reach Susan and get
her away was impossible, but he swiftly backed against a
pillar, his fists clenched, ready to fight again.

The Abbess had halted, undecided, half-way up the
aisle. A lull in the clamour enabled Charles to make his
voice heard, and he appealed to her :

'Reverend Mother, I pray you let me take her away.

On her account as well as my own, I swear that neither of us will say aught to anyone about what takes place here.'

'No! No!' came an angry chorus, and someone called, 'She should pay for having interfered with our lady Abbess's receiving the libation to Lucifer. Give her to the negro.'

The tall man who had first intervened shouted, 'I'll not have it! And you know who I am, Katie O'Brien. 'Twill pay you ill to cross me.'

The Abbess did know. He was a Duke and one of the wealthiest men in England. She was greatly averse to offending him, but loath to disappoint the many opposed to him, so she sought refuge in a subterfuge and cried :

'Brothers and Sisters, we are all equal here. We will put it to the vote. All those in favour of letting them go, put up their hands.'

A dozen hands were raised. Then she called, 'Now those who would have her pay a forfeit.'

Over twenty hands went up, a clear majority. 'So be it!' she cried, then beckoned to the negro. 'Come, Aboe, take her.'

Susan was being held, so could not get away. As the negro took a step forward, she screamed. At that moment the masked Duke sprang out of the crowd and dashed at him. To avoid the attack, Aboe stepped back and cannoned into the pedestal just behind him.

It went over with a crash. The oil that fed the flame in the centre of the chafing dish gushed out across the carpet. An instant later the flames caught the curtain with the *Yin* upon it. As it flared up the nearest cushion caught, then the flames seemed to leap from it to others.

Pandemonium ensued. Everyone was shouting, 'Fire!' and scrambling through billowing smoke toward the

entrance to the temple. Charles did not lose a second. No
sooner were the curtains ablaze than he swivelled about,
sprang towards Susan, grasped her by the arm and ran
with her toward the stairs. Rushing up them, they reached
the hall breathless. The footman there stared at them in
astonishment. Brushing past him, Charles wrenched open
the front door. Within two minutes of the fire having
started, he and Susan were out in the street.

Side by side they hurried to Charles's coach. He roused
the dozing coachman and told him to drive back to Berkeley Square. Susan was weeping and, getting into the
coach, huddled back into a dark corner. But Charles was
in no mood to be sympathetic, and demanded angrily :

'Since when have you become fascinated by the mys-
teries of the occult?'

'I am not,' she sobbed, 'and know nothing of them.'

'How then could you be so great a fool as to let Hawksbury take you to the Hell Fire Club?'

'I . . . I had no notion that is what it was. He simply
told me that . . . that he would like to take me to an amusing party for . . . for an hour or two. He said that it was
being given by one of his friends and . . . and that he would
bring me home well before the ball was over.'

'He deceived you, then. But that is no excuse for having
gone off alone with a man in the middle of the night. He
might well have taken you to his own apartment, or some
other place, and there seduced you.'

At that she, too, flared into anger. 'You are right ! As I
found him attractive, he might have. But had he
attempted me, the odds are that I should have prevented
him by saying that I had my affairs, and consoled him by
half-promises about the future.'

'You were then seriously considering taking him as your
lover?'

'Yes; and why not? I told you this morning that, while you sowed your wild oats, I should consider myself free to sow mine if I had a mind to it. But when you said that tonight you intended to disport yourself at a club that provided special diversions, I never dreamt that it would be in such company. Oh, Charles! How could you become a Satanist? The thought appals me.'

'I am not a Satanist, any more than were those distinguished men who belonged to the original Hell Fire Club. The ceremonies are only a means to render amorous encounters more exciting.'

'So you say. But you cannot deny that the occult enters into it, and that evil powers are invoked to better the prospects of those who attend these meetings.'

For a moment Charles was silent, then he replied, 'I believed it to be hocus-pocus. Although most members know only their introducer, the Abbess knows them all, so it would be easy enough for her to find out the state of their affairs through tittle-tattle and shrewd interpretation of their reactions to remarks made by her when conversing with them. I had no means of judging if her predictions are always right, and assumed that, in many cases, they enabled those to whom she made them to avoid threatened calamities or better their prospects by their own efforts. But tonight has proved me wrong. The powers of evil must have been potent in the temple, otherwise the powers of good would not have intervened to save us by causing that fire.'

'Indeed, you are right. The fire could have been no ordinary accident, occurring as it did at the critical moment. And, apart from having saved us, I do thank the good Lord that Captain Hawksbury took me there tonight, for it brought about your having to sever your connection with that abominable woman.'

Charles nodded. 'Yes. It seems that unwittingly you have played the part of my guardian angel.'

After a moment he added, 'It can as yet be barely two o'clock, so when we get home they will still be dancing; but some of the older guests may have started to leave. It would be awkward to encounter any of them, dressed as we are, so we'll go in by the tradesmen's entrance. Fortunately, I have a key to it. With luck we'll get up the back stairs to our rooms without being seen by any of the servants; but we may run into one of them. If so, we'd best start talking of a masque at Covent Garden, implying that we have returned after spending an hour there with friends.'

'I'd as lief no-one saw me dressed as a novice,' Susan replied, pulling off her coif. 'Let down the window so that I can throw this out, and the robe after it. Then, if I'm seen, I'll be ordinarily dressed.'

While Charles did as she asked, he said quickly. 'Of course. What a fool I am to have supposed that Hawksbury would have risked suggesting you should rid yourself of your dress and petticoats in the ladies' room, as did the other women before putting on their nuns' robes. I'll have to keep mine on, though, for I had to leave my coat, waistcoat and breeches with my cloak in the men's closet.'

'So you had made ready for the fray,' Susan remarked acidly. Then she went on, 'If we do meet any of the servants, they'll not think it so strange that you have exchanged your cloak for a friar's robe as they would if they saw me dressed to take vows in a convent.'

As she spoke, she was wriggling out of her white novice's attire, and she shivered from the blast of the chilly air now coming through the open window. Up till that moment her mind had been so agitated that she had not realised

that she had left her furlined cloak behind. Now she spoke
of her loss with bitter anger, wondering how she could
possibly explain its disappearance to Georgina. But when
she had thrown her white garments out of the window
and Charles had pulled it up again, he promised to go out
before midday and buy a similar robe for her.

At that she said in a calmer voice, 'Charles, it would be
most generous of you to do so, since 'tis no fault of yours
that I had to abandon such an expensive garment. I'll
admit now that I was plaguey foolish to let Captain
Hawksbury take me off on my own; and, but for your
presence in that house, God alone knows what might have
befallen me.'

'Then let us have no more recriminations, and say no
more about it,' he replied. Putting his arm about her, he
kissed her gently and they completed their drive back to
Berkeley Square in silence.

On entering the square, Charles told his coachman to
drive round the corner into Bruton Street. Before handing
Susan out, he took three guineas from his purse, gave
them to the man and said :

'Here, Jennings, is money enough to keep your mouth
busy for a long time with good ale; so you'll not open it
to mention to anyone that Miss Brook and I tonight
attended a masquerade. Is that understood?'

The man gave a broad grin. 'Indeed it is, m' lord, and
I thank 'e for this generous present. Hope be I'll drive you
and the young mistress to enjoy many a good lark, and
never a word will pass me lips 'bout it.'

Confident that the man would not now tell his fellow
servants about the night's doings, Charles led Susan
through the mews to the entrance at the back of the mansion. Unlocking the door, he opened it cautiously and
peered inside. No-one was about, so he whispered to her

to follow him in, and together they tiptoed up the back stairs. On the landing that gave on to their bedrooms, he said in a low voice :

'It will take me only a few minutes to put on suitable clothes, but longer for you to redo your hair, so when I'm dressed I'll come for you; then we'll go down together as though we had been sitting out a dance.'

Five minutes later he joined her in her bedroom and sat in a chair until she had finished making herself present-able.

When she had done, she turned to him and said :

'Dearest Charles. On the latter part of our drive home I did some serious thinking. That I should have caused the Hell Fire Club to be barred to you in future I have no regrets. But I realise that, as a man, you must satisfy your passions and, as I told you this morning, I now feel a simi-lar urge. Even if we refrain from telling each other of those with whom we indulge ourselves, neither of us can escape thinking of the other in such situations, and that will cause misery to us both. Rather than we should suffer that, I have changed my mind about insisting that I should enjoy another year of freedom to flirt with whom I will. Instead I have decided to accept your proposal that we should marry in the Spring.'

Sadly Charles shook his head. 'Alas, my love. I would we could, but it is now too late. Come Spring, I shall no longer be in England.'

Her eyes widened. 'Charles, what . . . whatever do you mean?'

His face suddenly became grim. 'You must have heard the taunt that Hawksbury flung at me after he had pushed me over into the gutter. He as good as called me coward, because while claiming to be a man well versed in the use of weapons, I was skulking in England instead of going to the war against our enemies in the Peninsula. The round of easy pleasures here have so filled my mind that such a thought had never before entered it. But he was right. It is my intention, no later than this coming afternoon, to see my trustees and have them purchase for me a commission in the Guards.'

5

A Tangled Skein

It was getting on towards mid-January, and a few mornings after Roger had learnt to his fury that, unless the *Cape Cod* chanced to meet with a British ship-of-war, he and Mary would be carried off to America, that Lady Luggala was sitting up in bed drinking her morning chocolate and Jemima came into her room.

No-one unacquainted with them would have taken the two women for mother and daughter. Maureen Luggala had kept her figure, but her brown hair was streaked with grey, her pale blue eyes had crow's-feet round them and she looked considerably older than Charles had taken her to be when he had seen her masked and rouged at the Hell Fire Club.

Jemima's hair was black, so were her heavy eyebrows, but her eyes were a deep blue, her complexion milk and roses and her full-lipped mouth sensuously attractive. She was tall, with a big bosom and hips, but narrow waist and carried herself well. With a cat-like grace she settled herself on a *chaise-longue* opposite the bed and flicked the skirts of her chamber-robe across her shapely legs.

The 'little season' was in full swing and the previous night they had both attended a ball given by Lord Ponsonby. Having greeted each other, the elder asked :

'Well, child, did you chance to learn anything of importance last night?'

Jemima shrugged. 'Little of value. Young Gorton told me that his regiment, the 42nd, is to form another battalion and he hopes to purchase a Captaincy in it. A Naval Lieutenant, who had landed at Portsmouth only two days since, bored me to distraction by an account of hardships endured in the Channel these winter months. His name I disremember, but his ship was the *Intrepid,* so she will be off station for several weeks while refitting. Out of Robert Henage I had hoped to get some tidings of Sweden's changing attitude, as he is in the Northern Department of the Foreign Office. On that account I gave him three dances and, half-way through the last, let him whisk me up to a room on the second floor. But his mind was so filled with the hope of seducing me that he'd give not a moment to serious conversation.'

'He is a valuable source, so I trust that you have kept him on a string by at least letting him hope that on some future occasion. . . .'

'No.' Jemima's voice was sullen. 'I did not even permit him the usual familiarities.'

'That is unlike you,' Lady Luggala remarked acidly.

'I admit it. Since half a loaf is better than no bread, and it is essential that I should protect myself from becoming known as a society whore by letting men go the whole way with me. But I was in no mood to have him frig me.'

'Why this sudden reluctance, and the aggrieved state of mind you still display this morning?'

'Because last night I was mightily disturbed concerning my own prospects. During a dance with Charles St. Ermins he exploded a bombshell beneath me. He told me that only that morning he had seen the Commander-in-

Chief at the Horse Guards, who has arranged a commission for him in the Coldstream Guards.'

Lady Luggala sat up with a jerk and exclaimed in consternation, 'It cannot be true! And this without a word of warning?'

Jemima nodded. 'I've seen him half a dozen times since Christmas, and he gave me not a hint of his intention.'

'But this is terrible. It means that within a few months he may be sent to the Peninsula.'

'In a matter of weeks, more like. He made it clear that he has not joined the Army simply to strut about in a fine uniform. He is going to the war as soon as he can get there. And, as he has influence, they will not keep him here for long.'

'Then, child, you must work fast, or you will lose him. Let him seduce you at the first opportunity. Then he'll feel in honour bound to become engaged to you. If fortune favours us, we might even rush the marriage through before he leaves for Portugal.'

'Do you think me such a fool that I have not thought of that?' Jemima's voice was angry. 'But my chances of doing so are slender. As soon as he has his uniforms he is leaving London for Canterbury to start his initial training.'

Lady Luggala wrung her hands. 'Oh, my! Oh, my! Just to think that after all we may lose him. I've thought so much on it. Yourself a Countess, and all his riches. His mansion in Berkeley Square and White Knights Park with its thousands of acres. His mother, too, is worth a mint of money. Two husbands have left her fortunes, and her father yet another. Charles is her only child and she dotes on him. When she dies, he will be one of the wealthiest men in the three Kingdoms.'

'Stop!' Jemima snapped. 'I know it all. But for months

you have been counting your chickens before the eggs were even warm from the hen's bottom. Charles likes me, finds me amusing and good company. I've given him cause, too, to know that I'd be all that he could wish for in bed. But he has never yet even got as far as hinting that one day he might ask my hand in marriage.'

'Yet recently he has shown his preference for your company over that of all other young women. The frequency with which he escorts Susan Brook counts for nothing. They were brought up together, and the attentions he pays her are no more than those to be expected from an affectionate brother.'

'You are right in that I credited myself with a good lead in the St. Ermins stakes and, given another London season, might have been first past the post. But now all is altered. How in a week or so can I possibly secure him? Unless . . . yes, I have it. You must seek the help of the Irish witch.'

'Alas!' Lady Luggala sadly shook her head. 'She lacks the means to help us. Had all gone well on New Year's Eve we would have had him in our power. We laid a pretty plot. She fixed the draw so that he should be my partner. In my nun's robe I had concealed a small pair of scissors with intent, when we had had a frolic, to snip off a small tuft of his pubic hair. I should have told him that it was my custom to secure such a souvenir from every man who enjoyed me; so he would not have objected. With that in our possession and a tuft from your own bush we could have cast a spell that would have made him crazy to have you; and, naturally, your price would have been marriage.

'But, as I told you afterwards, all was brought to ruin. And by Charles himself, through that fool Hawksbury having brought young Susan there without telling her

what to expect, and making certain that she would prove
an eager witness to our ritual. Since the little prude
objected, and Charles looks on her as a sister, one can
hardly blame him for carrying her off. That he should
have acted as he did proved disastrous. We were lucky to
have saved Bast, and that the men got the fire under control as quickly as they did.'

Jemima was silent for a moment, then she said, 'I
appreciate your good intentions on my behalf, but take it
hard that you have always refused to have me made an
initiate of the club. That Susan, although she proved un-
willing, should have been put forward rankles with me
still more, for she is only seventeen, whereas I am twenty.'

'I had my reasons for refusing you. And why complain?
Ever since I chanced upon you being straddled by that
stable boy in Ireland, you have never lacked for lovers.'

'True. But what lovers! To protect my reputation I
never dare let a man of quality have me, lest he talk. I
am compelled to make do with that bean-pole of a music
master once a week, who would never dare tell of it lest
he was prosecuted for slander and found himself in the
stocks. How infinitely more enjoyable I'd find it to participate in these luxurious orgies you have told me of.'

'That I understand, although I blame myself now for
having spoken to you so freely on these matters. Had I in
fact been your mother, I would never have done so. But
the major interests in both our lives are the same—to free
our dear Ireland from the tyranny of the hated English
and to enjoy to the full our amorous encounters. There is
no-one else I could trust to be my confidante and I'm
sure that you, as well as myself, have greatly enjoyed
discussing our experiences.'

'I have indeed,' Jemima agreed more warmly. 'Since
that day when I was little over fifteen and you caught me

being tumbled by young Conan, you have taught me much. Had it not been for your prompt dosing of me with ergot of rye, I'd have had a child by him and, on the few occasions since when over-eagerness has led me to be careless, you have got me out of trouble. But, knowing my love of variety in licentious pleasures, I still cannot understand why you refuse to have me initiated into the Hell Fire Club.'

'It is not I who refuse, but your mother.'

Jemima's blue eyes opened wide.

Lady Luggala gave a gasp of dismay. 'There! Oh, Satan help me! By throwing me into a tizzy about Charles going off to the war and our losing him, you've led me into disclosing that she is not dead, as I'd given you to understand.'

Springing up from the *chaise-longue*, Jemima cried, 'Who is she? Who is she? I insist that you tell me.'

'No, child! No! That I cannot do. I am sworn to secrecy.'

''Tis too late!' Jemima flared. 'To me it is a secret no longer. Who could have refused your request that I should be initiated into the Hell Fire Club? Only one person. The Irish witch. It is she who is my mother.'

Tears had filled the older woman's eyes. Stifling a sob she murmured, 'How can I deny it! But long since we agreed that we would always keep it from you lest you inadvertently gave it away, and so spoiled your chances of an advantageous marriage by everyone believing you to be the daughter of myself and an Irish baronet.'

Jemima had gone white, and she was biting her lower lip. Suddenly she broke out, 'I want the whole story. Everything! Everything about my birth.'

'That I refuse to tell you, girl,' Lady Luggala replied angrily. 'It is not my secret.'

'Very well, then,' Jemima retorted with equal anger. 'I'll go to my mother and find out. I'll go this very afternoon.' Then she flounced out of the room.

At three o'clock a hackney coach set Jemima down in front of the house in Islington. When a footman answered the door to her ring, she said, 'I am Miss Jemima Luggala and I wish to see your mistress on a matter of importance.'

The man bowed. 'You are expected, Miss.' Having taken her furs, he said, 'Be pleased to follow me,' then led her to a charmingly-furnished boudoir overlooking a small garden at the back of the house. The witch was sitting there, looking like no witch that Jemima had ever imagined, but a beautiful, imposing lady dressed in a flower-patterned satin gown with white lace fichus over her full breasts.

As Jemima's mouth fell open in surprise, the witch smiled and said, 'Come in, my child, and seat yourself on the other side of the fire. It is surprised you are by my appearance. No doubt you supposed me to be an evil-looking old crone. But Lucifer can prevent the appearance of lines in the faces of his votaries, which come with age in other women.'

'I . . . ' Jemima stammered. 'I hadn't expected . . . expected to find you so beautiful.'

'It is happy I am to reciprocate the compliment, although I am not surprised by your good looks, for I have seen you many times in my crystal. Now look you in the mirror over the mantel.'

As Jemima obeyed, a thing by which she had already been struck was brought home to her more forcibly. Except that her black eyebrows did not quite meet over her nose and it was less arched, she was extraordinarily like her mother.

'You see now,' the witch went on, 'why I refused to allow Maureen Luggala to make you one of us.'

'You mean on account of my resemblance to you? But she told me that everyone who attends your meetings does so masked.'

'That is true. But whilst in the throes of passion, masks can slip or their strings snap. Such accidents do not occur often, yet they have been known to at times. I meant to run no risk that you would be recognised by some gallant who might afterwards talk and so perhaps spoil the plan I had made with Maureen for you to become the Countess of St. Ermins.'

'Now, by evil chance, my hopes of that are sadly jeopardised. Charles has secured a commission in the Guards and . . .'

'I know it, and we will talk of that anon. Let us first go into the prime reason for your coming to see me. It is the circumstances of your birth that you wish to learn and why, for all these years, Maureen has passed you off as her daughter. Now she has given it away that I am your real mother, I see no point in concealing from you how that came about.'

'I thank you . . . Mama. I have wondered about my parentage ever since, by another slip, Lady Luggala revealed to me that I was not her daughter. It occurred when she caught me out in my first affair. The youth was handsome and merry, but only a stable boy. She reproached me angrily, not so much for the act as for my choice of a lover, declaring that my lack of good breeding showed in it, for no daughter of hers would have allowed herself to be seduced by a menial.'

The witch laughed. 'My dear, like many a woman of her class, Maureen is a stupid snob. 'Tis a man's physique and mentality that matter, not his blood. But she was right in that you cannot claim yours to be blue, for I was born out of a slut in a Dublin slum.'

'How came it then that you were able to foist me off on Lady Luggala as her daughter?'

'My grandmother was a follower of the Old God and learned in the secret rituals. When I was still quite young, she came from her home in the country to live in Dublin, and passed on to me much of her wisdom. That enabled me to transform myself from a child of the gutter into a seemly young woman, and secure a post as Maureen's lady's maid. By various means I was already able to foretell the future, and she was greatly intrigued by predictions I made for her coming to pass. They were mostly in connection with men whom she was eager to have as lovers. You must know her well enough to be aware that she is almost obsessed by thoughts of cooling the heat that generates between her thighs. A time came when I induced her to come with me to a meeting of my coven, where I promised that a spell could be put upon a young man she desired but who had so far rejected her advances. The spell had the desired effect, and she became a member of the coven. From then onwards it was in my power she was, because she knew that did she threaten me I could have her denounced as a witch. Then, without involving me, my associates could have brought enough evidence to have had her hanged.'

At the revelation of this terrible blackmail, Jemima paled a little, but she listened eagerly as the witch went on :

'It was about that time that both Maureen and I conceived. She desired a child, hoping that it would be a male and provide an heir for her husband, Sir Finigal. I could have rid myself of mine, but had no wish to, because I was in love with the man by whom I had become pregnant. Maureen gave birth five days before I did. She, of course, had her child in her lovely bedroom with me, a midwife and a doctor fussing round her. I had you in my ill-furnished upstairs room, without anyone in the household knowing. But Maureen, being aware that my time was approaching, had agreed to engage my grandmother as a temporary sewing woman. She looked after me and by her arts rendered the birth almost painless.

'That night I carried you down to Maureen's room and, while she slept, put you in her baby's cradle. Next morning she was amazed to find that the child she believed to be hers had grown and changed from fair to dark, so I had to tell her what I had done. Naturally, it was very angry she was, but she dared not reveal the substitution from fear that I would have a curse put on her, or worse.'

'But did not Sir Finigal notice the difference in appearance of his lady's child after you had changed it for myself?' Jemima asked.

'He was not there to do so. He had died some weeks earlier after being thrown from his horse in the hunting field.'

'And what became of Lady Luggala's infant?'

With a smile the witch drew a slim finger slowly across her throat. 'My grandmother took it away. To achieve some things the personal intervention of Lucifer is required. That entails a Black Mass and the offering up of the blood of a newly-born babe. The two infants might have been born as much as a month apart. Others than myself could have been prevented from seeing at close quarters the child in Maureen's room, but not Sir Finigal. For the deception to succeed he had to be disposed of. My grandmother had promised to offer up an infant in payment for his death.'

Jemima felt her spine creep and stammered, 'Then . . .

then you . . . you agreed that she should use her powers
to kill my father?'

Her question was answered with a shrug. 'Child, anyone who seeks the power to ensure that all his wishes in
life are fulfilled must put his scruples behind him. The
mite was too young to realise what happened to it and, in
any case, Sir Finigal was not your father.'

'Was he not?' Jemima exclaimed in surprise. 'Lady
Luggala has often spoken to me of him as an insatiable
lecher. She once said that when he had tired of her he
could not keep his hands from under the petticoats of any
new maid who had been in the house more than a week.
I am amazed that he did not invade the bedroom of a girl
as lovely as yourself.'

'Oh, he did. He had me many a time, but it was not
by him that I became pregnant.'

'I see. The reason for substituting your own child
for Lady Luggala's is obvious, and I am deeply grateful
to you. Had you not, I might well now be a servant girl
instead of a society belle. But it surprises me to learn that
neither of my parents was of gentle blood; that is, unless
the man who begot me on you was of the Dublin aristocracy.'

'Fie, fie, girl! I see you have imbibed something of
Maureen's snobbery. That you have health and good
looks is all that counts, no matter where they came from.
But, if you set a value on lineage, you may well be proud,
for in your veins runs some of the noblest blood in all Ireland.'

'It was then an Irish noble who sired me?'

'Nay. 'Twas no empty-headed lordling, but a hero
whose efforts to liberate our people cost him his life. No
lesser man than Wolfe Tone.'

'Wolfe Tone!' Jemima cried, her blue eyes lighting up.

'Then I am proud indeed. He was the greatest patriot of them all.'

'Child, you never spoke a truer word. A genius he was and had the heart of a lion, yet tender and gay. He was the very darling of a boy. Do you know much of him other than that he died for Ireland?'

'Only that he aroused in our people a great enthusiasm for the cause, came over with the French in an attempt to liberate us, was captured by the brutal English and, rather than allow himself to be hanged, cut his own throat while in prison. But that I am his daughter makes me impatient to hear all you can tell me of him.'

"Twas in the winter of '90/91 that I first met him. Rising twenty-eight he was then and already a well-known figure in Dublin. At both Mr. Greig's school and later at Trinity College he had been incorrigibly idle, yet he seemed to acquire knowledge as lesser men breathe in air. In the middle of the eighties he eloped with and married a girl of fifteen called Matilda Witherington. Martha he called her, but had not enough money to keep her, so they had to live with her family. Finding that insupportable, he went off to London and became a student-at-law in the Middle Temple. There he loafed again until he became reconciled to his father-in-law, returned to Dublin and in '89 took his degree of L.L.B. He practised as a barrister for a while on the Leinster circuit, but he detested the law and threw himself into politics.

'In 1790 there occurred the affair of Nootka Sound, about which I doubt you have ever heard. The place was a sheltered anchorage thousands of miles away on the Pacific coast of Canada. Both Spain and England claimed it and came to the verge of war. Wolfe's pamphlet on the subject, published under the name of "Hibernicus", first drew the attention of other patriots to him. In it he argued that Ireland was not bound by any declaration of war on the part of England, and ought to insist on remaining neutral.

'It was during the following winter that we secretly became lovers. I conceived so great a passion for him that I ceased to go with any other men and, when I knew myself to have become pregnant by him, refused to let my grandmother abort me. My greatest regret is that I failed to persuade Wolfe to join my grandmother's coven, for had he done so we could have invoked power to further his projects and protect him personally. It was no case of his being a bigoted Catholic. On the contrary, his secret intention was, when Ireland had become free, to work for a general revolt against all Christian creeds; although, in order to first achieve political freedom, he strove to unite Catholics and Protestants. His rejection of my pleas was due to the fact that he was fully occupied in forming a club with William Drennan, Peter Burrowes, Thomas Addis Emmet and other patriots.

'The news of the success of the French Revolution enormously increased the urge among our people to throw off the yoke of England—especially among the Scottish Presbyterians in northern Ireland. On July 14th they celebrated in Belfast with great rejoicing the anniversary of the fall of the Bastille. It was then that Wolfe issued his great manifesto, which ran, *"My objects are to subvert the tyranny of our execrable government, to break the connection with England, the never-failing source of all our political evils, and to assert the independence of my country."* And, although himself nominally a Catholic, he had the honour of being elected an honorary member of the first company of the Belfast Green Volunteers. It was in Belfast, too, that he assisted in the formation of a union of Irishmen of every religious persuasion; then he

returned to Dublin and, with James Tandy, founded the
club of United Irishmen, which became the mainspring
of all endeavours to achieve the Republican principles of
liberty and equality.

'All over Ireland there were demonstrations against the
English but, by '94, Wolfe and his friends realised that
if our tyrants were to be overthrown armed help was
needed from France. He prepared a memorandum declaring Ireland ripe for revolution, which was to have been
taken to Paris by the Reverend William Jackson, but Jackson was caught, tried as a traitor and died in prison. Wolfe
then emigrated to the United States and in Philadelphia
secured from the French Minister there an introduction
to the Committee of Public Safety which then ruled Revolutionary France. Although he could speak hardly a word
of French, he convinced the famous Carnot, who was
Minister for War, that, given armed support, a rebellion
by the Irish would prove successful, and Ireland could
then be made a base for the invasion of England.

'General Hoche was nominated by the Directory to
command the expedition, and Wolfe given a commision
as Adjutant-General. The preparations met with long
delays, but at length, in December '96, they sailed with
forty-three ships and fourteen thousand men. Alas, those
delays brought ruin to our hopes. Mid-winter tempests
four times dispersed the fleet, and it straggled back to
Brest.

'It was not until '98 that another attempt was made.
In May of that year the Wexford insurrection took place,
and Wolfe used the news of it to re-arouse French interest
in Ireland. General Bonaparte had sailed to Egypt with
the finest regiments of the French Army and the greater
part of the French Navy, so Wolfe could be given only
inferior ships and a few thousand men. Again misfortune

befell our hero. The expedition arrived off Lough Swilly early in October but, before the troops could be landed, a powerful English squadron arrived on the scene. Wolfe commanded one of the batteries in his ship and fought it for four hours most gallantly; but she was then forced to surrender and he, with the other survivors, was made prisoner.

'He was taken to Dublin, tried and condemned to death by his enemies. As an officer in the French Army, wearing the uniform of that country, he insisted on his right to be shot; but the vindictive English decreed that he should be hanged as a traitor. Rather than suffer such a disgrace, he took his own life. So ended the life of the valiant man who, for a brief season, I was privileged to have as a lover and whose daughter you are.'

The account of Wolfe Tone's ceaseless endeavours to free his country had brought Jemima to tears. Dabbing at her fine eyes with a wisp of handkerchief, she murmured. 'Thank you, dear mother, for revealing to me that my father was so splendid a man. How I wish I had had the opportunity to throw myself at his feet in admiration, and aid him in some way.'

The beautiful witch smiled. 'Although it is long dead that he is, you aid the cause for which he died. As indeed I have done for many years. France still remains Ireland's only hope, and may yet free our people. In his ill-starred attempt to conquer Russia, the Emperor lost a great army, but I know him to be back in Paris and, with his boundless energy, now raising another army. The coming summer may well see a revival of his fortunes and the defeat of his enemies on the Continent. We must continue to aid him by sending to Paris all the intelligence we can glean of England's plans and resources. You are well placed for such work and, through Maureen, have sent me many

useful items of information. Monsignor Damien was prais-
ing your efforts only a week ago.'

'Monsignor Damien? Who is he?' Jemima asked with
quick interest.

'I first met him in Ireland some years ago, and brought
him to England with me. He is a Frenchman who came
over to escape the Terror, and was later unfrocked for
insufflating pretty women who came to his confessional,
in order to seduce them.'

'Insufflating. What is that?'

'Breathing upon them. The practice arouses sexual
desire. When I learned of this I decided that he might be
the very man to act as High Priest for me, and he readily
agreed. He already had contacts with the French in Dublin, through whom he was sending information, and has
since made contact with a Dutchman, through whom we
correspond with Paris.'

After a moment's silence, Jemima said, 'Tell me now,
dear mother, can you aid me in the matter of Charles St.
Ermins?'

'The Powers help those who help themselves. He is an
honourable young man. If you could seduce him . . .'

Jemima shook her head. 'In the limited time I have at
my disposal, 'tis most unlikely that an occasion will arise
when I'd have the chance.'

'Then you must procure something for me impregnated
with his essence.'

'Lady Luggala suggested a snippet of his pubic hair,
but I can think of no means of procuring it. We are not
sufficiently intimate for me to request it of him without his
thinking me immoderately immodest, and so unfitted to
become his wife.'

'True; and to give him any such idea would be fatal to
our plans. Nail parings or a handkerchief he had used

would have no such suggestive association, but are second best. Even something he has worn could be used by me to cast a spell of sorts upon him. But something impregnated with his emanations I must have if I am to aid you. Eager as I am to help you, child, I must leave it to your ingenuity to get possession of some such thing and bring it to me.'

For another hour the mother and daughter talked on. They had not only the features but minds that had much in common, so they delighted in each other, and when they parted it was with expressions of deep affection.

One week later Jemima came to the witch's house again. She had seen Charles only twice since her last visit, as their mutual attraction had not reached a point of meeting in secret. Much as Jemima would have welcomed an afternoon drive alone with Charles, it was for the man to suggest any such rendezvous, and Charles had done no more than pay special attention to her in society, express his admiration for her and, on several occasions, embrace and snatch kisses from her when sitting out in secluded corners during dances.

But the previous night Lady Luggala had given a rout at her house in Soho Square. On the excuse of giving Charles some Irish linen handkerchiefs to take away with him, Jemima had got him up to her boudoir. She had hoped that he would take the opportunity to seduce her there, but his code forbade him to go so far with a young lady of breeding; so they had got no further than a passionate session on a sofa, which had left them both panting.

Having failed to entrap her quarry to a point where she could afterwards say to him with starry-eyed innocence, 'Charles, my love, we must let my mother and yours know that we are now engaged,' Jemima had had to resort to her second string. When they had got back their breath, she said with a deep sigh :

'Charles, I am desolate at your going away. I shall miss you most terribly. I pray you, give me something of yours that I may treasure in your absence.'

'I'll do so willingly, sweet Jemima,' he replied. 'But what?'

After a moment's apparent thought, she exclaimed, 'I have it! Let me cut off a lock of your dark hair. I'll put it in a locket, then wear it between my breasts at night and dream of you.'

Pleased and flattered to find her feeling for him deeper than that he had aroused in his other flirts, Charles readily agreed. Then, as they would not be seeing each other again before he left two days later, they embraced again in affectionate farewell.

The following afternoon, when Jemima related to her mother all that had taken place, and produced a small, enamelled box in which reposed a dark curl snipped from the back of Charles's head, the witch took it and said :

'In the circumstances, you have done well, my daughter. Were this his pubic hair, mingled with some of yours, I could bind him to you. That I cannot now do. But at least I can use this hair for his protection, so that he is neither killed nor injured while he is at the war. While there 'tis most unlikely that he will meet with anyone he wishes to marry; so, on his return, you will have another chance to make him yours. Come here again late tomorrow night; by then I will have kneaded his hair into wax and formed a puppet of it upon which we will perform a magic.'

When Jemima came again to the house, her mother showed her a wax figure, about nine inches high. Etched down the back was the name, Charles St. Ermins. They talked affectionately for some time while drinking a bottle of wine, then, a little before midnight, the witch took Jemima down to the temple.

It was lit as it had been for the New Year's Eve meeting. But in front of the altar there stood, instead of the curiously-shaped stool, a brazier filled with glowing coals, above which was an iron pan on a tripod. Both women stripped themselves naked, then performed certain curious rites that included the use of a leather phallus.

The witch then set the wax puppet upright in the iron pan and, while it melted, recited an invocation to the figure of Bast. The intention was to preserve Jemima's image in Charles's mind, and give him protection from all the normal hazards of war : from sword, lance, pike and bayonet, from lead bullets, fragments of iron cannon balls and explosions.

But they failed to include rope, and by rope a man may be hanged.

6

The End of the Road

On February 28th Roger and Mary landed in New York. For him, having all his life been a bad sailor, the voyage had been one of almost unmitigated misery. Sometimes for days on end the winter storms had churned the ocean into great masses of water, seeming mountain-high, that threatened to engulf the ship as easily as a whale swallows a herring. For hour after hour she slithered up the long green slopes until the crests of huge waves broke over her, then plunged at terrifying speed down into watery valleys. While she ran, often with bare masts and hatches battened down, before such storms, Roger rolled, sick and weak, on his narrow berth in the little cabin.

During the worst storms Mary had also been seasick, but she proved the better sailor and had tended him most of the time like a ministering angel. On days when the weather was less inclement she bullied him into staggering up on deck to exchange the stuffy air of the cabin for freezing wind and sometimes driving rain. On such occasions Silas van Wyck helped her with him and at other times, when Roger could not be persuaded to leave the cabin, gave her his arm on the heaving deck and proved a most pleasant companion.

For most of the time Roger had eaten very little and,

when he did feel well enough to join the others at table, he found the fare meagre and unappetising. This was because the ship had not been provisioned for an Atlantic crossing, so during the last weeks of the voyage both passengers and crew had to make do mainly on weevilly biscuits and brackish water.

Added to these discomforts Roger was greatly worried about what would happen to Mary and himself when they reached America. His expenses in getting out of Russia and while in Stockholm had sadly reduced the considerable sum he normally carried on him when abroad. In his money belt he had now only a dozen gold pieces and the little washleather bag containing a few small diamonds that he always kept there against emergencies. But how long would such slender resources last? And, above all, how could he and Mary possibly get home from a country at war with Britain?

During a spell of bitter weather, a few days before they sighted land, Roger had talked over his problems with van Wyck, and the friendly American merchant had proved most helpful. He could offer no suggestion about the Brooks' securing a passage back to England, but he said that his house in New York was large and comfortable, and insisted that they should be his guests there while exploring the possibilities of recrossing the ocean. In consequence, when they landed at the snow-covered dock in the Hudson river, they went ashore with him.

Van Wyck had not exaggerated about his home. It was a three-storey, brownstone mansion some quarter of a mile from the tip of Manhattan Island, looking across the water to Brooklyn village. His wife and family were naturally surprised and delighted to see him. Mrs. van Wyck was a rosy-cheeked, buxom lady in her early forties, and there were three teenage daughters: Prudence, Guelda and Faith. While the mother made the Brooks welcome, the girls smiled at Mary and dropped curtseys, then two young negress house slaves were sent bustling off to light fires in the upstairs rooms and prepare them for the visitors.

An hour later they all sat down to an excellent dinner to which, after their weeks of privation, the three voyagers did ample justice. Roger had lost nearly two stone in weight, and had come ashore in very poor shape; but after this hearty meal, washed down with an ample supply of red wine followed by port, he began to feel more like his old self.

There was little to tell of the war. After the disaster to the American force under General Van Reusselaer in mid-October, winter had closed in, rendering further major land operations impossible, and it was not expected that they would be resumed until mid-April. At sea the Americans continued to harass British commerce, but the British had considerably increased their squadrons off the United States coast, and it was feared that, as the weather improved, the ports in the north would be as closely blockaded as those in the south already were.

Roger had had no reason to fear that while in America any restriction would be placed on his liberty, because the States were at war with Britain. It was Napoleon who, after the brief Peace of Amiens in 1803, had originated the arrest and internment of all civilians who, later, were termed 'enemy aliens'. This innovation in warfare had profoundly shocked all other nations and had been generally regarded as a most barbarous infliction on thousands of harmless people. But Roger had anticipated that, although van Wyck had so generously offered Mary and him hospitality, owing to their being English, the majority of Americans would not conceal their bitter resentment at having had to resort to war with Britain in defence of their right to trade freely.

However, this proved far from being the case. During the next few days, having learned of van Wyck's unexpected return, scores of his acquaintances came to call on him. When introduced to Mary and Roger, they condoled with them on their plight, showed a warm friendliness and expressed the hope that they would be able to help in making the exiles' stay in New York enjoyable.

This attitude was due largely to the fact that, although some forty years earlier they had had to fight Britain to gain their independence and were now fighting her again, their sympathies were still with her in the desperate war she had for so long been waging on the Continent against the French.

Generals Lafayette and Rochambeau and numerous other French officers having come to the aid of the Americans during their revolution, had not materially altered the fact that, from the earliest times of settlement along the Eastern coast, in both the north and south, the French had been the hereditary enemy. Louis XIV had succeeded in establishing a thriving colony in New France, as Canada was first called, and another in Louisiana on the Gulf of Mexico. The former had not been conquered until fifty years earlier, when General Wolfe had scaled the heights of Abraham and defeated the Marquis de Montcalm; and the latter acquired by purchase from Napoleon as recently as 1803.

Roger soon learned that the New Yorkers differed greatly from the population of all other States in the Union. In the earlier part of the seventeenth century the two major British settlements in America had for many years been separated. That in the north was inhabited by the Puritan New England farmers, that in the south by the sugar and cotton growers descended from Catholic Elizabethans and Stuart cavaliers. Between them had lain Dutch and Swedish colonies, known as the New Netherlands, which consisted of Manhattan Island and the lands adjacent to the Hudson river, and New Sweden, north of Delaware Bay.

In 1655 the Dutch had attacked and absorbed the Swedish colony. Then, in the Anglo-Dutch war of 1673, while England had suffered the indignity of having a Dutch fleet sail up the Thames, on the other side of the ocean they had conquered the New Netherlands, and its capital, New Amsterdam, had been renamed by Charles II after his brother and High Admiral, James Duke of York.

These changes in sovereignty, together with the immigration of Italians, Germans, Spaniards, Portuguese, Swiss and others, after their countries had been conquered by Napoleon, had resulted in New York becoming the most cosmopolitan city in America; and, when Roger arrived there, it was said that the native tongues of its citizens ran to more than sixteen languages. Very few of the population had any longer a special loyalty to any European country, as for a hundred years the Dutch had placidly accepted British rule and, after the States had achieved independence, the English who remained loyal to the Crown had emigrated to Canada. All this resulted in the New Yorkers having become almost a race apart. The same applied to the New Englanders and the Southerners for, although they had all accepted the Constitution and, as the United States, were technically one nation, as yet they were far from having coalesced into one people.

Most of the houses in the city were built of wood, and down by the Battery, on the point, there were still some narrow streets of Jacobean buildings; but further inland

the streets were wider, with houses of brick or stone. To
the north there was open country, with many farms and,
along the bank of the Hudson, a number of mansions with
extensive grounds. They could not compare in size with
the stately homes of England, but they could in design,
as most of them were fine examples of the best Georgian
architecture.

The van Wycks took Roger and Mary to visit two of
these lovely homes, which belonged to friends of theirs,
and this resulted in a piece of great good fortune for
Roger. The owner of one of them was Gouverneur
Morris.

This distinguished American had been born in what
was known as Morrisania Manor and, many years later,
had purchased it from his brother. After holding several
important posts in the newly-formed independent Government of the United States, in 1789 he had gone to live in
France, and in '92 been appointed American Ambassador
there. A born aristocrat, he favoured strong government
by well-educated men of good birth. His open hostility to
the revolutionaries after they had imprisoned the Royal
family had led to the Convention demanding his recall.
But before returning to America he had spent four years
travelling in Europe, and for a considerable part of that
time he had lived in London. While there he had been
made a member of White's, and Roger had met him at
the club on several occasions.

Mr. Morris was now a man of sixty; cynical, intelligent, witty and having enormous charm. Like most New
Yorkers, he had been strongly opposed to this new war
with England, and when he learned of the plight of the
exiles he showed his sympathy in the most practical manner by asking Roger how he was placed for funds.

Roger promptly disclosed the slender state of his re-

sources, and added that as he was unable to produce
evidence that at home he was a man of substance, he
could not approach anyone in New York for a substantial
loan on his note of hand, even if they were prepared to
wait for repayment until after the war. To this Morris
replied :

'Mr. Brook, the fact that your father was a British
Admiral and that you are a member of White's is security
enough for me, and I should be happy to finance you to
any reasonable amount.'

It was then arranged that Roger should write a letter
to Hoare's Bank, informing them that Mr. Morris had
lent him five hundred pounds and that this sum was to be
repaid on presentation of the letter, together with the current rate of interest for loans from that date up to the date
of presentation. Mr. Morris said that he would have
the money next day, and invited the Brooks and the van
Wycks to dine with him so that he could hand it over.

When Roger and Mary were in bed on the night they
had received this generous assistance, he said to her :

'Mary, my love, although I have done my best to hide
it from you, I know that you must have guessed how desperately worried I have been about our situation here.
If we could have got a ship to land me in any European
port, either in Britain or, as the *Comte de Breuc,* anywhere on the Continent, I could with ease have procured
the money to pay our passage. But Silas van Wyck's enquiries among his shipping friends have made it certain
that no American merchant will any longer send one of
his ships to sea, owing to the certain chance of her being
captured by the British blockading squadron.

'That meant I would have to seek some clerical post
to provide us with the means of subsistence during our
virtually enforced captivity here; for we could not remain

as the good van Wyck's guests indefinitely. But now, with the five hundred pounds that Gouverneur Morris has so generously lent me, an alternative is open to us. With ample money to pay our way, we could proceed north to the Canadian border and, given good luck, succeed in crossing the war zone. Then from Quebec we'd have no difficulty in securing a passage home. What say you to this project?'

'That we must embark upon it,' she replied at once. 'The war may last for years, and working as a clerk in some merchant's office would be misery for you. The loan has proved a god-send, and the sooner we set out for Canada the better.'

After a moment he said, 'Were I alone I would not hesitate to do so. But nothing could induce me to leave you behind, and such a journey would prove no light undertaking for a woman. Once past Albany you would have to face great discomfort. Further north winter conditions still prevail : ice on the lakes, snow, possibly blizzards, and uncertainty about securing even barely edible food. Added to that, when endeavouring to cross the frontier, we would be in grave danger, not only from the Americans catching us and believing us to be spies, but also from falling into the hands of a band of Indians, who might treat us with the utmost savagery.'

'No matter,' Mary declared. 'No conditions could be worse than those we faced together in Russia. Mr. Morris's loan will not last indefinitely, and it would be misery for you to earn a pittance here in some subordinate position. And still worse for me, to witness your unhappiness daily for months, perhaps for years. If you refrain from asking Silas tomorrow to do what he can to facilitate our journey to the north, then I shall do so myself. Now, either make love to me, or let us go to sleep.'

Turning over, Roger took her in his arms and murmured, 'My sweet, brave Mary. Since you are determined to face this venture, I'll no further labour the risks we must take, for if we do not take them we condemn ourselves to an indefinite period of dreary frustration which would be near intolerable to support.'

The following morning they told their host and hostess of their decision to try to get home by way of Canada. Silas van Wyck endeavoured to dissuade them from the attempt, stressing the difficulties and dangers they would encounter. His wife added her plea, describing the discomforts she had once endured during a journey of only a week in a covered wagon. But Mary replied that she had suffered far worse, and Roger added that they could travel the greater part of the way by water.

This was true, as the supply route to the American forces on the St. Lawrence river front was due north from New York, first by way of the Hudson then across Lake Champlain, and there was a regular service of river boats up the Hudson as far as Albany.

Having failed to persuade his guests to stay on, van Wyck procured passages for them on the next boat going north, sailing on March 14th. That morning the van Wyck family accompanied them to the landing stage and, having said good-bye to these excellent friends Roger and Mary started on their long journey.

There had been settlements on both sides of the Hudson river for well over a hundred and fifty years, and there was a regular service between New York and the considerable town of Albany, so the boats were moderately comfortable. The passengers were mostly farmers or store keepers, some of whom were accompanied by their wives and negro slaves. There was also a group of Redskins, who had been down to New York to exchange furs for tobacco, powder for their muskets, fiery spirits and various domestic articles such as iron cooking pots.

Roger was told that the Indians were Mohawks, one of the tribes of the Five Nations that, united, were termed Iroquois. Hiawatha had been one of the founders of the Confederation, and it had the highest form of government of any Indian people north of Mexico. The group on the boat wore, beneath their furs, fringed tunics of fine deer-skin, and their moccasins were decorated with coloured beads. Their heads were closely shaved, except for the traditional scalp lock, from which a single eagle plume dangled over the left shoulder. Mary and Roger had seen a few Indians, mostly half-breeds, in New York, but they had been shoddily-dressed by-products of semi-civilisa-tion, whereas these Mohawk braves were obviously the real thing. All day they sat cross-legged, seldom speaking but passing their pipe and taking unhurried draws in turn from it. Thin-faced, with high cheekbones, hooked noses and impassive features, they presented a picture of proud independence. At night they remained on deck and slept wrapped in their bearskins.

It was very cold, but the weather was fine and the wind favourable. Every twenty miles or so the boat went along-side the wharf of a small township to disembark or take on passengers and stores; then, when she reached Albany, she berthed for the night before preparing for her return trip.

In Albany Roger and Mary stayed the night at an hotel the name of which had been given them by van Wyck. Fortunately, as it now turned out, they had bought fur coats, hats, gloves, muffs and fur-lined boots while in Stockholm, as further north it was still winter. Knowing that for part of their journey they would have to sleep rough, they went out the following morning and bought a number of things they might need, including beaver sleeping bags.

Next day they went aboard a smaller boat which would take them another forty-five miles up the river to Hudson Falls, which was the most northern point to which it was navigable. There they landed at Fort Edward, about which there had grown up a small settlement. In an open space some troops were being drilled, but otherwise there was little military activity, as the campaign was not expected to open for another three weeks. Nevertheless, owing to the place being on the supply route for the operations of the previous summer, it had grown considerably and now had several large rest houses, at one of which Roger was able to secure accommodation.

The next stage of their journey entailed twenty miles overland, past Glen Falls to Fort George, which lay at the southern extremity of the lake of that name. Again the past summer's campaign made their journey easier, for what had earlier been a rough track through the wilderness had been greatly improved to facilitate the passage of convoys. The scenery, with its rapids, waterfalls and wooded slopes, was magnificent, but the gradients were often steep, so it took them twelve hours to do this part of their journey in a covered wagon.

A settlement had also grown up round Fort George and, at a rest house that night, Roger made enquiries of the owner about transport up the lake. Next morning the man produced two Longhunters who were going north in their canoe and willing to take two passengers for a reasonable price.

The name of one was Ben Log, the other was known as 'Shorty'. Both of them were bearded and had mops of ill-trimmed hair under caps of skin which had been shorn of the fur. They were dressed in green hunting shirts, with girdles of wampum and breeches and leggings of buckskin, the latter laced at the sides and gartered above the knee with deer sinews. Each had a knife and a small hatchet thrust through his girdle and, hanging from it, powder horns and pouches. The rifles they carried were very long and the barrels polished to mirror brightness.

They naturally wanted to know why the Brooks wished to go north, and Roger produced a story he had thought up in New York. Knowing that they had no means of checking up his account of himself, he said he was a cartographer employed by the Government to make more accurate maps of the country south of the St. Lawrence. To support his story he had bought a theodolite, a number of maps and a big roll of paper suitable for making others. He added, before he could be asked why he was taking his wife into the wilds with him, that he, although an expert surveyor, was a poor hand at drawing, whereas Mary had a gift for it; so she was indispensable as his assistant.

By midday, the Brooks' baggage and gear—including a bivouac that Roger bought at the local store, as they would have to camp at nights on shore—had been carried down to the canoe and, with the two Longhunters paddling in prow and stern, they set off up Lake George.

The scenery on either side was more beautiful than ever for, on the east, the Green Mountains, and on the west the Adirondacks, ran down to the shores of the long, narrow lake. For most people who normally lived in comfort the prospect of having to camp out in such bitter weather would have been highly disagreeable. But after the terrible weeks that Roger and Mary had spent in the icy wastes of Russia, they could face it without apprehension. There, for a great part of the time they had had to fend for themselves; here they had with them two strong men who would do all the chores. There, too, towards the end of their journey, they had been near starvation; now they had ample supplies of food with them.

For many months each year the Longhunters lived far from civilisation, so making camp was for them a long-perfected drill. With a practised eye they selected sites where canvas could be stretched between neighbouring trees at an angle that would screen the campers from the wind. The canoe had no sooner grounded than they threw out fishing lines. Jumping ashore, they swiftly collected rotten branches and, starting it with a small log soaked in resin, within a few minutes made a good fire. While Shorty set up the bivouac and brought furs, stores and cooking utensils from the canoe, Ben Log went off into the woods with his long rifle to see if he could sight a bird or game for the pot. So they ate heartily every evening while the Longhunters remained with them off a fresh-caught fish or savoury stews of venison, hare, or turkey.

At the northern end of Lake George lay the settlement of Ticonderoga. There they had to land and cross a narrow isthmus to reach the far larger Lake Champlain. A party of Indians from among those who lived in the settlement was hired to do the porterage. Four of them carried the big canoe, the others the tentage, baggage and equipment.

Roger noticed that none of them wore feathers in his hair, and Ben Log told him they were known as 'naked foreheads'—men who had failed to pass the agonising ordeals by which an Indian became a 'brave'. They were, he added, squirting out the juice of a tobacco plug he was chewing, men of the Oneides tribe, who with the Mohawks, Onondagas, Cayuga and Senecas made up the Five Nations.

As they advanced up the long lake, whenever they

D

passed a small bay a part of which faced nearly northward, they noticed the ice there had not yet melted and
fringed the shore. Further up it made a white line all
along the coast, and the trees were still coated in snow.
Several times they had to turn their fur collars up round
their faces while passing through snow storms and, when
they went ashore, flail their arms to warm themselves up
until a fire could be got going. The Longhunters had
brought a good supply of spruce—a fiery spirit—with
them, and every night before settling down to sleep in
their beaver robes, they all drank a good ration of it.

Occasionally they passed other canoes, manned either
by befeathered Indians or bearded whites, and twice they
were passed by small sailing barques carrying troops up
to the front. But usually there were no other humans in
sight, and nothing moved except, now and then, a fish-
hawk diving on its unseen prey. For long spells the silence
was broken only by the rhythmic splashing of the
Longhunters' paddles as they drove the canoe steadily
forward.

Dusk still fell early; then, while they sat round the camp
fire, the denizens of the forest awoke to go on their nightly
prowl for food : coyotes barked, badgers screamed, owls
hooted and wolves howled. One night a small pack of
wolves, attracted by the fire, approached near enough
for their yellow eyes to reflect the light. Mary gave a little
cry of fright, and Roger quickly put his arm about her
while, with his free hand, he pulled out one of his pistols.
But the Longhunters did not even bother to pick up their
rifles. Shorty plucked a burning brand from the fire, hurled it at the nearest wolf and chuckled when it hit its mark.
The singed beast gave a high-pitched whine and bounded
away, followed by the others.

At that date the head of Lake Champlain, and the

Richelieu river, which connects it with the St. Lawrence, were in Canadian territory. Roger had been greatly tempted to offer the Longhunters a good sum to take Mary and himself as far as the border, but decided not to risk it. They were naturally posing as Americans, and as many New Yorkers had English accents, neither of the men had shown the least suspicion that they were not. But if they were given cause to think that their passengers meant to cross into Canada, they might very well guess the truth and cut up rough, which would be very awkward and dangerous.

In consequence the party landed at Plattsburg, which was about twenty miles below the frontier, and where Roger had originally hired them to take him. There was a considerable number of troops in the town, as it was the base for the northern front. In an open space a company of American troops was being drilled and, after watching for a few minutes, Roger took a very poor view of them. They were nearly all good specimens of manhood, strong-limbed and with healthy, bronzed faces; but their dress was slipshod, their movements had no snap and obviously they were recruits unused to discipline. Having spent much of his time for many years with both the French and British armies, he knew that one quarter of their number of Napoleon's Imperial Guard, the British Grenadiers or a regiment of the Line, would make mincemeat of the poor fellows.

Every foot of the original accommodation in the place was occupied, and many new huts had been built, but only as quarters for the military, so Roger and his party had to pitch camp on the edge of the town and sleep in their bivouacs. Normally the Longhunters would have gone off into the forest to shoot and trap game until they had collected as many pelts as they could carry back to

the lake and take down to Fort George for sale, but Roger
now made them a handsome offer to accompany him and
Mary westward as far as the St. Lawrence.

Next morning Ben Log succeeded in hiring a covered
wagon with a half-breed driver. That afternoon, having
loaded their tentage and freshly-bought stores, they set
off on their ninety-mile trek along a trail that had develop-
ed into a rough road after convoys and troops had so
frequently used it.

The forest trees were still bare of leaves, but Shorty
who, although uneducated, was by instinct a naturalist,
told Mary that in the autumn the turning leaves made a
sea of gold and pointed out to her the different barks on
giant hickories, beeches, maples, black walnuts, pines and
silver birches. Many of the tree trunks were overgrown
with moss and others half-smothered in tangles of ivy. He
warned her against the latter, as much of it was poison
ivy, and a very nasty rash would have resulted from touching it. Shorty could also tell the species of a bird from its
cry, and quite frequently they saw jays, ravens, hawks,
crows and catbirds sailing overhead.

On the fourth evening they came to St. Regis, where the
Sulpician Fathers had a mission which was part hospital
and part school to which Indian Chiefs sent their sons
to acquire a smattering of the white man's education. Two
days later, Thursday, April 1st, they reached French
Mills, now a fully-garrisoned American strongpoint within a short distance of the river. It had taken them nineteen
days to get there from New York.

The Fort itself consisted of two square, two-storeyed
block houses, with overhanging upper floors roofed with
bark. These were connected by palisades made of high
pointed and pitched stakes lashed securely together. The
palisade enclosed a large area into which, in times of

trouble, settlers with their families and livestock could take refuge. It was entered by a single sally port. Now that French Mills had become a frontier post during active warfare, the palisaded enclosure was nowhere near large enough to accommodate the garrison. In consequence, a cantonment had grown up round it, consisting of long hutments for barracks, storehouses and stables. Some of the troops were being drilled and others carrying out fatigues. Among the latter were a number of Indians and, at a cookhouse, Mary noticed with interest a number of fur-clad women collecting rations.

As Roger and his party approached the sally port his heart and Mary's began to beat a little faster, for they both knew that this might prove the end of the road for them. By suffering considerable hardships and discomfort they had succeeded in getting to within a mile of the Canadian frontier. If they could now manage to get across it, they were as good as home.

But there can be many a slip 'twixt cup and lip. Roger had long since learned that Mary had a natural gift for calligraphy, and could even write in Elizabethan script: so a few days before they left New York he had bought a sheet of parchment and asked her to write on it in copper-plate what appeared to be a letter of authority from the Department of Rivers and Forests stating that he was a surveyor.

When she had done so and he was about to sign it with a fictitious name, she stopped him and said:

'Would it not be better if we could secure the Minister's signature and I forged it?'

'Forged it?' he had repeated with a frown. 'Are you really capable of doing that?'

'Oh yes,' she laughed. 'When I was at my academy, on quite a number of occasions I earned a little money by writing essays for lazy rich girls in hands that were near enough to pass as theirs.'

'It would certainly make the document appear valid, and so save us from dire trouble if anyone to whom we showed it chanced to know the Minister's signature. But how could we get hold of it?' He asked and she had replied.

'You must recall that I bought an autograph book while we were in Stockholm, and that several members of the Royal family were gracious enough to sign it. I could add the signature of Mr. van Wyck, and copy from the draft he gave you last night that of Gouverneur Morris. I'd take my book to the Minister, get him to sign it, then copy his signature onto this document.'

Roger had agreed to Mary's plan and the following day she had succeeded in carrying it out.

But the document's acceptance by the Commanding Officer at French Mills still entailed one very nasty risk. If at his Headquarters there were trained mapmakers, it would soon be realised that Roger was entirely ignorant about such work. Suspicion of his bona-fides would be aroused, a careful watch kept on them, which would prevent their crossing into Canada, and a letter of enquiry about them dispatched to New York. It would emerge that the document was a forgery and further enquiries elicit the fact that they were English. They would then be arrested and charged with having come up to the war zone as spies.

Striving to hide their apprehensions under a calm, unconcerned manner, they walked towards the Fort, eager yet fearful to learn what Fate had in store for them.

7

Disaster

A SENTRY, smoking a pipe, was lounging by the entrance
to the sally port. Roger asked him where his commanding
officer could be found. The man jerked his thumb toward
the nearer of the blockhouses. 'Colonel Jason be yonder.'

Leaving the Longhunters outside, Roger and Mary
entered the stockade. After further enquiries they located
the Colonel in one of the buildings, sitting with another
officer at a rough, plank table in a back room. It had a dirt
floor, was sour-smelling and dim, the only light coming
from loopholes in two of the walls. The uniforms of the
two officers were dark blue serge, with dull red facings,
worn and grease-stained. They were sorting through a
small pile of papers, but, greatly to Roger's relief, there
were no maps to be seen, or other evidence that this was a
military headquarters similar to those he was accustomed
to frequent in Europe.

Bowing politely, he took a paper from his pocket,
handed it to the elder of the officers and said, 'My name,
Sir, is Roger Brook. Permit me to present my wife. These
are my credentials.'

As Mary curtseyed, the two men stood up and bowed.
The Colonel, who was grey-haired, with a lined face, took
the paper.

At Roger's dictation Mary had headed it, 'To whom it may concern,' then written :

'Mr. Roger Brook of this city is a qualified surveyor in the employ of my department, and his wife is his assistant. This is to request that every assistance shall be given to them to carry out their work and, where possible, accommodation be provided for them.'

Beneath this she had forged the signature of *Andrew Stapleton*—the name of the Minister concerned—then had carefully printed underneath : *DEPARTMENT OF RIVERS AND FORESTS.*

For a long moment they waited in acute suspense while Colonel Jason read it. He then looked up and, to their immense relief, showed no suspicion that the document might be a forgery. 'Well, Mr. Brook,' he said. 'What can I do for you?'

'As you must be aware, Sir,' Roger replied, 'the maps of this remote part of New York State are most indifferent. I have been sent here to make better ones. If you can provide my wife and me with accommodation we should be most grateful. And rations. For the latter I am, of course, quite willing to pay, as they will be charged to my department.'

The Colonel nodded. 'That's no great problem. The fort itself is fuller than a barrel of herrings; but, as you'll have seen, we've built scores of shacks nearby. Long huts for the men and cabins for the officers and some of the wives who've been living here with them all winter. But now the fighting'll soon start again, several of the ladies have already left.'

With a wave of his hand toward the other officer, he added, 'This is Captain Dayho. He'll take you along and allot you quarters.'

The Brooks exchanged bows with Dayho, then thanked

the Colonel. All had gone smoothly and they could now hope that within a few days they would be across the river.

The Captain, a sprightly, youngish man with bushy side-whiskers, escorted them to the sally port, where Roger presented Ben Log and Shorty to him. Accompanied by the two Longhunters, they walked for some distance through dirty slush along a path to a large clearing in which there were a score or more of cabins. Most of them were still occupied, but several had been abandoned, the wives having left and their husbands having moved into one of the long huts reserved for officers. After looking into several, Mary chose one which had been left in a cleaner condition than the others. It was furnished only with a broad, leathermesh bed on which there was a thin palliasse stuffed with straw, a rough-hewn table, several empty packing cases that could be used either to sit on or keep spare clothes in, and an iron brazier.

Smiling at Mary, Dayho said, 'Not much of a place for a lady like you, Ma'am, but it's the best we can do. There's a woodstack behind this row of cabins, from which you can collect logs for your fire, and any of the other ladies in the clearing will tell you where you can draw your rations. As you are from New York, I fear you will find social life here very dull. Colonel Jason takes the view that parties should be discouraged, as they distract his officers from their dooties.'

Turning to Roger, he went on, 'You suggested paying for your rations, Sir, but that is quite unnecessary. And we shall be happy to make you an honorary member of our Mess whenever you care to come to it. Now, if you will excuse me, I must get back, as we are exceptionally hard at it preparing for the new campaign.'

When he had left them Shorty went round to the woodstack, collected some logs and got a fire going in the brazier, while Ben Log went to fetch the covered wagon. They unloaded all their belongings, then Roger paid off the half-breed driver.

The Longhunters realised that now Roger and Mary had been installed in the camp they would no longer need their services so, after a drink of spruce all round, the good-byes were said. Roger offered them a bonus on the sum agreed, but smilingly they refused to take it, declaring that it had been a privilege and a pleasure to escort such a gay and uncomplaining little lady as Mary on a trek. Not to be outdone, she kissed them both on their bearded cheeks. Then, with their long, loping stride, these two of Nature's gentlemen went on their way.

After distributing their things about the cabin and arranging it as comfortably as possible, Roger and Mary went out to make acquaintance with their nearest neighbours. The men were on duty with their troops and there were only a few, furclad women about. They were all of a type that Americans describe as very 'ornary', and a little over-awed by Mary's ladylike appearance, which she could not disguise; but they were pleasant and helpful about telling of the life of the camp.

That evening Roger tactfully acted on Captain Dayho's invitation to make use of the Officers' Mess, and spent an hour or so drinking with several of the members to whom Dayho introduced him. As he had expected, only the few seniors were regulars, the others being Militia and mostly farmers or storekeepers from small up-country towns. Nearly all of them wished the war soon over, as their hearts were not in it, and Roger felt sorry for them because they obviously knew next to nothing about soldiering and could not hope to stand up against equal numbers of well-disciplined British troops.

When he got back to the cabin he found that Mary had succeeded in making a stew from some venison left them by the Longhunters, but it had proved a far from pleasant task, as the only means of cooking was the brazier and there was no chimney, only a hole in the roof to let out the smoke. The cabin was half-filled with it, and her eyes were smarting painfully.

She had also had an unnerving experience when going to the woodpile for more logs. Strange noises were coming from it, and she had feared they were from some wild animal. But she had been reassured by another woman coming up, who laughed at her, then told her it was only a chipmunk and quite harmless.

Anxious to get away as soon as possible from these comfortless conditions, they went out early the following morning, armed with Roger's theodolite and a book for making notes. On reaching the river they found, to their disappointment, that the bank there was a sheer cliff nearly a hundred feet deep, and that the river below was only partly frozen with, between the ice along both banks, a raging torrent caused by the melting snow.

Pretending to take observations now and then, they made their way upstream for several miles, only to find that, although dangerous-looking paths wound down the cliff here and there, at no place was it possible to cross the river. Next day they explored the territory in the opposite direction, but met with no better fortune. At one place there was a tangle of rocks where it would have been possible in summer to cross by scrambling from one to another, but now the rocks were half-submerged in clouds of white, foaming water cascading over them.

Their third day being a Sunday, convention prohibited them from appearing to do any work but, after attending service they went for a long walk. At dusk, tired and depressed, they were about to re-enter the camp when, just outside it, they came upon a group of men. In the centre was an Indian and standing round him were half a dozen soldiers. As Roger and Mary approached they saw that he was a youngish man and, by the scarlet feather that dangled from his scalp-lock, a brave. His furs had been taken from him, one of the soldiers had put a noose of rope over his head, while another threw the other end over the low branch of a big tree. Although the native was half-naked in the biting cold, and obviously about to be hanged, he stood erect and unmoving, his proud face showing no trace of fear.

Halting beside the group, Roger asked the sergeant in charge, 'Why are you about to hang this man?'

'Because 'e's a dirty spy, Sirre,' replied the N.C.O. 'We roped him in this mornin' an' we're wise to 'is tribe. 'E comes from over thar, across the river.'

Mary's heart was wrung with pity for the impassive brave, and she exclaimed to Roger, 'Can we do nothing to save him?'

Not wishing to show pity in front of the American soldiers for one of their enemies, she had spoken in French. Immediately the Indian was galvanised into speech. In the French patois that was the *lingua franca* of the Indians in Canada, his dark eyes flashing, he cried :

'I beg your help! I am a Christian. The rich furs you wear and those of he who is with you tell me that he is a great Chief. Beautiful lady, I implore you. I implore you do not stand by and let them take my life.'

Roger well knew that hanging was the normal penalty for any spy who was caught, but he also felt a natural pity for this brave man. Suddenly, he had had an inspiration, and said to the sergeant :

'As I am not one of your officers, I cannot give you an

order; but I can give you a very good reason why you should not yet hang this fellow. He tells me he is a Christian. As you probably know, nearly all Indian Christians in Canada have been converted by the Fathers. He is therefore a Roman Catholic. As such he naturally wishes to make confession before he dies, and receive absolution for his sins. It is only reasonable that he should be kept prisoner for a few days until one of the priests from St. Regis can be brought up here to perform the last rites for him.'

There ensued an argument between Roger and the sergeant, but one of the soldiers happened to be a Catholic, and broke in strongly to support Roger's contention; so it was decided that the prisoner should be taken to the fort and brought before the Commandant for his decision.

After a wait of half an hour the grey-haired Colonel Jason received them and listened to what Roger had to say. As the Colonel could speak no French and wished to interrogate the Indian, Roger acted as interpreter. It transpired that the man was a Cree Indian named Leaping Squirrel. He was twenty-four years old and son of a Sagamore who ruled over many lesser Chiefs. At the age of fourteen his father had sent him to the Jesuit mission at Caughnawaga, near Montreal. There he had been baptised and remained for two years, learning to read and write in French, and about the life of Jesus Christ. To prove his assertion he recited the Lord's Prayer and some passages from the Gospels.

There could be no doubt that he had been sent across the river to get some idea of the strength of the American forces in that area, so the Colonel was in no mood to show him mercy; but he did agree to grant a reprieve until a Catholic priest could be brought up from St. Regis to hear the man's confession.

Roger then said, 'That may take a week or more, Sir. In the meantime would you allow me to take charge of him? As a servant he could relieve my wife for a while of some of the menial tasks, to which she is unaccustomed. Moreover, since he must know a good deal about the territory in this neighbourhood, I have no doubt that he would be willing, out of gratitude, to help me with my surveying.'

The Colonel considered for a moment. As the Brooks were supposed to be Americans, they had agreed when leaving New York that Mary should be known as Mrs. Brook instead of Lady Mary. But on his visits to the Mess Roger had casually mentioned that he had been a friend for many years of Gouverneur Morris, and named several other prominent New Yorkers he had met while a guest of the van Wycks. In consequence the Colonel had come to regard him as a man with influence, whose wishes it would be wise to humour. Looking up, he said:

'Mr. Brook, realising that your wife is a lady of quality, I should have liked to provide her with a servant. But to do so would have been unfair to the wives of my officers, who have to fend for themselves. However, I see no reason why you should not have the use of this man while he remains with us. In the daytime, of course, you will be armed, so could shoot him if he attempts to escape. But what of the nights? I have no other prisoners as yet, every room in the fort is occupied, and I am loath to spare men to stand guard over him in a cabin.'

Roger swiftly countered that by saying, 'If he is given back his furs, Sir, he is used to sleeping in the open. He would be as much a prisoner if he dosses down within the compound as he would be in a cell, for without help he could not possibly climb out over the palisade.'

So the matter was settled. The thongs that bound the Indian's hands behind his back were cut, upon which he

knelt down before Mary and kissed the hem of her fur
robe in gratitude. His furs were brought to him and, as
night had now fallen, a soldier took him to a place along-
side the palisade where he could sleep. Then Roger and
Mary returned to their cabin to eat a cold supper.

Next morning they collected Leaping Squirrel from the
compound, gave him the theodolite to carry and set off on
their daily walk along the cliff. When they had covered a
couple of miles, Roger pointed to a small mound from
which anyone approaching could be seen from a distance,
and said, 'Now, let's sit down there and talk.'

When they were all seated, he addressed Leaping
Squirrel in French. 'You realise that, within a week at
most, one of the Fathers will have come up from St. Regis,
and that when you have made your confession there will
be no way in which you can secure a further respite from
being hanged?'

The Indian gravely inclined his head. 'I accept that.
Leaping Squirrel was told before he started on the trail
that if he fell into a snare his end would be as that of a
robbing stoat dangling from a tree. To you, noble ones
of the Americani, Leaping Squirrel is grateful for these
few extra days of life.'

'We are not Americani,' said Roger quietly. 'My wife
and I are Englesi.'

The dark eyes of the Indian suddenly lit up. 'Then
Leaping Squirrel is not the enemy of the noble ones, but
their little brother.'

Roger nodded. 'Yes. We three are as one people. My
wife and I are very anxious to get to Canada, but we cannot find a way to cross the river. By showing us a way
you can not only earn our gratitude, but save your own
life.'

No longer impassive, the Indian spread wide his hands,

bowed his fine head then exclaimed joyfully, 'Noble ones, the Lord Jesus sent you to Leaping Squirrel. You are to him as the hand of the Father when He held it over Daniel in the lion's den. Leaping Squirrel will lead you to Canada. But the trail is long. Three sleeps from here. No, four or more for the tender feet of the gracious lady, before we can cross the rushing water.'

'No matter,' Roger smiled. 'And the sooner we are on our way, the better. We will start tonight.'

The Indian's face fell. 'How is that possible, noble one? Leaping Squirrel is a captive. He sleeps within the stockade.'

'We will get you out. It means running a certain risk, but with a little luck it can be done. Fortunately, the moon is in its last quarter, so the stockade will be in semi-darkness; and you must pick a place in which to sleep where the shadow from one of the blockhouses will conceal you. I'll then throw a rope over to you so that you can haul yourself up and get over the palisade.'

'But what then, noble one? When it is found that Leaping Squirrel has escaped, Indian trackers will be sent after him. Given a few hours' start, he could outdistance them. What, though, of the gracious lady? She could not travel at such speed. After our first sleep, at best our second, they would catch up with us.'

That most unpleasant possibility had not occurred to Roger. As he looked anxiously at Mary, she said :

'It is a chance we must take. Unless we do, in a few days' time a priest will arrive from St. Regis to hear Leaping Squirrel's confession, and then he will be hanged. Besides, I am stronger than I look.'

Roger smiled. 'That's true, my love; and you are right about Leaping Squirrel. If we can get a good start, we should be able to throw any trackers off our scent. There is also the fact that, without a guide, the possibility of our getting across the river seems very slender. I think we should risk it.'

Having taken this decision, they left the mound and went into a nearby neck of the woods, with the object of sleeping through the afternoon, so that they would be able to travel all night without needing to rest. Leaping Squirrel gathered some young branches of sassafras to make a couch for Mary, then they settled down.

Early in the evening, filled with suppressed excitement, they returned to camp. While Mary went to the cabin to cook supper, Roger accompanied Leaping Squirrel into the stockade, and the Indian indicated the spot against the palisade where he would lie in his furs when night came. Roger, while apparently looking uncon- cernedly about him, counted the number of posts in the palisade from the spot chosen to the south-west corner. Walking out through the sally port he again counted the posts up to the same number, picked up a large stone and put it against the post, so that he could find it easily again; then he went to the Mess, bought a bottle of brandy, had his usual evening drink there, and afterwards rejoined Mary.

When they had had their meal, they packed all the belongings they felt they could not do without, and such food as Mary had been able to get hold of, into two bundles in the canvas of the bivouac under which they had slept on the way up to Fort George; but Roger had first tied the greater part of the ropes by which it was pegged out into one length of about eighteen feet.

Having completed these preparations, they had to wait with such patience as they could muster until the hour that had been agreed for Leaping Squirrel's rescue. For- tunately, the garrison at French Mills kept early hours.

One by one the lights in the other cabins went out, then they doused theirs and sat on the hard bed, with their arms about each other, occasionally kissing or talking in low voices. The time of waiting seemed interminable, although they had decided that, to get as long a start as possible, they would make the attempt as soon as it could reasonably be assumed that the officers and men who lived in the stockade were asleep. At length, at about eleven o'clock, Roger felt that they must risk everything to carry out their plan.

Each of them took a bundle and Roger, in addition, threw over his shoulder the rope he had made and the straw palliasse from the bed. Walking as quietly as they could, they made their way along the track through the wood until it ended a hundred yards or so from the fort. There, in the shadow of the last trees, Roger left Mary with the two bundles and continued on toward the stockade.

Since the river bank for several miles on either side of the fort was a high cliff, it was almost impossible to take French Mills by surprise, so no sentries were posted, except for one man inside the now closed sally port, and he was stationed there only to open it in the event of a despatch rider arriving during the night. Taking care not to tread on any small fallen branches, Roger advanced until he reached the large stone he had left outside the palisade. There he took from his pocket a whistle made from the wing bone of a turkey, which Leaping Squirrel had given him to signal with. He blew gently on it, so that the sound should not be audible at a distance of more than a dozen paces. It was answered from the other side of the palisade by the low hoot of an owl.

Standing well back, Roger threw the straw palliasse up so that it landed on the spikes of the eight-foot-high stakes forming the palisade. He threw after it one end of the rope, then tied the other end round his waist, so that he could take a strain upon it. A moment later it became taut and he caught the sound of a faint scrambling noise, then Leaping Squirrel's head appeared above the mattress. Wriggling over it, he slid down to Roger's side.

Five minutes later they were with Mary. The two men took the bundles and, in Indian file with Leaping Squirrel leading, they set off, three silent shadows, into the almost dark woods.

For about two hours the moon, filtering through the bare branches of the trees, continued to give them just enough light to see their way. By the time it set they were sufficiently distant from the camp for there to be no risk of their being seen on the open ground along the cliffs by any restless person who had left his quarters to go for a midnight stroll; and, for the remainder of the night, the dim illumination from lingering patches of snow enabled them to press on without any danger of walking over the edge of the cliff. By dawn, although leaning on Roger's arm, Mary had to admit that she could not go a step further. But her dogged courage had enabled them to cover the better part of fifteen miles.

As it was unlikely that Leaping Squirrel's escape would be discovered before dawn, and after that some little time would elapse before a party of trackers could be sent in pursuit, they reckoned that their night march had given them about eight hours' start. Having rested for ten minutes every hour, Mary had been able to keep going, but Roger realised that unless fatigue should overcome her later, they must now sacrifice several hours of their lead; so he called a halt and they made camp.

At ten o'clock, after a good sleep, they roused and

Roger set about collecting sticks so that they could get a
fire going and cook a meal. But Leaping Squirrel stopped
him, giving the disquieting reason that they were in
Mohawk country, and the smoke of a fire might be seen
by an Indian out hunting. If that happened, he would
fetch others, and they would be lucky if they were not
scalped and killed.

Having made do on cold food, they set off again, re-
entering the forest, as the river curved away in a great
arc at the place where they had slept, and Leaping
Squirrel told them it would save many miles if they cut
across it. After they had penetrated for some way among
the trees, the Indian asked them to wait where they were
for a while. He then padded to and fro, sometimes dis-
appearing for several minutes; but at length he beckoned
them to follow him. When they had done so for two hundred yards or more, he pointed to a gash about five feet up
on a big tree, where the bark had been chipped away.
Turning east, he walked on some distance, then pointed
to a similar gash on another big tree, and told them these
were the marks by which he had blazed a trail on his
outward journey, so that he could easily find his way
back.

Just as evening was closing in, he stopped beside one
of the blazed trees which also bore a buzzard feather
wedged in the bark. With a stout stick, which he had
picked up an hour or so earlier, he began to dig in the
earth behind the tree, and soon turned up a foot-long
package. Unwrapping a covering of elk skin, he showed
them a chunk of dried bear meat and some strips of pem-
mican. Roger was delighted at this unexpected addition
to their supplies as, although they had brought all the
food Mary had had in the cabin, he had feared it would
not last them for more than a few days; and his pistols

were useless for hunting, owing to their short range.

After eating, they slept for some hours. When they awoke, moonlight lit the glade, so they made the most of it to cover several more miles; then, when the moon set, they slept again.

Half-way through their second day's trek, Leaping Squirrel, who always led the party, suddenly halted, swung round and put his finger to his lips to enjoin silence. He then signed to them to take cover among some blackberry bushes, which were the only low-growing vegetation within sight. Reluctantly, but seeing, from the alarmed expression on the Indian's face, that danger threatened, they waded in among the long, prickly stems and crouched down among them.

For several minutes Roger and Mary could hear nothing, although they listened intently. Then they caught the faint sound of snapping twigs. Peering out from their hiding place they saw a dozen figures some twenty yards away. It was a party of Mohawk warriors, moving silently in single file and resembling a band of gliding spectres.

Fortunately they were heading in the direction of the river, but a good ten minutes elapsed before Leaping Squirrel signed to his companions that they might leave their cover. They emerged from the tangle of bushes with several nasty scratches, and Roger's buckskin leggings had been badly torn on a cat briar.

Roger and Mary feared that the Indians they had glimpsed were trackers sent out from French Mills. Leaping Squirrel reassured them that the men were a party of hunters intent on their own business, and to be avoided only because they might have proved hostile. But, he added grimly, their lead must be lessening, as they had to take much longer rests than the trackers would need, and

the time had come when they must try to hide their trail
by wading in a lake which he knew lay a few miles
head.

That evening they came to it and, for a quarter of an
hour, splashed through the bitterly cold water along its
shore, entering and leaving it several times to confuse their
pursuers.

Now that the danger of capture had become ominously
nearer, Roger could not keep his mind off that possibility.
It would certainly mean death for Leaping Squirrel.
There was no way of preventing that. But what would
happen to himself and Mary after they had been marched
back to French Mills?

Colonel Jason could hardly have failed to connect their
disappearance with Leaping Squirrel's escape on the same
night. In any case, their being captured with him would
be indisputable evidence of it. What, Roger wondered,
was the penalty for assisting an enemy spy to escape? Almost certainly a sentence of several months in prison. But
would matters end even there? At French Mills there was
no prison, so he would be sent down to Albany, or perhaps
New York. A trial would also lead to an investigation of
his past. It would emerge that the document stating him
to be a surveyor in the employ of the Ministry of Rivers
and Forests was a forgery; and, quite possibly, that he was
an Englishman. The discovery of his nationality, together
with the fact that he had secured a guide known to be a
spy to get him over the frontier into Canada would
lead to the assumption that he, too, was a spy. The possible result could be, not months, but years in prison, or
worse.

And what of Mary? It was hardly likely that they
would imprison her. But she would be stranded. As the
van Wycks knew the truth about them, they would almost

certainly help her. Even so, she could not live on them indefinitely. She would have to take some dreary job in a shop, or become a dressmaker, and live in constant misery at the thought of him in prison.

It was not to be wondered at that, during their third day in the forest, Roger was constantly looking over his shoulder, and frequently tempted to force the pace. But he could not do that for, although gallant little Mary trudged doggedly on, she had now to lean on his arm for most of the time, and was fast approaching exhaustion.

At last, on the Friday, their fourth day after leaving French Mills, they emerged from the forest to see again the valley through which the St. Lawrence ran. A high cliff still prevented them from getting down to the river, but Roger heaved a great sigh of relief when Leaping Squirrel told him that within two hours they would be across it.

After walking for a little over a mile, the Indian led them to the edge of the cliff and pointed to the right. Immediately below them were rapids with water foaming between a number of big, flattish rocks, and nearer the bank several large, swirling pools. But further along the cliff was rugged and broken, where there had been a landslide, making it possible to climb down to the water, and there it was smooth.

For some minutes they gazed down at the river; then, just as they turned away, a great bald-headed eagle swooped, screeching, down upon them. Evidently its nest was below the place where they were standing on the edge of the cliff, and it feared they were about to harm its young.

Mary gave a cry of fright and swiftly backed away from the big, terrifying bird. Next second she uttered a piercing scream. She had retreated too far and put a foot over the cliff edge. Roger dashed forward, but was too late to grab her. Flinging himself flat, he looked over, praying that she might have landed on a ledge. But she had not. His eyes starting from his head, he saw her, a whirling bundle of furs, hurtling downward until, with a great splash, she hit one of the pools and disappeared.

8

News out of Portugal

IT was on the evening of April 6th, while Roger and Mary were on their way with Leaping Squirrel from French Mills to the place at which the latter hoped to get them across the St. Lawrence, that a Captain John Harley of the 47th Foot delivered to Lady Luggala's residence a packet addressed to Jemima. She did not receive it until she returned from a rout soon after two o'clock in the morning.

Seeing that it was addressed in Charles's writing, Jemima bade Lady Luggala a swift goodnight, went straight up to her room and tore open the packet with eager fingers. To her delight, she found that it contained a letter several pages in length. Its opening, *'Most beautiful and adorable of the Sex'*, caused her to flush with pleasure, and quickly she read on :

'You will, I trust, have received my missive despatched by a sloop sailing from Lisbon within a few hours of my landing, just to inform you that, although we met rough weather in the Bay of Biscay, being a good sailor I arrived none the worse for that.'

Jemima had not received such a missive, but at once assumed that either it had gone astray or the sloop had been sunk. The letter continued :

'In Lisbon I spent several very pleasant days, as I had

*brought with me a letter of introduction to the Rt. Hon.
Sir Charles Stuart, our Minister in that city; and, after
reporting to the Garrison Commander I went straight to
the Legation. There I was most kindly received by Sir
Charles and his lady, who insisted I should be their guest
until I received orders to proceed to the front.*

*'At two dinner parties given by the Stuarts, and other
entertainments to which I was invited, I met as well as
numerous British officers several Portuguese Generals and
Ministers and their wives, and all cannot speak too highly
of His Grace of Wellington's conduct of the campaign.
And well they may, since with an army that until recently
rarely numbered more than sixty thousand men, for four
long years he has bedevilled the French, who at times had
four hundred thousand men in the Peninsula, driven them
from Portugal and has now freed half Spain.*

*'The Stuarts have living with them their niece, Deborah
—a poor, pale hop-pole of a girl who suffers from shyness,
but is a kindly creature. On two occasions I drove out,
with her as my guide, to see the now famous "Lines of
Torres Vedras", behind which our army remained secure
during the winter of 1810-11. The earthworks and
innumerable bastions in this great double line of forti-
fications are of such amazing strength that no-one, having
seen them, can be surprised that Marshal Masséna,
despite his great superiority in numbers, realised that any
attempt to force them would have led to the massacre of
his army. For his failure to make the attempt Bonaparte
recalled and broke him. That, to my mind, was cutting off his nose to spite his face, for it is generally
held that Masséna was the ablest of all the French
Marshals.*

*'It transpired that Deborah had known Uncle Roger,
as he stayed here with the Stuarts during the Spring of*

1811. At that time she had with her an ex-school friend, one Lady Mary Ware with whom, I gather, Uncle R had a secret affair, during which Miss D acted as their confidante. The last Miss D heard of Lady M was in the following autumn—that she was about to marry a wealthy merchant. Since then D's letters have been returned marked "gone from here", and I could give her no news of Uncle R, since he left England on one of his secret missions some fifteen months ago.

'I need no telling how distant our war here is to people at home in England. It is scarcely even mentioned by society belles like yourself, except when news comes of some relative killed or seriously wounded. And I'll confess that I hardly gave it a thought myself except when there had been occasion to celebrate a victory. But now that I am involved, I feel you will want to know something of the situation in the Peninsula and of our prospects.

'It has been a grim struggle and our army would long since have been defeated and driven into the sea had it not been for the brilliance of our great commander, and the fact that the enemy had for years to hold down all but a tiny corner of Spain, and the greater part of Portugal. It is this last that, in spite of their enormous superiority in numbers, has prevented them from ever being able to bring against us in the open field a force greatly exceeding our own. And the Duke is truly inspired. Again and again, whenever he has found himself in an unfavourable position, he has had the courage to invite censure by retiring, as he has twice done from Madrid; yet, time after time when opportunity offered, he has caught the French off their guard by clever stratagems, launched a lightning attack and destroyed whole divisions of them.

'We also owe far more than people realise to the Portuguese and the Spaniards. While behind the lines of Torres

Vedras the Duke embodied and trained many regiments of the former. They are well disciplined troops and in battles since have displayed high courage. The contribution by the Spaniards has been still greater, although at times their forces have proved a dubious asset.

'As at least you will know, owing to Cadiz being situated at the end of a narrow eight-mile long peninsula the Spaniards succeeded in retaining that city and there formed a Junta which, after the flight of their King, assembled a Cortes that declared itself the government of Spain, and later entered into an official alliance with us. Incited by their fanatical priests, all but a very small part of the population in the north and south of Spain accepted the orders of the Junta and rose in revolt against their conquerors. Not only did they raise half a dozen armies, but also innumerable bands of fierce irregulars living in the mountains have constantly harassed the French from one end of the country to the other, cutting their communications and capturing convoys of supplies.

'Most unfortunately, the generals of their regular forces have proved both incompetent and unreliable; so that on numerous occasions during battles in which they took part with us, they failed to carry out the tasks allotted them by the Duke, with the result that we were deprived of what should have been complete victory. Last autumn the Cortes decreed that its generals should no longer act independently, but come under the Duke, as Generalissimo. So far, only the Spanish army in Galicia has given us full co-operation, but in this year's campaign, we are hoping that others will also prove of value.

'However, the fact remains that the Spanish regular and irregular forces have compelled the enemy to distribute his men in several armies, each of which is separated from the others by great ranges of mountains, so that none of them is readily able to come to another's assistance.

'The hatred displayed by the Spaniards and French for each other is almost unbelievable. Neither take any prisoners and butchers the wounded without mercy. When the French take a town, they massacre everyone they find in it and burn it to the ground. When the Spaniards capture a convoy or small body of troops, they torture them to death, often nailing them to doors and roasting or skinning them alive.

'Only on the east coast have the French succeeded in pacifying the country and this because, alone among the Marshals, Suchet decreed a policy of conciliation, spared the towns he took and even allowed their own Mayors to continue in authority. Yet his sixty thousand men are as severely harassed as are those in other parts of the country. Spanish forces constantly attack them. They are always defeated by Suchet's troops, but fade away into the mountains, only to reappear after a week or so and again attack.

'Bonaparte's eldest brother, Joseph, whom he made King of Spain, theoretically commands all the French in the Peninsula, but I am told has little say in directing operations. He is said to be an honest, easy-going, good-natured fellow who takes his sovereignty seriously, and does his best to protect the interests of his Spanish subjects. But the row he has to hoe must be a hard one. He is, in fact, no more than a nouveau riche bourgeois, and the Spanish aristocracy who reluctantly form his Court are the most tradition-bound and stiff-necked in the world. Moreover, poor Joseph is no general, and the Marshals hold him in contempt. It is also our good fortune that the Marshals are intensely jealous of one another and, even *when in a position to do so, frequently refuse to come to one another's aid.*

'Masséna was replaced by the young and energetic Marshal Marmont. For a while he gave our army considerable trouble, but his own conceit led to his downfall. Last July the Duke, with a force of some forty thousand men, had fallen back on Salamanca. Marmont was following him up with about the same number and, only two days' march behind, King Joseph was coming to the Marshal's support with a further fifteen thousand men. But, rather than wait for the King and have to play Number Two to him, Marmont wanted all the credit for a victory, so impetuously attacked us. The Duke gave him a tremendous trouncing, he was severely wounded by a cannon-ball and, but for the ability of General Clausel, who took over, the whole of Marmont's army would have been destroyed.

'It was from the time of this battle that the tide of war in the Peninsula really began to turn in our favour. King Joseph beat a retreat as quickly as he could to Valencia, and took refuge with the powerful army under Suchet. This opened the way for the Duke to capture Madrid and delivered both Leon and the Castiles from enemy occupation.

'As the only possible hope of regaining his capital the King had to call on Marshal Soult, who for three years had been holding down the south with another great army and reigning in Seville like an independent sovereign. His march toward Valencia raised the siege of Cadiz, freeing the Anglo-Spanish-Portuguese force that has held out there for so long, and gave the Cortes there undisputed power over the whole of southern Spain.

'Soult is one of the ablest of the Marshals, and his joining up with Suchet at Valencia gave King Joseph an army *of ninety thousand men. In addition, the remains of the French army from Portugal had joined with other forces in the north, giving General Clausel another army of some forty thousand in the neighbourhood of Burgos. Against this one hundred and thirty thousand and many thousands more French troops garrisoning Spanish cities, the Duke could bring only sixty thousand; so, although by his operations he had liberated all Portugal and a good half of Spain, he wisely decided to give up Madrid, for while Suchet remained in Valencia Soult was advancing on the capital with one hundred thousand men. The retreat continued until mid-November, by which time the Duke had fallen back on Ciudad Rodrigo, and the French, constantly harassed by Spanish irregulars, were so exhausted that they could press on no further.*

'However, this set-back was of no long duration. Shortly after Christmas they learned here of the appalling disaster that had befallen Bonaparte in Russia. It is now confirmed that he left behind him, to die in the snow, no fewer than half a million men. This is greatly to our benefit, as he has withdrawn from Spain twenty-five thousand of the most seasoned officers and men to reform his Imperial Guard, several able Generals and, last but not least, our most dangerous adversary, Marshal Soult.

'This still leaves some two hundred thousand French in Spain, but they have been much disheartened by losing so many of their veteran officers and N.C.O.s, while reinforcements during the winter have brought our army up to seventy-five thousand, the highest number the Duke has ever had at his disposal. Moreover, the greater part of the French army in eastern Spain is now entirely occupied in endeavouring to keep open their communications with France, which are seriously threatened by thousands of irregulars operating from the mountains of the Asturias

and Navarre, under the Spanish General Mina. So we now have opposed to us only King Joseph, with Marshal Jourdan as his adviser—an ageing General of the Republican wars. We are, therefore, in great heart regarding our prospects in the coming campaign.

'Reverting to myself. After five nights with the hospitable Stuarts, I was ordered to join a convoy and, with my man Briggs, took the coast road north. For many miles beyond the Lines of Torres Vedras the country is in a sad condition, since before retiring behind the lines the Duke secured the agreement of the Portuguese to lay bare the countryside, in order to deny the French sustenance and shelter. All livestock was removed, farms and barns emptied of their contents and left roofless, the people of the towns were brought into Lisbon and the peasants took to the mountains. The abandoned land is now being brought under cultivation again, but many vineyards are still thigh-high in weeds and brambles, making one highly conscious of the loss and distress inflicted on the hapless poorer sort by the wars of the mighty.

'By way of Caldas, Alcobacca, Leiria and Pombal we reached the considerable town of Coimbra. From there we turned inland through the mountains, then by way of Guardaz and Pinzio crossed the frontier to Ciudad Rodrigo. As the crow flies, the latter is no more than two hundred miles from Lisbon, but the winding road through the mountains adds half as much again to the distance to be covered.

'The scenery along the coast road was most picturesque, particularly as the many varieties of trees were beginning to show their young Spring green, and in the clear air of the mountains breath-taking panoramas opened up at every turn of the way. Before the war the tracks must have been impassable for transport other than by mule, but our

engineers have done much to widen them and, in the worst places, lessen the gradient; so it took the convoy no more than a fortnight to reach its destination.

'To do so was a considerable relief to me for, the effects of war apart, Portugal is in the main a desolate and poverty-stricken country. At such miserable inns in which, now and then, I spent a night, there were no beds, but legions of bugs infesting the walls of the rooms, no fresh meat but goat, and little other food but goat's cheese and some bread, washed down with a resinous wine that made one gasp. Fortunately, the Stuarts had warned me what to expect, so I took with me a good supply of hard tack to lessen the monotony of the army ration; although that, I will say, was good and ample, for the Duke has ever held it a first principle that his troops should never lack for food, and they love him for it.

'On my arrival at headquarters, my Lord Duke received me very graciously and promised to find me a post suitable to my rank—I do not imply my rank as an officer for, as you know, nothing higher than a Lieutenantcy could initially be purchased for me, although as an officer of the Household Brigade I carry the seniority of a Captain when with other units of the Army—but as an Earl.

'A few days later it emerged in conversation that, having lived on the Rhine with dear Mama when she was married to that brute, von Haugwitz, I speak German fluently. Thereupon His Grace promptly told me I was just the man to fill the rôle of an extra A.D.C. and Liaison Officer with the Duke of Brunswick.

'The Duchy of Brunswick now forms part of Westphalia, which Bonaparte created as a Kingdom for his youngest brother, Jerome. The late Duke, a Prussian commander of distinction, was killed at the Battle of Auerstadt in 1806 and his son, Duke Frederick William, upon

E

whose staff I now am, nurses a most bitter hatred against the French for having deprived him of his dukedom. He is a charming and most courageous man. In 1809, he led a revolt in an endeavour to free Brunswick but, owing to the strength of the French garrison, it failed. Undismayed, the Duke and the troops who had risen in support of him retired into Bohemia; then they carried out a most remarkable enterprise—no less than fighting their way right across Germany until they reached the North Sea. British warships took them off and conveyed them to England, where the King gave them the name of his "German Legion" and, at their leader's request, sent them to serve with our army against the French in the Peninsula.

'*So you see I am now well settled and eagerly anticipating the opening of the new campaign next month. Being a liaison officer I need spend only part of my time with the Germans, and at the Duke's headquarters I now have a number of congenial companions, with several of whom I had been acquainted in London, and most of them senior to me by only a few years.*

'*An officer of the 47th Foot who has to proceed to London in order to unravel certain complicated matters with the Paymaster's Department will convey this to you. By the same hand I am despatching a missive to my beloved mother, and have endeavoured to divide my news between you; so each of you must read the other's letter.*

'*Owing to Boney's enormous losses in Russia, one can hardly doubt that the back of his main army is broken; and, now that the Prussians have united with the Russians against him, it seems there is a good chance that by summer this war of a life-time will, at last, be over. My Lord Duke is in hopes that we will drive the French back over the Pyrenees before they are finally defeated by the Allies in Germany. Be that as it may, when the news does reach*

London that the French have been forced to surrender, I bid you, my dear love, to lose not one moment in setting about the preparation of your trousseau; for on my return I'll brook no delay in putting an end to our six years' engagement and making you, sweet Susan, the bride I have so long dreamed of.

'Your ever devoted and adoring
Charles.'

On reading those last few lines, Jemima's mouth fell open, her dark eyes started from her head and, trembling with anger, she had to throw the letter from her to prevent herself from tearing it to pieces.

The mentions in it of 'Uncle Roger' had seemed strange, as Charles had never used that term to her on the very few occasions he had spoken of his mother's great friend, Mr. Roger Brook. But, in every other way, the letter was one that Charles might have written to her and its opening had thrilled her with the belief that he was much more deeply in love with her than he had led her to suppose. Only the very end had revealed the horrid truth. He had written three letters at one sitting and, by mistake, put a friendly one for her in the packet addressed to Susan and his mother.

At one blow, all her hopes for the future had been shattered. How utterly wrong she and Maureen Luggala had been in their belief that the mutual affection displayed by Charles and Susan when together was due only to their having been brought up as brother and sister. It was now clear beyond all doubt that, ever since they had been old enough to feel attraction to the opposite sex, they had been in love and had planned to marry in due course. The fact that, during the past year or two, both of them had carried on flirtations with others meant nothing. Her face red with renewed anger, Jemima visualised them telling each other about their affairs and laughing together over the conquests they had made.

Snatching up the letter, Jemima jerked open her door, flounced across the landing and, without knocking, erupted into Lady Luggala's room. The older woman was seated at her dressing table in a peignoir, smothering her face with grease while her yawning maid braided her hair for the night.

Imperiously Jemima snapped at the girl, 'Get out! I wish to talk to Her Ladyship.'

Maureen Luggala had found Jemima difficult enough to handle before she had discovered that she was a cuckoo in the Luggala nest. Since then Jemima had learned that her real mother supplied the funds for the Luggala ménage, and that the woman she still called 'mother' in public was no more than a puppet who received her orders from the Irish witch. Headstrong and imperious by nature, Jemima had lost no time in making use of her knowledge. During the past few months she had dominated the household and the servants no longer dared question her orders.

After one scared glance at Jemima, the maid dropped the rope of half-plaited hair, gave a quick curtsey and, only too glad to get to bed, hurried from the room.

Being by now aware that in an angry exchange with Jemima, she would only get the worst of it, Maureen closed her thin lips firmly for a moment, then asked resignedly, 'What brings you here at this hour?'

Still flushed with wrath, Jemima waved the letter. ''Tis this! A letter from Charles. A pox on him! Would you believe it; after playing up to me in no uncertain manner, he was all the time affianced to that bitch Susan, and plans to marry her the moment the war is over?'

Lady Luggala gave a gasp and her painted eyebrows

shot up. 'It cannot be true! The fondness he shows for her is no more than brotherly.'

'Brotherly, my arse!' exclaimed Jemima furiously. 'He addresses her as "most beautiful and adorable of the Sex." This letter was for her, but the fool put it in a cover addressed to me.'

'Oh, mercy me! Then we are indeed undone.'

'Undone I may be, but I'll have his guts for this.'

'Your disappointment is understandable. But you can hardly accuse him of having jilted you. According to the account you gave me, he did not even have you, let alone promise you marriage.'

'True. Yet he gave me good cause to believe myself a hot favourite in the St. Ermins' stakes. In no other girl did he show such interest. And I've not a doubt that all the time he was telling Susan that I was mad about him; while she, each time she saw me, must have pissed herself with secret laughter at my expense.'

"Tis possible your case is not so ill as you suppose. There's much in the old saying that "men were deceivers ever." Maybe he is playing a double game. He could have become affianced to Susan when they were only boy and girl, and he now regrets it, yet lacks the courage to break it off. There is at least a chance that, although he may not mention marriage in his letter to you, there will be evidence of great affection in it; so still hope for the future.'

For a moment Jemima was silent, then she said, 'That might be so. I must find out. By now Susan will have read the letter meant for me and guessed that I, or some other person, received hers through Charles's carelessness. To-morrow, or later today rather, I'll take her letter to her.'

'Some weeks have now elapsed since she and the Duchess left town. The odds are they're at Newmarket

with the old, bed-bound Duke; but they may be elsewhere. In any case, it will mean a journey, so we had best
take things for the night. No doubt they will offer to put
us up.'

'There is no need for you to do so. If you prove right
and Charles has shown real warmth for me in his letter,
that could lead to a confrontation between me and Susan.
I'd prefer to face that red-headed bitch alone. Where
they are I'll ascertain in the morning.' Calmer, but still
frowning, Jemima wished the woman she now regarded
as no more than a spineless duenna a surly 'Good night',
and left the room.

Jemima had received a bitter blow, but she was not the
type of young woman to cry herself to sleep, and she was
resilient by nature. The odds on becoming Countess of St.
Ermins now seemed to be a hundred to one against her;
but she did not mean to give up her attempt to get Charles
as a husband. When she had seen Susan she would better
be able to judge the depth of the girl's feeling for Charles.
After all, Maureen might well be right, and the bond
between them no more than a tacit acceptance of an
agreement made several years before.

That did not appear to be the case as far as Charles
was concerned, or he would not have urged Susan to be
ready to buy her trousseau in a hurry; but it might well be
with Susan. Perhaps she would be glad of an excuse to be
free from her engagement. If so, Jemima meant to win
her confidence and incite in her a resolution to break it
off; or, failing that, by some subtle means sow dissension
between them.

9

The Power of the Frog

ROGER had barely glimpsed the splash made by Mary's body as it struck the water sixty feet below when his ankles were seized, and he was jerked away from the edge of the cliff. Fearing that, as had happened with Mary, the overhang of the precipice would give way beneath Roger, Leaping Squirrel dragged him back to safety.

When the Indian released his legs, Roger remained flat on his face, unmoving, his mind benumbed by horror. Only a few minutes ago, Mary had been beside him; gay, loving, courageous little Mary. He could still hear her laughter. Now she was gone—gone for ever.

It seemed impossible; he must be in the middle of a nightmare, the victim of an evil dream. Yet he knew that he was not. It had happened—happened within a yard of him. At one moment he had been looking up at the swooping eagle. The next, Mary's scream had pierced his ears. He had flung out a hand to grab her, but too late. Already her head was on a level with his waist, her mouth gaping wide, her eyes starting from her head with terror, as she shot down into the void.

He had been married to Mary for only just over three months but, apart from their earlier affair in Lisbon, ever since he had come upon her again by chance in St. Petersburg, the previous October, they had not only lived together, but had hardly ever been out of each other's sight.

Unlike the majority of couples, separated for the greater part of their waking hours, the man earning his living, the woman running the home, they had spent day after day for all that time either riding and walking side by side, together in the narrow confines of a ship's cabin, or cheek by jowl in canoes and covered wagons. In Russia they had shared burdens while trudging through hundreds of miles of snow, and slept in one sleeping bag. Crossing the Atlantic they had endured sickness and tempest. More recently they had again faced below-zero temperatures and, muffled in furs, fed primitively round camp fires.

They had thus attained a greater degree of intimacy than could have been achieved by years of normal marriage. Their minds had become so closely attuned that they could anticipate each other's thoughts. They had not had a single quarrel; and physical desire, which inevitably declines between lovers with long, constant association, in their case had not had time enough to wane.

It was not to be wondered at that Roger felt as though half of his own being had been suddenly torn from him with Mary's plunge to death over the edge of the cliff.

When, years before, he had arrived in Martinique to learn that his wife, Amanda, had just died in giving birth to Susan, he had been so grief-stricken that he had made himself drunk for a week. Now he felt that, even had he unlimited liquor at hand, no bout of drunkenness, however long, could bring him to accept the loss of Mary.

They had been within an hour of getting safely over the border into Canada. Once there, it would have been only a matter of two or three months at most before they could be back in England. Only now he realised to the full how immensely he had been looking forward at long last to putting behind him the hazardous life he had led and making a home with Mary at Thatched House Lodge.

To return there without her would be an utterly different matter. Bitterly he recalled the year he had spent in England before, out of restlessness and boredom, he had accepted the mission to Sweden which had led to his again becoming involved with Napoleon and taking part in the retreat from Moscow.

In March 1810, he had persuaded his beloved Georgina to marry him as soon as he could get back to England. In June he had actually been about to take ship from Hamburg when arrested and accused of the murder of von Haugwitz, tried and sentenced to death. His sentence had been commuted to ten years' imprisonment. The following October he had escaped and succeeded in reaching London, only to learn that Georgina, believing him dead, had succumbed to the pleading of the old Duke of Kew, and married him.

During the greater part of 1811 he had lived at Thatched House Lodge. Whenever Georgina had been in London, the two life-long lovers had again spent glorious nights together of companionship and passion. But for months at a stretch she had had to live in the country, and they had been able to snatch only occasional meetings. After the intensely active life he had led for so many years, those long periods of lonely inactivity had driven him to distraction.

Since the Duke had been stricken by paralysis, his doctors said that he might continue to live like a vegetable for many years. Meanwhile Georgina would remain tied to him. So, on returning to England without Mary, Roger would again be faced with the dreary, frustrating life he had lived in 1811. At the thought, he groaned aloud.

Ever since dragging him back from the precipice, Leap-

ing Squirrel had been kneeling beside him, endeavouring
to comfort him. Roger heard his words only as a murmur
and their sense failed to register in his stunned brain. But
now the Indian grasped his shoulders, shook him violently
and cried in his Canadian-French patois :

'Noble one, we cannot remain here. So far we have been
fortunate in keeping lead of Mohawk trackers sent after
us from French Mills; but travelling with the poor, beautiful one put brake upon our pace. Our enemies cannot now
be far behind. Once across river we shall be safe. But we
dare not delay. I beg you rouse yourself.'

With a groan, Roger forced himself to his feet, took a
last, despairing look at the ground, now forming the edge
of the cliff, which had given way under Mary. Then he
automatically fell into step behind Leaping Squirrel.

When they had covered about four hundred yards they
came to a gully which led to a narrow, zigzag path
descending to the river. Between the water and the cliff
lay a bank of pebbles about four feet wide. Turning back,
they followed it toward the cluster of large rocks, separated here and there by narrow channels, through which
rapids roared, but the rocks were not sufficiently far apart
to prevent a bold traveller from stepping from one to
another and so crossing the river.

They were just passing the pool beneath the overhang
into which Mary had fallen, when Leaping Squirrel gave
a loud shout and pointed. The nearest of the rocks, now
only a hundred yards ahead, had a flat surface sloping
slightly upward. On it, half out of the water, lay a large,
furry bundle that, in the distance, might have been taken
for a drowned bear.

Running and slipping on the large, uneven pebbles, the
two men raced toward it. Within two minutes, outpacing
Roger, the Indian had scrambled on to the rock and

turned the bundle over. As he had supposed, it was Mary.

Gasping for breath, Roger joined him and stared down at the motionless figure. He was now a prey to the most agonising suspense. Was she dead, or had she only fainted? Obviously the racing river had cast her up on the rock. She could hardly have been submerged long enough to drown, but had her plunge into the icy water killed her by a heart attack?

Leaping Squirrel tore open her furs. Roger thrust his hand between them, down to her bosom. A second later he gave a shout of joy, 'Her heart's still beating! She lives! She lives!'

Outside, her furs were soaking, but their thick skins had, in most places, protected her body from the water. Frantically they pulled off all her furs and, while Roger slapped her ribs, Leaping Squirrel massaged her hands and feet.

A few minutes later she opened her eyes, then screwed up her face, gave a cry of pain and jerked her right foot away from the Indian's grasp. He then realised, from the limpness of her foot, that her ankle was broken. Meanwhile, Roger was smothering her face with kisses.

As soon as Mary was sufficiently recovered, the two men stopped massaging her. Roger wrapped her in his fur coat, and Leaping Squirrel put his fur hat, gloves and moccasins on her; then they set about the difficult task of getting her across the river.

Where the big rocks had flat surfaces, she was able with Roger's support, to hop along on her sound leg, but over the rougher stretches they had to carry her; and, as some of the chasms between the rocks were nearly a yard wide, getting her safely from one to another was a nerve-racking business. The roar of the rapids was so loud that, as they passed her wet furs done up in a bundle and their camping equipment, across the rushing spates of water, they had to shout to make themselves heard.

In his bare feet the Indian was sure-footed, but Roger was far from being so. Several times he stumbled, and once his heart was in his mouth, for he tripped on a jagged stone, which caused him to let go of Mary a moment too soon. As she slid from his grasp toward the water, he was momentarily petrified by the fear that he had lost her, after all. But, just in time, Leaping Squirrel shot out a hand, caught her arm and hauled her to safety.

When over half an hour had gone by, Roger began to fear that they would never reach the opposite shore. The foaming cascades of white water sent spray that half blinded them high into the air and soaked them all from head to foot. But, at last, chilled to the marrow, with shivering bodies and chattering teeth, they crossed the final chasm and tumbled exhausted on the pebbles of the Canadian beach.

Leaping Squirrel was the first to recover. Roger had given his fur coat to Mary, so he had suffered the most severely from the icy spray. Taking off his furs the Indian threw them over him, then crossed the pebbles to a strip of earth that lay beyond them further inshore, and began to run for a hundred yards each way up and down it until he had fully restored his circulation.

On the Canadian side of the river, instead of a steep cliff, the ground rose in a gentle slope, closely covered with fir trees, few of which exceeded twenty feet in height. Having warmed himself up, Leaping Squirrel became as active as ever, darting in among the trees and collecting armfuls of small, dead branches, which he piled near his companions. Within ten minutes he had a fire going.

Meanwhile, Roger had recovered sufficiently to get out the bottle of brandy he had brought against emergencies.

All three of them took several pulls at it, and the fiery spirit soon warmed them up enough to sort out their belongings. Leaping Squirrel insisted that Roger should keep his furs until Mary's had been dried at the fire; but he took back from her his moccasins and produced a towel in which to wrap her feet.

Before doing so, Roger examined her injury. The ankle was already badly swollen and obviously broken. She said that, as far as she could judge, the water into which she had hurtled had been about twenty feet in depth, so was deep enough to break her fall, but not enough to prevent her plunging to the bottom where she had struck the rock hard with her right foot. It was the awful stab of pain as her ankle broke that had caused her to faint before coming to the surface.

Roger began to get out their provisions, with the intention of cooking a meal, but the Indian checked him, saying, 'We are not yet safe, noble one. Leaping Squirrel made this fire only to dry clothes. If Mohawk trackers reach cliff opposite while it still daylight, they see smoke, come across rocks and capture us. Hold furs to fire while Leaping Squirrel find safe place to spend night.' Then turning away, he ran off down river.

Half an hour elapsed before he returned, dragging behind him two twelve-foot-long saplings from which he had trimmed the branches with Roger's tomahawk.

'What are those for?' Mary asked.

He gave one of his rare smiles. 'Leaping Squirrel has found good place not far off. With these we make Indian sleigh to draw beautiful one. In old days we use squaws or big dogs to draw, but since Pale Faces come, we use horses.'

Laying down the two long poles about two feet apart, he began to make a cradle between their thicker ends, using the sleeping bags, small branches of fir and such cord as they had with them. By the time he had finished, their furs were dry enough to be worn again without discomfort. Dusk was now falling, but he took the precaution of kicking the fire to pieces, then threw the still-smouldering branches into the river. Their belongings were piled on the rear of the cradle, where they would form a rest for Mary's back. Having laid her on the cradle, the two men got between the slender ends of the poles, which now formed the shafts of the sleigh, picked them up and drew her along behind them.

For Mary it was bumpy going and every few minutes the jerking caused her to grimace from the pain in her ankle, but on rounding the corner of a bend in the river they saw not far ahead a cluster of great boulders. It was the place Leaping Squirrel had chosen for them to spend the night, as smoke could not be seen during darkness, and from the midst of the boulders a fire would not be visible from the opposite bank.

Leaving Mary there, the two men collected more fallen branches and soon made another fire. The Indian smoked some strips of meat on it, while Roger made a rough splint for Mary's leg from two of the straightest sticks he was able to find. This first hot meal they had eaten for several days, together with the knowledge that they were now on Canadian soil, cheered them mightily and, soon afterwards, having made themselves as comfortable as they could, they all fell sound asleep.

Leaping Squirrel was up early, and when the others awoke they found he had just returned from the forest with a big bundle of young sassafras shoots to make a more comfortable seat for Mary on the improvised sleigh. As soon as they had made a meagre breakfast of biscuits, they set off along the shore, the two men drawing Mary behind them as they had done the previous evening. When they had been on their way for about an hour, the forest on their left gave way to stony outcrop which soon became a cliff, some thirty feet in height. Having followed it for about two hundred yards, they came upon the entrance to a low cave. The Indian called on Roger to halt and crawled into it. A moment later he gave a cry of delight, and emerged dragging after him a small, birchbark canoe. He had come up-river in it and had hidden it there, but feared that it might have been found and stolen in his absence.

It was just large enough to hold the three of them, with Roger in the stern, his legs apart so that Mary could lie between them and rest against him, while Leaping Squirrel knelt in the prow and steered the little craft by dexterous twists of his paddle.

As they were going with the current, their speed was several times as swift as it had been while dragging Mary on the sleigh and it was infinitely more comfortable for her. During the course of the next three hours they travelled at least thirty miles; but it was dangerous going as, here and there, rocks and shallows had to be avoided, and with the canoe so heavily loaded a single mis-judgment in steering by the Indian could have proved disastrous.

Well before midday they left the wide St. Lawrence for a tributary, which made the going very much harder and slower as they went upstream. Leaping Squirrel began to sweat profusely and, from time to time, had to pull into the bank so that he could rest. But after an hour and a half of laborious paddling he had a piece of good fortune.

They came to a cliff from which protruded a small, wooden staging about six feet above the water. On it an Indian, who had climbed down from the cliff top, was fishing for salmon by means of a pole, at the end of which there was what looked like a huge, coarse-string butterfly net. Leaping Squirrel hailed him and they spoke together in their native tongue, then the Indian picked up two fish he had caught, scaled the cliff and disappeared into the forest that fringed it.

Turning back to his companions, Leaping Squirrel said, 'That man is an Onnchataronon; not of Leaping Squirrel's tribe. But, like all tribes north of Great Lakes, we have in common the Algonquin tongue—while the Five Nations, who live south of lakes, all speak Iroquois tongue. If he is good runner, within two hours he be with Leaping Squirrel's people. For taking message he receive good reward. Help will be sent and, instead of making camp again, before sunset big welcome by great chief Morning Star, Leaping Squirrel's father.'

He then recommenced to paddle, but less strenuously, so that in the next three hours the canoe progressed up stream only a few miles. On rounding a bend in the river they saw coming rapidly toward them a big war canoe. As it approached, they could see that it was manned by twenty warriors; then, when it turned about, that it was made from one huge, hollowed out tree trunk. There were loud, happy shouts of greeting, a rope was thrown to Leaping Squirrel and, towed by the big canoe, the small one was borne upstream at a fine, steady speed.

Later that afternoon the canoes drew in to a landing stage, inland from which was a large clearing in the forest. They had been sighted some way off by a look-out, and his horn blowing had brought scores of braves running from the Indian settlement. At the sight of Leaping Squirrel there were excited whoops of joy. In spite of his tattered garments he made a figure of great dignity as he stepped ashore, and was received by an elderly warrior wearing a mantle of wolf-skins and a head-dress from which rose buffalo horns.

For some moments Leaping Squirrel spoke in his own language to this dignitary, who then welcomed Roger and Mary in French-Canadian patois, and earnestly assured them that his whole tribe was their debtors for having saved the Chief's son. An Indian carrying-chair, with a comfortable bark seat, was brought and Mary lifted into it; then, with the whole company chattering excitedly, they were escorted to the big village, which was hidden from the landing stage by a grove of chestnut trees, just showing their young green. Through them ran a narrow, twisting path, along which the company, led by Leaping Squirrel, wound its way in a single file.

Beyond the grove lay an open space some two acres in extent. The greater part of it was enclosed by a palisade of stakes, with bands of porcupine quills round them. Backing on to the palisade was a great circle of tepees and wigwams, the former round-roofed, the latter tent-shaped. In the centre of the enclosure there rose a carved and painted totem pole, twenty feet in height with, beside it, a much shorter, uncarved pole painted bright red. Beyond them was a habitation many times larger than any of the others, which Roger knew must be the Longhouse, in which the Chief lived and where councils were held when the weather was inclement.

Leaping Squirrel led his visitors to a tepee which had already been prepared for them. It contained no furniture, except for two big tubs full of fresh water for washing in. It was spotlessly clean and two thick piles of furs and blankets spread on the beaten earth floor promised to serve as comfortable beds. He said that after their fatiguing journey they needed a few hours' rest, then he would present them to his father. Meanwhile, refreshments would be brought and Mary's ankle would receive attention.

A quarter of an hour after leaving them he returned with several young squaws, some carrying bowls of broth and others of rice mixed with deer meat; others brought flagons of Indian beer and spruce, with handleless cups to drink from. Both the bowls and cups were beautifully carved, and when Roger remarked on this, Leaping Squirrel said that his people were good carvers and spent much of their time in the winter making such articles, and animals or toys for their children, out of yellow pine, walnut and black cherry.

Roger also expressed surprise at there being rice with the deer meat, as he had seen none in New York or on their journey north. 'It is wild rice,' his host told him. 'It grows in the swamps on shores of the Great Lakes. Every season many squaws go there in canoe, gather armfuls of the rice and flail kernels into baskets.'

When the meal was finished and the things cleared away, Leaping Squirrel brought in two very old squaws, who removed the splint from Mary's ankle, carefully examined it, smeared it with a pungent grease, then re-bandaged it. With much salaaming they left the tepee, drawing the curtain of hides that served as the door. Then Roger and Mary dozed for two hours in the semi-darkness.

Twilight was falling when Leaping Squirrel came to them again, followed by two naked 'foreheads' with a carrying-chair, into which Mary was lifted. As they left the tepee, she and Roger saw that the great open space was now occupied by several hundred people.

Furthest from the centre there stood long lines of squaws wearing gaily-coloured blankets, and forehead bands of bright beads which kept in place their long, dark hair, parted in the centre and falling to the shoulders. Nearer in there squatted semi-circles of braves, dressed in a variety of fringed garments made from the skins of animals and decorated with tufts of bright feathers, bear claws, opossum and beaver tails. Some wore necklaces of shells, others of intricately-carved wooden beads or semi-precious stones. Their headbands were of painted leather, from the scalp lock of each dangled a single, scarlet feather, and their expressionless faces were daubed with circles and lines of red, yellow and black paint.

Facing them, in a single semi-circle, sat the elders of the tribe. Their garments were richer; ermine and sable, with belts of wampum, and they wore necklaces of stone beads as large as pigeon eggs. All of them, with one exception, wore head-dresses of eagle feathers reaching to their shoulders. The exception was Leaping Squirrel's father, Morning Star, who sat in the centre with his back to the totem pole. His head-dress fell on either side of his lined face, right to the ground, and his robe was made of supple skin, from which all the hair had been removed so that hieroglyphics representing his deeds of valour could be painted on it. He was wearing a number of medals presented to him by Governors of Canada for the assistance he had given the British. His leggings were of snake skin and he wore heavy bracelets and anklets of gold.

Although it was dusk, as Leaping Squirrel led Roger and Mary forward they were able to take in every detail of this colourful spectacle by the light of the flames from a big fire that blazed in the space between the braves and the elders. Within a few yards of his father, Leaping Squirrel halted and, speaking in his own tongue, began to address him in a loud voice that all could hear. His oration lasted a good twenty minutes. During that time the elders maintained a dignified silence but, now and then, the braves broke into whoops of applause; so it was obvious that he was describing how he had been captured by the Americans and saved from death by the Pale Faces whom he had brought back with him.

When he ended, the braves and elders all stood up. Morning Star stepped forward, placed one hand on Roger's shoulder and the other on Mary's head, and spoke in French-Canadian patois:

'Sagamore Morning Star speaks for all his people. To the noble ones now our guests we owe a debt that all the shells of the Quahagclam that we possess could not repay. As long as they live, anything they may ask of any member of our tribe shall be given to them, and given willingly. I, Morning Star, have spoken.'

The assembly gave a great shout of assent. Mary was then carried back to her tepee, accompanied by the two old squaws, while the Sagamore led the way to the Longhouse, followed by Roger, Leaping Squirrel and the elders. Another big fire was blazing in front of it, throwing up the complicated patterns with which it was painted in red, blue and yellow. Inside, the greater part of it consisted of one big room, on the walls of which were many trophies of the chase; heads of bison, bear and lynx, old-fashioned British Tower muskets and horrifying masks worn by the medicine-men of the tribe for certain ceremonies.

When they had sat down, cross-legged, in a circle, a feast was served, everyone helping himself with his fingers from the many dishes. Roger enjoyed the fresh-caught salmon and a pigeon stuffed with sage. He also recognised the bear and deer meat, but other foods were strange to him. After trying the fungus fried in fish oil, he hastily helped himself to a cornmeal cake covered in honey. One *ragoût* was pressed upon him as a great delicacy and he found it very tasty, but felt distinctly queasy when, having asked Leaping Squirrel what it was, he learned that it was stewed dog.

The feast over, the ceremonial pipe of peace was brought to the Sagamore. He lit it, drew on it, exhaled the smoke, then passed it to Roger, who did likewise, then passed it to Leaping Squirrel who was seated on his other side. Complete silence was maintained until the pipe had made the full circle, then it was emptied of its remaining tobacco and returned to the place where it had hung on the wall. As the slow, measured talk began again, nearly all the elders produced their own pipes and began to smoke. The bowls of the pipes—for which the Indian word was *calumet*—were beautifully-carved stone of many colours, their stems long tubes of wood. Later Roger learned that many of the younger braves who could not yet afford such valuable pieces used their tomahawks as pipes by hollowing out the handle of the weapon and grinding a bowl in the thick end of the axe.

Although there were several round holes in the roof of the Longhouse to let out the smoke, so much of it lingered in the big room that Roger's eyes soon began to smart. After his long day he also felt very tired, but feared that it might be regarded as bad manners if he, as the guest of honour, asked permission to leave the party. Fortunately, his drooping eyelids were noticed by Leaping Squirrel, who whispered to his father. The Sagamore at once stood up, and all the others followed suit. When Roger had expressed his thanks, his host touched him on the arm and wished him good rest. All the elders came forward in turn and did the same, then Leaping Squirrel took him to his tepee where, in English fashion, they shook hands. Inside the tepee a single rush light was burning, and Mary, he was pleased to find, was fast asleep, with one of the squaws seated silently beside her. After whispering a few words, the old woman glided out, and ten minutes later, he too was fast asleep.

In the days that followed Roger learned a lot about Leaping Squirrel's people from him. In earlier times the eleven tribes of the Algonquin nation had lived further south, but they had been defeated in a great war with the Iroquois and driven north of the St. Lawrence and the Great Lakes. Having settled in Canada, they had become firmly attached to the French, but after their defeat the Algonquin had sided with the British against the Americans. Pointing to the red-painted post that stood near the totem pole, Leaping Squirrel had added, 'Whenever our tribes go to war with *Americani,* such posts are set up in all villages to show that we are allies of the *Englesi.*'

Leaping Squirrel also said that, although the Iroquois were now fighting for the Americans, they did so only from fear that, if they refused, they would be driven from their present settlements. When Europeans had first come to America, but for the help the Indians had given them it is doubtful if they would have survived; yet, again and again, their kindness had been repaid by treachery. As the numbers of American settlers increased, they had pushed further and further inland, driving the Indians before them, and depriving them of their hunting grounds. Many treaties had been made, and when an Indian Chief gave his word and a wampum belt, he regarded his promise as sacred. But the land hunger of the Americans had caused them to break treaty after treaty; so, from south to north, they were hated by every tribe.

Mary had to keep to her bed for her ankle to mend, but on some days Leaping Squirrel took Roger hunting. Outside the palisade there was a large area where various crops, including tobacco, were grown; but the patches were irregular, because the Indians could cut down trees but had no means of dragging out the stumps of big oaks, elms and sycamores. Here and there among the patches were small platforms raised a few feet from the ground. On asking their purpose, Roger was told that, when the crops ripened, either children or squaws who were too old for other work, sat on them as living scarecrows, to drive off the crows.

Beyond the cultivated area virgin forest stretched for miles, where game abounded and innumerable grouse and pigeons. Leaping Squirrel would not let Roger use a gun, as a single report scared the wild life for a long way round. Instead, he taught him to use a bow and arrows fletched with turkey feathers. Small game was also caught in snares made from grass and reeds. The forest alone would have provided ample food for the tribe, but they also netted a variety of fish from the river, and it was so plentiful that they often deliberately caught more than they needed to eat, allowing the surplus to go bad so that it could be used as manure. Yet their staple dish was neither fish nor game. They seemed to prefer *Scuccotash*—a mixture of corn and beans cooked in meat broth.

Roger was surprised to find that couples did not live together. Early every summer there was a great ceremony. The young squaws were paraded, and the virtues of each in turn extolled by one of the old women. The girl was then chosen by one of the braves, who took her off into the forest. On their return she went back to the squaws' tepees and in due course had her child; but not until the child was a year old was the father, or any other man, allowed to take notice of her again. Even if the parents met on a narrow path she had to stand aside while he pretended that he had forgotten even her name.

A large part of the squaws' time was occupied in collecting birch bark, and they were often to be seen doing so with a young *papoose* strapped to a board on their backs. The bark was used to make canoes, tepees and wigwams, the latter having a framework of pine poles. The long, thin roots of tarmac trees were used to sew the strips of bark together, then the seams were waterproofed with the heavy resin from gum trees.

In the winter the squaws made leather sacks to hold corn, waterskins, clothes and fishing lines. Many of the young ones were good-looking; but, close to, they smelt unpleasantly of rancid grease, owing to their custom of plastering their hair, during the period when the moon was waxing, with the fat of animals whose virtues they wished to possess: a deer's for swiftness, a beaver's for industry, and an owl's to make them wise at night.

Apart from this unpleasant habit of smearing grease on their hair, Roger found the Indians surprisingly clean. Both the men and women bathed regularly in the river, rubbing their bodies with a type of fern that made a soapy lather. At times they also took sauna baths in tepees set apart, where they turned water into steam by pouring it over heated stones. Instead of shaving, the men plucked the hairs from their faces with bone tweezers, and without even wincing, for it was part of a brave's training to show no evidence of feeling pain.

To qualify for the red feather, they went through hideous ordeals. Leaping Squirrel had held a red-hot stone under his armpit for ten minutes, without flinching. Until well into middle age, they kept themselves extraordinarily supple and muscular by constant exercise. Their favourite game was lacrosse, played so ferociously with wooden clubs and a stuffed deerskin ball, that broken heads were not uncommon.

At their first meeting, Morning Star had asked Roger

tribes of your people spend their lives delving in darkness far underground. Others labour from childhood to old age in tepees fifty times the size of this Longhouse. In them they work streaming with sweat as they feed roaring fires, deafened by the thunder of machines, rendered breathless by steam hissing from huge iron cauldrons and poisoned by noxious fumes. It is too late for them to stop. They must go on until all your people, but for a very few, are forced to become machines themselves. They will build more and more of those great tepees until you have no forests, no open country left. Their bodies will deteriorate from lack of sunshine, of clean air, or healthy exercise. How much better is our way of life : to cultivate the land and enjoy its produce, to hunt in the forests and fish in the rivers, to fashion our simple requirements by hand, and dance and feast here round our totem poles.'

Many of the expressions actually used by the Sagamore Roger found difficult to understand, but in the main he absorbed their meaning; and, recalling the journeys he had made in the Midlands and north of England, where the Industrial Revolution had taken place toward the end of the previous century, he felt bound to agree.

After a moment's silence, the Sagamore resumed, 'But it is not of these things that Morning Star wished to speak to the noble one. It is clear that, although a Christian, he recognises that form of worship to be new compared with others. Therefore, he cannot believe that the Christian Father God created the world.'

'No,' Roger replied. 'He was simply adopted by the early Christians from the Jehovah of the Jews, and there were many other beliefs far older than theirs.'

'The noble one speaks truly, and the origin of all is embodied in our totem pole. Does he know its meaning?'

'Leaping Squirrel told me that the eagle at the top

represents the Spirit of the Air, the wolf the Spirit of the Land, the whale the Spirit of the Sea, and the frog at the bottom the union of Earth and Water.'

'The Frog represents more than that, for he moves by leaping, so he is also symbolical of Air. Thus he is the basis of all things. I cannot confer upon the noble one the ability to leave his body at will, but I am a son of the Frog and can confer his power on one other person before I die. This way Morning Star will pay his debt.'

'I . . .' Roger hesitated. 'I . . . no, Sir. No, this should go to your heir, Leaping Squirrel.'

The Sagamore's heavily-lidded eyes showed a gleam of appreciation, but he shook his befeathered head. 'Leaping Squirrel is wise and brave. He will make a good Chief and Morning Star has no fears for him; whereas his spirit tells him that a time may come when the noble one's need may be great. I have spoken. Now, bare your right arm.'

As Roger obeyed, the old Indian drew a sharp knive from his wampum belt, bared his own left arm and made a slight nick in it, then he nicked Roger's arm. Globules of blood welled up from both arms and they held them together for a minute so that their blood mingled. Then the Sagamore rose, and said, 'Come with me.'

Outside the Longhouse the village was now very quiet. All but a few braves, squatting by the watchfire, were sleeping. The moon was nearly full and only occasionally obscured by small, scudding clouds. By its light Roger followed Morning Star out into the woods, and along a winding path through them for about half a mile until they came to a big lake. On the shore the Sagamore halted and made sounds like the croaking of a frog.

A moment later a large frog jumped out of the water. It was followed by others, until the whole shore for yards round was covered with a mass of them, leaping and croaking, and Roger marvelled that so many could come up out of one lake. Morning Star then addressed them:

As he began to speak, they all fell silent, and their protruding eyes stared up at him. Roger never knew what he said, because he spoke in his own language; but when he ceased speaking, the frogs all gave one loud croak, then tumbling over one another, jumped back into the lake.

Morning Star's lined face broke into a smile. Putting an arm round Roger's shoulders, he said, 'The noble one is now my brother and my equal. The Frog People have accepted him. Henceforth, when evil threatens, he can thwart it by calling on the great spirit that embodies the Power of the Frog.'

10

Plot to Supplant a Rival

ON the morning of the day that Roger and Leaping Squirrel got Mary across the St. Lawrence, Jemima came downstairs grimly determined to face Susan and learn her reactions on being given the letter received the previous night.

While taking her morning chocolate and fresh rolls in bed, Jemima had had a running footman despatched to Berkeley Square, and he had just returned to report that Miss Brook and the Duchess were not at Newmarket, but at the latter's old home, Stillwaters, near Ripley in Surrey.

Jemima was already dressed for the road, and had a night bag with her. The Luggala coach had been ordered round from the nearby mews, and by eleven o'clock she was on her way out of London.

Very soon she had left the streets behind and was covering the miles of semi-open country to the south of the capital where, between ancient villages, numerous mansions standing in small parks were scattered among farms, orchards and market gardens. Gradually the buildings grew fewer and fields separated by patches of woodland lined the road until they reached Ripley.

There Jemima's coachman pulled up at the Talbot Inn, to enquire the whereabouts of the house, and was told that they had passed the entrance to the estate half a mile

back. The man then remembered noticing the handsome
iron gates described. Ten minutes later, they had been
opened by a lodge-keeper, and the coach was rolling up a
long drive, bordered on either side by woods.

In the Spring sunshine, the country was looking its best,
and Jemima had enjoyed the twenty-mile drive. Now she
looked about her with special interest, for she had often
heard of Stillwaters and how, in the latter years of the
previous century, its beautiful mistress had held fabulous
parties there, entertaining royalties, ambassadors and
ministers.

Among the trees there were big patches of primroses
and, farther on, glades in which hundreds of daffodils
were in bloom. As the coach emerged from the drive,
Jemima caught her first glimpse of the stately mansion
and the terrace, with its stone urns and statues, which ran
the whole length of it. Through the other window of the
coach, she saw the close-cropped lawns running down to
the lovely lake that gave the place its name. At this sight,
the bile of covetousness almost choked Jemima. If only her
hopes that Charles would marry her had been better
grounded, not only would she have become the mistress
of his mansion in Berkeley Square and his seat at White
Knights Park but also, when his mother died, of this magnificent domain.

The footman on duty met the coach at the door.
Jemima learned from him that Susan was out riding, but
he offered to take the visitor's name in to the Duchess; and
five minutes later she was being received by Georgina.

When Jemima wished to please, she was an adept at
it; her manners were admirable and her conversation
intelligent. On these grounds and her dark good looks
Georgina, being confident that no woman could replace
Susan in her son's heart, had thought Jemima very suit-

able to provide him with a temporary amusement, particularly as her psychic sense told her that the girl was very far from being a prude, and was therefore just what Charles needed as an outlet for his urges until the time came for him to marry.

In consequence, she gave Jemima a smiling welcome, and said at once, 'My dear, I can guess the reason to which we owe the pleasure of seeing you here. Only this morning one of my grooms brought me from London a packet from Charles. In it there was a letter for myself and one for you. The foolish boy must have sent it with mine instead of one for Susan, and you have received the one for her. Am I not right?'

'Indeed, Your Grace has guessed aright.' Jemima curtseyed again and, with a flourish, produced the letter for Susan from her reticule.

Smiling again, Georgina took it. 'How very sweet of you to have brought it all this way yourself. Susan is out riding with Lord Bellsavage and Mr. ffoulks. But they will soon be back. You will stay and dine, of course. And afterwards, if you prefer not to make another twenty-mile journey this evening, we should be happy for you to stay the night.'

'You are most kind; and, unaccompanied, I'd be a little scared of falling a prey to a highwayman after dark. So I brought a night bag, meaning to get myself a room at the inn. Naturally, I'd liefer accept Your Grace's hospitality.'

'That's settled then.' Georgina sent for Madeira and biscuits to refresh her guest and shortly afterwards Susan came in, accompanied by the two men. Mr. ffoulks was quite young and evidently a beau of Susan's. Lord Bellsavage was in his thirties and, Jemima guessed, having an affair with the beautiful Duchess.

The two girls went into the adjoining room and there exchanged letters. Jemima read hers with some degree of satisfaction. It was much shorter than the one to Susan, and contained no expressions of fervid attachment; but it showed sufficient warmth for Jemima to believe that if Susan was secretly averse to marrying Charles she might yet get him for herself.

For Jemima to have known that the letter she had received was intended for Susan she would have had to read it to the last paragraph. Realising this, Susan said to her :

'Jemima, dear. This letter has apprised you of the secret that Charles and I have long been engaged; but we also agreed to indulge ourselves in the pleasure of flirtations for a while before entering on married bliss, so I do pray you breathe not a word to others of our intentions.'

'You have my word that I will observe your wish,' Jemima replied, a little coldly, 'although I fear you must both have found food for laughter in my having such a predilection for your Charles.'

'Nay. I know him to be too honest a man to have led you to suppose that he had serious intentions toward you; that being so, I can hardly think you would expect more of him than admiration and affection. Life at our age would be dull without kisses. And, believe me, I do not grudge those Charles may have given you, any more than he would me those I have let Harry ffoulks and others take off me.'

'Dear Susan, we are at one in our ideas,' Jemima laughed, 'and I pray that you may enjoy many a warm embrace before Charles returns to claim you.' But secretly she was thinking, 'You self-confident little fool. With luck, you'll overplay your hand and find yourself desperately

F

enamoured of one of the men you toy with so lightly. Then, if Charles finds out, he'll repudiate you and be easy game for me.'

Georgina had invited some neighbours, mostly young people, over for dinner that day, so Susan lent Jemima an evening dress, and they sat down eleven to table. It proved a gay meal, and afterwards, to the music of a still-room maid who played the pianoforte and an undergardener who was a good fiddler, they danced. Jemima thoroughly enjoyed herself and, the following morning, drove back to London in a much more optimistic frame of mind than she had left it.

However, she had been badly shaken by learning that Charles, far from looking on Susan as a sister, was secretly her fiancé, and gave the impression in his letter of being deeply in love with her; so, having told Maureen Luggala all that had occurred at Stillwaters, Jemima decided that afternoon to consult her mother.

When she arrived at the house in Islington, the footman told her that his mistress had a gentleman with her, but he would let her know that Miss Luggala was asking to see her. After Jemima had waited for a few minutes in the hall, the man returned and showed her into the pleasant room at the back of the house where the Irish witch had first acknowledged Jemima to be her daughter and in which they had since frequently spent several hours together.

On this occasion there was a short, tubby, middle-aged gentleman with her mother. He had rubicund cheeks and a genial manner. Jemima was introduced to him as Miss Luggala, and her mother went on :

'My dear, this is Mynheer Cornelius Quelp, a Dutch gentleman, but French on his mother's side. It is he who carries the information we gather to Paris, by means of a smuggler's craft that runs cargoes between England and Holland. It was only last night that he landed in Essex, and is giving me the latest news from the Continent.'

To the plump man she added, 'You need have no apprehension, Mynheer, regarding the discretion of this young lady. She and her mother, Lady Luggala, are among my most valuable sources for collecting useful tittle-tattle in high society, and both are as devoted as you or I to the Emperor's cause.'

The Dutchman kissed Jemima's hand and expressed his pleasure at meeting so charming an ally; then they seated themselves and, speaking fluent English with only a slight accent, he went on :

'I was just saying how happy I am to be able to report that His Imperial Majesty's affairs are in far better shape than any of us had reason to expect after the terrible disaster he met with last winter. His vitality and resource are truly inexhaustible. The negotiations for an armistice, which were begun in February, are still proceeding and if one can be arranged that will be all to the good, since it will give him more time to equip and train the new army he is forming.

'Fortunately, last September, while still in Moscow, he had the forethought to send orders back to France for the call-up of the class due for conscription in 1813, and it is estimated that will bring him some one hundred and thirty-seven thousand new troops. Further levies are being raised in Italy, the Netherlands, Westphalia, Bavaria, Saxony and other German lands. Including those he is withdrawing from Spain, he should have under his hand nearly six hundred and fifty thousand men by the summer. A great part of these have yet to be embodied and trained, and he still has a heavy commitment in Spain, but already over two hundred thousand are available in the army of the West, and they hold all the fortresses on the Elbe, the Weser and the Oder.'

'That is indeed good news,' smiled the beautiful witch. 'But what of our enemies?'

'The pursuit of the *Grande Armée* cost the Russians dear, Madame. They suffered almost as severely as the French from campaigning in such intense cold and living on starvation rations. So poor is their condition that General Kutusov is known to favour entering on a peace, as opposed to the Czar, whose ambition has been fired by his success in driving the French from his country. He has ordered the formation of a reserve army, but the Russians are poor organisers and have great distances to cover, so it will probably be many months before these new conscripts are available for operations. In the meantime, it is believed that the Russian army in the field has been reduced to not much more than one hundred thousand men.'

'And the Prussians? I recall that General von Yorck, who commanded the Prussian contingent in the invasion of Russia, ratted on his chief, Marshal Macdonald and, in the last stage of the retreat, slunk off to Poland without his men having fired a shot.'

'That is true, Madame; and it has since been learned that he had been secretly instructed by his King to avoid giving aid to his French allies, wherever possible. It was the same in the case of General von Schwarzenberg, who commanded the Austrian Corps on the other wing.'

'What shameful conduct!' exclaimed Jemima. 'I only pray that events will enable the Emperor to punish both sovereigns for their treachery.'

Cornelius Quelp nodded. 'The summer campaign may well enable him to do so, at least in the case of the King of Prussia; but at the moment the situation is extremely confused. Technically, Russia and Prussia are still at war, and King Frederick William is too cowardly a man to defy the Emperor by openly changing sides. Yet von Yorck and the army he commands have as good as done so, for he has made a pact with the Russian General Diebitch, which allows the enemy to advance along the Prussian coastal roads without opposition.

'Still more embarrassing for the pusillanimous King is the attitude of his people. For years past, men like Fichte, Stein and Steffens have been inciting the German masses to revolt and drive the French from their territories. Even Scharnhorst and Gneisenau, the King's principal military advisers, are pressing him to break with France. But should he do so, it will be at his peril. It is doubtful if Prussia could raise an army of forty thousand men. The Danes are our staunch allies, also Bavaria and Saxony, and Marshal Davout holds Hanover in a grip of iron. After the retreat from Russia we still had a garrison of thirty thousand in Danzig alone, General Regnier retired on Warsaw with forty thousand, Prince Eugène lies behind him with a field army of sixteen thousand. In Brandenberg and the fortresses we have at least another thirty thousand; so, with the addition of the great reinforcements that the Emperor is sending across the Rhine, even supported by Russia what chance would those miserable Prussians have?'

'So far, Mynheer, you have said naught of Austria,' the witch remarked shrewdly.

'From that direction lies our only danger,' Quelp replied. 'She is still allied to France, but only keeping up an appearance of hostilities against Russia. She is known to be bringing her army up to one hundred and fifty thousand men and, did she once again turn her coat, that would give our enemies parity.'

'You fail to take into account the genius of the Emperor,' put in Jemima.

'No, no!' Quelp smiled. 'I am far from doing that. And, since the councils of the others would be divided, I doubt not he would emerge victorious.'

For a further half-hour they continued to discuss the situation on the Continent, marvelling that Napoleon had made such a swift and remarkable recovery after his defeat in Russia, and with their confidence renewed that he would yet again defeat the combination which was forming against him. Then Mynheer Quelp took his leave.

As soon as the door had closed behind him, Jemima told her mother about the letters from Charles, then said how shattered she had been to learn that he was engaged to Susan, and apparently still deeply in love with her. When she had done, her mother said thoughtfully:

'It is just possible that Maureen Luggala is right in that Charles now regrets having become affianced to Susan, but lacks the courage to break it off. Yet I am inclined to doubt that. Were it so, having no reason to suppose that Susan would ever see his letter to you, he would have expressed himself much more passionately in it.'

Jemima made a grimace. 'Alas, that is what I also feel. And worse—his stating that he means to marry Susan the moment he gets back from the war sadly reduced my hopes. Charles has no streak of cruelty in him, so would never have confirmed her belief that he intends to make her his wife did he not consider his promise binding.'

'Then we must find some other husband for you. What think you of Lord Broughton? It is a fine place he has in Yorkshire, and he is mightily good-looking.'

'Nay. He is a most consummate bore, and can talk of naught but dogs and horses.'

'Everard Winstanley, then? Although he has no title,

he is one of the richest men in England.'

'He is so inveterate a gambler that he may not remain so for much longer. 'Tis said that but a se'nnight since he lost five thousand guineas wagering that one raindrop running down a window in White's Club would reach the sill before another.'

'The Earl of Tulloch? His Scottish estate alone is near the size of a county, and he has others in Wales and Somerset.'

'I thank you, no. He openly boasts that no bawdy house in London procures a new girl of any beauty but he's the first to have her. He'd give me the pox before I'd been married to him a month.'

'Young Hector Vaughan is both personable and witty, and he will inherit much property in London and Ardesley Hall when the old Lord, his father, dies.'

'I've no mind to make do on an allowance while waiting for dead men's shoes.'

'Sir Denison Hever-Crew then. He . . .'

'No, mother, no!' Jemima interrupted impatiently. 'My mind is set on having Charles. His letter to Susan has revealed that all the odds are now against me. Or would be, had I not you for my mother. But you are not as other mothers. You are versed in the secret arts that can alter people's destinies. Use them for me, I beg.'

'There are limits, child, to what can be done in that way. To influence a person in a matter concerning them so vitally as turning love to dislike it is necessary to have frequent converse with them. Could you bring Susan here to me so that I became well acquainted with the girl I could, in time, dominate her mind. But that is not possible because, as you will recall, that fool Hawksbury brought her here last New Year's Eve without preparing her for what would take place. The little prude was shocked and Charles wrought havoc with our ceremony to get her away. Since we were face to face, 'tis certain she would recognise me. Knowing me for what I am, she would instantly oppose my every thought, and as soon make friends with the Devil as with myself.'

'Were matters otherwise, how would you proceed to turn her mind against Charles?'

'By mesmerism.'

'I have heard the term, but know little of it.'

' 'Tis a form of occultism introduced by a Dr. Anton Mesmer. In Paris, just before the Revolution, he opened a clinic and there performed many miracles of healing. But it can also be used for other purposes. People can be made to believe that when drinking water it is wine. By a series of treatments they can be persuaded that their friends are really enemies, and to perform acts that they would recoil from in horror had their minds not been distorted by this mysterious influence.'

'Can anyone learn to use this power?'

'Given sufficient concentration, the majority of people can.'

Jemima's dark eyes suddenly lit up. 'Then I pray you, mother, teach me this strange art. Yesterday I was made most welcome at Stillwaters. It should not be difficult for me to become Susan's bosom friend. Then, if I had this power, I could secretly employ it gradually to dominate her mind.'

The Irish witch smiled. 'You are indeed my daughter. So be it then. You shall practise with my guidance on the servants here, daily for the next few weeks. If your thought forces became really potent, the game will then be in our hands. You will have the power to cause Susan to doubt Charles's love for her, or if need be become so mentally ill as to be unfit to marry.'

11

Home Again! Home Again!

ROGER had kept a record of the days, and it was the morning of April 19th when he and Mary left the Indian settlement in which they had stayed nine days. One of the big war canoes had been made ready with a good supply of provisions and tentage in it. Leaping Squirrel took twelve braves with him to propel the canoe, and four naked 'foreheads' as servants. With a specially-shaped paddle he steered the canoe from the stern, while Mary and Roger sat in front of him on piles of blankets.

They had some eighty miles to go, the latter part of the way lying through places where the river was so wide that it really formed a series of lakes; but, as they were heading downstream both along the tributary and later when they turned east into the St. Lawrence, they travelled at a good speed.

That night they landed and made camp on the south side of the river, for at that date the State of Vermont extended only to the latitude of Rouse's Point, at the head of Lake Champlain, and all the territory north of it was still part of Canada. Having no fear of hostile Indians there, a camp fire was made and a good meal enjoyed; but afterwards they were put to the inconvenience of shifting camp a quarter of a mile further along the shore, as a swarm of huge, black ants had been attracted by the smell of cooking.

The following morning they made an early start and soon after midday emerged from a lake, crossed narrower water to the north shore, and landed on the island of Montreal.

Before leaving the settlement Mary had given two little, silver-topped bottles, one of which contained smelling salts and the other a residue of opium to dull pain, to the old squaws who had tended her. Now, wishing to leave the twelve braves some small souvenirs, she cut into strips a gaily-coloured, silk scarf that she had bought in New York, and tied a strip round the arm of each man. Their gratitude was profound and, kneeling in turn, they kissed the hem of her fur coat. Meanwhile, Roger had presented Leaping Squirrel with his sword, and nothing could have more delighted their cherished Indian friend.

After taking an affectionate leave of him, they hired a carriage on the waterfront and were driven to the Governor's residence. Their clothes were so worn and stained that when Roger asked to see the Governor, the footman who had admitted them looked at him askance. Ignoring the man, Roger sat down at a table in the hall which had writing materials on it, and wrote a brief note, handed it to him and said abruptly:

'Don't stand there staring. Take that to His Excellency and be quick about it.'

Impressed by Roger's air of authority, the servant's manner instantly changed. Bowing, he took the paper and said, 'His Excellency is from home, Sir, down at the headquarters in Ottawa. But I'll take this to his deputy, Brigadier General Sir Wallace Warren.'

Roger had written in the note, '*My wife, Lady Mary*

Brook, and I have recently succeeded in crossing the border from the United States. While there I obtained information that may be of value, and request the honour of an interview.'

His mention of Mary had been deliberate, as he felt certain that, on realising they were people of quality, the Governor would not fob them off on some subordinate. After a few minutes the footman returned, led them down a passage and ushered them into a handsome, book-lined room.

The General proved to be a short, stout little man with a rubicund face and slightly protruding blue eyes. Standing up, he came round his desk and greeted them cordially. In the course of the next few minutes Roger gave an abbreviated account of how they came to be in America and their adventures since leaving French Mills, then he said :

'Perhaps, Sir, you would be good enough to give me the name of the best hostel in the city, where we can lodge in reasonable comfort and replenish our sadly depleted wardrobes before proceeding on our journey. I will, of course, wait upon you again at any time that may be convenient, to give you, or one of your officers, such particulars as I can regarding the forces of our enemy.'

'No, no!' the General protested quickly. 'You must be our guests while in Montreal, and it is now too late in the day for you to purchase your requirements. Tomorrow will be time enough. My wife will be happy to lend Lady Mary a change of clothes for this evening, and we will dine informally.'

Roger gladly accepted the offer. A little later, Lady Warren joined them. She was elderly, white-haired and limped in, using a stick, as she was a martyr to arthritis. But her forbidding expression became a kindly one when

she was told what Mary had been through and, with
motherly concern, she took her upstairs. Sir Wallace then
turned Roger over to his valet. An hour later, when they
met again, bathed and in borrowed plumage, they felt
like different people.

At dinner, besides themselves and the Warrens, there
were only the A.D.C. and his wife : a pretty, snub-nosed,
vivacious young woman. Over the meal the four residents
were fascinated by the account Roger and Mary gave of
their stay in an Indian settlement. Afterwards, when the
ladies had retired, the General suggested that they should
take their port into the library.

There, while the A.D.C. took notes, Roger gave particulars of the military situation on the other side of the
river. Having spent so many years with armies, he was a
highly-trained observer, so was able to provide an expert
appreciation of the strength, morale and communications
of the United States forces on that front.

During the three days that followed, Roger and Mary
re-equipped themselves with clothes, portmanteaux and
other necessities, mainly at the Hudson's Bay Company's
store. They were surprised to find how large a proportion
of the inhabitants of the city were of French descent and
still spoke Canadian French; but they had been under
British rule for fifty years and, their hereditary enemies
having been the Americans, there could be no doubt where
their loyalties lay. They had also largely contributed to
making Montreal a more pleasant place in which to live
than most American cities, for they had retained the cul-
inary art of their ancestors. Roger and Mary discovered
this on their second day, when the A.D.C. and his wife
took them to dine at a restaurant in the old French quarter. It was the most sophisticated meal they had enjoyed
for many a day.

On April 23rd they took leave of the hospitable War-rens, and went aboard a brig in which the General had secured passages for them down the freely navigable stretch of the St. Lawrence to Quebec.

The wind being favourable, the brig covered the one hundred and sixty-odd miles in good time, and they landed in Quebec on the 25th. Sir Wallace had provided Roger with an introduction to the Governor, Vice-Admiral Sir Cyprian Crow, so they were welcomed by him at Admiralty House that evening, on his return from inspecting the Royal Marine Depot. In the meantime they had been entertained by a Mrs. Rusholm, the Admiral's widowed sister who, as he was a bachelor, had come out to run his house for him. She had at once invited them to stay and the Admiral became even more genial when it transpired that he had been a junior Captain under Roger's father, the late Admiral Sir Christopher Brook.

That night there was a dinner party at which most of the other guests were officers, and Roger found that he shared mutual acquaintances with several of them. As Mrs. Rusholm employed a French chef, the meal was excellent, and the glasses were kept well filled throughout, so it proved a merry evening. After the loyal toast, the Admiral proposed, 'To Hell and Davy Jones with the Americans', which was drunk with enthusiasm by all.

Next morning Roger consulted his host about a passage back to England, Gouverneur Morris's loan enabling him to add that he could afford to pay for the best accommodation available. Upon which the jovial sailor exclaimed:

'Pay be damned! If my old chief's son is not entitled to a free passage home, who in thunder is? I've a frigate with despatches sailing in the course of a week. You met Captain Saunders at dinner last night. He's the "owner". You and your lady will sail with him. Meantime, we'll do our best to make your stay in this town of friendly frog-eaters as enjoyable as possible.'

So the matter was swiftly settled. During the next six days Roger and Mary were taken to see the Heights of Abraham, scaled in the night by General Wolfe's troops to take by surprise in the morning and defeat those of the Marquis de Montcalm; to the great Château named after Cardinal de Richelieu who, long ago, had made eastern Canada New France; to see an inspection of recently-landed British reinforcements for the Army; for drives in the surrounding country and to dine and dance.

On May 2nd, they were welcomed by Captain Saunders aboard the thirty-two gun frigate *Albatross* and, a few hours later, to the thunder of a Vice-Admiral's salute, waved good-bye to Sir Cyprian and his sister as the ship set sail for England.

During the voyage Roger suffered from his habitual sea-sickness, but neither so frequently nor so badly as he had done on his way to America, as that had been in mid-winter, whereas now summer, with mostly blue skies and calmer seas, was the order of the day.

On the evening of Friday, June 11th, they docked at Portsmouth. The Lieutenant-Colonel carrying the despatches landed at once, to take them with all possible speed to the Prince Regent, and the Commander-in-Chief at the Horse Guards. Roger and Mary went ashore the next morning and drove to London in a hired coach.

As was his custom whenever he returned from abroad, Roger went straight to Amesbury House in Arlington Street, where his greatest friend, Lord Edward Fitz-Deverel had an upper floor as his personal suite, and always put him up. As it was the height of the London season, Roger felt certain that 'Droopy Ned'—as Lord

Edward was known to his friends, owing to shortsighted-
ness which caused him to have a permanent stoop—would
be in residence; but a footman told him that he was staying the night with friends at Twickenham, to attend a
masked ball at the Duke of Northumberland's mansion,
Sion House. Neither was his lordship's father there, for
the Earl, now being over seventy and in poor health, rarely
came to London.

However, the major-domo, who had known Roger
since he was a boy, was sent for, greeted him warmly and
assured him that Lord Edward would take it most ill if
he and his lady slept elsewhere that night. So rooms were
swiftly prepared for them, and a welcome supper sent up.

In the morning they rose late and, on going downstairs,
learned that Droopy was not expected back until the late
afternoon. Roger then took the first step in a policy that
he had already decided to adopt. Fond as he was of Mary,
he had no intention of being tied to her apronstrings, or
ever giving anything but a vague indication of his doings
when away from her. So, having settled her comfortably
in the small library with the latest periodicals and news
sheets, he said:

'My love, I am now going out, and I'll not be back for
luncheon, as I have various matters to attend to. Some
time, too, I must wait upon Lord Castlereagh to give him
the latest news from America; but, while I am absent, I
am sure that you will be well looked after.'

As he had expected, Mary, knowing that all his life he
had been involved in foreign affairs at the highest level,
made no great demur. Having kissed her good-bye, he
took his hat and went out into the June sunshine.

But he did not proceed in the direction of Whitehall.
Instead, on reaching Piccadilly, he turned left and walked
down the hill to Kew House, one of the fine mansions that

looked out over St. James's Park, for it was there that his beloved Georgina normally lived during the London season, as she preferred it in the summer to Charles's house in Berkeley Square.

To his great disappointment he learned that Georgina was not in residence, and was further distressed on being told that, a week before, the horses of her carriage had bolted, resulting in an unpleasant accident. She had suffered no serious injury, but her face had been badly bruised and she had broken her collar bone; so she had gone down to the country until she was sufficiently restored to appear again in society. However, on enquiring the whereabouts of Miss Brook, he was told that his daughter was there; so he had himself shown up to her boudoir.

It was over eighteen months since he had seen Susan, so he found that she was now a nearly full-grown woman, and a very pretty one. She embraced him with delight, then introduced him to, as she said, her dearest friend, Miss Jemima Luggala, who had been sitting gossiping with her.

As Jemima curtsied, Roger took in her tall figure and dark good looks with an appreciative eye, and thought what a pleasant contrast in colouring the two young beauties made. She at once offered to leave father and daughter together, but when it transpired she had been asked to luncheon, Roger said that of course she must stay, and invited himself to join them.

Having listened to particulars of Georgina's accident, Roger said that he would take an early opportunity of going down to Stillwaters to see her. To his great annoyance, Susan told him that she was not there, but with her old Duke at Newmarket. His annoyance was due to the fact that at Stillwaters he and Georgina would have been alone together, whereas at Newmarket the Duke's elderly sister was in permanent residence, and the only time he had stayed there she had made things so unpleasant for Georgina and him that they had decided it would be better if he did not visit there again.

The time sped swiftly by as Roger told Susan about the new wife he had brought back with him, and how they had been carried off to America. And Susan told him about Charles having bought a commission and gone to Spain; although how he was faring she could not say, as it was a long time since she had had a letter from him.

They were joined at lunch by Great-Aunt Marsham, who had played the part of a mother to Susan during Georgina's absences from home, and was now acting as chaperone, so that Susan might continue to enjoy her nightly engagements during the London season. Over the meal he entertained them with accounts of the strange life led by Red Indians.

When he arrived back at Arlington House it was well on in the afternoon, and he found that Droopy Ned had returned earlier than expected. With him was his cousin, Judith Stanley, whose husband was with Wellington in Spain. She was staying in the house, and had accompanied Droopy down to Twickenham for the ball on the previous night.

Mary had been about to cross the hall as they came in at the front door, and had explained her presence to them a trifle nervously; but in a moment they had put her at her ease by their delight on hearing that Roger was safely home again, and that he had at last married an English girl as pretty and charming as herself.

She had already given them an outline of happenings to Roger and herself since they had left Sweden; but there was so much to tell that they talked on about the war with the United States and escaping across the St. Lawrence, with a break only while they changed for a late dinner. When the ladies had left the men at table, Droopy smiled across at Roger and said :

'Congratulations, m'dear. I find your little Mary charming, if a little shy. She may not have the devastatin' looks of your late lamented, but she's far more to my taste.'

' "Late lamented" does not apply to Lisala as far as I'm concerned,' Roger smiled back, 'despite the fact that I was responsible for her death and that of that brute, von Haugwitz—although without intent. The female form divine never harboured a more evil mind.'

Droopy nodded, 'You're right in that; and 'twas only by God's mercy that, when tried and condemned for their deaths, you got off with a ten-year prison sentence, then escaped.'

'I'm highly conscious of it, Ned. And nine years of that sentence, all but a few months, still stands against me did I get caught in Prussia. But that I'll never be. It's close on four years now since I formed the wish to go adventuring no more. I must have been out of my mind when I let patriotism get the better of my common sense, and allowed m'Lord Wellesley to talk me into accepting that mission to Prince Bernadotte. It involved me again in so many dangers.'

Droopy was one of the very limited number of people who knew about Roger's secret activities. Having told him how he had had to go from Sweden to Russia, then became involved in the retreat from Moscow, Roger added, 'But now, I vow, I'll ne'er set foot on the Continent again.'

'You honestly believe that your restless nature will allow you to settle down?'

'I do. Admittedly, I found it difficult when I had the chance before and could spend happy hours with Georgina only infrequently. But now I have Mary, matters will be very different.'

'Did you know that poor Georgina was the victim of an accident from which she is now convalescing?'

'Yes. This day I took luncheon with Susan and learned of it from her. To my fury she told me that instead of going to Stillwaters, Georgina is at Newmarket.'

Droopy shrugged. 'She has ever kept the pact she made with old Kew when she married him—that, however she chose to amuse herself in private, she would maintain the outward appearance of being his good Duchess. To do that she must needs spend a fair part of the year at Newmarket; so doubtless, being temporarily incapacitated, she felt this a good opportunity to put in some weeks there.'

'Then I must resign myself to waiting a while before I have the joy of beholding her again. Now, Ned, what of the war? You ever have your ear to the ground, and I know no better source of reliable information.'

'The best news is that the new Coalition, which I gathered from m'Lord Wellesley you initiated by bringing Sweden and Russia together, has matured into a formidable combination. Both countries have since openly broken with Bonaparte and become our allies. In March Prussia also threw off the hated yoke, and made a fourth, sworn to put an end to French aggrandisement. The latest is that, on June 4th at Pläswitz, an armistice was agreed which is to last until July 20th.'

'Now that we again have allies on the Continent, I regard an armistice as deplorable. Napoleon's army having been so vastly weakened by his disaster in Russia, he should have been harassed without respite until totally defeated.'

'Maybe that could have been done had this new Coalition been formed earlier; but, throughout the winter, all was sixes and sevens. In Poland and Prussia the utmost confusion reigned. There were still many thousands of French troops in those countries—enough at least for Prince Eugène, who was given command there, to form a formidable army and to continue maintaining garrisons in all the principal fortresses. On his right flank, Schwarzenberg defected and marched his Austrians home, and on his left flank von Yorck defied his King and took his Prussian Corps over to the Russians; but the Muscovites had been so weakened by their long pursuit of the French that it was mid-January before they had recruited their strength sufficiently even to cross the Vistula.

'Meanwhile, as you can well imagine, back in Paris Bonaparte had been far from idle. The reinforcements he sent to Eugène and St. Cyr enabled them to check the Russian offensive on the line of the Oder. It was nearly the end of February before King Frederick William plucked up the courage to sneak away from his French masters in Berlin and, having reached Breslau, disclose the fact that he had entered into an alliance with Russia and ourselves.'

'Every musket that can be turned against Napoleon is a help,' Roger remarked. 'But, unfortunately, Prussia is very far from being what she was in Frederick the Great's day. When Davout defeated them at Auerstadt, with the odds of three to one against him, and Napoleon chased them from the field at Jena, that took the heart out of their army. Then, by the treaty of Tilsit, the Czar and Napoleon between them brought the country near to ruin. They reduced her territory to four provinces and her population to a mere four and a half million.'

''Tis true she's been sadly crippled, but I'm told they are arming every man between the ages of sixteen and sixty, and that even women are volunteering.'

'I can well believe it. Two autumns ago their hatred against the French had already reached such a pitch that they were ripe for revolt. It was an anti-French riot by students that enabled me to escape from prison. It's on the cards that, now they've been given their heads, they'll fight as fanatically as the Spaniards.'

'I'm told, too, that in addition to von Yorck they have some good Generals.'

'Yes. Scharnhorst and Gneisenau are both most able men. There is also old Blücher. He is said to be a rough diamond with little education, but makes up for that by his fiery patriotism and fighting spirit. He is a veteran whom his men would follow anywhere.'

'Scharnhorst is no more. He was killed in Silesia.'

'That is bad.'

'He lost his life in one of the first clashes with the Prussians that occurred after Bonaparte arrived to take command of the French forces in person.'

'When was that?'

'Toward the end of April. He had mustered two armies, one commanded by Ney on the lower Main, and another by Eugéne on the middle Elbe. They concentrated under him between Halle and Jena, then advanced on Leipzig. At that point he was greatly superior to the Russians and Prussians, having two hundred thousand men against their eighty thousand; and, at a place called Gross-Görschen, near Lutzen, he inflicted a severe defeat on them.'

Roger sighed. 'It seems that other Generals stand little chance against his genius. Somehow he always succeeds in forming these concentrations against inferior forces at exactly the right place and time. What then?'

'Bonaparte passed on swiftly to Dresden, while Ney pushed back the Prussians under von Bülow. The allies

withdrew behind the Spree to Bautzen and there, on high
ground, made a stand. But you are so right, Roger. The
Devil himself must inspire that Corsican brigand. The
allies mustered only one hundred and ten thousand men.
He attacked their centre himself with one hundred and
twenty thousand, brought Ney up on the right with
another eighty-five thousand, and still had Davout with
thirty thousand more on the Elbe. Fortunately, he lost so
many thousands of horses in Russia that he is still very
weak in cavalry; whereas the allies are strong. It was that
alone that saved them from complete defeat.'

'The picture is much worse than I had supposed,'
Roger said glumly, 'and I see now why the allies agreed
to an armistice.'

'It could prove of advantage to either side. The levies
Bonaparte is calling up from France, Italy and Illyria will
be reaching him in greater numbers, and the veterans he
is recalling from Spain. On the other hand, further divisions are on their way from Russia; and, about a fortnight
since, Prince Bernadotte landed in Stralsund with a
Swedish Army of twenty-four thousand men, which has
not yet been in action. But bringing about the armistice
was mainly due to Prince Metternich.'

'Is Austria still allied to France?'

'Nay, she has become neutral, and the Prince is playing
a most skilful game. He is greatly averse to Bonaparte
continuing to dominate Europe, and equally so to Russia
becoming more powerful. In the hope of preventing
either, he is now acting as mediator, and hopes to bring
about a permanent peace. Meanwhile, he is rebuilding
the Austrian Army into so powerful a force that, if flung
in on either side, it could prove the deciding factor.'

Roger nodded. 'With the one exception of my old
friend, Talleyrand, I count him the cleverest diplomat of

our age. Have you any idea what his proposals are for converting this armistice into a permanent peace?'

'Yes. I had them from m'Lord Castlereagh himself. The price Metternich is demanding of Bonaparte for Austria not joining the allies is that both the Grand Duchy of Warsaw and the Confederation of the Rhine, created by him as vassal states, should be abolished, the re-establishment of the Free Hanse Towns, the return to Prussia of the territories of which she has been robbed since 1805, and the return to Austria of her Illyrian provinces. Knowing the Corsican so well, Roger, think you he will agree?'

Roger helped himself to another glass of port before replying:

'I would were I in his shoes, Ned, for those conditions are not unreasonable. He would be left with a France considerably larger than when the Bourbons ruled it, Holland, Switzerland, the Belgian lands and the greater part of Italy. After twenty-odd years of war, France has been bled white, and I'd wager any money that her people would gladly give up every conquest the Emperor has ever made, if only he would give them peace. Spain has long been a running sore and, as I learned from Susan this noon when she told me young Charles is now there, the Duke is besting in turn every Marshal sent against him.

'Yet I greatly doubt if the Emperor will accept Metternich's terms. The devil of it is that these past few years he has become the victim of *folie de grandeur*. He'll no longer listen to the wise counsel of his old friends, and counts himself omnipotent. He will persuade himself that, as he has an Austrian Princess for wife, his father-in-law can be counted on to hold Metternich back and that then, with only the Russians, Prussians and Swedes against him, he'll be able to perform another miracle.'

'I pray God he doesn't,' Droopy said soberly. 'England

needs peace near as badly as France. His damnable Continental System has brought thousands of our merchants to ruin. Yet, whatever happens, we must see it through to the end. If only Austria would come in before the winter, we might hope for final victory.'

Roger raised his glass. 'Let's drink to that. But I've now played my part and, victory or defeat, I'll not be there to see it.'

12

Seen in a Crystal

On the Monday morning, while Judith took Mary shopping, Roger borrowed a mount and rode down to Richmond. For many years, during his long absences abroad, old Dan Izzard had acted for him as the faithful custodian of Thatched House Lodge; and eighteen months earlier, as he had not expected his mission to Sweden to take more than eight to ten weeks, he had kept on Mrs. Muffet, his cook-housekeeper and one maid, arranging for them to be paid by Hoare's Bank while he was away.

He found them all well, and happy to see him again after so long. Everything was in good order, the reception rooms needed only the removal of the covers from the furniture, and the garden was a blaze of flowers. Well pleased, he informed them of his marriage, and told Mrs. Muffet to engage two extra maids, then he sat down to write a letter to Georgina.

In it, having condoled with her about her accident, he told her that a strange twist of fate had enabled him to take her advice and marry Mary; that he would tell her when they met of the unexpected happenings that had kept him abroad for so long and, with all the eagerness he would have felt had he been twenty years younger, he prayed that might be soon. He begged her, if she must yet remain unable to re-enter society for a few weeks, to remove forthwith to Stillwaters, or to her *petite maison* in Kensington, so that, 'by the world forgotten and the world forgot', they might glory once again in being alone together.

Giving Dan a handful of guineas, he sent him off with the letter to Newmarket, charging him to give it into Her Grace's own hand.

On his return to London, he told Mary that he had found everything at Thatched House Lodge in good shape, and the memory of how delightful she had thought it on the one brief occasion that she had been there made her eager to move at once into her new home. But Roger said they must give Mrs. Muffet a few days to install two more maids, and Droopy and Judith both pressed them to stay on at Amesbury House for at least a week, so it was agreed that they should not move down to Richmond until the following Monday.

The week in London gave Roger the opportunity to present Susan to Mary, to introduce her to a number of his friends, to give Lord Castlereagh an account of the situation in America, and to resume his acquaintance with many of his fellow members at White's. On the Thursday, Droopy gave a *soirée* to enable Mary to meet many leading members of society and soon afterwards invitations to numerous functions began to come in. It was, too, on Thursday morning that Dan arrived with a letter from Georgina in reply to Roger's.

Having expressed her unbounded delight at his safe return, she went on, '*Recalling what you told me of your Mary, after your affair with her in Lisbon, I am certain you have been wise to make her your wife, for there is no change in the condition of my poor old Duke. It seems that he was blessed—or rather, now, cursed—with an iron constitution, and the doctors say that, although since his stroke he has become no more than a vegetable, he may yet survive for many years; so clearly Fate decreed that we should never marry. But, Roger my love, unfaithful as we have ever been to our spouses, in this new situation we must use the utmost discretion. Mary must never be given cause to suspect that we are more to each other than life-long friends. I will remove to Stillwaters in ten days or so, in order that we may again rejoice in being under one roof; but no more than that. You must bring her with you, and I suggest for a long week-end from Friday, July 2nd until the Monday or Tuesday; as it would be unreasonable to ask her to leave her new home for longer until she has been in it for the best part of a fortnight. Later in the month I will come to London. No doubt to discuss some affair of State, or a punch-drinking with your men cronies will also necessitate your spending a night or two in the capital, and then! then! then! Roger, my own, we'll roll back the sheets, and with them the years.'*

The letter went on to tell of her accident, of Susan and the numerous beaux whom she enjoyed pursuing her while Charles was in Spain, and ended by saying that the news that Roger was safely back in England had been like a draught of the Elixir of Life to her.

Despite Roger's impatience to hold her in his arms again, he was well pleased with her letter. Over the years, the long periods they had had to spend apart had armoured them both against any feeling of jealousy concerning their relations with others; nevertheless, he was touched by this evidence that Georgina's mind was still so closely attuned to his own, in her determination to protect Mary from unhappiness.

On the Monday afternoon Mary could hardly contain her delight when Roger took her over Thatched House Lodge, and she unpacked her things in the best bedroom.

During the ten days that followed, they went several times to balls and routs in London, returned tired but happy in the early hours of the morning. Then, on July 2nd, they drove down to Stillwaters.

When Roger had told her of the invitation and that he had accepted it, she had been far from happy at the idea of leaving her new home even for a week-end. But she had not shown it, for Roger had often spoken to her of Georgina, as his boyhood sweetheart before he had run away to France, and his friend of a life-time, so she did not protest at his being eager to see her again.

As Roger had expected, the meeting of the two ladies proved most pleasant. Georgina told him later that she thought Mary pretty enough to please most men, and with an intelligence and sense of humour much exceeding the majority of her sex; while Mary said to him of Georgina that her graciousness was surpassed only by her beauty, and it seemed impossible to believe that she was over forty.

Susan had come down for the week-end, bringing Jemima with her and, to entertain the two girls, Georgina had invited their latest beaux : the Honourable Ivor Tavistock and Captain Hercules Hunt, so they formed a merry party. Roger had long since warned Mary always to give out that they had met again in Copenhagen and make no mention of their terrible experiences in Russia, as he had then been on Napoleon's Staff, and that would have taxed even his ingenuity to explain; but during the evening they told of their adventures while in America, and Captain Hunt discoursed at some length on the war in Spain.

For some days past the Peninsula had again become a principal topic of conversation, because on June 21st the Duke of Wellington had achieved an outstanding victory.

At Vittoria he had inflicted a crushing defeat on King Joseph and was now said to be pursuing the remnants of the French army, with a view to driving it over the Pyrenees.

On the Saturday morning all the young people went riding, but Georgina, although now recovered from her injuries, said she did not feel inclined to ride again yet and Roger, delighted at the prospect of getting an hour or two alone with her, said he would remain to keep her company.

Highly conscious that if they remained in the house together, she might be persuaded by Roger to let him make love to her, and determined to take no risks, Georgina promptly announced that, as it was a lovely day, they would take a walk round the garden. Knowing very well what was in her mind, Roger gave a wry grin and agreed.

As they strolled along arm in arm, he was able to tell her how he had really met Mary again in St. Petersburg, and of their ordeals during the retreat. When he had ended with their escape to Sweden, Georgina said :

'What you tell me of her courage and unfailing good humour in such circumstances makes me more certain than ever that you were right to marry her. It is your nature, dear one, that you must ever have constant excitement or congenial companionship. That became all too evident during those last eight months you spent in England. It was our tragedy that, believing you to be dead and not caring what became of me, I should have allowed old Kew to persuade me to marry him. But, once his Duchess, I had to abide by the conditions I had myself made—to be his wife only in name, but to take no lover openly. That meant our never being together for more than a few nights in succession, and that oft with weeks between. I could not wonder at your becoming bored and miserable. But now you will have little Mary, and we can still snatch . . .'

Pressing the hand that rested on his arm, he interrupted impatiently, 'But when, my sweet, when?'

She considered for a moment. 'It would be wiser if you did not take your first night away from Mary too soon; so I'll not come up to London until after next week-end. Let us make it Wednesday, the 14th. Come to the studio at seven o'clock that evening. Harriet married last autumn, so be not surprised when a new maid lets you in. Her name is Jane. She is devoted to me, and so is entirely trustworthy.'

'Twelve more days to wait,' Roger sighed. 'I can hardly bear it. But you are right. For Mary's sake we must not rush our fences; and now, at last, I'll not be tempted to leave England ever again.'

Entering a big, domed glass house, they walked to the far end. Inside were growing palms, orchids and tropical creepers with great leaves that would prevent anyone passing outside from seeing them. He took her in his arms and pressed her to him. After several long, sweet kisses she suddenly broke away from him and exclaimed breathlessly:

'No, Roger, no! Lud, how I long for you! But desist, I beg. I'll trust neither you nor myself if you go further. Take me out of here.'

As they left the hothouse, both of them were trembling, and he said, 'To be with you again after all these months, yet unable to possess you will drive me crazy. So I'll make some excuse to take Mary home on Monday, instead of Tuesday as we planned.'

She nodded. 'Yes, that would be best, for I feel the same.'

Back at Richmond he resumed with Mary the pleasant

life they had been leading before their visit to Stillwaters. The following Sunday he mentioned casually that he would be from home on the coming Wednesday night, to attend a gathering at a club of which he had long been a member, and where he would again meet old friends he had not seen since his return.

Having never before moved in London society, Mary was unaware that such men's drinking clubs were a feature of it; so when he was about to mount his horse on the Wednesday afternoon, her kiss was a little cold as she wished him a merry evening.

Having stabled his horse at Amesbury House and spent a pleasant hour with Droopy Ned, Roger took a coach out to Georgina's villa-studio which stood on the rise north of Kensington village. Her new maid, Jane, proved to be a buxom wench with a merry smile and red-gold hair.

An adept at making himself agreeable to servants, when she opened the door to him he said with a laugh, 'M'dear, your hair is the same colour as my money.' Taking a guinea from his breeches pocket, he held it up against her nearest ringlet, then pressed it into her palm and kissed her lightly on her rosy cheek. Blushing with pleasure, she ushered him into her mistress.

Georgina, as ravishing as ever, her black curls tied back with a broad red ribbon and clad only in a silk chamber robe, was reclining on a sofa. Jane had barely left the room before Roger was kneeling beside her, smothering her face with kisses, inhaling the special, delicious scent she used only for their secret meetings, and with eager hands exploring for the thousandth time the hidden glories of her lovely person.

As they had so often done before, when Roger had changed into a chamber robe she kept there for him, they feasted off pâté, lobsters, glazed duck garnished with red cherries, and nectarines, washed these good things down with goblets of champagne, teased each other, recalled old times and laughed until they cried. Then, at length, he picked her up and carried her into the next room, where Jane had already turned down for them the black silk sheets of the big bed.

Alternately they made ecstatic love and dozed, embraced, until the morning. At eleven o'clock Georgina rang for Jane, who brought them a freshly opened bottle of champagne and iced melon. After they had breakfasted, Roger reluctantly began to dress. As he tied his cravat before the mirror, he said:

'What would I not give to be able to spend the day and yet another night here, as I have oft done in the past.'

Georgina yawned, then replied with a smile, 'Yes, to be out of the world together for two or three days at a stretch was truly heaven; but, until Mary has become more used to your absenting yourself, we must make do with single nights.'

'That's a sound reason why we should not too long delay our next.'

'I think we should restrain our impatience for ten days at least.'

Turning, he shook his head, 'Nay, sweet. 'Tis already July 15th. Come the end of the month the season will be over. In August London will be as empty as a drum, providing no possible excuse for you to come up from Newmarket. Before the calendar imposes on us eight weeks or more of abstinence, we must indulge ourselves again at least twice.'

'To start with, weekly meetings were more than I intended. Yet, with the desolate weeks at Newmarket to be faced, I've not the strength of will to refuse you. Having but recently returned after so long an absence, Mary should not regard it as unreasonable if you wish to attend the last two meetings of this club you've told her of before everyone leaves town.'

Thus the matter was agreed, and on the evening of Wednesday, the 21st, Roger was again admitted by pretty Jane to his earthly paradise.

During the past week, memories of the previous Wednesday night had been so frequently in his mind that, if possible, he was more eager than ever to have Georgina in his arms, and she received him with equal fervour.

Again they feasted, laughed, loved and drank the night away until, as daylight was showing between the chinks of the curtains, satiated, blissfully happy and without a care in the world, they fell asleep.

It was about an hour later when Roger was roused by Georgina crying out in her sleep. 'O God! No! No! No!'

To wake her from her nightmare, he put a hand on her shoulder and gently shook her. With a start she sat up, covered her face with her hands and sobbed through them in agonised tones, 'No, no! It can't be true! Oh, God, please don't let it be true.'

Roger threw his arm about her shoulders, drew her to him and asked anxiously, 'What is it, my sweet? Please! You'll be all right in a moment. You've only had a horrid dream.'

As she took her hands from her face, he saw that her great eyes were brimming with tears. She shook her head and the tears ran down her cheeks as she sobbed:

'It was Charles. He was riding through a wood with half a dozen other mounted men. Suddenly they were fired upon. They had run into an ambush. Charles and his men broke into a gallop. One of them was hit and fell from his horse. The others got away—except for Charles. His horse was shot under him. A score of French soldiers

G

ran out of the wood. Charles had scrambled to his knees. They seized him and hauled him to his feet. He . . . he's been taken prisoner.'

Frowning, Roger strove to comfort her. 'Beloved, it was only a dream. Nothing but a dream. You've been worrying about him too much.'

Swallowing hard, she said hoarsely, 'Yes, a dream; but a true dream. It was in colour. Oh, what will happen to my darling boy?'

Roger knew of old the psychic powers Georgina had inherited from her gipsy mother, so he feared she was right and did not argue with her. Instead he said:

'There are worse things than being captured. At least for a few months, until it can be arranged for him to be exchanged for a French officer of equivalent rank, he'll be in no danger of being killed or wounded. And as an officer he will receive decent treatment.'

'Perhaps. I can only pray that it will be so. But by some accounts the French have become savages. I must find out. I must find out what the future holds for him.'

As she spoke, Georgina scrambled out of bed, went to a bureau, took her crystal from a drawer in it, put it on a small table nearby and, sitting down, riveted her gaze on the globe. For several minutes she was silent, then she murmured:

'I can see him. He looks well, except that there is a bandage round his hand. I see him again. This is much later, and he has grown a beard. I think he is in a castle. But not in a dungeon. There is plenty of light. He is with other officers, but their uniforms do not look like those of Englishmen. Some of them are playing cards. Charles is laughing. How strange that I should have a son old enough to grow a beard.'

As she sat at the table she was still naked. Now that

Roger could believe that Charles would be safe and well
cared for, he allowed his mind to dwell on her beauty.
She was sitting in profile to him, her dark ringlets falling
to her shoulders and hiding her face, except for the corner
of an eyebrow, thick, curling black lashes, well-modelled
nose and one side of her very full, red-lipped mouth. As
she leaned forward, her breasts rested on the edge of the
table, an upturned nipple protruded from the semi-circle
of brown corona. Below the table, her powerful hips
tapered to smoothly-rounded knees then, drawn back
beneath them, perfect calves, slim ankles and arched feet.

She had remained silent for several moments. Suddenly
she gave a gasp of horror, thrust the table violently from
her so that the crystal rolled across the carpet, jerked herself erect, gave a piercing scream and fell in a dead faint
on the floor.

Leaping out of bed, Roger seized her shoulders and
cradled her head in his arms. Jane came running in, her
mouth agape. Together they got Georgina back into bed.
Roger sent Jane for brandy, and forced Georgina to swallow a little of the spirit. She began to moan, then opened
her eyes and looked desperately about her.

'What did you see, my poor sweet?' Roger asked her
frantically. 'Tell me! Tell me! What did you see?'

She groaned again. 'They . . . they're going to hang
him. He . . . he was standing beneath . . . beneath a tree.
It was in a long avenue. There were . . . French soldiers
round him. They . . . Oh God! . . . his hands were tied
behind him and . . . and they were just about to put the
noose of a rope round the neck of a comrade standing
near him.'

Roger signed to Jane to leave them, then took both
Georgina's hands and said firmly, 'Light of my life, I do
not believe one word of this. The whole thing is a fantasy.'

'But I saw it! I saw it. And my crystal never lies to me. Remember how in the autumn of 1809 I saw you with a pastor in a cell for the condemned. We persuaded ourselves it was a glimpse of the past, when you were in Guildford gaol. But it was not. I was seeing you many months later, after you were tried for murder in Berlin.'

'True, but I was reprieved. And this vision of yours lacks all credulity. Charles is an officer, and officers condemned to death are shot. They are never hanged.'

'Roger, I saw it as clearly as I see you now. That avenue of tall trees and Charles standing among their fallen leaves with . . . with other prisoners who were already hanging from the branches of the trees.'

'It would then be in the autumn.'

'Yes, yes, it was autumn. 'Twas this morning he was captured. Of that I'm certain. But in a few months' time he . . . he'll do something . . . then . . . oh, is there nothing we can do to save him?'

As her big eyes, misty with tears, stared into Roger's, he knew what she was thinking. He knew, too, that she would not ask it of him; but there was something that could be done, and he was the only man in England who might be able to do it.

On the Continent, wherever France's writ ran, he was *Colonel Comte de Breuc,* a Commander of the Legion of Honour and an A.D.C. to the Emperor. He had for years formed one of Napoleon's intimate circle, and a single prisoner would mean nothing to a man whose prison camps held many, many thousands. He had only to go to the Emperor and ask for an order for Charles's release, and he had not the least doubt that it would be given him.

Through Roger's mind raced distressing thoughts of what such a commitment would entail. He had vowed never again to leave England until the war was over. His desperate craving to be done with risks and to lead a life of ease must go by the board. Once more he must face the chance that he would be found out to be an English secret agent. But that was not all. There was Mary. She had been settled into her new home barely a month. Must the man she loved so devotedly be snatched from her, and her happiness be turned for many weeks into miserable anxiety at the thought that she might have lost him for good?

It was not as though he could hope to accomplish such a mission in a fortnight by a swift crossing of the Channel and return. The Emperor was in Germany and Charles in Spain. To reach northern Germany, ride all the way across the Rhineland through France, find Charles, secure his release, then get home, could easily take two months.

But wait! Was it necessary to go to the Emperor? No. Roger knew King Joseph well, and Napoleon's eldest brother was a kindly man. It was men of his army who had captured Charles, and he could easily be persuaded to give an order for the boy's release. To go direct to Spain would save a month or more. And time was important, for any unforeseen delay in the much longer journey could mean not reaching Spain until the autumn, and perhaps too late.

Roger had as good as made up his mind that he must inflict a month or so of misery on poor little Mary when another thought struck him. If Georgina's vision had been a true one, no order for Charles's release could prevent his standing beneath a tree about to be hanged. In that case, any attempt to save him must prove, as near as made no odds, futile.

Again his thoughts raced furiously. Himself apart, Georgina loved her son more than anyone in the world. How could he possibly tell her that, unless the crystal had misled her, there was no hope for him? Besides, while there is life, there is always hope. She had not seen Charles hanging, only about to be hanged. It might be that his captors were only threatening him with death as a means of wringing some information from him. That was a possibility as slender as a gossamer thread. On such a chance to shatter poor little Mary's happiness and resume the dangerous game that, with fantastic good fortune, he had survived for so long was, when regarded cooly, sheer madness.

But wait! Perhaps Georgina's vision had been sent her as a warning—a warning of a fate likely to overtake Charles unless some action was taken to prevent it. There had been many instances of people who had appeared to stand no hope whatever of escaping execution, yet had been saved from death by some quite unexpected intervention. All forecasts of future events were, Roger knew, no more than probable indications of the course fate would take. None were inevitable.

With sudden resolution he took Georgina's hands firmly in his and said:

'I will go to Spain and spare no effort in an attempt to save him.'

13

To Go, or not to Go

It was with a heavy heart that Roger rode home that afternoon, to face Mary and tell her of the scurvy trick fate had played them. Anxiously he wondered how she would take the news that he must leave her. Very badly, he was certain, and he was terribly distressed at the thought of the grief he must inflict on her.

He was also grimly conscious of his own misfortune. Gone was the future to which he had looked forward for so long: to leading the life of a well-to-do gentleman of leisure, mingling with high society at gay balls and routs, frequenting the most exclusive clubs and discussing there with the best informed men of the day the latest news from courts and camps, pleasant visits to Brighton and big country houses, sleeping always in comfortable beds, hearing Mary's merry laughter daily, having Susan and Droopy to stay and, as a priceless spice to life, from time to time renewing his youth by revelling in a hectic night with his beloved Georgina.

Instead, he was doomed, for a time at least, to a renewal of the hard and dangerous existence he had led for so long. He knew from bitter past experience how easy it was, once on the Continent as *Colonel Comte de Breuc,* to become involved in hazardous undertakings. They could lead to having to spend days on end in the saddle until he was half-dead from exhaustion, to sleeping wrapped in a cloak on the hard ground, to coming unexpectedly face to face with someone who knew him to be an Englishman and who might denounce him as a spy; or, once again, having to gallop through smoke and musket balls carrying orders from Napoleon during one of his battles and fearing every moment to be killed or maimed for life.

But Mary was his immediate worry. In vain he had racked his brain for a way to soften the blow, but there was no avoiding having to deliver it. However, on one aspect of the matter his mind was made up. In no circumstances must she be allowed to know that it was for Georgina's sake that he was leaving her. And, fortunately, he thought he had the means of preventing her suspecting that.

Following a procedure he had decided upon during his ride from London, when Mary ran out of the house to greet him as he crossed the garden from the stable yard, he gave her only a pale smile and kissed her in a slightly off-handed manner. When she asked him how he had enjoyed his dinner the previous night, he replied, 'Oh, well enough,' then said that after freshening himself up he had some letters he must write.

Although he did not put pen to paper, he remained in his small library until the gong sounded for dinner, moodily contemplating the distressing task before him. Over the meal he appeared distrait and answered Mary's questions only very briefly. She waited until the parlour-maid had put the dessert on the table and left the room. Then she asked with deep concern :

'Roger, whatever ails you? I've never known you like this. Are you in some trouble?'

Beginning to peel a peach, he replied, 'I am not, but

someone very dear to me is and, alas, it entails great un-happiness for both of us.'

'For us? But why, and in what way?'

'Because, my dearest, I'll have to leave you for a while.'

Mary's mouth dropped open and she exclaimed, 'Leave me! Oh, no! You cannot mean it.'

'I do. I hope not to be absent for more than a few weeks, but I have to go abroad again.'

'Abroad!' Mary gulped, then her eyes became angry. 'Roger! When we sailed from Sweden, you swore to me that you would never accept another mission. Yet you must have. And we've been living for scarce a month the life I've dreamed of. Oh, how could you? How could you?'

' 'Tis not a mission. I mean, this is no matter of going to the Continent again as a secret agent. It is a personal affair. Young Charles St. Ermins has been taken prisoner.'

Mary lowered her eyes. 'I am indeed sorry to hear that. But I do not see what you can do about it.'

'Joseph Bonaparte, as King of Spain, is the titular com-mander of the army there so it was his troops that cap-tured Charles. I have known the King well for many years. I have no doubt whatever that I can obtain from him an order for Charles's release.'

Again Mary's glance was angry. 'As an officer he will be well treated, and in due course an exchange will be arranged for him. At best you could only spare him the inconvenience of a few additional weeks in captivity. And anyway, why should you go there on his account?'

'Because, Mary, he is my son.'

'Your son! You mean that he has no real right to the Earldom? That you fathered him upon Georgina?'

For a moment Roger was tempted to accept the con-clusion to which she had jumped, as it would have strengthened his case for going to Charles's assistance. But swiftly he realised the danger of acknowledging this tie with Georgina.

'No, no,' he shook his head. 'I mean only that Charles is the nearest thing to a son I've ever had. As you know, he and Susan were brought up together by Georgina, so I have always looked on both of them as my children.'

The nearest thing to a sneer that Roger had ever seen on Mary's face crossed it for a moment, then she snapped, 'So you think of yourself as his father! A fine father I must say! Why, it will be near three years since you even saw the boy. And when you were last in England for any length of time, he was for most of it at Eton. Did you come face to face with him in a street tomorrow, I doubt me if you'd know him.'

Roger sighed. 'Mary my love, what you say is true enough. Yet I feel this to be a duty I cannot shirk.'

'You mean you learned this from Georgina and have given way to her pleading that you should desert me to go in search of the son she so dotes upon?'

'Georgina does not enter into this.'

'Oh, but she does! Your story to me that she has been your lifelong friend is true enough. But there is more to it than that. Do you suppose there are no malicious tongues among the society women with whom I have become acquainted during this past month? Several of them have been at pains to inform me that Georgina was your mistress for many years, and sweetly congratulated me on having supplanted her in your affections.'

'That we were lovers when young I'll not deny,' Roger replied smoothly. 'But that is a long time ago. Not one of those scandalmongering jades could provide a tittle of evidence that I've been aught to Georgina between her marriages but a frequent escort when in London.'

'Yet you must have been with her at some time during the past twenty-four hours. How else could you have learnt that Charles is a prisoner?'

Roger had agreed with Georgina that, to make certain the news about Charles did not get to Susan's ears and cause her great distress, she should tell no-one of her dream or vision in the crystal. So he was able to reply :

'I learnt it last night from the Minister of War, who made one of our party. Charles's capture was mentioned in a despatch he had received that morning from His Grace of Wellington. Knowing my connection with the boy, he told me of it, but he'll not make it public, in order to spare Georgina the anxiety she would feel.'

The plausible lie temporarily stilled Mary's suspicions, but she continued to argue that she had a bigger claim on him than Charles, and to plead with him to forgo his intention of going to Spain.

He had assumed she would be tearful but submissive, so her persistence, added to her unexpected suspicions about Georgina, annoyed him. Sorry as he was for her, and the more so from knowing that he was making her unhappy to undertake a journey that might very well prove futile, he was not the man to change his mind once he had made it up, let alone go back on his word to Georgina. At length, pushing back his chair, he said :

'M'dear. When we first met in Lisbon I told you that, being near twice your age, I was too set in my habits to change them. I have never yet allowed a woman to interfere with any project I have set my mind upon. I can only say that since I love you very dearly, I will return to you as soon as possible.'

Thereupon Mary burst into tears. But he ignored her, left the table and walked from the room.

She did not join him in the library, and he spent the

next few hours putting his affairs in order. By the time he had finished, he had decided that the only way to ensure against Mary making further trouble in future, when she disapproved of his arrangements, was to teach her a sharp lesson. So, when he went upstairs, instead of going to their bedroom he went to his dressing room and slept the night there.

He had hoped she would come to him and seek a reconciliation; but as she had not he was in no mind, when he went downstairs in the morning, to take the first step himself. She did not join him for breakfast, so when he had finished he sent for her maid, and said :

'As Her Ladyship is still up in her room, I assume she is feeling indisposed. Be good enough to tell her that I shall shortly be leaving for London, but expect to return in time for dinner.'

To his surprise the girl faltered, 'But Her Ladyship is not there, Sir. She got up early, ordered the coach and left an hour since. I . . . I thought you knew.'

With difficulty concealing the anger he felt at having to show ignorance of his wife's plans, he asked, 'Did she say where she was going, and what time she is likely to be back?'

'No, Sir. But she had me pack a small night bag to take with her.'

Dismissing the girl with a nod, Roger poured himself another cup of coffee, then sat back to consider this unexpected development. Mary had clearly taken the bit between her teeth, but where the devil was she on her way to? She had no relatives with whom she could stay while endeavouring to bring him to heel, and no money of her own. He had started to make her a generous monthly allowance, but she could not have put aside out of the first instalment sufficient to keep herself for any length of time.

During the past few weeks she had made a number of acquaintances, but was not yet intimate enough with any of them to ask them to put her up—except Droopy Ned. Yes, that was probably the answer. She had gone off to pour out her trouble to him.

Roger had meant to look in on Droopy that day and, as he had no secrets from this best of friends, tell him that he was going to Spain, and why. Now he decided against doing so, for he had no intention of letting Mary think he had come hot-foot after her.

Half an hour later he was on his way to London, and by mid-morning at the Admiralty, where he sent up his card to the First Sea Lord, an acquaintance of long standing, who was one of the comparatively few people who knew of his past activities as a secret agent.

After a short wait, the Admiral saw him and they talked for ten minutes or more about Roger's experiences in Russia and America, then he said, 'My Lord, I am anxious to get to Spain as soon as possible. I must not conceal it from you that this is on private business; but if you could help me I'd be deuced grateful.'

The old sailor smiled. 'Having in mind your past services to the nation, Mr. Brook, we'd be mightily ungrateful if we couldn't stretch a point for you. The frigate *Pompey,* Captain Durrant, will be sailing from Greenwich three days hence. You're welcome to a passage aboard her, and I'll notify her commander accordingly.'

Well pleased, Roger made his way to White's Club. As he hung his beaver on a peg in the inner hall, it crossed his mind how manners and fashions had changed since he had first become a member. Then, all the hats had been tricornes and many edged with gold lace. Now, they were all toppers of various colours, some, like his own, rough-surfaced, others of smooth, shining silk.

At the far end of the billiard room he found Droopy, playing backgammon. He peered at Roger with his short-sighted eyes, then greeted him cheerfully, but said nothing of Mary. As soon as the game had ended, Roger drew him aside and asked if she was at Amesbury House.

'No,' replied Droopy in some surprise. 'At least she was not there when I left an hour agone. Why, think you she might be?'

Over a decanter of Madeira, Roger told him what had occurred. After a moment's thought, Droopy said, ''Tis plaguey hard upon you both, though she will be the greater sufferer. Loath as you are to go abroad again, at least you'll be fully occupied, whereas poor Mary will have naught to do but wait and pray. Wherever she is gone, since she has little money she'll not remain away from home for long; and, when she does return, you must not upbraid her for this display of temperament, for 'tis love for you that is the cause of it.'

'You're right, Ned. And it troubles me mightily to have to inflict this pain upon her. Yet how could I possibly leave Georgina without a single hope?'

'In view of what you have always been to each other, you could not. To that I agree. Yet, if her vision be a true one, your hope of saving Charles is no better than that an angel should appear at the critical moment when the rope is put about his neck.'

'Dam'me, I know it! And my wrath at being forced into undertaking a mission so likely to be foredoomed to failure is exceeded only by my sorrow that it seems the boy is fated to die. Although I've done little, other than buy him presents when a child and later teach him enough of sword play to make him a dangerous antagonist. I've loved him both as my sweet Georgina's son and for himself.'

Droopy nodded. 'I, too, will share Georgina's grief and yours. Since he could toddle, I have ever been his "dear Uncle Ned". Indeed, over the years I have seen much more of him than yourself, and he was fast becoming a man of whom we could all be proud.'

In due course, Roger accompanied Droopy back to Amesbury House, to make certain that Mary had not arrived there while they had been at White's. Then Roger rode back to Richmond.

Half an hour after he reached home, he heard his coach drive up to the front door. Hurrying to it, he met Mary on the doorstep. Holding out both his hands to her, he said with a smile :

'Mary, my love, wherever have you been? Your driving off without a word to me this morning, and taking a night bag with you caused me great concern.'

She returned his smile. 'For that I'm sorry. But this was an occasion when I felt that I, for once, must undertake a mission.'

He frowned. 'I trust it was successful . . . but I do not understand. And why did you take a night bag?'

'Because I thought I might be asked to stay the night. And it was successful. You need not now go to Spain.'

'What the devil are you talking about?'

Taking a letter from her reticule, she handed it to him. He saw Georgina's crest on the envelope. With a sudden frown, he ripped it open and read :

'Dear Roger,
'Mary tells me that Charles has been taken prisoner and that, having learned of this, it is your intention to proceed to Spain in the hope of obtaining his release. Naturally, this news greatly pains me and I feel sure that it was rea-

*lising how much it would do so when I heard it that
prompted your generous intent. But though I'd derive
great comfort from knowing that you were going to
Charles's assistance, I cannot allow it. I have no doubt that
His Grace of Wellington will speedily arrange for his
exchange; and the anxiety you would inflict on Mary by
leaving her could not possibly be justified in order to
spare the boy a few extra weeks of captivity.*

    'Ever your loving friend,

                    'Georgina.'

As he finished reading, Mary said, 'I thought her to be
at Stillwaters, so drove down there this morning, only to be
told that she left for London the day before yesterday
and . . .'

'And her letter makes it obvious that when you found
her at Kew House you told her about Charles.'

'Of course. It was to do so that I sought her out.'

Roger had told Mary that the news of Charles's capture
was to be kept secret, in order to spare Georgina. Her
letter showed that she had kept to their agreement to speak
of it to no-one, so that Susan should not learn of it. Coldly,
he said :

'Did it not occur to you that telling Georgina would
cause her great grief and anxiety?'

'Well . . . yes,' Mary faltered. 'But to appeal to her was
my only hope of preventing you from leaving me.'

Obviously Georgina had said nothing to Mary of her
vision in the crystal, and to write that letter, foregoing the
one possible chance of saving her son must have cost her
dear. Yet it was typical of the generous and courageous
spirit that Roger loved in her. Slowly he tore the letter
across, again and again, let the pieces flutter to the ground,
and said harshly :

'Madame, your callous act has failed to achieve its purpose. I do not take orders from Georgina. For your information, in three days' time I am sailing for Spain.'

Then he turned his back on Mary and strode into the house.

An hour later, her eyes red from weeping, she came down for dinner. As Roger did not appear, she thought he must have failed to hear the gong, so told the parlour-maid to sound it again. For the second time that day the girl showed surprise, then faltered:

'Did you not know, m'lady? The master ordered his horse and half an hour since rode away.'

When Roger reached London he still felt very bitter about Mary; for he considered she had betrayed his trust and taken a step which, had his beloved Georgina not already known about Charles, would have caused her great grief. Within a few minutes of entering Kew House he had even greater reason for his anger. Georgina was in her boudoir and, as the door closed behind the footman who had shown him up to her, she said:

'I take it you have had my letter?'

He nodded. 'Yes; it is about that I am come.'

'So I imagined. I hope you have given that wife of yours a beating for the damage she has done.'

'A callous act, yes; but damage, no. You already knew about Charles.'

'Certainly. But Susan did not, and she was with me when the little fool blurted out about your going to Spain, and the reason for it.'

'What?' Roger roared.

'Yes; and it was for her sake we agreed to keep the matter secret. The poor child was distraught. Driven frantic. Naturally, she still knows nothing of my vision, but she imagines Charles to be in some noisome cell, living on meagre prison fare. I had a terrible hour with her. She is now in bed, sleeping I trust, for I gave her a potent draught.'

'Hell's bells! Mary told me naught of this. To show my disapproval of her conduct, I left the house without telling her I was riding up to London, but I had intended to return tonight. Now, devil take me, for this I'll leave her to stew until I return from Spain.'

'But, Roger, you had my letter. And what I said in it I meant. How could I refrain from taking pity on her? 'Tis true that she was thoughtless in showing no consideration for my feelings, but not wicked. You must go back, forgive her and endeavour to put this whole wretched business out of your mind.'

'I'll be damned if I will. When I had to tell her yestere'en that I was going abroad again, I was mightily unhappy for her. But after what she has done to Susan, I am so no longer. I sail from Greenwich three days hence. Till then I'll stay with Droopy Ned.'

Georgina shook her head. 'I've long since learned 'tis useless to argue with you. And, sorry as I am for her, 'twill comfort me greatly to know that you are doing what you can to save my boy. But if you wish to avoid further wrangles with your wife, you had best not stay with Droopy. 'Tis the first place she will go to look for you. I suggest you should stay here.'

'I thank you, dear one, but I'll not do that. You're right that she will seek me at Droopy's. Failing to find me there, she will next come to you. She already suspects that there is more than friendship between us, and I am greatly averse to strengthening that impression, for both your sake and hers. I have it, though. The perfect hide-out. Your studio.'

'By all means. But I'll not go out there with you. To disport ourselves as we have so oft done there one needs a carefree mind.'

Roger sighed. 'Alas, you are right. Without it our bodies would take no real joy of one another.'

'You will find your chamber robe and toilet things in their usual place, and I'll send out a footman to valet you. Also, if you wish to lie low there, one of my under-chefs to cook your meals.'

'I thank you, but I'll not need the last, as I'll eat out. I would, though, that tomorrow morning, dressed in plain clothes so that it will not be known that he is one of your people, the footman should take a coach out to Richmond with a letter to old Dan, telling him what I require packed for my voyage, then return with my valises.'

After a by no means cheerful supper with Georgina, Roger rode out to Kensington, stabled and fed his horse, then undressed. He had never slept alone in her big bed and, as he was about to get into it, he was suddenly conscious of a feeling that to do so would be a sacrilege against their abiding love, so he spent the night in the room that buxom Jane occupied when her mistress was staying there.

In the morning the footman arrived with a supply of food, and cooked breakfast for him, then set off for Richmond with the list of things that Roger wished Dan to pack. By midday he was at White's and sent a note to Droopy, asking him to look in at the Club.

An hour later Droopy joined him. Georgina's guess had been right. Mary had arrived at ten o'clock, and poured out her woes to Judith, who was still trying to comfort her when Droopy came downstairs. Both he and Judith had quite truthfully assured her that they had no idea where Roger was, and offered to put her up until she had news of him. She had been grateful, but declined, saying that

she would next try Kew House and that, if Roger was
not there, would go home and stay there as—not knowing that he had had his things collected that morning—
she felt sure he would return to get them before leaving
England.

When Droopy had been told of the latest developments,
he shook his head. 'I think you're wrong, Roger, to treat
her so harshly. 'Tis true that by her impetuosity she has
caused young Susan needless suffering; but remember that
she knows nothing of this threat to Charles's life, only that
he is a prisoner. It is natural that she should resent your
leaving her, solely to save the boy from a few extra weeks'
captivity.'

'How could I tell her of the vision, Ned? Had I done
so, I would have had to admit to having been secretly
with Georgina. That would have made them enemies for
life, and might have wrecked our marriage for good. In
any case, it would have meant that every time in the future
that I spent a night away from her, there would have been
a most awful rumpus; and that I will not have.'

'I take your point. Nonetheless, 'tis clear that what she
did was done on account of the great love she bears you.
I pray you think on that.'

'I will,' Roger promised. But as soon as Droopy had left
him to keep an appointment, his thoughts reverted to
his poor young daughter and the misery Mary had so
selfishly brought upon her.

On the two days that followed, he killed much of the
time by taking long walks through parts of the metropolis
he did not usually frequent. It was several years since he
had done so, and he was sadly shocked by the change that
had taken place. Many of the shops were closed and
shuttered, their owners having gone bankrupt. Groups of
men stood about on street corners, obviously out of work;

their clothes were ragged and they looked half-starved. Even many of the more prosperous citizens lacked spring in their step and had gloomy expressions.

It brought home to him the fact that Napoleon's Continental System was at last having its effect, just as the British blockade of the Continent was ruining the French. Both nations were utterly weary of the war. That England would never give in he was fully convinced, but the sight of so much suffering was heartbreaking. He could only pray that Austria would join the Coalition and, in the autumn, finally defeat the terrible Corsican egoist who for so many years had inflicted widespread misery on the peoples of a dozen nations.

On the morning of Sunday, the 25th, Roger had his valises loaded into a hired coach, lavishly tipped the footman who had looked after him, and drove to Kew House to say good-bye to Georgina, as had been arranged when he last saw her. To his amazement and intense annoyance, he was told that both Her Grace and Miss Brook were no longer there. Georgina had left a scribbled note for him, to the effect that an emergency had necessitated Susan and herself leaving for the country. She added that she would be constantly thinking of him and praying for his success and safe return.

Greatly disgruntled, he wondered what possible emergency could have caused her to let him leave England without a farewell meeting. As he got back into the coach and ordered the driver to take him to Amesbury House, it occurred to him that she might have received news that her old Duke had died, and felt it incumbent on her to set off for Newmarket immediately. If so, that would be all to the good as, on his return, she would be free to be with him more frequently. But they could not marry, for he now had Mary.

At the thought of Mary, he sighed. For the past few days he had determinedly put her out of his thoughts, but now he wondered if, by not returning to Richmond even to say good-bye, he had not punished her too severely. After all, Droopy had been right in that what she had done she had been driven to by love. Well, it was not too late to send her an affectionate message, and reassure her that it was not his intention to leave her permanently.

In the courtyard of Amesbury House, Droopy's coach was waiting as, whenever possible, he saw Roger off. Roger had his luggage transferred to it, then went inside the house, to find Droopy waiting for him with a bottle of fine Bordeaux wine that had just been decanted.

When the two friends were half-way through it, Roger said :

'About Mary, Ned. I did not take your advice, and now regret it. Please see her for me and tell her I'm sorry I pained her so; also that she has no need to worry about money. Yesterday, when I filled my money belt with gold at Hoare's Bank, I transferred ample funds to her account for her to draw upon.'

Twenty minutes later, they were on their way to Greenwich. As the coach pulled up at the jetty off which the frigate *Pompey* lay, Roger noticed that another coach was standing there. When he got out, he saw to his delight that it was Georgina's. At the same moment, followed by Susan, she emerged from it. His daughter ran forward and threw her arms round his neck. Having fondly embraced her, he took Georgina's hand, kissed it and said with a smile :

'You've played a pretty trick on me, and I suppose driving out to Greenwich could be termed going to the country. My departure, though, is hardly an emergency. But no matter. I am overjoyed to see you.'

She returned his smile. 'Nothing would have deterred me from bidding you farewell. But this is an emergency. At least I thought it so, knowing you to be about to cut off your nose to spite your face.'

He gave her a puzzled look. 'What mean you? I fail to understand.'

Droopy had led Susan aside; so, as Georgina took Roger's arm and led him towards her coach, he guessed that his friend must be in on this little plot, whatever it might be. On reaching her coach, Georgina pulled open the door, stepped back and gave Roger a swift push which sent him sprawling on the step, with his head inside the coach.

The interior was in semi-darkness but, after a second, he realised that the female figure sitting back in the far corner was Mary. It struck him at once that the women had thought up this trick to stop him, at the last moment, from going to Spain.

Mary leaned forward and spoke in a trembling voice, 'Roger, dear love, I am truly repentant for the unhappiness I caused Georgina and Susan. They have both forgiven me, and . . .'

'And laid this trap in an effort to make me change my mind about leaving England,' he cut in angrily.

She shook her head. 'No, not that. We know that none of us could change your stubborn mind. Dear Georgina brought me here only that I might beg your forgiveness too, before you depart.'

'Ah, that's a very different matter,' he exclaimed joyfully. 'And I am truly glad she did so. But, Mary, it is I who should ask forgiveness. It was only out of love that you tried to stop me, and I should not have held it against you. I am ashamed now to have treated you so brutally these past few days. I should not be long in Spain. With luck I'll be away only a few weeks, and on my return we will resume our happy life together.'

Three-quarters of an hour later, Droopy and the three ladies, all of whom he loved so dearly, waved him away from the jetty, and he went aboard *Pompey*.

Captain Durrant proved a pleasant, youngish man and, *Pompey* being his first command, he showed Roger over the ship with pride. Roger had realised that the advance of Wellington's army during the present campaign would make it unnecessary to go all the way down to Lisbon and had expected to be landed at Corunna; but Captain Durrant told him that Bilbao had recently been liberated, and it was to that port they were bound, thus shortening Roger's land journey across northern Spain by several days.

So far it had not been a particularly good summer, but the weather had improved during the past week, and it was a sunny afternoon when *Pompey* dropped down the Thames.

For the next few days the sky remained almost cloudless, and the sea calm, so for once Roger was not sick when crossing the Bay of Biscay. On the 29th, they entered Bilbao harbour and when he went ashore the heat was grilling. On enquiring of a passing British officer, he learned that General Graham had set up his headquarters in the castle, so he had himself driven there in a *carrozza* and sent up his name.

Graham, Sir Thomas Picton and General Hill were the Duke's principal commanders, and Roger had met them all in Lisbon in the days when the British Army had been entrenched behind the lines of Torres Vedras, so the General received him as an old acquaintance.

Roger made no mention of Charles to him, but simply that he had to go to the Duke's headquarters, and would be grateful for facilities to do so. Graham readily agreed to provide him with a horse, and an escort of Dragoons as a precaution against his being attacked by French deserters, hundreds of whom were hiding in the mountains. He then offered Roger accommodation in the castle for the night, and said he would look forward to seeing him at dinner.

Over the meal Roger learnt from Graham and his Staff officers the events that had led up to Wellington's decisive victory five weeks earlier at Vittoria.

In the first place, two ill-judged decisions by Napoleon had helped to make it possible. Encouraged by the successes of their compatriots in other parts of Spain the guerrillas in Biscay, Navarre and Aragon had greatly increased their numbers and redoubled their efforts. Under their Chief, Mina, they became such a serious threat to the French army's line of communications that the Emperor had allotted forty thousand men, under the command of General Clausel—who had brilliantly saved Marshal Marmont's army from total destruction after he had been seriously wounded at Salamanca—to clear northern Spain of these great bands of fanatical patriots. This had resulted in weakening the main army of King Joseph to a point which, at last, gave Wellington superiority in numbers.

Napoleon's other blunder had been to recall the Duke's most efficient opponent, Marshal Soult, leaving as the King's senior adviser the elderly and ailing Marshal Jourdan—whose sole claim to fame was a General of the Revolution at the Battle of Fleurus where the enemy, when attacking up a hill and being met by a heavy cannonade, had panicked.

But it was the Duke's clever strategy that had been the main cause of this outstanding victory. He had led the

French to believe that Braganza and not Ciudad Rodrigo was his base and that he meant to attempt to outflank their left wing, whereas he had pushed Graham's corps up along the coast on their right. Owing to the country there being very mountainous, Jourdan had thought such a move unlikely and detailed only light forces to hold it. Time after time they had been pushed back, necessitating withdrawals by the outflanked main army. The British had advanced five hundred miles in six weeks, until Jourdan had felt compelled to make a stand on the Zadorra river.

Marshal Suchet, who commanded the other main army in Spain, could not come to Jourdan's assistance as he had all he could do to hold down Catalonia and prevent the advance of a British force under General Sir John Murray that had landed, in Valencia, from Sicily; neither could General Clausel, as the King had recalled him from the north too late.

As the battle was joined, Graham had again driven back the French right and succeeded in cutting off their retreat by the great highway leading to San Sebastian and Bayonne. Meanwhile, Picton and Hill had forced the French centre and left to fall back on the Zadorra and the town of Vittoria. Once the French were broken they had no way of escape except through the town, then along a narrow, mountainous road that led to Pamplona. Under the bombardment of the British guns, the town had become a shambles and the retreat a rout of men running for their lives, pursued by Hussars and Dragoons.

The French were forced to abandon everything. The whole equipment of their army was captured, every single gun, hundreds of carriages laden with the loot of cities they had sacked, and one million pounds in their Paymasters' chests. King Joseph fled on horseback, and when he reached Pamplona had only a single gold piece in his pocket.

When the tale had been told, General Graham said to Roger, 'But now tell us of the war in the north; for you must have much later news of that theatre than we have here.'

'I've no idea, Sir, how up to date you are,' Roger replied. 'But so far neither side has reaped much advantage from this year's campaign. Following Napoleon's disaster in Russia, Prince Eugène was forced to fall back to the Elbe, but the French still had strong garrisons in all the big fortress towns of northern Germany. After the great Kutuzov died in March, General Wittgenstein was given command of the Russian army, but he was later succeeded by Barclay de Tolly—ever a cautious man—so the best advantage was not taken of the situation.

'By early May the Emperor arrived in Saxony with great reinforcements to take the field in person. At Lützen the allies should have gained a victory, but were foiled by Marshal Ney's determined stand at Gross Gorschen. In the battle General Scharnhorst was killed; a great loss to the Prussians, but they still have Gneisenau and Blücher. I gather that the old man is a real tiger. He has never got over his men being driven from the field at Jena, and has sworn to have his revenge on Napoleon, or die whilst seeking it.

'Later in the month, to cover Silesia, the Emperor crossed the Spree and there was another great battle at Bautzen, which again ended in a stalemate. After it the French succeeded in raising the siege of Breslau, while the Emperor retired on Dresden.

'It was shortly afterwards that he made, to my mind, a great mistake. The allies had failed in their attempts to induce the Saxons and the Danes to come over to their side, and both the Prussians and the Russians were tired and downhearted. Had Napoleon realised that, one more battle might have finished them. But he evidently believed the forces arrayed against him to be much more formidable than they actually were, so he sent Caulaincourt to the Czar Alexander to propose an armistice. The Austrians acted as mediators and it was agreed that hostilities should cease from June 4th to July 20th, and just before I left England I learned that the armistice had been extended for a further month.

'There can be no doubt that Napoleon's object was to gain time for further reinforcements from Spain and Italy and fresh levies from France to join him and give him superiority in numbers. But things may well go the other way. It gives the allies, too, time to regroup and increase their forces. Prince Bernadotte has landed in Stralsand with a Swedish army that has not yet been in action, and he is an extremely able General. Last, but not least, the Austrians have not forgotten that Napoleon has twice occupied Vienna, and has robbed them of many provinces. They are still sitting on the fence; but as their price for remaining neutral they are demanding the return of Illyria, the restoration to Prussia of her stolen territories and many other concessions. To submit to such humiliation I judge to be contrary to the Corsican's nature. And, if the Austrians do come in against him, 'tis my belief that his goose will be cooked.'

On the following morning Roger set out for Wellington's headquarters, and he reached them two afternoons later. The French armies of both King Joseph and General Clausel had been driven across the Pyrenees, but as General Graham had told Roger, it was not the Duke's intention to follow them until he had captured two important fortresses: Pamplona and San Sebastian, both still strongly garrisoned by the French.

Roger had first met Wellington when he was a Colonel

in India, but more recently he had brought him valuable information about the enemy's intentions in Portugal and Spain; so when, after a brief wait, an adjutant led Roger from the blazing sunshine into the cool shade of the Duke's marquee, he received a pleasant welcome.

When he had congratulated the great commander on having just received his Field Marshal's baton in recognition of his brilliant victory at Vittoria, the Duke said:

'Sit down, Mr. Brook, and tell me what brings you here.' Then, being one of the very limited number of people who knew of Roger's second identity as one of Napoleon's A.D.C.s, he added with a smile, 'I hope it is to tell me that you again mean to present yourself at the enemy's headquarters and bring me back all you can learn about his latest plans.'

Roger returned his smile. 'Indeed, Your Grace, I do intend to go there, if you can provide me with the uniform of a dead French officer—preferably a Colonel. And you may be sure that I will do my utmost to return with information useful to you. But it was not that which brought me here. A young officer very dear to me was taken prisoner by the French only a short time ago. I know King Joseph well, and have little doubt that at my request he will release the prisoner on condition that, on rejoining your army, he should be sent to England, so that he is of no further value to you.'

The condition was not an unreasonable one, and Roger had thought of including it in his request because, if Charles could be got away from Spain, there would be no likelihood of his being captured a second time and Georgina's vision coming true.

'There will be no difficulty in getting a suitable uniform for you,' the Duke replied. 'There are hundreds of wounded in the hospitals. But who, may I ask, is this young man whom you are so anxious to relieve of the tedium of captivity?'

'Tis the son of my greatest friend, a lady whom you must have met when in London. She is now the Duchess of Kew, but was formerly the Countess of St. Ermins. It is her boy, the young Earl.'

The Duke ran a finger down his high-bridged nose, then shook his handsome head. 'I am much distressed by what I have to tell you, Mr. Brook. Soon after the Earl arrived at my headquarters, on learning that he spoke fluent German, I attached him to the Duke of Brunswick's staff. When it became known here that Prussia had declared war on France, Brunswick naturally wished to take his German Legion back to fight on their own soil. His request was granted, and they were shipped to Germany. St. Ermins had formed a strong attachment to the Duke, and I allowed him to go with them. I fear you have had your journey to Spain for nothing. He must be a prisoner somewhere in Saxony or Silesia.'

14

The Greatest Statesman of His Age

Two factors accounted for the Duke of Wellington's out-standing success as a General: his unceasing care that his men should be well-fed, well-shod and suitably clothed, and the unusual combination in a military commander of the resolution to launch sudden offensives with the utmost vigour but coupled, normally, with almost excessive caution.

It was the latter which had determined him—although his army could now have invaded France almost unopposed—not to cross the frontier while leaving the two great fortresses of Pamplona and San Sebastian still in the hands of the enemy and therefore capable of interfering with the smooth running of his lines of communication.

On learning this, Roger realised at once that it might be several weeks before the British army crossed the Pyrenees, so he must do so on his own; and since it was evident that Charles had been captured somewhere in Germany, he must make his way there as quickly as possible.

A quarter-master secured for him the uniform of a French Colonel of Chasseurs, who had recently died from wounds, and an additional horse to carry his baggage, including a sufficient supply of food and wine to last him several days. A staff officer showed him on a large-scale map the disposition of the French forces in the mountains, as far as they were known, and provided him with a *laisser-passer* to show any British or Spanish advanced patrols that he might encounter. Then, on the morning of August 2nd, he took leave of the Duke and set out for Paris, the first five-hundred-mile stage of his long journey.

Owing to Napoleon's heavy withdrawals of troops from Spain for his campaign in Germany, and the almost total destruction of King Joseph's army six weeks earlier at Vittoria, it was known that the French forces along the Pyrenees were comparatively few in number and still in a state of grave disorder. So Roger decided that, rather than make a long detour round their left flank, he would risk approaching the mountains direct in the neighbourhood of Tolosa, which lay half-way between Pamplona and San Sebastian.

His first day's ride proved extremely fatiguing, as the heat was torrid, and he gained only temporary relief by resting for two hours in the shade of a wood during the early afternoon; but by evening he was well up into the foothills of the mountains. As the sun was setting he came upon an isolated farmhouse and, on learning that he was an Englishman, the owner willingly gave him a meal and a bed for the night.

By midday the next day, in a much more pleasant climate, he entered a pass high up in the mountains. He was halted there by the most advanced of the numerous Allied patrols that had stopped him, and ordered to show his papers. The troops were Spaniards recently embodied from what had previously been a guerrilla band, and their leader, now an officer, gave him useful information about the situation of the French units on the far side of the pass.

Shortly before reaching the highest point in the pass he

came upon a side track leading into an area of large, tumbled rocks. Having made his way along the path for a few hundred yards, he tethered the horses, ate a picnic meal; then, hidden by big boulders, unpacked his valise and changed into the French Colonel's uniform. As he had no further use for his civilian clothes, he buried them under a pile of shale, and he abandoned his spare horse, since having it would conflict with the story he meant to tell on reaching the French lines. He remounted his own horse, returned to the rough road through the pass and proceeded on his way.

It was not until nearly an hour later, on rounding a corner of the downward slope, that he encountered a French vedette. It consisted only of a sergeant and four men. They were naturally greatly surprised to see a senior French officer alone up there in the mountains; but he told them that he had succeeded by night in getting through the British who were besieging San Sebastian, and was on his way to King Joseph's headquarters, with an urgent plea that the King should attempt to relieve the city, otherwise it must soon surrender. The sergeant willingly gave him directions on how to reach the nearest main road, and by nightfall he entered Bayonne.

At headquarters there Roger learned that the Emperor, infuriated by his brother's defeat at Vittoria, had recalled both the King and Marshal Jourdan in disgrace, and, in July sent Soult post-haste back from Germany to resume command of the army now defending the Pyrenees. This could, Roger felt, be bad news for Wellington when he received it, for after Davout and Masséna, Soult was considered to be the most able of the Marshals and, as a strategist, could be counted on to make the Allied invasion of France much more difficult than would one of the braver but less brainy Marshals, such as Ney or Augereau.

H

The Duc de Dalmatia was not at his H.Q., as he had gone up country with his staff to make a personal reconnaissance before launching a new offensive; but the able General Clausel, whom Roger had met on numerous occasions, was there. Roger told him the story of having been caught in San Sebastian, and his success in having got by night through the British lines, in the hope of securing aid for the beleaguered city. The lie provided yet another episode to support the legend in the French Army which had led to his becoming known as 'le brave Breuc,' and Clausel praised his courage, but said there was little hope of relieving San Sebastian unless the Marshal Duke's projected offensive proved successful.

Clausel had no news of the situation in northern Europe. As far as he knew, the armistice agreed at Pläswitz, which had been reinforced by the Treaty of Reichenbach later in June, still continued and, in view of Roger's reputation, he asked him to remain in a post on his staff. But Roger replied that only circumstances over which he had had no control had compelled him to remain in Spain, and now that he had got out of that miserable country it was his duty, as one of the Emperor's A.D.C.s, to return to him.

That night, at dinner in the headquarters Mess, he met several old acquaintances, and passed an enjoyable evening. Then he set off again early the next morning, on the road to Paris. He had travelled it several times before, so knew well the cities through which he passed : Bordeaux, Angoulême, Poitiers, Tours and Orléans. There being no urgent necessity for speed, he did not tire himself unduly, and was content to cover an average of something over fifty miles a day. This gave him ample opportunity to observe conditions in the cities and the countryside along the way, and he found them deplorable.

In his youth, before the Revolution, and even after it during the Directory, the Consulate and the early years of the Empire, the towns had been a bustle of healthy people, going eagerly about their business; fat, jolly women behind market stalls heaped high with produce, the narrow streets jammed with carriages, wagons and horsemen; while in the fields and vineyards sturdy men worked and chaffed beside buxom peasant girls; there were herds of fat cattle and goats, big piggeries and many haystacks.

Now the population of the urban areas was old, slow-moving and looked half-starved. The only young males among them were one-legged, hobbling along on crutches, blind and tapping their way along with a stick, or with bodies hideously distorted by war wounds. In the streets there were no carriages, few wagons and no horsemen, while two-thirds of the market stalls were empty. Between the towns things were little better. Only cripples and grey-beards now worked in the fields beside the women. The herds were gone, all but a few scraggy cattle and horses had been commandeered, and not more than once in a mile could a haystack be seen.

To this terrible state, by his insatiable lust for power had the Corsican brigand reduced the once fair land of France.

On Thursday, August 14th, Roger reached Paris, and rode straight to Talleyrand's great mansion in the Rue St. Florentin. He arrived there just before six o'clock in the evening. As that was a favourite hour for gallants to dally with ladies they wished to seduce in their boudoirs, and knowing the brilliant statesman's insatiable zest for amorous encounters, Roger feared he might be engaged. But that did not prove to be the case. His Exalted Highness Charles Maurice de Périgord, Prince de Benevent, Vice Grand Elector of the Empire, was at home and, on Roger's

name being brought to him, at once ordered the footman
to show him in.

Talleyrand was at this time fifty-nine years of age. As
the eldest son of an ancient, princely family, he would
normally have gone into the Army, but an accident while
still a child had lamed him for life, and led to his being
made to go into the Church. Few men could have been
less fitted for the priesthood, as he was venal and so licentious that he was reputed to have slept with scores of the
loveliest ladies at the Court of Versailles. That had not
prevented his becoming Bishop of Autun, and a leading
figure among those who brought about the liberal revolution of 1789. He was among the first to defy the Pope and
adhere to the new French National Church, but with the
coming of the Terror he was forced to go into exile, first
in England then in the United States. From that time he
threw off even the pretence of being a Churchman, and
later married.

Never having been officially listed as an émigré, he was
able to return to France soon after the fall of Robespierre
and, under the Directory, began his brilliant career as the
manipulator of France's foreign policy. Although Paris
was then still dominated by the new ideas brought in by
the Revolution, he contemptuously refused to conform,
continued to dress in silks and satins, wore his hair
powdered and lived again as a great noble.

By '99 France was bankrupt and the whole country in
a hopeless state of disorder. Realising that solvency and
law and order could be restored only by government under
a strong dictator led to his conspiring with the redoubtable
Fouché to bring about the *coup d'état* of Brumaire, which
led to young General Bonaparte being made First Consul
on his return from Egypt. For the greater part of the ten
years that followed Talleyrand, as Foreign Minister, and

Fouché, as Chief of Police, had been, after Napoleon, the most powerful men in France.

To begin with, Napoleon, knowing nothing of foreign policy, had allowed himself to be guided by Talleyrand; but as the years passed, the Emperor had become ever more convinced of his own omnipotence, and had acted contrary to his Minister's advice. He had, as Talleyrand had believed he would, brought order out of chaos; but, again and again he refused all opportunities to make peace, and Talleyrand saw that, having restored France, he was now destroying her by his ceaseless wars waged for his own aggrandisement. In consequence, in 1807 he had resigned his portfolio and refused to serve the Emperor further.

Nevertheless, Napoleon was so bewitched by Talleyrand's genius for statescraft that, having made him a Prince and one of the six Great Dignitaries of the Empire, he continued to consult him on all important questions.

Talleyrand had known Roger ever since he had first come to Paris as the youthful secretary to the Marquis de Rochambeau. In those pre-revolutionary days the Abbé, as he then was—although he had already taken to wearing the lay clothes of a Court exquisite—lived in a small house in the suburb of Passey. After an attack by footpads, Roger had been carried there unconscious, and his babblings had revealed the fact that he was an Englishman. A friendship had sprung up between them and, several years later, it was Roger who had secured the papers that had enabled Talleyrand to escape the guillotine and get safely out of France.

That was one reason why, still later, even when Roger had re-appeared in Paris as an A.D.C. to Napoleon, Talleyrand had kept it secret that Roger was the son of a British Admiral. But there was also another reason. From the very beginning, the great statesman had held the conviction that there could be no lasting peace in Europe unless France and Britain ceased their long enmity and became allies—a belief that Roger fully shared. To that end Talleyrand had ever worked secretly and consistently, and he had astutely decided that if Roger was a secret agent the damage he could do France was outweighed by his usefulness as an abettor of his own intrigues; as had proved the case at the time of the *coup d'état*. More recently, when he had secured actual proof that Roger was a spy, he had still refrained from denouncing him because, when at last the Emperor's downfall could be brought about, Roger would prove a trustworthy go-between to vouch for it to the British Government that he, Talleyrand, had contributed to that fall and was the most suitable man to guide France into an *entente cordiale* with Britain.

In consequence, on this August evening the two met as old friends, although on Talleyrand's part with pleased surprise. Limping forward from behind his huge, mahogany desk, he laid a beautifully-manicured, beruffled hand on Roger's arm and exclaimed :

'*Mon cher ami!* How delighted I am to see you. I had believed you long since dead in those accursed Russian snows.'

Roger returned his smile. 'Nay, Prince. 'Twas a devilish near thing, and by ill chance I became separated from the Emperor, so had to hide while the tide of war swept over me. But after several nightmare weeks, half-frozen and starving, I succeeded in reaching Reval. Thence I took ship to Stockholm, where I was kindly received by Bernadotte.'

'How fares that Gascon rogue?'

'I found him in excellent trim. As Crown Prince he has

become very popular with his Swedes and, as you must know, has had the good sense to enter into an alliance with both Russia and Britain.'

'Indeed I do, for they have paid his price—a free hand to oust the Danes from Norway. He offered to remain neutral if the Emperor could give him that, but Napoleon dared not, otherwise he would have lost the Danes as allies.'

'I had no idea that Bernadotte had been playing with both sides.'

'Ah, he's a sly one. But, mark my words. The new Coalition will derive little benefit from the army he has landed in Stralsund. He'll let the others do the fighting, and just stand by to pull his share of chestnuts out of the fire when all is over.'

'Think you this autumn's campaign will at last see an end to the war?'

Talleyrand had told the footman who had shown Roger in to bring champagne. The man now returned with it. While it was being poured and until the man had left the room, the statesman remained silent. Then, raising his glass, he said, 'Here's defeat and damnation to the scourge of France. But when it will come no man can say. Everything is still in the melting pot.'

Roger willingly drank the toast, then frowned. 'I am at a complete loss to understand why, after he had lost his army in Russia, the Prussians did not seize the chance to turn on him at once and, with the Russians, finish him off.'

'In last winter's campaign, the Russians suffered nearly as severely as their enemies. After they had driven what remained of the *Grande Armée* over the frontier into Poland, they were too exhausted and wasted by disease to launch an offensive. Remember, too, that although our field army had been almost annihilated, we still had many thousands of troops in Poland, Prussia, Saxony and other German States, and garrisons in every fortress city of importance. When Murat abandoned the command the Emperor had left with him, and made off to his Kingdom of Naples, Prince Eugène, who took over, could have held the line of the Oder. That he later fell back to the Elbe was a strategic blunder, but he can hardly be blamed, since he could not know the weakness of the enemy confronting him.

'As for Prussia, you know as well as I do what a gutless fellow Frederick William is. Even when his own General, von Yorck, took his army corps over to the enemy, the King could not be persuaded by Scharnhorst, Gneisenau and Blücher to declare openly against France. Admittedly he was in Berlin, which was held by us; but even after he had sneaked away by night to Breslau, it was well into Spring before he could be persuaded to enter into an alliance with the Russians.

'No-one can at least accuse our little man of dragging his feet. By mid-December he was back here working twenty hours out of every twenty-four, recalling troops from Spain and Italy and pouring into new regiments every male between sixteen and sixty who could be laid hands on. Ah, even the deaf, the one-eyed and men who were still partially disabled from old wounds. By April the reinforcements he had despatched to the army of the north made it superior in numbers to those of Russia and Prussia combined, and several of his best Marshals; Ney, Marmont, Macdonald and Oudinot all commanding corps. Early in May he arrived to take command in person. There followed the battles of Lützen and Bautzen.'

Roger nodded. 'Yes, I have heard accounts of them,

and I gather that at both he gave the Allies a tremendous pasting.'

'He did indeed. They were most bloody encounters, with heavy losses on both sides, and from both he emerged victorious. But in neither case did he follow up his success. Had he done so after either, as he would have done in the old days, he might well have inflicted a final defeat on the Allies and forced them to sue for peace. But he is no longer the man he was.'

'For that at least we can thank God. What thinks Your Highness of the armistice which he agreed early in June? Will he benefit from it when the conflict is renewed, or the reverse?'

Talleyrand smiled. 'With luck, it will prove his undoing, and I was largely responsible for it. As you know, I have long been in secret correspondence with Metternich and, in addition, had the ear of Prince Schwarzenberg while he was Austria's Ambassador here during the winter. I persuaded them to build up their army to the maximum possible extent, then use the threat of it to coerce our mass-murderer into agreeing terms which would lead to a permanent pacification of Europe.'

'I heard something of this just before I left England in July, and more talk of it at the Duke of Wellington's head-quarters, from whence I have just come. According to these rumours, the Austrian terms are so harsh that I judged it unlikely that the Emperor would accept them.'

'I think them not unreasonable. They are that the Grand Duchy of Warsaw and the Confederation of the Rhine should be abolished, that the Illyrian provinces should be restored to Austria, that the Hanse towns and other territories of northern Germany which were annexed in 1810 should be restored, and that Prussia should be re-established in as favourable a situation as she was in

1805. This would leave France considerably greater in area than she was under the Bourbons, and with the natural frontiers that she has always desired. But you were right, *cher ami*. Our egomaniac ruler cannot be persuaded to give up his dreams of world conquest, so Austria will join the Coalition against him.'

'God be praised for that!' Roger exclaimed. 'I was given to understand that the armistice ended on July 20th, and although it is now August 14th, there is still no news of its cessation, so I feared the Austrians had after all become afraid to take the plunge.'

'Nay.' Talleyrand took a pinch of snuff, then carefully brushed off the grains that had fallen on his lace cravat and the lapels of his black satin coat. 'Metternich would have preferred a settlement, because with France defeated and greatly weakened, that would leave Russia far stronger than he wishes to see her. For that reason he has given the Emperor a further three weeks, hoping to the last that he would see sense. Yet Austria dare not stand by and risk Prussia and Russia being forced to make a separate peace, lest next year, for the third time, the conqueror decides to march on Vienna. Metternich realises now that there is nothing for it but to fight, and even as we sit here the die is cast. I had secret intelligence of his decision three days ago. But you said a moment since that you are just come from Spain. Tell me now how go things there, and what brings you again to Paris.'

After describing the situation in the Pyrenees, Roger went on to relate how he had returned to the Continent in order to find the young Earl of St. Ermins and secure his release.

When he had done, Talleyrand nodded. 'The Ministry of War should have lists of all the officers in prisoner-of-war camps, but it may take some while to locate your young friend. In the meantime, I shall be most happy if you will be my guest here. There are many matters upon which we can discourse with mutual interest, and you have not yet told me what you have been up to since you left Stockholm. But you must forgive me if I leave you now, as I have an appointment with the Duc de Bassano, who succeeded me as Minister of Foreign Affairs, and still holds that post.'

Standing up, Roger replied, 'I am most grateful to Your Highness for your generous offer of hospitality; but from my youth, whenever in Paris, I have always stayed at *La Belle Étoile*, hard by the Louvre. The owner is a treasured friend of mine, who has often given me valuable information on the trends of popular opinion in Paris. Moreover he stores there for me a trunk containing a variety of clothes, weapons and other things which I am anxious to go through. I trust you will excuse me if I take up my old quarters there; but I shall be most happy to wait upon Your Highness daily and learn at what hours it would be convenient for you to receive me.'

'As you will.' The Prince nodded. 'In any case, join me for dinner tomorrow. I have a number of people coming, most of whom will be known to you.'

The reason that, on reaching Paris, Roger had gone straight to Talleyrand's mansion, was because he knew that the Prince was the one person in the city from whom he could learn if Austria had backed down or if there was still a possibility of her joining the Allies against Napoleon; and that decision was of immense importance to all Europe, not least to Britain whose people, after twenty years of conflict, were now so utterly war-weary. He would otherwise have gone first to *La Belle Étoile*.

Now, greatly cheered by the possibility that within a few months the slaughter might at last cease, having taken leave of the statesman he made his way to the ancient hostelry where many times he had known fear and joy. But on his arrival his elation was soon changed to grievous sorrow.

The grey-haired ostler in the stable yard greeted him with the news that the old landlord, Maître Blanchard, had died of a burst stomach ulcer the previous winter, and his widow had soon afterwards sold the property and returned to her native Normandy to live with her sister.

On the first evening after arriving in Paris Roger had always supped with the good couple in their private parlour off his favourite mushroom omelette, and duck cooked in the Normandy fashion, which was Madame Blanchard's speciality. He had been looking forward to that excellent meal, washed down with a couple of bottles of the Mâitre's best Burgundy, while the three of them gossiped cheerfully over old times and new. Now, never again would he enjoy that good cheer, and the companionship of the honest, big-hearted couple.

The new landlord was a much younger man and, when he learned that Roger was *Colonel Comte de Breuc,* well known as one of the Emperor's paladins, became unattractively servile. Bowing and scraping, he led Roger up to his old room, which happened to be free, and had his big, round-lidded trunk brought down from the attic. In it, among other clothes, he had a spare uniform, medals and an A.D.C.'s sash, so he was able to change into his proper military attire.

While doing so, he was prey to many disturbing memories. It was there he had lived, posing as a terrorist during the darkest days of the Revolution, while the good Blanchards had kept the secret that a few years earlier, in his true rôle as an exquisite, he had frequented the Court of Versailles. There, too, he had for a while concealed the beautiful Athénais de Rochambeau, later enjoyed the clandestine visits of Napoleon's lovely, lecherous sister, the Princess Pauline, and still later also made love to his divine Georgina when she had been secretly in Paris.

Next morning, he went to the Ministry of War and sent his name up to the Minister, General d'Hanebourg Clarke, Duc de Feltre, who was an old acquaintance. After a wait of ten minutes or so, Clarke received him and, knowing that he had been with the Emperor in the retreat from Moscow, heartily congratulated him on his re-appearance alive and well.

Roger told him of his escape to Sweden and that from Stockholm he had gone to England. The General expressed surprise and wonder that, as a French officer, he had not been kept there as a prisoner-of-war.

Raising his eyebrows, Roger replied, 'I thought you were aware, as most of my friends are, that although I was born in Strasbourg, my mother was Scottish and that when she died I was sent to England to live with her sister. I was educated there, and returned to my own country at the time of the Revolution, as a young journalist inspired by the new doctrine of Liberty, Equality and Fraternity. I have numerous relatives in England who believe that I've spent the greater part of my life travelling in distant lands while, in fact, I have been serving as an A.D.C. to the Emperor.'

It was the story he had told for many years, and it was believed by everyone in the French Army who knew him well. After a moment, he added, 'The Emperor, of course, has long been aware of this and, on more than one occasion, I have gone back to England in order to report to him upon conditions there. That is why, on escaping from Russia, I took the opportunity to do so again, which brings me to the matter upon which I have come to see you.'

When he had told the General of his anxiety to trace Charles St. Ermins, whom he stated was his nephew, Clarke replied, 'Certainly I will do what I can to help you and, as you are so close to our master, I've no doubt he will grant your request to have this young milord exchanged as soon as possible. But we have many thousands of prisoners in camps here in France, in Saxony and also in Holland and the Rhineland, so it may take several days before I can let you know in which he is.'

Having thanked him, Roger enquired about the prospects of the present campaign.

The General shrugged. 'As you must be aware, much depends on whether Austria comes in against us. But, even should she do so, I think our chances of defeating this new Coalition far from bad. According to my latest intelligence, the Russian field army is some one hundred and eighty thousand strong, the Prussians about one hundred and sixty thousand, the Swedes and Mecklenburgers about thirty-nine thousand. That totals approximately three hundred and eighty thousand men, and between them they have some one thousand one hundred guns. Should Austria join our enemies that would bring the Allied strength up to roughly six hundred thousand men and one thousand four hundred guns. Against that, we and our allies have over eight hundred and sixty thousand men under arms. They are not, of course, all with the Emperor but, including reinforcements now on the way to him, he should have well over six hundred thousand in the German lands.'

When Roger left the Ministry, he was considerably perturbed by the figures that had been given him. A large percentage of Napoleon's troops must, he knew, be raw recruits, and also he was short of cavalry. But, although Austria was coming in, he would still have superiority in numbers; and, while it was certain that the councils of the Allies would be divided, the Emperor alone would control the dispositions of his great army. Moreover, he was unquestionably a greater strategist than any of the Generals opposed to him.

Among those of the twenty-four people known to Roger who sat down to dinner at Talleyrand's that afternoon were Goudin, Duc de Gaëte, once a junior official at the Treasury, whom Napoleon, on becoming First Consul, had made Minister of Finance and who had by his brilliant measures rescued France from bankruptcy, and Cardinal Fesch. The latter was the half-brother of Napoleon's mother. As an Abbé, at the time of the Revolution, he had fled with the Bonapartes from Corsica to the South of France, but there renounced the Church to become a supplier of army stores, and in that capacity accompanied Napoleon on his first victorious campaign in Italy, returning to Paris with an ill-gotten fortune. Later, feeling that it could prove useful to have a prelate in the family, Napoleon had made him Bishop of Lyons then, on the rapprochement with the Papacy, a Cardinal and Grand Almoner. 'Uncle' Fesch, as he was known, was a sly fellow and insatiably avaricious. Like all the other Bonapartes, he showed little gratitude for his elevation and, as Ambassador to Rome, had proved an expensive failure; but he had great influence with his half sister *Madame Mère*, and was not a man of whom to make an enemy.

Later that evening Roger told Talleyrand that *La Belle Étoile* had changed hands, and he did not at all care for the new landlord, so the Prince renewed his invitation which Roger now gladly accepted, and the following morning he moved into the mansion.

That day he attended the levée of the plump, stupid young Austrian Arch-Duchess Marie Louise, who was now Empress of the French, and made his bow to her son, the King of Rome, a charming little boy who was old enough to stand beside her, dressed in a miniature uniform.

From the Tuileries, Roger went on to pay his respects to *Madame Mère*, the only other Bonaparte then in Paris. The gaunt old lady had a forbidding presence and could be very tart at times; but she liked Roger because he had never shown any fear of her, and talked to him in her atrocious French for over half an hour about Napoleon and her other children, whose well-being was the one concern of her life.

Having made his duty calls, Roger rode out on the Sunday to Malmaison, to see the ex-Empress Josephine. They had been friends for many years. She received him with delight, took him round the hothouses, in which she grew a remarkable collection of tropical plants, and insisted that he stayed on to dine with a number of other friends she had coming out to visit her.

In her youth and the early years of her marriage to Napoleon, while he was absent on his campaigns she had given free play to her amorous inclinations; but, belatedly, she had fallen in love with her husband and became furiously jealous about his affairs with other women. At the time of the divorce, losing him had been a more severe blow to her than losing her position as Empress. But Roger was glad to find that she had become resigned to living in retirement at Malmaison which, with her boundless extravagance—paid for willingly by the Emperor—she had made one of the most beautiful homes in France and where, owing to her intelligence and charm, she never lacked for company.

During the days that followed Roger found plenty to occupy him. When it became generally known that Aus-

tria had declared war on the 14th, distinguished visitors
to Talleyrand's mansion, who wished to discuss the new
situation, became more numerous than ever. Old acquaintances of Roger's invited him to their houses, and
on two further occasions he rode out to Malmaison and
spent several hours with Josephine. Having heard nothing
from Clarke by the Friday, he called again at the Ministry of War, but the General told him that there were still
a whole series of files to be gone through. Impatiently he
waited until the following Monday. That evening a note
was brought to him, which read :

'My dear de Breuc,
'I much regret to have to tell you that we have drawn a
blank. My people tell me that after the Brunswickers were
shipped by the English from Spain they were landed in
north-west Germany and employed there against the
forces of the Marshal Prince d'Eckmühl in Hanover; so
your relative is probably in a prisoner-of-war camp in the
Prince's command; and of the occupants of these we have
no records.
'With my most distinguished sentiments, etc.'

Giving a sigh, Roger laid the letter down. Obviously
the mission on which he had set out was not yet anywhere
near accomplishment.

15

The War Reopens

As Roger had had good reason to expect that Charles
had been sent south to a camp somewhere in France or,
at the worst, in the Rhine Provinces, General Clarke's
letter was a grievous disappointment. Not only did it mean
another journey of at least six hundred and fifty miles, but
the Prince d'Eckmühl was Marshal Davout, a dour man
who had no liking for Roger, so it would be useless to go
direct to him. The only course was to go first to the
Emperor and obtain from him an order to the Marshal to
release Charles.

All that was known in Paris of the situation in the north
was that the French were holding the line of the Elbe and
that the Emperor's headquarters were somewhere in the
neighbourhood of Dresden. So, on the morning of August
24th, Roger took leave of his charming host and set off
in that direction.

Again averaging fifty miles a day, he travelled by way
of Chalons, Nancy, Strasbourg, Stuttgart, Nürnberg,
Plauen and Chemnitz.

At officers' Messes in garrison towns through which he
passed he picked up news of the conflict that had re-
opened when Austria entered the war. On the 18th Marshal Macdonald's army in Silesia had been defeated by
Blücher and forced back over the river Katzbach; but on

the 21st the Emperor had arrived on the scene and restored the situation. Two days later he hurried back to
Dresden. Macdonald was said to have believed that the
allies were retiring, but they were not, so the two armies,
this time unexpectedly, again came into collision.
Blücher's Prussians were severely handled, but the Russian
cavalry broke through the French flank and drove the
centre of Macdonald's army in great confusion down into
the flooded river Neisse. After further severe fighting, by
September 1st the allies had driven the French out of
Silesia, so could claim their first substantial victory.

In the meantime, on August 22nd, Prince Karl von
Schwarzenberg, who had been nominated Generalissimo
of the Allied forces, had invaded Saxony with his Austrians, and advanced on Dresden. As the Emperor had
by then gone to the assistance of Macdonald in Silesia, the
city was covered only by St. Cyr's corps. Schwarzenberg,
presumably unaware of this, and at all times a hesitant
General with an obsessive fear of Napoleon, decided to
await further reinforcements; so he did not open the
attack until the morning of the 26th, and then only half-
heartedly.

But for this dilatoriness he could almost certainly have
taken the Saxon capital. As things turned out, St. Cyr's
three divisions proved staunch enough to hold off the first
assaults and, that very morning, Napoleon returned.
Halting on the bridge over the Elbe, he swiftly deployed
the army he had brought back with him from Silesia, and
despatched General Vandamme with a strong force to
Pirna, from where he could fall on the Allies' rear.

Early on the 27th Napoleon launched a full-scale attack
and, although the Allied army exceeded the French by
some forty thousand men, by afternoon their left wing
had been shattered, which led to a general retreat. The

weather was appalling, the roads bad and that night Russians, Prussians and Austrians were fleeing in hopeless disorder. They had lost ten thousand killed and wounded, and fifteen thousand had been taken prisoner. On the following day they were relentlessly pursued, and lost a further five thousand men.

Such was Napoleon's great victory at Dresden, but he was robbed of its fruits a few days later. While the Allies strove to stem the retreat and bring up reinforcements, the King of Prussia appealed to the Russian General Ostermann to use the reserve division he commanded in an endeavour to check the French advance. On the 30th the fifteen thousand Russians fought heroically against great odds, lost half their number, but succeeded in holding Vandamme before Kulm. By the following day von Kleist's Prussians had outflanked the French, and both the Russians and Austrians, now fifty thousand strong, attacked them fiercely. At Kulm two divisions laid down their arms, and ten thousand prisoners were taken, including Vandamme himself. For him this was a great misfortune, as he was one of Napoleon's ablest Generals and, but for this defeat, might soon have been made a Marshal.

Such was the situation, as far as it was known to Roger, when he rode into the great camp just outside Dresden on the afternoon of September 6th.

Whenever Roger rejoined Napoleon, it had always been his custom first to see Duroc, the Grand Marshal of Palaces and Camps, who had long been a close personal friend of his, to learn from him how matters were going and the mood of the Emperor. Stopping a Lieutenant, he enquired of him the whereabouts of Duroc's quarters.

The young officer looked up at him in surprise and replied, 'Did you not know, Sir, the Duc de Friuli is dead? He was killed by a cannon ball that ploughed right through the Emperor's staff on the day after the battle of Bautzen.'

This was a great blow to Roger, as he knew it must also have been to the Emperor, since for nearly twenty years Duroc had been Napoleon's constant companion, and a man for whom he had a very deep affection.

For a few minutes Roger remained seated on his halted horse, his head bowed in sadness; then another horseman cantered by, glanced at him in passing, abruptly pulled up and exclaimed :

'*Mon Dieu*! If it's not *le brave Breuc*! We thought you long since dead on the plains of Russia.'

Swinging round, Roger recognised Caulaincourt, Duc de Vicenza, a soldier-diplomat whom he had known for many years, and said, 'I got cut off, but had the good luck to escape. At the moment though, I am quite overwhelmed, for I have only just learnt that poor Duroc is dead.'

The *Duc* nodded. 'Alas, yes. Without him at headquarters things will never be the same. Neither will the Imperial Guard without Bessières as its commander. He was killed at Lützen.'

'I must then condole with the Emperor on the loss of both when I report to him.'

'You would do better to wait for a more propitious moment, both to report and to condole. He got back to Dresden from one of his reconnaissances in force only this morning, so is up to his eyes in business and in a far from good humour. Wait until this evening, and in the meantime accompany me to my quarters, where I can provide you with refreshment and you can rest for an hour or two.'

Roger happily agreed, as Caulaincourt was one of the Emperor's closest confidants. He came of a noble Picardy family and, when Bernadotte was Minister of War, had been given by him the command of a crack cavalry regiment. Under the Consulate Talleyrand had, on discovering that Caulaincourt had an excellent brain, sent him as Ambassador to Russia. On his return Bonaparte had made him an A.D.C., and it was then that Roger had first come to know him.

Later, when Napoleon had become Emperor, he had made Caulaincourt Grand Equerry then, in 1807, sent him again as Ambassador to Russia. He had got on excellently with the Czar and his advisers, and done everything he possibly could to prevent war between the two countries, but failed. Having accompanied Napoleon in the retreat from Moscow, he had left the shattered army with him when he abandoned it to return in haste to Paris, and since had handled the negotiations that had led to the armistice of June-July.

In his marquee, over a bottle of excellent hock, he gave Roger the inside information about what had been going on. As one of Napoleon's most loyal subordinates, he lamented the state into which his master had fallen. He said that the Emperor, unlike his old self, was now a prey to constant indecision, wasted hours and sometimes days in sleeping or lazing about and, instead of concentrating his forces, tended to disperse them. It was his failure to follow up and swiftly support Vandamme which had led to that General's defeat and capture; and his attempt to take Berlin had been both ill-judged and disastrous.

Roger had heard nothing of this last. Napoleon had always disliked Bernadotte, so had displayed ungovernable rage when he learned that his ex-Marshal had actually brought Sweden into the war on the side of the allies, and had sworn to be avenged on him. When the war reopened, the allies had put Bernadotte in command of their army of the north, which consisted of some one hundred and twenty thousand Prussians, Russians and Swedes. Instead of concentrating all his forces against the Allies' main army on the far side of the Elbe, Napoleon's personal hatred of Bernadotte had led him in mid-August to despatch Marshal Oudinot with sixty thousand men, and General Girard's division of fourteen thousand in support, to capture Berlin.

French intelligence reported that there had been dissension among the Allies. Bernadotte, afraid to try conclusions with Napoleon, had been for retiring behind the Havel and Spree, but the Prussians were determined to die if they had to in front of their capital rather than behind it, and had pushed the Swedish Crown Prince into letting them have their way. After some initial successes, Oudinot was surprised by an independent corps of Prussians on his right; his centre, under Regnier, was driven back and, a few days later, Girard's division was almost annihilated. So this pointless attempt against Berlin had led to another defeat for the Emperor, and the loss of some ten thousand men.

The bottle of hock being finished and Roger having given a brief account of his movements since escaping from Russia, he took his ease while Caulaincourt settled down to work at his desk. An hour or so later an adjutant brought him a despatch. Having glanced at it, he sprang up from his chair with an excited shout :

'Here is splendid news ! That traitor Moreau is dead. His legs were blown off by a cannon-ball during last week's battle.'

Moreau had first become famous as a General during the wars of the Revolution and, while Bonaparte had been in Italy, won the great battle of Hohenlinden. But he was a die-hard Republican, and his enormous popularity with

the people had made him an obvious leader of any movement to curb the powers of a dictator, which Bonaparte
as First Consul was already showing signs of assuming.
To forestall any such danger to his position Napoleon had
had him and a number of other Jacobins brought to trial
for conspiring against the State. They had been condemned—in Moreau's case probably unjustly—but, fearing a popular outcry, Bonaparte had not dared order the
hero's execution, so had sent him into exile.

Roger had not heard of him for a dozen years and, sitting up, exclaimed in surprise, 'Moreau? I thought he was
in the United States.'

Caulaincourt shook his head. 'Nay. He was, but had
recently returned, hoping that the time had come to take
his revenge on the Emperor. He was received with the
highest honours by the three Allied monarchs, and has
since been acting as military adviser to the Czar Alexander. I must take these great tidings to our master. Personal
feelings apart, he will be delighted, for Moreau was a very
able General, and so a danger to us. Come with me and
you can be assured of a good reception from His Majesty.'

Ten minutes later they were both in the presence of the
Emperor. In the nine months since Roger had last seen
him, he seemed to have aged several years. His paunch
was even more prominent, the dark hair brushed across
his big head was thinner, his stoop more pronounced and
his face, always pale, now had an unhealthy look.

When Caulaincourt announced his news, Napoleon's
fine eyes suddenly lit up, and he cried, 'So that treacherous
pig is dead, eh? What a splendid bonus to our recent victory. God be praised for yet another mercy.'

Then his glance lit on Roger, who had been standing
a little behind Caulaincourt and in his shadow from the
big lantern that lit the marquee. Leaning forward he

scowled for a moment and thrust out his powerful jaw. Then he suddenly laughed :

'Breuc, or I'll be damned! I swear you have nine lives like a cat. How did you get out of Russia?'

Bowing low, Roger started off, 'May it please Your Imperial Majesty . . .' then gave the account of himself that he had told both Clarke and Caulaincourt. That Roger had been in England did not surprise the Emperor, as his memory was prodigious, but when it emerged that, from Sweden, Roger had been carried off to the United States, Napoleon's interest immediately quickened.

'Ha! Then you can tell me about the war the Americans are waging against the accursed English. You shall do so while I eat.' Turning, he called in his heavily-accented French to his secretary, Baron Méneval, who was working at a desk at the far end of the marquee, 'Have my dinner brought.'

Méneval was absent only a few minutes. During that time Roger continued his account of how he had succeeded in rejoining his master by way of Spain. Then Rustom, the Mameluke slave whom Napoleon had brought back from Egypt as his personal body servant, came in carrying a single dish under a silver cover.

Napoleon had never had any interest in food and at meals in his Palaces had tended to embarrass his guests by the swiftness with which he despatched course after course, evidently grudging the time that had to be given to eating. When in the field he ate irregularly and, in order that he should not be kept waiting whenever he felt hungry, day and night his chefs put a fresh chicken on the spit every ten minutes or so, in order that one should always be sufficiently roasted to be served immediately.

While he ate voraciously of this single course, washing the meat down with gulps of red wine, Roger told him all he had gathered about the Anglo-American war on land and sea. When he had exhausted the subject, he went on smoothly :

'You will recall, Sire, that I have English relatives. While I was in London I learned that a young nephew of mine, the Earl of St. Ermins, a Lieutenant in the Coldstream Guards, who was attached to the Duke of Brunswick's contingent, had been taken captive. I have reason to believe that he is now in one of the Prince d'Eckmühl's prisoner-of-war camps. The boy's mother is a dear friend of mine, so I should take it as a great personal favour if Your Imperial Majesty would give me an order for his release. It could be executed without his becoming aware that I am in fact a loyal Frenchman and in your service. He could be told that his liberty has been restored owing to an exchange with the Prussians, on condition that they send him home and he remains a non-combatant for the duration of the war.'

The Emperor considered for a moment, wiped his mouth on a napkin, then replied, 'Why not? It will make one less mouth for us to feed and, God knows, supplies in this damn' country are devilish hard to come by. My poor army is now living on starvation rations.' Turning to Méneval, he added :

'Write an order to Davout, or whom it may concern, in accordance with Breuc's wishes, and let him have it.'

Ten minutes later, with the order in his hand and greatly elated by his success, Roger was bowing himself out of the marquee. But his elation was short-lived, as Napoleon said curtly :

'I can't let you go off to Davout to arrange such a minor matter yet, though. The campaign has already proved most costly, and I am short of A.D.C.s. With your long experience you will prove most valuable to me. You must remain until I've taught those treacherous Austrians a lesson and dealt with the rest of the rabble that has combined against me. When I've done that, it will be time enough for you to restore this youth to his mother's arms.'

'To hear is to obey, Sire.' Roger forced himself to use cheerfully the *Gasconade* with which he had often before taken the Emperor's orders. But, as he made his way to find the quarters which Caulaincourt had promised to have allotted to him, he was greatly worried. It was already September. Charles was menaced by death when the leaves began to fall, and that would not now be long. It might be months before a decisive battle was fought, and he dared not flout the Emperor's orders by leaving him at once. He must remain for a week or two at least, but it had become imperative that he should not remain longer with Napoleon. He made up his mind there and then that at the first chance, during a reconnaissance or skirmish, he would disappear, leaving it to be believed that he had been killed or captured, and make off with all speed to Davout's headquarters.

Next day Roger learned that the Emperor, still obsessed with his desire to defeat and humiliate Bernadotte, had, on the 5th, sent Ney with his corps to reinforce and take over the command from Oudinot for another attempt to capture Berlin. On the 7th Napoleon, with further divisions and his staff, including Roger, left Dresden to support this new opposition.

The Emperor's position was now a far from favourable one. Since the recommencement of hostilities, he had lost one hundred and fifty thousand men and three hundred guns. His communications were under constant attack from German irregulars, it was becoming more and more difficult to supply his army, and he had at least three hostile armies of mixed Allies threatening him from dif-

ferent quarters, the exact positions of which were unknown
to him.

Not long after leaving Dresden he received a despatch
from Ney, reporting that his opening move had proved
successful and he had driven the enemy back on Jüterberg.
But on the following day intelligence was received that the
army of Silesia was again advancing on Dresden; so, instead of continuing north to join Ney for a concerted
attack on Berlin, Napoleon turned his army about, to
defend the Saxon capital again.

The Emperor's failure to support his Marshal, coupled
with Ney's misjudgement in ordering Oudinot to reinforce their front on the north bank of the marshy Ahebach,
brought about disaster. Courier after courier brought
tidings of the ever-worsening situation. In the neighbourhood of Dennewitz, Bülow's Prussians drove in the French
right. Ney made a desperate attempt to break through the
Prussian centre, but failed. Oudinot was unable to get his
troops back across the marshy little river in time to turn
the tide of battle. Before he could do so, the cautious
Bernadotte had decided to commit his Swedes. As darkness fell, the French broke and fled. The second attempt to
take Berlin had failed lamentably and cost the French
twenty-two thousand men.

With this depressing news, Napoleon returned along the
road to Dresden. On the morning of September 12th, before breaking camp to make the last day's march, he sent
for Roger and gave him a despatch for St. Cyr who, as before, had been left to defend the Saxon capital, and told
Roger to ride on ahead with it.

This was just the kind of opportunity Roger had been
waiting for. Once clear of the army, instead of going to
Dresden, he could turn off along a road leading west, then
make his way north to Davout's headquarters in Ham-

burg. To have carried out his plan would have been impossible had he had a long distance to cover, through territory made dangerous by partisan bands that roamed the country harassing the French whenever opportunity offered, as he would have had to take an escort. But Dresden was only twelve miles off and, as it was the Emperor's main base, there were constant troop movements taking place in the vicinity, making the area too dangerous for German irregulars to operate in.

Normally he would have taken his orderly but, with so little time to plan his venture, he could think of no excuse by which he could rid himself of the man later, and it was important that he should disappear without trace. So, while his charger was being saddled up, he said to the man:

'I have been ordered by the Emperor to ride on ahead, but I'll have no call to dismount before reaching Dresden, so I'll not need a horse-holder. You are to remain with the column, and when you reach camp, keep a sharp eye on my baggage.'

A moment later he had mounted and set off. Within a quarter of an hour he was clear of the advance guard and cantering cheerfully along, greatly elated by the thought that at last he was free of Napoleon and, within a few days now, should be finished once and for all with this unfortunate business that had yet again brought him unwillingly back to the Continent.

During the next half-hour he passed several tracks leading into the wood that bordered the road, but he knew that a mile or so further on there was a highway to the west, and it was this he intended to take; for he was well aware that in the country that lay between Dresden and Hamburg, a solitary French officer was liable to be attacked unless he kept to the main roads.

He was within a mile of the highway leading west when the unexpected happened. Suddenly a shot rang out. He felt a blow as though he had been hit by a musket ball on the calf of his right leg. His horse gave a loud neigh, reared and attempted to bolt. With an effort he checked it and brought it to a halt. For a minute the animal stood with its head down and legs splayed, quivering, then it slowly sank to the ground.

Roger had ample time to free himself from his mount as, panting heavily, it rolled on to its side; but, as he put his weight on his right foot, the numbed leg gave under him and he fell on his knees beside the horse. One glance at his leg confirmed his worst fears. He had been shot through the calf and the bullet had then penetrated the horse's belly.

The nature of his attacker he had already guessed. No band of German irregulars would have risked operating so near Dresden. It must be a solitary farmer or woodsman who lived in the neighbourhood. All over Germany there were now thousands of such men, embittered by years of French tyranny, who would not leave their homes to serve in the armed forces, but took a fanatical delight in taking pot shots at their hated enemies whenever they could do so with a good chance of escaping capture.

On his way up from the Rhine Roger had nearly always remained in close contact with French troops, as he had heard several accounts of attacks made on French couriers, and other soldiers who had become temporarily detached from their units. He knew, too, the sequel that often followed when the German succeeded only in wounding the man at whom he had fired. He waited for a while, until his victim had become weakened by loss of blood, then suddenly emerged from his cover to fire again at close quarters and so finish him off.

Whipping out one of his pistols, Roger crawled behind his fallen horse and anxiously scanned the wood from which the shot had come. He could see no sign of movement, but knew that death lurked there waiting to claim him. Looking down again at his leg, he saw that it was now bleeding badly, and he had no means of stopping the flow of blood. Soon it would have weakened him to a point where he no longer had the power to resist.

As he lay there, his mind seethed with anger, frustration and self-reproach. For many years he had diced with death. There had been unpleasant chances in battles afloat and on land that he had been compelled to take; but nearly all the worst dangers he had run had been calculated risks. He owed his survival very largely to careful preparation of his plans and never taking any chance that could possibly be avoided. But that morning, in his elation and haste, he had neglected the rule of a lifetime. A moment's thought should have told him that only a half-witted French officer would set off unaccompanied to ride through German forests, now that the country had become hostile. He should have taken his orderly and, as the man would not have dared disobey him, kept him for company all the way to Hamburg.

Now he was to pay for his stupid thoughtlessness. Gone now was all hope of saving Charles; while he, after succeeding in so many brilliant exploits, was to die uselessly, murdered in a ditch by a German peasant, who was no better than a human animal.

16

A Hideous Affray

ROGER had only just completed his swift survey of the wood opposite when the musket banged again. Instantly he ducked his head. The bullet went nowhere near it, but thudded into the horse's neck. Blood gushed from the wound, the animal made an ugly choking sound, writhed for a few moments, then shuddered and died.

The second, ill-directed shot at least showed that Roger's would-be killer was a poor marksman, which was some comfort. It meant that he would have to come out of the wood and much closer to ensure hitting his victim in a lethal spot—perhaps even close enough for Roger to use his pistol with effect and so turn the tables on him.

But Roger was very far from sanguine about his chances. There was always the possibility that French troops might appear on the scene, but he had passed only one troop of cavalry since leaving the main army, so he had little hope of being rescued by such means before he would have to make a last, desperate attempt to save his life. He could only pray that the attack would come soon, while he still had the strength to meet it.

For the next ten minutes he remained acutely alert, listening with faint hope for the distant sound of horses' hooves approaching along the road and, with fear, for a nearby rustle in the undergrowth, indicating that his enemy was about to attack him; but the silence remained unbroken. Meanwhile he lay at full length alongside the carcase of the horse, occasionally taking a quick peep over its belly, to make certain that he was in no danger of being crept up on and taken by surprise.

By then his leg was beginning to pain him badly. Obviously the muscle of his calf must have been torn right through, and blood was still seeping steadily out of the hole on each side of his riding boot. If only he could have got the boot off, he could have bandaged the wound and stopped the flow. But to get the boot off without help was quite impossible. Even normally he had to use a jack or have his servant pull his boots off. Yet he knew that if he could not somehow stop the bleeding he would become easy game for the man who was waiting to kill him.

It then occurred to him that he might open up the boot by cutting down either side of the leather so, laying his pistol aside, he got out a sharp knife which he always carried, and set about this onerous task. The leather, although as soft as velvet to the touch, proved unexpectedly tough, and every time he put pressure on the knife an agonising pain shot through his calf. He was also hampered by the fact that he dared not raise his head, so had to work in an awkward position, doubled up, to remain behind the cover of the horse. Within a few minutes he was streaming with sweat and, after cutting through only two inches of the leather, gave a loud groan, then relaxed.

The groan must have been taken by the man who was waiting to kill him as a sign that he was no longer capable of putting up a fight, for a moment later there came a scampering sound on the far side of the horse and a brief order shouted in a German patois that Roger did not understand.

Next second, to his horror, the reason for the scamper-

I

ing and the order was made clear : a big wolfhound suddenly came bounding round the buttocks of the dead
horse. The brute had been sent by its owner to flush Roger
out. He had laid aside his pistol, but was still holding the
knife with which he had been trying to slit his boot open.

With a ferocious snarl the beast leapt at him. He was
lying at full length. To have scrambled to his knees, so
as to be better able to meet the attack would have been
fatal, for he had no doubt that his enemy had now come
out of the wood and was only waiting for him to raise his
head above the level of the horse to put a bullet through it.

The wolfhound's jaws gaped wide. Another moment
and his gleaming fangs would have fastened themselves in
Roger's throat and torn it out. In a bound the beast was
upon him, pinning down his hand that held the knife.
There was only one hope of saving himself. Clenching his
left fist, he drove it straight into the big dog's mouth. Automatically the jaws snapped to. Roger gasped as the sharp
teeth bit into the sides of his forearm, but the sustained
force of the beast's spring and the thrust of Roger's fist
had carried his hand right through the slobbering mouth
and down into the animal's gullet. The yellow eyes dis-
tended to their fullest extent, it snorted fiercely in a vain
endeavour to draw breath. Choking, it reared up and
thrashed wildly with its forepaws on Roger's chest as it
strove to wriggle free. Its efforts to draw away released
Roger's right hand, in which he still held the knife.
Savagely he thrust upward with it into the brute's belly,
then turned the weapon in the wound. Next moment a
warm mess of blood and guts were pouring out over his
arm and body. The great dog jerked spasmodically, tore
its mouth free of Roger's left arm, gave a whimpering
howl and collapsed upon him.

Roger's heart was pounding fiercely as he lay motionless, the strength temporarily drained from all his limbs. But his mind was working frantically, for he was acutely aware that he was still in deadly peril. To have survived the attack by the savage hound was more than he could have hoped for when he first heard it snarl and saw it come bounding towards him. But he had yet to escape death at the hands of its master, whom he knew must be lurking only a few yards away on the far side of the horse, with his musket at the ready.

Making a great effort he pushed the dead hound half off him, pulled his knife out of the gaping wound and transferred it to his left hand; then, with his right, he groped for and found his pistol.

Now, having got his breath back he was, for a moment, sorely tempted to end matters, one way or another, by taking a gamble with fate. Being a crack shot with a pistol, he felt certain that if he suddenly sat up and his enemy was within fifteen paces, he could kill him. But he had only the one bullet, and no means of reloading. The second he exposed himself the man would bring his musket to bear and, if he was further off, the odds would be in his favour.

On the other hand the man must know that his hound was dead and possibly think that Roger had died in his struggle with it; or at least have been rendered helpless. Within a few moments it was certain that he would come round to find out what had happened. To do so he would have to expose himself, and be within easy range. Having considered these alternatives, Roger's native caution decided him to ignore his impulse and lie doggo.

The greatest danger entailed by his decision was that he had no means of guessing whether his enemy would come round by his horse's head or its tail and, lying at full length as he was, he could not keep his eyes fixed on

both simultaneously. All he could do, while glancing first
one way then the other, was to strain his ears for sounds
of the killer's approach.

He waited in an agony of apprehension. Time seemed
to stand still. The suspense was almost unbearable. Again
he was seized with the temptation to sit up, but fought
it down. He knew that with his right leg useless, his left
arm torn and aching from the dog's fierce bite, weakened
by loss of blood and lying there on his back, he was no
match even for an active, well-grown boy, let alone a cun-
ning and stalwart peasant; yet he longed desperately for
an end to this hideous uncertainty.

At last it came, and when it did come took him by
surprise. His only warning was the sound of a few swift
footfalls on the muddy, rutted road. But his enemy
appeared neither round the head nor tail of the dead horse.
He ran straight at it, looming suddenly above the saddle,
with his musket pointed down at Roger.

He was a tall man with gangling limbs, wearing a
worn, rabbit-skin jacket over filthy rags. His hair, a dirty
brown streaked with grey, was an untidy mop, standing
out in tufts where it had been roughly cut. A straggling
beard covered his cheeks and chin. His lips stood out
red and thick, his eyes were small, dark, and glaring
hatred.

Caught off his guard, Roger had no chance to use his
pistol, for to aim it he would have to throw his right arm
across his chest. His eyes started from his head as he stared
up into the barrel of the musket. The man's finger was
upon the trigger and he was just about to fire. The dead
dog still lay half sprawled over Roger's body. Inspiration
from beyond suddenly came to him, as it had several times
before when his life had been in dire peril. Instantly he
acted on the thought that he knew had been sent to him

unconsciously by Georgina's spirit which was bound so closely to his own. With all the power he had left he jerked up his good leg. It threw the dog up from midway down his body, so that its dead head landed on his face. A fraction of a second earlier the musket had been fired. The bullet ploughed through the wolfhound's head instead of Roger's.

Even as the dog's blood and brains poured over Roger's face he realised that he still had a chance to save his life; but that it would last only the next few moments. He must get the better of his attacker before he had time to reload his musket, otherwise he would be irretrievably lost.

Thrusting aside the horribly shattered carcase of the animal, he shook his head violently to get the filthy muck out of his eyes, then sat up. His right eye was still blinded by a fragment of the dog's flesh, but with his left he could hazily make out the form of the peasant. He had the musket between his knees and was in the act of pouring powder from a horn that hung from his belt down the barrel. Roger swivelled his pistol, strove to steady his quivering hand, aimed for the man's chest and pulled the trigger. To his utter dismay, nothing happened.

The reason flashed upon him. The powder had become wet with the dog's blood. By then the peasant had taken a bullet from his pouch, and was about to drop it down the barrel of his musket. In desperation Roger hurled the now useless pistol at him. It caught him sideways on, full in the face. With a howl he let the musket fall, clutched at his broken nose, then staggered and fell.

For Roger to have remained where he was would have been fatal. The injury he had inflicted on his enemy was not sufficient to prevent him from coming to his feet and completing the reloading of his musket. Transferring his knife to his right hand, Roger heaved himself and, dragging his wounded leg behind him, scrambled over the horse's body. The peasant had come to his knees and stretched out a hand to grab his musket. Suddenly both of them went still and remained for a moment as though frozen. Simultaneously they had caught the sound of horses' hooves coming up the road from the direction of Dresden.

In the violence of the struggle neither had heard them in the distance, but now they were loud and coming on at a canter. Evidently the horsemen had been alerted to trouble ahead by the firing of the musket that had shattered the dog's head.

Wiping the blood from his face with the back of his hand, the peasant gave a frightened glance down the road; then, abandoning his musket, turned to make off into the woods. With a lightening glow of elation Roger knew that he was saved, but he was not content to let his would-be murderer go.

When in Spain he had learnt how to throw a knife. Drawing back his hand, he sent the sharp blade with all the strength he had left whizzing after his enemy. He aimed to strike the man between the shoulder blades, but by then he had become so weak that the force behind the throw was insufficient, even at that short distance, to carry the knife high enough. Yet it scored a hit, slicing into and cutting a tendon at the back of the peasant's left knee.

He let out a scream, staggered and fell. Scrambling to his knees, he attempted to run on, but his left leg had been rendered useless. The moment he put his weight on it he fell again. By then a small party of Chasseurs had rounded the corner and were approaching at the gallop. Clawing at the muddy road, the man made frantic efforts to drag himself up a low bank into the thick undergrowth.

Roger, still gasping for breath, was sprawled across the

body of his dead horse. Although he was covered from head to foot in blood and muck, his uniform was still recognisable as that of a French officer. The leader of the Chasseurs, a young Lieutenant, had grasped the situation in a glance. Drawing his sabre, he rode at the peasant, intending to sever his head from his body at a stroke. But Roger raised a hand and cried in a croaking voice :

'Don't kill him ! I want that man alive.'

A moment later the Lieutenant and his four companions pulled up and dismounted. Two of them seized the man and dragged him to his feet, while their officer hurried over to Roger. In a few words he confirmed the fact that he had been ambushed, then added jerkily :

'A sabre slash or a bullet is too swift a death for that . . . that swine. I want him hanged . . . but not with a running noose. Just have a loop of rope put over his head and . . . and string him up to the nearest tree. When his friends find him, he'll be an example to them. They'll see from his face that we left him to dance on air till . . . till he slowly strangled, instead of our pulling on his feet to give him a quick end.'

The Lieutenant had already seen from Roger's rank badges that he was a Colonel, so did not demur. One of his men produced a lanyard, tied one end of it to the stout branch of a tree that protruded about seven feet above the road. The struggling peasant was pushed up the bank and the other end knotted round his neck. His legs were then kicked from under him, and he swung out above the road.

His shouts ended abruptly, his little eyes bulged, and his limbs began to jerk like those of a puppet on a string. His neck had not been broken by a drop of several feet and, as the noose was loose, it would not immediately choke him. It could be anything up to a quarter of an hour before the strain of the weight of his body on his neck caused his torture to end in oblivion. Roger was not by nature cruel, but he had suffered such agony, both physical and mental, inflicted on him in this terrible encounter, that he felt fully justified in exacting vengeance.

By this time the head of a column of wagons had appeared round the bend of the road, and Roger learned that it consisted of supplies being sent up to the Emperor's army. On hearing that the Emperor was on his way back to Dresden, the Lieutenant agreed that it was pointless to proceed further, and ordered his column to turn about. He also called up a sergeant to whom Roger gave the despatch he had been taking to St. Cyr, and ordered him to ride off ahead at full speed with it.

Meanwhile, two of the soldiers had cut Roger's riding boot away and pried his injured leg from it. As the bullet had gone right through his calf, he was spared the probing needed for extraction, but the muscles had been torn to pieces and, although he was nearly fainting with pain as they bound up the pulpy mess with a field dressing, his vanity was piqued by the gloomy thought that never again would fair ladies comment on the perfection of his legs when wearing silk stockings. He had, as he had feared, lost a lot of blood, so was very weak and now unable to stand unless supported. As several of the wagons were loaded with hay, they were able to make him fairly comfortable in one of them and he was conveyed to a nobleman's palace in Dresden that had been turned into a hospital for officers.

There they gave him opium to dull the pain of his wounds, then stripped him of his filthy clothes and bathed him thoroughly. The thickness of his tunic had prevented the hound's teeth from biting deeply into his left forearm but, after his leg had been properly dressed, he had to submit to the further ordeal of having the bites cauterised.

Next morning he gradually roused from a heavily-drugged sleep to contemplate the extremely worrying situation in which he had landed himself by his hasty decision to set off without an orderly. Failing to take that precaution had led to his coming within an ace of losing his life; but he endeavoured to console himself with the thought that although, had he been accompanied by an armed companion, the peasant would never have dared attempt to finish him off, that could not have prevented the man from shooting him through the leg in the first place.

When the surgeon made his rounds, Roger asked anxiously how soon he would be able to ride again. The reply was not for a month or, at the least, three weeks, and then only for a mile or two at a time at walking pace. That was what he had feared, and his heart sank. If Georgina's visions had been true foresight, young Charles was due to die with the fall of the leaves, and it was already September 13th.

Fate, Roger thought bitterly, had been against him all the time in this nebulous mission, about the success of which he had, from the beginning, considered the odds greatly against him. Georgina had seen Charles in her crystal actually about to be hanged, and for his would-be rescuer to take steps in time to prevent that now seemed most improbable.

Yet for Georgina's sake he had felt it imperative to do his utmost to render her vision false by finding the boy and getting him back to England before the autumn. To do that there should have been ample time; but again and again he had been thwarted, first by Charles having left Spain, next by learning that he was not held prisoner in France, but was somewhere in Davout's command based on Hamburg, thus necessitating the long ride up to Dresden. And Hamburg lay to the north-east, over two hundred and fifty miles away. How, now that he was crippled, could he possibly hope to cover that distance before every tree in north Germany was bare of leaves?

17

The Battle of the Nations

THAT afternoon the Emperor sent to enquire after Roger. From time to time, his friends on the Staff came to visit him and he learned something from them of the progress of the war, although it had again become a most complicated picture.

The three armies opposed to the French now greatly outnumbered them, but the weakness of the Allies was that their forces, which roughly formed a semi-circle east of the Elbe, were widely separated. One army covered Berlin, while the others were in Silesia and Bohemia. Napoleon, in accordance with his habitual strategy, aimed to concentrate his army and defeat each in turn before they could join forces against him; but his plans were seriously bedevilled by the fact that since he was operating in hostile country he could secure no reliable information about the whereabouts of his enemies.

His strongest card was that, owing to his unique reputation as a General, all the Allied Commanders were frightened of him. Bernadotte had been one of the ablest Marshals, yet he had no confidence at all in his own ability to defeat his old master, so kept his Swedes well to the rear of the battle zone. Schwarzenberg, who was technically Commander-in-Chief of all the Allied forces, was an able diplomat but a craven soldier, and became scared out of his wits every time he heard that Napoleon was approaching. Barclay de Tolly had, again and again, perhaps wisely, scurried off with his army rather than stand and fight during the French advance to Moscow in the previous year; and the other Russian Generals were equally cagey about taking on the redoubtable Corsican. Old Blücher and his Prussians alone showed a determination to lose no opportunity of attacking the enemy, but the veteran was too shrewd to take the offensive with his limited forces unless he could be assured of the support of the Russians and Austrians.

This fear of Napoleon by the majority of the Allied Generals did not prove altogether to his advantage, since although it enabled him to move the bulk of his army wherever he wished, every time he advanced against one of the enemy armies it withdrew. The result was that he was constantly exhausting his troops by long marches in most evil weather, without being able to bring any of his opponents to engage in a pitched battle. For the remainder of September, during which there was hardly a day upon which it did not rain, he forced the pace in desperate efforts to catch up with and defeat one of the Allied forces, only to hear that another was again threatening Dresden, so was forced to break off the pursuit and change direction in order to protect his base.

By the end of the month Roger was able to get about on crutches, but for him to have ridden any distance would have been certain to re-open his wound, so he began to contemplate the possibility of hiring a coach and leaving the city clandestinely one night. But once more his plans were frustrated. The Emperor's Chief-of-Staff, Marshal Berthier, Prince de Neufchâtel, happened to hear that he was able to get about again, so sent for him.

As Roger was that comparatively rare product, a *beau*

sabreur who also had brains, during periods when Napoleon had not been engaged in active operations he had oftent lent him for a while to Berthier; so he was well acquainted with the Chief-of-Staff, and the complicated work for which he was responsible.

The Prince, an ugly little man with an enormous head that held a card index brain; he was most unpopular and ill-tempered but, recognising Roger's capabilities, had always been polite to him, and he now explained that he was in the devil of a mess.

The constant changes of direction by the Emperor and the other widely scattered French forces, were making it near-impossible to carry out his task of re-routing supply columns and keeping a record of units available, together with their whereabouts; so Roger's help would prove invaluable. His request, as the senior Marshal in the Emperor's army, was tantamount to an order so, for the ten days that followed, Roger had to labour for hours on end, working out statistics from maps and schedules.

Meanwhile, Blücher, inspired by Gneisenau and encouraged by both his King and the Czar, had determined on a flank march which would enable him to join up with Schwarzenberg's Austrians, south of Leipzig. A few days later the Emperor, hearing that the Prussians had crossed the Elbe, charged Murat with the defence of Leipzig and St. Cyr once more with that of Dresden, then hurried north-west, hoping to crush his most inveterate enemy while on the march and encumbered by his baggage. Having sent Ney forward to fall on the rear of Blücher's army, Napoleon waited further news for four days in the dank, fogbound castle of Duben. When it came he learned that Blücher had turned westward, thus disclosing his intention of joining Schwarzenberg.

Promptly the Emperor devised a new plan to disconcert

his enemies. The great fortresses on the Elbe were all still in his hands; he would march to the Elbe and cross it. But the whole of his Staff considered this so reckless that they confronted him in a body and begged him to abandon this idea. Reluctantly he agreed, but only to substitute the still more venturesome design of first crushing Bernadotte, then crossing the Elbe at Torgan and circling round to strike at Schwarzenberg near Leipzig.

Had his men been tireless machines, this might have been possible, but for two months they had been marching and counter-marching, for a good part of the time in pouring rain. Their uniforms were sodden, their boots worn out and, owing to insufficient supplies to feed them, they were suffering from semi-starvation.

The Emperor had gained a great victory at Dresden, but his Marshals had been defeated in five major battles : at Grossbeeren, Hagelsberg, Katzbach, Kulm and Dennewitz. At the beginning of the campaign he had commanded half a million men but, mainly through his own ill-conceived strategy, frittered away over half of them. The hospitals were crammed, tens of thousands were suffering from minor wounds. Utter weariness and a spirit of despair now permeated the whole army.

By October 10th he had been forced to the conclusion that he dared take no further risks and now, if he were to save Leipzig, even abandon the middle Elbe in order to concentrate all his forces in the neighbourhood of that city. On the 11th, Berthier received orders to move the Imperial Headquarters to Leipzig, and a frantic packing of documents began.

During each of the past few days Roger had spent from a quarter to half an hour on a quiet horse, but he had not yet dared trot, and it was obviously out of the question for him to make the eighty-mile journey on horseback. In consequence he arranged to travel in one of the Mess carts, a small, two-wheeled, covered wagon.

All through the night and the following day the long columns of silent, depressed troops made their way westward and, late in the evening of the 12th, Roger reached the city to find that Berthier had taken over a Saxon noble's palace as a headquarters. Knowing that his leg wound pained him when going upstairs, one of Roger's brother officers had kindly reserved for him a large clothes closet on the first floor, and had a bed put in it. Tired out after his long journey, he pulled off his clothes, tumbled into bed and was almost instantly asleep.

On the 14th the Emperor arrived, bringing with him the unfortunate King and Queen of Saxony, whom for so long he had dragged at his chariot wheels while almost totally destroying what had once been their fair realm. With him, too, he brought the worst of news, which he had received a few days earlier. His hitherto most loyal ally, the King of Bavaria, had defected and entered into a pact with Austria that, in exchange for his putting thirty-six thousand troops at her disposal, she would guarantee a continuance of his sovereignty.

Having left the Saxon sovereigns at their palace, Napoleon pressed on to Wachau, a village about three miles to the south-west of the city, at which Murat had his headquarters. It was the central point opposite the arc from east to south where the allies had massed their main forces. Murat was superior to them only in cavalry, and his gloomy report conveyed the fact that he had not used it with his old dash and ability. The fact was that he was utterly sick of the war, and thought only of how soon he could get back to his Kingdom of Naples.

A similar spirit was displayed that evening by the other Marshals when the Emperor summoned them to a con-

ference at the village of Reudnitz. Among others he bitterly reproached Augereau for no longer being the intrepid
leader he had been at the battle of Castiglione; to which
the Marshal replied with equal bitterness, 'Give me back
the old soldiers of our Italian campaign, and I'll show you
that I am.'

But Napoleon himself was not the man he had been,
otherwise he would not have let the 15th drift by without taking any action, thus giving the Allies an extra day
to complete their concentration. During that time
Schwarzenberg was able to send a Corps across the rivers
Pleisse and Elster in order to threaten Leipzig from the
direction of Lindenau on the south-west and also, with
new divisions that came up, extend the right of his semi-
circle.

That night Marmont, whose corps was stationed in the
northern suburbs, reported watchfires, indicating that yet
another enemy army was mustered there. Actually it was
Blücher's Prussians, but the Emperor refused to believe his
Marshal's warning of this new threat and, continuing to
suppose that his only serious danger lay in the south-east,
ordered Marmont to be ready to march his troops through
Leipzig to support the attack he intended to launch
against Schwarzenberg.

Thus, on the morning of October 16th, when the Battle
of the Nations opened, one hundred and fifty thousand
weary and dispirited troops—all that remained to Napoleon—were opposed to three hundred thousand enemies
determined to destroy him and ready to advance simultaneously from the south, east and north of the city.

The Emperor's forces were disposed on a convex front
centred on Liebertwolkwitz, immediately to the east of
the city. The enemy were stretched over a much wider
arc, so he counted on being able to equal their numbers at

any point; and, having driven Schwarzenberg's army from the field in disruption, deal later with Blücher and Bernadotte about whose positions he was still in ignorance.

Berthier and the rest of the Staff had left the city to join Napoleon at his battle headquarters. As Roger was still unable to ride either fast or for any distance, he would have been useless as an A.D.C.; so, considerably relieved at having a valid excuse to escape the hazards of the battle, he remained behind.

Having breakfasted, he painfully climbed the stairs to the attics of the palace, found a skylight and crawled through on to the roof. From that height, with his spy glass he could get a good view of the greater part of the country surrounding the city.

At nine o'clock the opening shots were fired by the Allies from the heights they held opposite Liebertwolkwitz, and these were followed by a furious artillery duel that lasted for six hours. The Emperor then launched the two cavalry corps of Latour-Maubourg and Pajol. Led by Murat, these twelve thousand charging horsemen provided an amazing spectacle. They scaled the muddy slopes, sabred the gunners and enveloped the Russian squares. So deep was their penetration that the three Allied sovereigns who had been watching the battle from an eminence were forced to beat a hasty retreat. But Murat had forced the pace too early. His horses and men had not the stamina left to resist the counter charges by Pahlen's Cossacks and the Silesian Curassiers. The French were driven back in confusion, with the loss of both their Corps commanders.

Meanwhile, an Austrian attack on Lindenau had been beaten off, but on the west side of the city, at Möckern, the French received a most unpleasant surprise. In accordance with Napoleon's orders, Marmont had begun to move south when he was suddenly attacked by Yorck's Prussians. Ney's corps should have supported Marmont, but was also on the move. Berthier sent a confused order for Ney to turn about, with the result that his fifteen thousand men spent the greater part of the day marching to and fro without participating in the battle, and arrived too late to help Marmont. He defended Möckern with great determination, and it proved the most bloody engagement of the whole war, ending by the French being driven out and left with greatly reduced numbers to endeavour to check Blücher's advance from the north.

During the day the French had inflicted more casualties on the enemy than they had sustained, but they had lost at least twenty thousand men and had no means of replacing them. St. Cyr's corps of twenty-seven thousand men was far away at Dresden, and Davout's army, which had been strained to the limit in holding down north-west Germany, was still further away in Hanover; whereas Bennigsen was now rapidly approaching with the Russian Army of Reserve, numbering forty-one thousand men, and the ultra-cautious Bernadotte had belatedly begun to march south from Halle with his sixty thousand Swedes.

On the following day, a Sunday, the general gloom in Leipzig was added to by the Saxons and other German troops, under General Reynier, becoming disaffected and threatening to desert; also by pouring rain. Experience had shown during this awful autumn campaign that in such weather infantry became almost useless, because the powder for their muskets could not be kept dry. This may have been one reason why the battle was not renewed but, in Napoleon's case, the malaise and indecision which had recently afflicted him played a part. Instead of planning a break-out, he spent most of his time dozing, then decided to send the captured Austrian General, Merveldt, to his Emperor with proposals for an armistice. But at last the

Allies were beginning to realise that Napoleon was not invincible, and that now was their chance to make an end of him; so no reply was sent.

On learning that Blücher had now advanced far enough from the north-west to threaten the only French line of retreat, the Emperor instead of taking time by the forelock and ordering a retreat to start that night, merely directed that his drenched and famished troops should withdraw nearer the city. He then fell asleep.

Next morning, the 18th, the Allies launched a general offensive. Again Roger went up to the roof of the palace and watched the battle. From the south-west right round to the north-west, the city was ringed by over a thousand flashing guns. Cohorts of cavalry and great masses of infantry were pressing forward on every side but, as on the Saturday, clouds of dense smoke soon hid most of the fighting. Later in the day he learned that at Paunsdorf, to the north-east, the Allies had broken through the ring of the defence, owing to three thousand Saxons having gone over to the Russians and taking with them nineteen guns which they promptly turned on the hated French.

By evening Roger decided that the battle was now irretrievably lost and that, for him, it was time to go. His friend having had a bed put up for him in a clothes closet now proved a piece of unexpected good fortune as, on his hazardous way up to Hamburg, civilian clothing would protect him from stray bands of Germans. When he tried on some of the clothes, he found that they had all been made for a man a few inches shorter than himself and much fatter; but that could not be helped. He chose two cloth suits, some shirts and other garments, packed them, with his own possessions, into a portmanteau and hobbled downstairs with it.

Berthier had left all the headquarters transport in the

palace stables, and the Mess cart in which Roger had
travelled from Dresden was among it. The name of the
man who had driven it was Dopet. Routing him out from
among his fellow drivers, Roger said he had been ordered
to leave the city at once with certain important papers, to
ensure that they should not fall into the hands of the
enemy; then had him put the portmanteau in the Mess
cart.

Accompanied by Dopet, he went to the kitchen and
collected ample stores for the journey. Next, he secured
two muskets and a good supply of ammunition from the
guardhouse. Finally, while Dopet harnessed a stout little
cob between the shafts of the cart, Roger made himself
a comfortable seat in the back from half a truss of hay.
Then they set off into the semi-dark streets which resem-
bled an oasis in an inferno, as on the outskirts of the city
there were constant explosions and many houses in the
suburbs were on fire.

Under Roger's direction they reached the bridges to the
west of Leipzig. Only in that quarter was there now no
fighting in progress, but considerable numbers of men
were crossing the river. Roger guessed that they were deserters, and in fact they were only anticipating the
Emperor's order given to Berthier a few hours later that
night, that the whole army should retreat.

Later Roger learned that he had been lucky to get out
of Leipzig when he had, as during the night the bridges
became ever more crowded and on the following morning
it was only with difficulty that a way was made for the
Emperor's coach. By then all that was left of his army
was converging from south, east and north on to the one
road leading west. The narrow streets of Leipzig were
half blocked by abandoned guns and wagons. Between
them squeezed solid masses of panic-stricken troops,

breathlessly fighting their way toward the bridges. Hundreds of bursting cannon-balls, coming from three directions, added to the horror and confusion. Dead and wounded alike were trampled on by those still capable of making a desperate attempt to escape from that inferno. Many buildings were on fire, and in the suburbs Austrians, Russians, Prussians, Swedes and Saxons drove the wretched French from building to building, until tens of thousands of them had been forced out of the city in helpless herds.

The bridges were hopelessly inadequate for such masses to cross except in a comparative trickle. Early in the day the situation was still worsened by one bridge collapsing and another—the largest—being prematurely blown up owing to an error by a nervous Sapper. In desperation the fleeing host sought to escape by swimming the river. There followed a scene reminiscent of the crossing of the Beresina during the retreat from Moscow the previous winter. Hundreds of missiles exploded in the water and on both banks, creating a holocaust. Thousands of men were killed and thousands of others caught up in a tangle of bodies, and drowned.

Among the latter was the gallant Prince Poniatowski who for so many years had loyally led his Polish division in Napoleon's battles, vainly clinging to the faithless Corsican's promise that in due course he would restore Poland as an independent Kingdom. The Prince's death was the more tragic in that, only the previous day, Napoleon had made him a Marshal.

During those terrible twenty-four hours that saw the final defeat and utter rout of the great army that Napoleon had mustered in Germany early that summer, Roger succeeded in getting well clear of the battle area and the early deserters who had crossed the bridges the previous evening, as he had. They naturally took the roads to the south, hoping to reach the Rhine and the protection of the many French-held fortresses along it; whereas Roger's destination was Hamburg, so he had Dopet take a by-road leading north-west.

By morning they had covered some twenty miles and when full daylight came he decided that they must give the little cob several hours' rest. The most likely way of avoiding dangerous encounters was to spend the time in a wood, so when they next came to a track leading into one, he told Dopet to drive up it. At a brook they watered the animal, fed it, ate a meal, then made themselves as comfortable as they could in the Mess cart.

About midday they roused and had another meal. During it Roger told Dopet that they were going to Hamburg, so would have to pass through country where they were almost certain to run into bands of German irregulars. He then opened the suitcase, showed Dopet the two civilian suits, and said, 'We are going to change into these, then we can pass as Germans. That is, provided you don't open your mouth. I speak German quite fluently enough to be taken in these parts for a Rhinelander, so if we are challenged, I think we should get by without trouble.'

Dopet was a sturdy, unimaginative young Fleming, and although he would have much preferred to travel south rather than north, he had been in the Army long enough to know that one did not argue with officers. When they had changed, both showed amusement at the other's appearance. Dopet being shorter than Roger his trousers were the right length, but he had powerful shoulders, so when he struggled into the coat it burst at one of the seams; while Roger's coat fitted fairly well, but his trousers were absurdly short. They got over the fact that the owner of the clothes had had a large paunch by folding the slack under tightened belts. However, their appearance was a matter of no great concern, as they were not attempting to pass as persons of quality, and at that date clothes were so scarce in Germany that those they were wearing might easily have been bought second-hand.

Having packed their uniforms in the suitcase, they set off, and by late afternoon had covered another fifteen miles. They then rested again for several hours in the neck of a wood. From a map Roger had brought with him, he knew that the little town of Sangerhausen lay some twelve miles ahead, and he wanted to pass through it during the hours of darkness; so at about one o'clock in the morning they took the road again. Well before five o'clock they were clear of the sleeping town and, a few miles beyond it, settled on another suitable spot for a long rest.

By moving from Dresden to Leipzig Roger had reduced his distance from Hamburg by about fifty miles, and now they had come another fifty; but they still had a hundred and fifty to cover and, anxious as he was to reach Hamburg, he felt that the utmost that could be expected of the little cob that drew the Mess cart was twenty-five miles a day.

Since he had been used, when on an urgent matter, to ride a hundred or more miles a day, he found this slow pace terribly frustrating. Yet there was no alternative. Even if he could have secured a horse, he would not have dared ride at more than walking pace with his terribly torn leg only recently healed. Walking beside the cart, for a good part of each day while Dopet led the cob, was better for his leg.

While he limped along, he became ever more depressed at the probable outcome of his journey. Admittedly, he had never known one of Georgina's predictions about the future fail to come to pass, yet fundamentally her vision of Charles was absurd, because whatever crime Charles had committed, he was an officer and if he were condemned to death, he would not be hanged but shot. Yet, adoring Georgina as he did, how could he possibly not have volunteered to undertake this forlorn hope of changing the course of Charles's fortune by getting him back to England? He could only console himself by the thought that, having spent three months journeying from one end of Europe to the other, in another few days he would have done all he could and at last learn if Charles was already dead or still alive.

As they slowly wound their way northward they met other travellers with some of whom Roger discussed the war. The news of Napoleon's crushing defeat at the Battle of the Nations had sped ahead of them, and the inhabitants of every German village were wild with delight. Here and there they were passed by bands of irregulars, all now marching south, with the hope of joining in the pursuit of the broken French.

It was not until they reached Brunswick that they saw any French troops at all. But the city was an important junction so Davout still kept a strong garrison there, and the citizens were clearly overawed by the groups of surly-looking Grenadiers who patrolled the main streets or lounged, silent and unhappy, in the cafés.

While working with Berthier, Roger had frequently heard Davout's position discussed. After the retreat from Moscow, the Emperor had made him Governor of the Lower Elbe, and instructed him to turn Hamburg into an impregnable fortress from which, in conjunction with their Danish allies, he could hold down the whole of northwest Germany.

No choice for such a task could have been better than the 'Iron Marshal', as Davout, Prince d'Eckmühl and

Duc d'Auerstädt, was called by the Army. He was the only Marshal who had studied and understood Napoleon's revolutionary methods of warfare, so was a very formidable soldier. He was also an able administrator, completely ruthless and the strictest of disciplinarians.

In Napoleon's two bids, earlier in the year, to take Berlin, he had hoped that Davout might come to the assistance of Ney and Oudinot. That he had been unable to do, because his limited forces were already stretched to the utmost putting down patriotic risings in Hanover, Mecklenburg and Brunswick; but he had carried out his assignment regarding Hamburg with an iron hand. The whole of Germany being in a state of semi-starvation, to conserve his supplies he had first forcibly evacuated three thousand children; then, also as useless mouths, all the elderly people in the city. To reduce to a minimum secret subscriptions by citizens to patriotic societies and subversive movements, he had inflicted taxes on the wealthy that had reduced them to near poverty, and imprisoned many of the leading merchants as hostages. His dread tribunals sat daily, and sent to execution anyone found guilty of having offended against even his minor ordinances.

The state of gloom and terror existing in the great port on the Elbe had been confirmed by several Germans to whom Roger had recently spoken; so when, on October 27th, he came in sight of the city spires, he knew how matters stood there, but he did not intend to enter the city. Some three miles outside the walls he had Dopet turn into a coppice and there the two of them changed from their ill-fitting civilian clothes back into uniform. They then took a side road to Herrenhausen, which lay just outside the city. Near it stood an ancient castle that, until the end of the past century, had been the residence of the sovereigns of Great Britain when they visited their King-

dom of Hanover. It was there that Davout had had his
headquarters in 1810 when, before the Russian campaign,
he had been commanding in Hamburg and Roger had
been sent to him on a mission.

It was soon after midday when the Mess cart, now
driven by Dopet and with Roger riding in it, pulled up
outside the great gate of the castle. As Roger got out of
the cart the sentry came smartly to attention and presented
arms. Roger's surmise that Davout had again made the
place his headquarters proved correct. The sergeant of the
guard sent a man to show Dopet where to stable his cob
and cart, and another to escort Roger up to the Marshal
Prince's quarters.

Having announced himself as *Colonel Comte de Breuc*
to an adjutant there, Roger learned that Davout had ridden in to the city that morning, but was expected back to
dinner. Deciding to put his necessary wait to good advantage, Roger asked to be conducted to the department that
dealt with officer prisoners-of-war. He was taken to a room
in one of the towers, where a sergeant was shuffling
through some papers. Duly impressed by Roger's sash,
which proclaimed him to be an A.D.C. to the Emperor,
the sergeant hastened to produce a ledger and he was soon
able to tell Roger that Charles was a prisoner with some
hundred other officers at Schloss Bergedorf, which was
some ten miles distant.

Immensely relieved to learn that Charles was still alive,
and at having at last run his quarry to earth, Roger went
down the spiral stairs, enquired the whereabouts of the
anteroom to the Marshal's office, and sat down there to
await his return.

The wait was a long one, but at about half-past four
Davout, grim-faced as ever, came striding in, his spurs
clinking and his riding boots resounding on the parquet.

Roger promptly stood up, came to attention and saluted.

Halting abruptly, the Marshal gave him an unsmiling stare and asked, 'What brings you here, Breuc?'

'I come, Your Highness, from His Imperial Majesty,' Roger replied.

Davout motioned toward his office. 'Come in then, and give me such news as you have of him.'

When Roger had followed him in and been waved to a chair, he said, 'Alas, Your Highness, I can tell you no more than that I last saw the Emperor in Leipzig shortly before disaster overtook our army. But I have a warrant from him that he ordered me to present to you.'

As he spoke, Roger produced the paper he had obtained from Napoleon, ordering that Charles should be handed over to him, and placed it on Davout's desk.

Passing a hand over his bald head, the Marshal read it through quickly, then asked, 'What is the reason for this? Why does the Emperor wish me to transfer the custody of this young Englishmen to you?'

'Because I have a special interest in him, Your Highness. As you may know, my mother was English, and this youth is my nephew. The Emperor graciously agreed that, if possible, I should be allowed to make arrangements for him to be sent back to England, on condition that he did not serve actively again in the war against us.'

Davout frowned. 'I am most strongly opposed to sentiment being allowed to interfere with war. You should be engaged on your proper duties instead of travelling many miles to secure the release of a relative who is an enemy. However, that is not in my jurisdiction, and the Emperor's command must be obeyed. I will find out where this officer is being held prisoner.'

'While awaiting your return I took the liberty of doing so, Your Highness. He is at Schloss Bergedorf.'

'Schloss Bergedorf!' repeated Davout, with a sudden lift of his grey eyebrows. 'Then he may no longer be there. Some days ago, when the prisoners at the Schloss learned of our defeat at Leipzig, they got out of hand. There was a mutiny. Several were shot, but twenty-seven broke prison and escaped.'

Roger went pale. He swallowed hard, then gasped, 'Do you . . . do you know if St. Ermins was among them?'

The Marshal's face took on a vicious look and his voice was almost a snarl. 'No, I do not. But one thing I do know. I have given orders that any of the escapers who are recaptured are to be hanged.'

'Hanged!' Roger came to his feet. 'But you can't do that! Even if you condemn them to death, which would be unjustifiably severe, they are officers, so they have the right to be shot.'

'Silence!' Davout snapped. 'Who are you that you should dare to tell me my business? To hold down these German curs is the hardest task I have ever had. Officers they may be, but they are Germans and, until recently, our allies. By turning their coats they have become traitors. The penalty of a traitor who is caught is to be hanged, and this will serve as a warning to any of their compatriots who are my prisoners and tempted to make trouble.'

'I pray to God then that none of those who escaped will be recaptured.'

'Then you'll pray in vain,' the Marshal retorted harshly. 'Nine of them were recaptured this morning. They will be given a few hours to see priests if they wish, and make known their last wishes. But before sunset they will be dancing at the end of ropes.'

18

Fate Strikes Again

FOR a moment Roger gazed at the Marshal in horror.
Several of the prisoners had been shot while trying to
escape, and now nine who had been recaptured were to
be hanged. He had no doubt that Charles was among the
latter.

Fantastic as it seemed, the scene Georgina had witnessed in her crystal had, after all, been a true vision of
the future. Even more fantastic, Fate had caused him to
travel many hundreds of miles uselessly and delayed him
again and again in his search for Charles, yet brought him
within a few miles of the place where a rope was to be put
round his neck, on the very day he was condemned to die.
Clearly this was the work of Providence; there could be
no doubt of that.

But suddenly it flashed into Roger's mind that the issue
was not yet settled. Unless he could reach Schloss Bergedorf within an hour or so it might be too late. He might
find Charles's body, with that of eight others, dangling
from the branches of trees. Without another word to
Davout, he turned and strode toward the door.

'Halt!' came the sharp command from behind him.

Automatically he obeyed and again faced the Marshal,
who glowered at him and said, 'You seem to have forgotten the respect due to a senior officer, Colonel.'

Roger saluted. 'My apologies, Your Highness. The peril in which my nephew stands drove all other thoughts temporarily from my mind.'

'You seem very attached to this nephew of yours.'

'I am indeed.'

'Yet you are citizens of different countries, which have for many years been at war. You cannot have seen him since he was a child.'

Galling as it was to Roger to have to waste precious moments giving an explanation to the Marshal, there was no avoiding it, and he replied, 'As I stated a moment back, Highness, by blood I am half English. Moreover, I was brought up there, and still have many acquaintances in that country who believe me to be an Englishman. His Imperial Majesty has long been aware of this, and on numerous occasions has sent me to England in secret to report to him upon the morale of our enemies. During these visits, which were at times several months in duration, I naturally saw a great deal of my relations.'

Davout nodded. 'So that is the way of things. Even so, you could not have known that the boy was likely to be hanged, and merely to obtain his release I marvel that you should have risked showing yourself in northern Germany.'

'I see no reason why I should have feared to do so,' Roger replied, inwardly fuming at having to carry on this conversation when every minute was so precious. 'Your Highness's being in command of this territory is guarantee enough that, apart from exceptional circumstances, all French officers are safe here.'

'You are right, but you mention exceptional circumstances—and they apply to you.'

'In what way, may I ask?'

'Surely you have not forgotten that in 1810 you were

tried by a Prussian court for the murder of your wife and the Baron von Haugwitz, found guilty and condemned to death?'

Roger frowned. 'I recall very vividly, Highness, that most unpleasant experience, resulting from my being unable to prove my innocence. Also that I owe my life to your having induced the King of Prussia to commute my sentence to ten years' imprisonment.'

'I felt that I could do no less for a French officer whom I knew to have served my Emperor well on numerous occasions. But I was thinking of the present. When we met again last year in Russia, you told me that you served only a few months of your sentence, then succeeded in escaping when being transferred from one prison to another, through an attack on the convoy by a mob of rebellious students. Now that Prussia has betrayed us and become our enemy, owing to the great scarcity of food bodies of Prussian troops frequently raid my territory in the hope of securing supplies. Should you run into one of these raiding parties and someone in it chances to recognise you, I've not a doubt but that they'll carry you off with them to serve the other nine years or more of your sentence.'

Giving a hasty glance at the clock with frantic anxiety, Roger saw that it was now past five. As it was late October there could not be much more than an hour of daylight left. Swallowing hard, he said, 'That is a chance, Highness, that I must take. I beg you now excuse me.' Then he saluted and ran from the room.

Below in the stables he found a sergeant farrier, who picked out for him a good, strong horse and had it saddled up. Since being shot through the calf, Roger had ridden only on a few occasions and then at a walk. He had not yet even attempted to wear riding boots, but swathed his legs in spirals of blue cloth. Now, ride he must and at the fastest pace he could manage, for Charles's life hung on a matter of minutes.

While the horse was being saddled he got out his map to make certain of the road to Bergedorf. It lay on a main road south-east of Hamburg and he must have passed within three miles of it that morning. Mounting the horse he found it more mettlesome than he could have wished, and had difficulty in holding it back to a trot as soon as he had passed out of the great gateway.

Now that he was trotting for the first time, the pressure of his wounded leg on the horse's side hurt less than he had expected; so, having covered half a mile and knowing only too well the necessity for speed, he broke into a canter. Another mile and the leg began to hurt him so he eased the pace, for he dared not risk his wound opening again and cause him to lose his grip, with the risk of being thrown from the saddle.

Luckily, the way was fairly flat, with no steep gradients which would have put a further strain upon him. But by the time he had covered half the distance he was sweating profusely and with each jolt of the horse a sharp stab of pain ran up his leg.

With half-closed eyes and clenching his teeth, he pressed on, trotting and cantering alternately. At last he sighted the Schloss, standing on a rise above a village, but it was still two miles off. Glancing down at his burning leg, he saw that the blue bandage was now stained with crimson. As he had feared, the wound had re-opened and must be bleeding freely. By the time he was clattering on the cobbles through the village street the whole of his lower leg was covered with blood and it was dripping from his boot. But there could be no question of pulling up. Rounding a bend he came opposite the gates of the Schloss. At the sight of his uniform a sentry presented arms. But Roger ignored him. It was all he could now do to keep in the saddle.

Ahead, leading up to the Schloss stood a long avenue of lindens. His sight misted by pain, he saw that several score of troops were gathered in the avenue. They formed two long lines and there were several smaller groups beneath the trees. As, with his last reserve of strength, he galloped up the slope, his vision cleared. The nearest group of soldiers was standing below a body that swung from the branch of a tree. The next group was hauling on a rope to hoist a second victim. Beyond, hatless and with their hands bound behind them, stood seven escapers among other groups. In the queue awaiting death Roger saw Charles.

In front of the two lines of soldiers stood several officers. One, obviously the commander of the garrison, was walking slowly up and down. He came to a halt as Roger approached and stared enquiringly at him. Roger pulled up beside him and slid from his horse. As his wounded leg touched the ground, it gave under him and he caught at the arm the officer extended to him. Next moment, as they stood face to face, they recognised each other. The garrison Commander was a Colonel Grandmaison, with whom Roger had served in Austria.

'Why, 'tis the *Comte de Breuc*!' Grandmaison exclaimed. 'How come you here, my dear fellow, and in such a state?'

With one hand Roger drew the Emperor's order from his pocket and thrust it at his friend; with the other he pointed at Charles and gasped, 'That man . . . the last but three in a row. The Earl of St. Ermins. This . . . this is a reprieve . . . an order that he is to be handed over to me.' Then he fainted.

K

When he came to, he was inside the Schloss and being carried up a stone staircase on a stretcher. Soon afterwards he was laid on a table. Colonel Grandmaison and several other people were gathered round him, one of whom was an army surgeon. He was given what he realised was an opium drink, then most of his clothes were taken off. Several men held him down while he squirmed and yelled during the agonising process of having his injured calf disinfected and sewn up again. After he had been put to bed in another room he managed to ask Grandmaison if Charles could be sent to him.

The Colonel agreed, and five minutes later the soldier who had been left to supply Roger's need of anything let Charles in. His face was still drawn and pale from having recently so narrowly escaped death, but his eyes lit up and he was about to rush forward and pour out his thanks to Roger for having saved his life, when Roger put a finger to his lips enjoining silence.

Having sent the soldier from the room, Roger beckoned Charles to his bedside, made him kneel down and said in a low voice, 'I have told the Emperor and Marshal Davout that you are my nephew; but they, and everyone else in the French Army believe me to be a Frenchman, born in Strasbourg, the son of a Frenchman who married your aunt. In England it is known only to a few statesmen that I am a Count and Colonel in the French Army. Everyone else believes me to be an English eccentric who has spent the greater part of his life travelling in distant lands. Remember these things, Charles, for my life depends on them, and avoid talking about me whenever possible.'

Charles, weeping with gratitude, readily promised; then, having given Roger another opium drink, sat by him until he managed to get off to sleep.

The days that followed were agonising for Roger and

very anxious ones for Charles. Twenty-four hours after his arrival at Schloss Bergedorf, Roger's leg began to swell and the wound go purple at the edges. There could be no doubt that the blue dye in the strips of cloth he had wound round his leg had got into his bloodstream and poisoned it.

He had to submit to the pain of having the gangrenous strips of flesh cut away and the wound being restitched. But that failed to avert the menace. The following day the signs of poisoning appeared again, and the surgeon gave his opinion that the only certain way of saving Roger's life was to amputate his leg below the knee. However, on being pressed by Charles, the sawbones admitted that there was just a chance that further cutting away of the flesh might make amputation unnecessary. Upon this the wretched Roger, his brain a prey to delusions caused by opium and three-parts drunk on brandy, yet still capable of feeling acute pain, submitted for the third time to the surgeon's knife and needle.

A period of great anxiety followed, but on November 1st, Roger's sixth day at Schloss Bergedorf, the surgeon was satisfied that the second operation had been successful. These days of constant pain had cost Roger a stone in weight. Combined with the loss of blood and fear of being crippled for life, they had left him very weak. It was no surprise to him, therefore, when he was told that it would be several weeks before he could hope to travel and, anxious as he was to get home, he made no protest.

*   *   *

It was during the time when Roger was so desperately ill that an event occurred in London which was to bring Susan into dire peril.

One morning towards the end of October, just as
Jemima was about to go out shopping with Lady Luggala,
a running footman arrived with a letter for her. It was
from her mother, and asked that both of them should
come to her as a matter of the utmost urgency. As their
carriage was already at the door, they drove straight to
Islington.

There they found the witch's house a scene of great
activity. The servants were packing silver and linen into
hampers in the hall, while the witch and her high priest,
the lean Father Damien, were busily parcelling up magi-
cal implements and packets of precious drugs in the drawing room.

No sooner had the door closed behind her visitors than
the witch cried angrily, 'My dears, it is a shocking blow
that we have suffered. That fool Cornelius Quelp has
allowed himself to be trapped.'

'Oh dear!' exclaimed Jemima. 'How did it happen?'

'A French émigré, one of the old, sour kind who refused
to return to France when the Emperor proclaimed an
amnesty and has long been in the pay of the English,
wormed his way into the Dutchman's confidence. He was
arrested yesterday and charged at Bow Street with being
a French secret agent. The evidence against him was
irrefutable and it is in the Tower that he is now. A friend
of his brought the news to me in the middle of the night.'

'Obviously you are leaving, so I take it you fear he may
betray us,' said Maureen Luggala unhappily.

It was Father Damien who answered her. 'The Mynheer is a courageous man and much attached to us, so I
do not believe he would betray us lightly, but the brutal
English may force him to.'

'The English are not brutal in that way,' Jemima volunteered. 'They have long given up torturing prisoners.'

'There are other means of securing information from prisoners,' the priest retorted. 'They could promise to release him if he provided them with a list of his associates.'

'It is that I fear,' the witch put in, 'and Father Damien and I would head the list, since it was from us that he obtained the greater part of the information he took to France.'

'Oh my! Oh my!' Lady Luggala wrung her hands. 'Then all of us are ruined.'

'Nay. 'Tis I who am ruined. Another year or two in London and I could have made a fortune out of the Hell Fire Club. Now I must abandon it and leave the country.'

'You mean to return to Ireland?'

'Yes, although since the English rule there, even that may be dangerous if Quelp discloses his dealings with me. Where else could I go?'

'You might find a smuggler who would run you over to France,' Jemima suggested.

'It would take time to find one, child, and time is precious. Besides, the stars are no longer favourable to the Emperor. He is far from finally defeated yet, but Leipzig was, I am convinced, the turn of the tide for him. This latest combination of so many nations allied against him must end in his downfall. Those stupid Bourbons will then return. But they are not such fools as to neglect having all the secret papers they secure gone through most carefully. Quelp's will show the sums paid to me for the information supplied to him. Then, should I be in France, I'd be in constant danger of being identified and sent to the gallows. No, Ireland it must be; and that, Maureen, is why I sent for you.'

'You mean to take Jemima and me with you?'

'No, no!' the witch spoke impatiently. 'The fact that

you both met the Dutchman here a few times is no proof
that you were involved in his activities, any more than
were the men and women who came to participate in our
Hell Fire orgies. Neither of you is in any danger; but I
need your help in securing a safe refuge in Ireland. I dare
not settle in Dublin. It is too well that I am known there.
And I've no mind to pig it in some peasant's cottage. It
occurred to me that Father Damien and I could lie low
in that castle of your late husband's, at Luggala. But I'll
need a letter of authority from you for us to occupy it.'

Greatly relieved that she would not, as she had feared,
have to flee the country, Maureen replied eagerly, 'What
an excellent idea. I'll write to the bailiff with pleasure.
But you do realise, don't you, that the castle has not
been lived in for many years, so a lot will have to be done
to make it really comfortable.'

'That is of no great moment. Father Damien and I will
need the use of only a few rooms, and your bailiff can
get people in from the village to clean them up for us.'

While they were talking, the priest had left the room
and returned with a decanter of Madeira. As he poured
the wine for all of them, the witch finished packing the
last bag of herbs into a straw basket. Sitting down, she
asked Jemima :

'Tell me, child, how do your relations with young Susan
progress? It is some weeks since we have talked of this.'

Jemima pulled a face. 'Alas, I cannot tell you that they
do progress. It is now long since I established myself as her
best friend. We see one another frequently and talk with
the greatest intimacy. She has no secrets from me—that
I'll swear. And in many things I can influence her without
difficulty, yet I am no nearer dominating her mind than I
was six months ago.'

'That is disappointing. I'd hoped with time you would

achieve hypnotic power over her, and so be able to make her commit acts which would ruin her in Charles's eyes when he returns.'

'I have tried, Mama, but my efforts have proved in vain. It is not that she is a prude or sexually frigid. Indeed, she confessed to me not long since that, at the time Charles made that unfortunate scene here during a meeting of the Club, she was in half a mind to take a lover and, heaven knows, there are a dozen beaux into whose arms I have tried to push her. Yet she'll not give more than a kiss to any of them. She says that when Charles went to the wars, she vowed to herself that she'd remain a virgin until his return, however long that might be.'

'It may not now be very long, for all the portents tell me that, in a matter of months, the war will be over. I've not told you of it, child, but in recent weeks I've been much worried for Charles. Some great danger seemed to hang over him; something quite unforeseeable, for owing to the ritual that you and I performed upon his leaving, he is protected from all the normal hazards of war. But he has passed through this period of adversity unharmed.'

'Thanks be for that,' Jemima sighed. 'Yet, since my hopes of having the gossips dub Susan a society whore have failed so lamentably, my chances with him will be no better than when he went away.'

The witch patted her daughter's cheek. 'Do not lose heart, little one. We will lure Susan to Castle Luggala. You must bring her there as your guest, and then . . .'

'But, Mama, she would recognise you at once. How could she fail to do so, having seen you that night when Captain Hawksbury brought her here and she ruined your celebration? She'd flee the place the moment she set eyes on you.'

'Nay, you are in error there. She might wish to flee, but

I'd find no difficulty in holding her at the castle against her will.'

Father Damien chuckled. 'And we would put her to good use. I recall her well from the night she made that grievous scene here. The thought of her nude makes me lick my lips. I'd take great joy in relieving her of her virginity.'

'You lecherous fellow,' Maureen Luggala smiled at him. 'The very thought of you forcing her makes me feel randy.'

The lean priest gave a grin, leaned forward and took her by the arm. 'If that's the case, m'dear, let's go upstairs to my room. It wouldn't be the first good bout we've had together, and maybe we'll not have a chance to have another for some time.'

Maureen gave a breathless little laugh, and stood up. 'I regret only that, in the circumstances, it must be a short one.'

When they had left the room together Jemima remarked to her mother, 'How Maureen can possibly enjoy being had by that repulsive man passes my comprehension.'

Katie O'Brien shrugged. 'My dear, had you been had by him yourself you would understand it. He is a stallion of the first order and positively tireless. To any woman passionate by nature he is a gift from the gods. I have even seen women faint with pleasure under him. His control is perfect and he can bring me to a climax four times to his once.'

'What!' Jemima's eyes widened and she exclaimed. 'D'you mean you've actually allowed that loathsome creature to make love with you?'

'I have indeed. And so has every female member of the Hell Fire Club. It is he who initiates them.'

'Mama, you amaze me! How can they possibly bring themselves to submit when knowing nothing of his special power to drive them half crazy with sexual enjoyment? The very feel of his slobbering mouth on mine would make me vomit.'

'They are warned beforehand that they may find their initiation an ordeal, so steel themselves to it. Besides, there is an occult significance to the act. In the old days it is said that to become a member of a coven a woman had first to copulate with Satan. That too may have actually occurred, as in witch trials the accused frequently confessed it and told of their initiation as a mixture of ecstatic delight with hideous pain. They described Satan's member as huge, as cold as ice and barbed like an arrow, so that its motion tore their vaginas and they bled profusely even while screaming from a succession of erotic climaxes more rewarding than any human had ever given them.

'Yet, I doubt not that in most cases it was a man designedly made hideous who performed upon them. In any case, willing submission to a repulsive being was the price they had to pay if they wished to achieve occult power. And that is why I selected Father Damien to play the part of Satan.'

Jemima sighed, 'Eager as I am to become a witch, I find him so disgusting that I fear I could never bring myself to let him have me.'

'That, child, is unfortunate, as I know that ever since he first set eyes on you he has desired you. In fact, more than once, he has begged me to let you be initiated with that in view. You know my reasons for having refused. I'd not risk it even becoming rumoured in London society that you had become a member of the Club. But the Club is now finished, so when you come to Ireland that will not apply. I am in hopes that you will think again upon it and overcome your repugnance to him, at least for once, in order that you may attain occult power.'

'I'll consider it,' Jemima agreed reluctantly, 'although the idea of having that old goat naked upon me fills me with disgust. And did you really mean that you would force Susan to let him take her virginity?'

'I might if it suited my purpose. The thing is do you think you could persuade her to accompany you to Ireland?'

'Yes. I'm confident that I could, without much trouble.'

'Then you need no longer worry your pretty head about the future. I will so handle matters that, soon after Charles returns from war, he will make you Countess of St. Ermins.'

*　　　*　　　*

It was not until the last week in November that Roger was able to leave his bed. While confined there everything possible was done for him. Dopet was sent for from Herrenhausen to act as his soldier servant. His old friend, Colonel Grandmaison, visited him daily and, although food throughout the whole countryside was terribly scarce, saw to it that the invalid had the best of everything that could be procured. Now that Charles was officially Roger's prisoner, he was no longer confined with his German fellow captives, and was allowed out for walks on parole, but he spent a good part of his time at Roger's bedside, either reading to him or bringing such news as there was.

No-one knew for certain what was happening in the south, but it was said that the survivors of Napoleon's army had straggled back to the Rhine, and at that river, on which there were many fortresses strongly garrisoned by the French, the retreat had been checked. The Emperor, it was rumoured, had reached Paris on the 9th and was frantically at work there raising yet another army. Meanwhile, the Austrians and Russians were cautiously infiltrating into the Rhine Provinces, delaying to advance further before reducing French-held cities in them.

After Roger had been able to get up for a few days Colonel Grandmaison placed at his disposal a carriage in which to go for drives with Charles. Twice they drove into Hamburg and were shocked by the woebegone appearance of the remaining, half-starved inhabitants.

These drives along the shore also filled them with an infuriating frustration. Ever since Sweden had joined the Allies, the Baltic had again been open to British shipping, and the Skaggerak swarmed with British warships. Almost daily they bombarded the Danish ports and the fortresses of Hamburg. Often they sailed impudently up and down the mouth of the Elbe, within easy swimming distance of the land. If only Roger and Charles could have got aboard one of them, that would have been an end to their troubles. But Davout kept his shore patrols extremely alert, to prevent Hamburgers getting out to the ships with useful information; so, even had Roger been his old self, any attempt to swim off one night would have entailed great danger. As it was, still crippled and very weak, such a project was out of the question.

Never before had Roger and Charles spent so long constantly together, and both derived great pleasure from getting to know each other really well. Charles had always admired his 'Uncle Roger', but had been a little awed by him, while Roger had previously looked on Charles as no more than a promising youth. But now they were able to appreciate each other's real qualities and talked together as equals. As Roger's health improved, they discussed more frequently what they should do when he was well enough to leave Hamburg, and they came to the conclusion that their best plan would be to endeavour to reach France as, with Roger's long experience of that country's northern ports, they offered the best prospect of contacting a smuggler who would run them over to England.

To have again used the Mess cart that had brought Roger to Hamburg would have meant travelling very slowly, so Colonel Grandmaison agreed that Roger might take the smallest of three coaches that the owner of the castle had left in the coach-house before taking to flight, and their departure was fixed for November 30th.

As the state of the country was so unsettled, it was decided that they should travel in civilian clothes; so, on the day before they left, they went into Hamburg where Roger bought a suit for Charles, another, better-fitting one than that in which he had left Leipzig for himself, and a suitable costume for Dopet who was to act as coachman. Then all three of them packed their uniforms in a valise.

On the 30th, with the good wishes of Colonel Grandmaison, the surgeon who had looked after Roger, and numerous other people, they set off. By this time Roger had only enough money left to see them back to France, and to bribe a smuggler to put them across the Channel would require a considerable sum, so he decided to make first for Paris, as there he could draw from the Paymaster at the Ministry of War as much as he required.

The most direct route to Paris lay by way of Bremen, Osnabrück, Münster, Dortmund, Cologne and Rheims, but such scant intelligence as they had implied that the Prussians had already reached the lower Rhine and the frontier of Holland. In consequence Reger decided that in order not to run the risks of crossing a battle area it would be wiser, instead of heading for Cologne, to make a considerable detour and head for the Frankfurt-Mainz area which had for years been so strongly held by the French that it would almost certainly still be in their hands. So, from Dortmund, they turned south-west and took by-roads through the Westerwald and Tannus on their way to Mainz.

Two afternoons after leaving Dortmund they were approaching Wiesbaden. On rounding a bend in the road, to Roger's surprise they suddenly came on an outpost of Prussian infantry. A Captain called on them to halt. The coach pulled up and Roger put his head out of the window. The officer asked where they had come from. Roger replied 'Dortmund'. There followed other questions, to all of which Roger glibly gave answers which he had already thought up in case of such a challenge. The Captain seemed satisfied, until he asked them to produce proofs of their identity. That they could not do. His face then took on a stern look and he said :

'I regret, *Herrschaft,* but there are many adherents of the arch-fiend Bonaparte still at large on this side of the Rhine, and some of them are spies. I must search your luggage.'

At that Roger went slightly pale, for he knew that they were now in a very tight corner. With apparent calm he shrugged and agreed. Anxiously he watched as their portmanteaux were unstrapped and taken down by some of the soldiers from the coach roof. The first to be opened was that which held the uniforms and there, neatly folded, right on top, was Roger's dark-blue tail coat with its gold epaulettes and the cross of a Commander of the Legion of Honour on the breast.

Too late he cursed himself as a fool for not having left

it behind. But he had expected to change into it after crossing the Rhine, as once in France, it would have assured him a coach with four horses and priority at the Posthouses for the remainder of their journey to Paris.

'*Donnerwetter*!' exclaimed the Prussian officer. 'What have we here?'

'A souvenir, *Herr Kapitan*,' Roger asserted swiftly. 'I acquired it for twenty marks from a hospital orderly in Münster.'

'*Ach so*!' the Captain scowled. 'That we shall see.' Picking up the coat with one hand, he drew a pistol from his belt with the other, pointed it at Roger and added:

'Get out of the coach. Hand the pistol in your belt to my sergeant, then take your coat off and put this one on.'

There was nothing for it but to obey, so Roger stepped down into the road and put on his uniform coat. It fitted like a glove.

'As I thought,' sneered the Prussian. 'You are a dog of a Frenchman, trying to get across the river to your swinish countrymen.'

While he had been speaking a sergeant had taken from the portmanteau the soiled but still bright scarlet uniform of the Coldstream Guards, in which Charles had been captured. The Captain stared at it for a moment, then said, 'That is not a French uniform. Surely it is English. How comes it here?'

'It is mine,' declared Charles in his excellent German. 'I am a British officer.'

'If that be so, what are you doing in the company of this French spawn of hell?'

Charles smiled. 'I am his prisoner, *Herr Kapitan*, or was until you appeared on the scene and rescued me. I am travelling with him only because he had captured me and, in exchange for my life, I gave him my parole.'

For a moment Roger was quite shocked that Charles should have so brazenly gone over to the enemy. But then he saw the sense of it. Not to have claimed immunity as an ally of the Prussians would have been absurd, and had their positions been reversed it was what he would have done himself.

The third uniform was obviously Dopet's and, as he could speak only a few words of German, he was swiftly identified as Roger's servant. A soldier mounted the box in his place and he was ordered into the coach. Roger was told to change back into his civilian coat and the three uniforms were repacked in the portmanteaux. The Captain then put his Lieutenant in charge of the prisoners and despatched them in the coach with a small escort up the road.

After about a mile it emerged from the pine woods to some open farmlands, on the far side of which was a fair-sized farmhouse. The coach pulled up in front of it. The prisoners were ordered out and marched inside. In a room on the right of the entrance an adjutant was sitting at a table on which there was a litter of papers. The Lieutenant reported to him and the prisoners were brought it.

Roger now had a choice. He could swear that he was in fact a British secret agent, and hope that Charles's testimony would convince them that he was speaking the truth; or admit that he was a French officer. But he feared that if he took the former course it was more likely that Charles's testimony in his favour would make the Prussians believe that Charles was a liar and also a Frenchman in disguise. In consequence, when questioned by the adjutant, he decided that it would be better to ensure at least Charles's continued freedom by maintaining his own supposed rôle and by giving his high rank in hope of good treatment.

To have been caught like this when so nearly out of the wood was utterly infuriating, but he endeavoured to console himself with the thought that it was unlikely that he would remain a prisoner for very long. The Emperor's army had been shattered. It would prove impossible for even him to raise another of even a third the size of the forces now arrayed against him. North, south, east and west, he was menaced and surrounded by bitter enemies who were determined to put an end his career as a wholesale murderer. Either he must save all that remained to him of his Empire by agreeing to an humiliating peace in the near future, or be completely crushed soon after the New Year. So, in either case, Roger felt that he could count on being restored to liberty within a few months at most.

He had only just given particulars of himself to the adjutant when a babble of guttural German voices sounded in the narrow hall of the farmhouse. A Colonel put his head round the door and looked in. The adjutant cried to him joyfully.

'*Herr Oberst,* we have just taken an important prisoner. No less than *Colonel Comte de Breuc,* a Commander of the Legion of Honour and one of Napoleon's A.D.C.s.'

The Colonel turned and spoke to his companions outside. Next moment they came pressing into the room, led by a burly figure with a grey, walrus moustache, dressed in a plain, ill-fitting jacket, wearing a floppy, peaked cap and smoking a meerschaum pipe. Roger recognised him at once from descriptions he had had, as Blücher.

At that date the veteran was seventy-one. He was a rough, illiterate man who had the sense to realise his shortcomings as a strategist and rely for planning on his brilliant Chief-of-Staff, Gneisenau; but he was a fearless, ferocious leader and, in spite of his age, still seething with fiery energy. The previous May he had put up a magnificent resistance against great odds at the battle of Lützen. Later at Katezbach, he had defeated Marshal Macdonald, captured eighteen thousand prisoners and over one hundred guns. It was he who had delivered the most telling assault on Leipzig and had been made a Field Marshal for it.

For a moment he regarded Roger with interest. Then the excited voice of a young Uhlan officer in the background suddenly cut the silence, 'Breuc, did you say? The *Comte de Breuc*?'

The adjutant looked in his direction and replied, 'Yes, von Zeiten, this is the *Comte de Breuc*.'

'*Gott im Himmel*,' cried the Uhlan. 'It is the murderer! It was he who foully did to death his wife and my uncle, von Haugwitz, at Schloss Langenstein in 1810.'

Roger swung round to face him and retorted hotly. 'That is a lie. I was accused of their deaths, but was innocent.'

Young von Zeiten pushed his way to the front of the group and thrust out an accusing arm. 'I recognise you now. I was in court when you were tried and condemned to death.'

'Why, then, is he still alive?' asked Blücher gruffly.

'His sentence, *Herr Feldmarschall*, was commuted to ten years' imprisonment. But he escaped after a few months.'

Roger had not yet recovered from the shock of once more being identified as the man found guilty of the double death at Schloss Langenstein. His brain was whirling, but not so confused that he could not guess the awful fate that now threatened him. Next moment the doom he dreaded was pronounced by Blücher.

'Then send him back to Berlin to complete his sentence.'

As the Fieldmarshal turned away, Roger stared at the ring of hostile faces, rendered speechless by this terrible blow that Fate had dealt him. Whether, in a few months' time Napoleon agreed to an humiliating peace or was utterly crushed and dethroned could now make no difference to him. Instead of regaining his freedom, his lot was to suffer imprisonment among enemy criminals for all that remained of the best years of his life.

19

The House with the Red Shield

BLÜCHER and his staff left the room. The guard was summoned to take charge of Roger and Dopet. As the former was led away he was careful not to look at Charles. He knew how distressed the boy must be, and for him to have shown sympathy for his supposed enemy might have aroused the Prussians' suspicions that he was not, after all, a British officer. To Roger it was at least some compensation that he had saved the life of his beloved Georgina's son, and that Charles was still free to rejoin her as soon as he was able to do so.

From the hallway Dopet was pushed out of the farmhouse toward some tents in a nearby field; but Roger was taken downstairs and locked up in a cellar which still contained two flitches of bacon hanging from the ceiling and a few sacks of meal in a corner.

The cellar was lit only by a small, iron grille near the ceiling. In the dim light Roger sat down on one of the sacks and ruefully contemplated his misfortune. To have to face years in prison without hope of remission was in itself one of the most terrible things that could befall a man; but in his case it would prove even more insufferable than simply confinement and being debarred from all life's pleasures. This he knew only too well after having spent three months in a prison outside Berlin. There he had been in the position of a solitary Frenchman among Germans. Such had been the hatred of the Prussians of all classes for the French as despoilers of their country that the other convicts had done everything they could to make his lot more miserable. Although regulations decreed silence when exercising in the yards, they always exchanged the news that came through the prison grapevine, and talked in whispers. But Roger had been denied even this small relaxation, because they had sent him to Coventry That had also prevented him securing assistance to attempt an escape which might have been arranged with careful planning by a group, but was impossible for him unaided. And he had no doubt at all that, once he was back in a Prussian state prison, he would be treated by his fellow convicts as he had been before.

After about two hours a sergeant and two troopers came for him. They then escorted him upstairs and out of the farmhouse to the coach in which he had arrived, which was waiting outside the door. The sergeant, a big man with a walrus moustache, a mane of yellow hair and bright blue eyes, produced a length of cord, tied one end of it round his left wrist and the other round Roger's right. They then got into the coach. The two troopers mounted on to the box. One took the reins, shook them and the coach moved off.

When they had covered a mile or so they came to a signpost and Roger saw from it that they were taking the road to Frankfurt. That surprised him, as he had imagined that stronghold of the French to be still in their hands and that they would have strong outposts ringing the city for some miles round. But as the coach rolled on, the only soldiers to be seen were occasional troops of Uhlans, Prussian grenadiers and convoys supplying Blücher's army.

The December afternoon had been drawing in when they started, and by the time they had covered the fifteen miles to the city it was fully dusk. The coach pulled up at an indifferent-looking inn a few hundred yards past the splendid Gothic Staathaus. With Roger still tied to him the sergeant showed the landlord a billeting order and parleyed with him for a few minutes, then Roger was taken upstairs to a room on the second floor.

Having untied the cord attached to their wrists the sergeant, who spoke a little French, made it clear that if Roger attempted to escape he had orders to shoot him, and that during the night one of his men would sleep in the passage on a palliasse outside the door. Then he locked Roger in.

Going to the window, Roger parted the worn curtains and looked out. The room was at the back of the house and below him lay the stable yard. A man carrying a lantern was watering a horse down there, and by its light Roger could faintly make out the outline of the buildings round the yard. Up there on the second floor he was at least twenty-five feet from the ground, but the roof of the lowest floor projected about two feet from the wall of the building. By hanging from the window sill his toes would have been only about five feet from that projection. Even in full health and not crippled, to risk a drop on to such a narrow ledge would have been extremely hazardous. As it was, still weak from his recent illness and with his right leg as yet barely able to take his weight, he realised that to attempt the drop would be madness. He would certainly break his leg as it hit the ledge and, on falling from it, probably his neck.

With a sigh he turned away and sat down on the edge of the bed. Looking out of the window had brought home to him acutely that, in any attempt to escape, he must not

count on using even moderate strength; his only hope lay
in outwitting his escort.

Presently a tray was brought in to him by one of the
troopers. On it there were two *brodchen* filled with
leberwurst, a piece of *apfelstrudel* and a mug of cheap
draught wine. Slowly he ate his supper, pondering possible ways to fool the yellow-haired sergeant, but could
think of none.

There was no heating in the room, so it was bitterly
cold. Having examined the bedclothes he found they were
far from clean, as might be expected in a second-rate inn.
To sleep between them in only his underclothes would
be to invite the attention of bed-bugs and probably lice.
So he shook them all out, lay down fully dressed, then
piled them on top of himself for warmth.

Having snuffed the solitary candle that the landlord had
lit before leaving him in the room, he thought for a while
of Georgina and wondered if he would ever see her again.
Then he thought of poor little Mary, whom he had
deserted to come on this ill-fated mission. He now felt that
he had treated her unduly harshly for having interfered
in his affairs. But they had made it up before parting, and
he could only hope that she would find some way of
making a not too unhappy life for herself when Charles
got home and told her that her husband was in
prison, with little hope of returning home for years
to come.

After a while he began to wonder how the war was
going, as for a long time past he had heard only vague
rumours about it. That the French had been driven from
Frankfurt showed them to be in very poor shape. But he
thought it probable that they still held Mainz, as the
barrier of the broad Rhine would prove a serious obstacle
for any considerable force; and the dynamic Blücher's

headquarters being on the right bank seemed a cer
indication that the French were holding the left
strength. He was still vaguely speculating on how long th
war would continue when he drifted off into an uneas
sleep.

He was roused by a persistent tapping, occurring at
brief intervals. As his mind cleared, he realised that it came
from the window. Thrusting the blankets from him, he
limped quickly over to it and pulled aside the curtain.
It was pitch dark below, but outlined against the star-lit
winter sky were the head and shoulders of a man.

With sudden hope leaping in his heart, Roger strove
to get the window open. It had probably been shut for
years and resisted all his efforts. He dared not break the
glass, for fear that the noise would rouse the soldier who
was sleeping outside his door. Now desperate at the knowledge that the chance of escape was so near, yet still barred
to him, he racked his brains frantically for a means of
prising the window up. A possibility flashed into his mind.
Hurrying back to the bedside table, he picked up th
tray on which his supper had been brought, shot the contents on to the bed and re-crossed the room with it. The
tray was oblong, about fourteen inches by twenty-four and
made of iron with plain, thin edges. Holding it by the
sides, he jammed one of the narrow ends into the crack
between the frame of the window and the sill. Using all
his force he managed to insert it far enough to grip; then
using it as a lever, heaved back on it. The wood groane
and gave a trifle, so that the tray came free. Thrustin
in again, Roger repeated the process. With a sigh of
he felt a rush of cold air as the window open
good inch. Eager hands from outside grasped and hea
it up.

'Charles, bless you !' Roger whispered.

'Dam'me, I thought you'd never hear my tapping,' Charles replied with a low laugh. 'Come now, can you manage to follow me down this ladder?'

'Yes,' Roger nodded. 'I'll be all right.' Then, as Charles descended a few rungs to make way for him, he scrambled over the window sill out into the dark night.

When they reached the yard Charles murmured, 'Had I not had the luck to find this ladder, God knows how I could have got to you. But if we leave it where it is it will be seen by anyone coming to the stables and give premature warning of your escape.'

Taking the ladder away from the wall they carried it into the shed where Charles had come upon it, then he said, 'Now we must find you a horse. Soon after you were taken from Blücher's H.Q., I made off with a mare on which to follow you, but ...'

'Charles,' Roger interrupted him. 'You have performed a feat that does you the greatest credit. I'm truly proud of you, as your dear mother will be when I tell her of this night's work, and prodigiously grateful. You can scarce imagine the horrors you have saved me from and, crippled as I am, my chances of escaping were next to nil. Speaking of which, though I can mount a horse, I'm not yet capable of riding either fast or far. I gravely doubt me if we could keep a lead for long, once they send mounted men in pursuit of me.'

'What alternative have we but to attempt that?'

'To lie low here in Frankfurt until my leg is again sufficiently strong to stand up to a hard day's riding. Our problem is to find trustworthy people who would be willing to hide us. I know of only one, and him I have not seen for many years. Even to reveal our identities to him will prove a gamble; but I judge it to be a risk worth taking.'

'Who is he?' Charles asked as they moved out into the deserted street.

'He is a Jew, and it is all of eighteen years since I had dealings with him. It was in September '95, a year or so after the fall of Robespierre. A reaction against the Terrorists had set in, and it was thought possible that one of the Republican Generals might be induced to bring about a Restoration, as did General Monk in the case of your ancestor King Charles II.'

Roger had already turned in the direction of the *Stuathaus* and, as they walked along together, he went on, 'It was decided that, for our purpose, the best bet was a very able General named Pichegru. At that time he was commanding an army with his headquarters at Mannheim, and in the same theatre General Jourdan was commanding another on the north bank of the Necker. They were some distance apart, but both operating against two Austrian armies, commanded by Generals Wurmser and Clerfayt, and a third force of Royalist Frenchmen under the Prince de Condé.

'The mission on which Mr. Pitt sent me was, first to see the Prince and obtain from him a signed promise that Pichegru should be made a Duke and receive numerous other benefits including a large sum of money, then take it to Pichegru and endeavour to persuade him, in exchange, to lead his army on Paris instead of against the Austrians.

'I succeeded in getting Pichegru's agreement, but for one thing. He required an assurance that when he arrived outside Paris with his army, the bulk of the population in the capital would not be opposed to a Restoration. The only way to make certain of that was for me to go there and find out.

'That I was willing to do, but time was a vital factor.

It had already been agreed by Jourdan and Pichegru that the latter should make a dash on Heidelberg. By joining forces there they would have been in a position to defeat the two Austrian armies one after the other. To bring about an end to the war was the main inducement for the Parisians to welcome a change of Government, so if the Austrians were defeated and sued for peace, Pichegru would have no case to call for a Restoration.

'As England was providing the money to bribe Pichegru, I had been entrusted with an open order on the British Treasury. To gain the time needed to save the situation I offered to pay Pichegru a million francs if he would postpone his march to join up with General Jourdan, and so save the Austrians from defeat.'

'A million francs!' exclaimed Charles. 'That is a mint of money.'

'Yes, fifty thousand pounds, and I had to find the money in gold at short notice. I shudder now at my own temerity. Had things gone wrong, or he gone back on his word, I should have been held responsible. Through other causes we failed to bring about a Restoration, but he sent only two divisions, instead of his whole army to join General Jourdan; so the Austrians were saved from a major defeat, which might well have put them out of the war, and that was worth the money. I got it from this Jew to whose house we are now going. I only hope that he is still alive and will prove friendly.'

As Roger had been telling of this mission he had undertaken during the wars of the Revolution, they had repassed the *Staathaus* in the main square of the city and, after taking several wrong turnings, he recognised the entrance of the narrow street he had been looking for.

'Ah, this is it!' he exclaimed. ''Tis called the *Judengasse*. In the old days not only were all the Jews in the city compelled to live here but chains were actually pad-locked across this entrance to keep them in at night. It is at least one thing to be said for the Revolution that, wherever the French went, they opened up the ghettoes.'

The street was so narrow that only a single vehicle could have been driven down it. As they advanced, Roger kept his eyes fixed on the upper storeys of the houses, from which hung signs of various designs, just visible in the starlight. Recognising one by its shape he pointed to it and said :

'That shield is painted red. Comparatively recently this family of Jewish bankers changed their name and took a new one from the shield. They are now known as the Rothschilds.'

As he spoke he turned and hammered with his clenched fist on the stout, iron-studded door of the house. There was no answer, so he told Charles to create a louder summons by kicking the door with his riding boot.

At length a light appeared, a grille in the door opened and a pair of dark eyes peered through. 'We are friends,' said Roger in German, 'and I wish urgently to speak with Herr Maier Amschel.'

'To our sorrow, my master died fifteen months ago,' replied a gruff voice.

'Then I must speak with one of his sons. You can say that I am an Englishman and that the British Treasury has already had dealings with this house through me.'

The grille closed, there followed an interval of about ten minutes, then came the sound of bolts being drawn back and the door was opened, but only a few inches, and it remained secured by a heavy chain.

A man in a loose robe, wearing a skull cap, surveyed them with shrewd, dark eyes and said, 'I am Anselm

Maier, the senior partner of this House. Why do you come here at this hour of the night?'

'You will not remember me,' Roger replied, 'for it is eighteen years since I was here. But you may recall the transaction, since you and two of your brothers were with your father at the time. In four days you succeeded in securing for me a million francs-worth of gold coin against an order on the British Treasury.'

The banker nodded. 'I do remember, because it was our first transaction of real importance with the English. And now, high-wellborn one, I vaguely recall your face.'

As he spoke he undid the chain, opened the door and bowed them in. His servant, who stood behind him, re-locked it while he led them through his counting house to a room behind it, lit candles and begged them to be seated at a round table of finely-polished, beautifully-grained wood.

Roger introduced himself and Charles by their proper names, then came at once to the point. 'I am in trouble with the Prussians. They believe me to have committed a murder of which I am innocent. I was being sent under escort to Berlin to be imprisoned, but tonight Lord St. Ermins here rescued me. Owing to a severe leg wound I have for some time been unable to ride fast without incurring great pain, so did we take horse from the city tonight we would almost certainly be caught. Our best hope is in lying low for some days. We will then stand a much better chance of getting away. I know no-one but yourself in Frankfurt, and I have no claim on you; yet I make so bold as to ask if you will allow us to remain in hiding here.'

Anselm Maier's expression did not change but he said quietly, 'I think, high-wellborn one, that you do have a claim on my house. Do you recall my second younger brother, Nathan?'

'Yes. He was then a young man of about eighteen. I have met him since, some years ago in London. He told me that he had spent some time in the north of England, and made a handsome profit in Manchester goods before moving to the capital.'

'That is correct. But you seem to have forgotten that he consulted you when we first met on the prospects of making good money in England. It was on your advice that he went there, and you fulfilled your promise of putting in a good word for him with a Mr. Rose, who was then head of your Treasury.'

Roger laughed. 'Yes, I recall that now. May I take it then that you will give Lord St. Ermins and me sanctuary for perhaps a week or so?'

'You will be my honoured guests, high-wellborn ones; and now permit me to offer you some refreshment.'

Standing up, Anselm Maier left the room and returned a few minutes later, followed by his servant. A bottle of wine was opened and dishes of motzas and saffron cakes set on the table. While enjoying a splendid Hock, they talked of the war and its recent developments, on which the Jewish banker proved to be extremely well informed.

He said the Allies had been very tardy in their advance after Leipzig, but had now reached the Rhine in a number of places. However, typhus was rampant among their troops, so it would probably be some time before they felt strong enough to cross the river. An Austrian army had entered eastern Switzerland, and a Prussian army under von Bülow had crossed the Dutch frontier. Bernadotte had left his allies to march south and swung his Swedes north-west through Hanover, with the obvious intention of besieging and capturing Hamburg from his hated enemy Davout.

At these last words Roger sadly shook his head and murmured to Charles, 'Had we only known, we could have remained in Hanover until the Swedes overran it. Then Bernadotte would have put us on a British ship, and in a week or so we'd have been safely home.'

The banker went on to tell them how, after Leipzig, Napoleon's Confederation of the Rhine had fallen to pieces. The score or more of petty Princes who had licked his boots and supplied him with troops and money for a generation had hastened to transfer their allegiance to Austria. To be allowed to rule independently again in their pocket kingdoms, they had promised to raise between them a quarter of a million men.

'It was through handling their business that the fortune of your family was founded, was it not?' asked Roger.

'Indeed yes, high-wellborn; particularly that of the Landgrave of Hesse, whose territories are far greater than those of any of the others. He was one of the richest sovereigns in Europe, and owed the greater part of his fortune to England. Before the coming of Napoleon all the common people in the Principality were serfs. Every year the Landgrave had the young men rounded up, at times as many as twelve thousand, and sold them as soldiers to the English, who sent them to fight in the Americas. He then lent the money to the always needy King of Denmark, and we acted as his agents.'

'Now that he is once again master in his realm, do you think this wicked traffic in men will be resumed?' Charles asked.

Anselm Maier shook his head. 'No, high-wellborn. Having tasted freedom, the people would not submit to it. And if it did the House of Rothschild could now afford to refuse such unsavoury business. I remain at the centre of things here. My second brother, Solomon, is now well established in Vienna. Nathan, as you are aware, has already become a power in the financial world of London, and my youngest brothers, Karl and James, have recently opened branches in Paris and Naples. We have perfect trust in one another, and always act in concert. Together we decide how to utilise our now considerable resources, and always support causes that we believe will benefit humanity.'

A grandfather clock in a corner of the room struck three o'clock. Glancing at it the banker said, 'High-wellborn ones, half the night is already gone. Permit me to conduct you to a room where you can get some sleep.'

They readily agreed and he took them up to a room on the third floor, in which there was a large, comfortable-looking bed. After wishing them good sleep, he added, 'I am confident that I can trust all my people, but others come to the house, so it would be best if you remained here during your stay, and I will have your meals sent up to you.'

Having expressed their gratitude they quickly undressed, blew out the candles and were soon asleep.

During the three days that followed, they were well cared for. Several times Anselm Maier came up to bring them books, talk with them and see that they had everything they wanted. But they were extremely worried, because they had learnt that not only the Main, upon which Frankfurt stood, but the greater part of the east bank of the upper Rhine were now in the hands of the Prussians. It was certain that by this time a full description of both of them would have been circulated, and all troops ordered to keep a look-out for them. Roger's leg had suffered no permanent damage, except that a large piece of flesh from his calf had had to be cut away, but for many weeks he would have a limp which he would be unable to disguise and to put a strain upon his leg for any length of time still pained him considerably. And they were now faced with the problem of crossing both the Main and the Rhine before they could hope to be safely back in French-held territory.

20

In the Toils Once More

FOR hours Roger and Charles discussed their problems. Even if they could cross the bridge over the Main, which would not be heavily guarded, without being recognised, Roger could not ride far enough to reach the Rhine in a single night. If they hired a coach they would have to risk the driver, or an ostler at one of the post houses realising that they were the wanted men; and in these German lands everyone was only too eager to get his own back on the hated French. If they walked, that would treble the time needed to reach the great river, and along the roads they would be exposed to the scrutiny of many more people. Even if they succeeded in reaching the Rhine, there would remain the hazard of crossing it. The river was much too broad and fast to swim it, and it was certain there would be pickets all along the banks, so it would be very difficult to steal a boat and get any distance without being fired on.

They were still at their wits' end about the best course to take when, on the morning of December 15th, Anselm Maier came up to see them and said:

'During these past few days I have been trying to think of a way to get you safely out of Frankfurt so that you need not expose yourselves to possible recognition, and I think I have hit upon one, provided you are willing to put up with a certain amount of discomfort.'

L

'That's very good of you,' Roger replied, 'and we'd be glad to hear what you propose.'

'As I have informed you, the Allied armies do not by any means form a continuous line from Holland to Alsace. There are still large areas which they have not yet occupied, and fortresses strongly held by the French. One such is Ehrenbreitstein, which dominates the junction of the Rhine and Moselle at Coblenz. During the course of the war, my House has naturally had many dealings with the French as well as with their enemies. And for both we have frequently handled valuable consignments of works of art as well as currency. If the high-wellborn ones are prepared to lie hidden in crates for perhaps two days I could have them sent down the river by barge, consigned as precious porcelain, to my agents at Coblenz.'

'Two days!' exclaimed Charles. 'During so long a time we would die of thirst.'

'Nay. The crates would be roomy enough for you to feed yourselves, and both provisions and flasks of wine would be put inside with you.'

Roger did not at all like the idea of being boxed up in what amounted to a coffin, but the banker assured him that the crate lids would be so loosely nailed down that they could be kicked off if the necessity arose.

'What of the Prussians, though?' Roger asked. 'They control the area. Are they not likely to hold up any goods being sent down river to a city still held by the French?'

Anselm Maier smiled and shook his head. 'I should send with the crates one of my people who would be in our secret. He would have the crates with him in a cabin on the barge and carry all the necessary documents relating to their supposed contents. The high-wellborn ones may rest assured that the House of Rothschild is now held in

such respect that goods consigned by us to anywhere in
Europe would never be interfered with.'

Charles and Roger exchanged a quick glance of agreement, then thanked the banker for having thought of this
way of getting them safely out of Frankfurt.

That afternoon two large crates, made of light wood
and measuring six feet by three feet by three feet, were
brought up to the room. Both were so constructed that
half-inch-wide spaces between each three side planks
would let in ample air. They contained well-padded palliasses to lie on, pillows and supplies of food and drink.
Laughing a little sheepishly to conceal their reluctance to
be imprisoned in them, Roger and Charles stretched
themselves out on the palliasses and listened to the lids
being nailed down. By forcing their elbows against the sides
of the crates, they prevented themselves from being thrown
about while they were carried downstairs and loaded on
to a wagon. It rumbled off over the cobbles and half an
hour later they suffered further jolting as the crates were
loaded on to a barge. After that they were left in silence
and darkness.

The hours that followed seemed to both of them interminable, each hour a day, each day a week. From time
to time they managed to doze a little, but had no idea
whether it was night or day. The only way in which they
could break the awful monotony was to fumble blindly
among the packages that had been put in with them;
then, lying awkwardly on one hip, swallow food or drink;
but after a while they both realised that they must resist
the temptation to resort to this distraction too frequently
or they would soon find that they had consumed all their
supplies. Very occasionally they caught the murmur of
voices, but for hour after hour the only sound they heard
was their own breathing and they lay, their arms stretched

out along their sides, in the darkness and silence of the
grave. There were times when, only half asleep, their
minds became a prey to awful nightmares, during which
they were seized with panic and for a few moments
believed they had been buried alive. Then the realisation
of their true situation returned to them only just in time to
stop themselves from screaming and striving to batter a
way out of what they had imagined to be a coffin.

Their ordeal seemed as though it would never end, and
they could hardly believe the evidence of their senses when
a mutter of voices was followed by the crates being lifted.
They were again subjected to considerable jolting, but
welcomed it as evidence that they were at last near their
journey's end. Twenty minutes later, to their unutterable
relief, the crates were prised open.

They were so stiff that at first they had difficulty in
sitting up and, after being so long in darkness, were semi-
blinded by the daylight. But when they had been helped
out of the crates, they saw that they were in a small ware-
house half-filled with other crates, trunks and boxes. With
them were two Jews. One introduced himself as having
brought them from Frankfurt, the other as the Rothschild's agent in Coblenz. The latter asked if he could be of
any service to them, to which Roger replied :

'I should be grateful if you could get a coach to take us
to Ehrenbreitstein.'

He and Charles were then taken across a courtyard to
a house and given glasses of wine, while a servant went to
fetch a coach. It arrived shortly after midday, and having
thanked the two Jews for their help, they drove off to the
great fortress.

Neither of them was yet fully recovered from the mental suffering they had endured during the past two days,
but as the high castellated walls came into sight, Roger

pulled himself together sufficiently to say in a low voice to
Charles :

'I shall of course, announce myself as *de Breuc*, but
the story you gave before, on the spur of the moment, that
you are my prisoner and remained with me all this time
because you had given me your parole, is too much to
ask them to believe. As I cannot say you are an Englishman and your French is so indifferent that I cannot possibly pass you off as a Frenchman, it would be best, I
think, if I told them that you are my orderly officer and a
Bavarian who remained loyal to us after Bavaria went
over to the Allies. Have you any suggestions about a name
for yourself?'

After a minute's thought, Charles said, 'What think you
of Lieutenant Count von Schweibacker-Erman? That
would fit in with the coronet and initials on my underclothes should a servant chance to notice them.'

Roger laughed for the first time in many hours. "Tis
one hell of a name, but most suitable. You're a fine fellow,
Charles, with a good brain as well as courage.'

At the great gate of the fortress he paid off the coach
and after a wait of three-quarters of an hour they were
taken up to the office of the General commanding the
garrison. Roger had never met him, but when the name
of *de Breuc* was brought up to him he had made enquiries
of his staff and now had with him a Colonel Orton of the
Engineers, who had known Roger during Napoleon's
second occupation of Vienna; so, in spite of his rumpled
civilian clothes and unshaven face, the Major was readily
able to identify him.

Roger's story was that he and his companion had
become separated from the Emperor at the battle of Leipzig, and that he had been severely wounded during the
retreat. Fortunately they were then in the neighbourhood

of a house owned by a widow lady who was a relative of Count von Schweibacker-Erman. She had agreed to hide them from their enemies. His wound had then become gangrenous, and he had been so ill that they had had to lie up there for many weeks. When at last he had become fit to travel, they had made their way, mostly by night and hiding by day, toward the Rhine. Then, hearing that Coblenz was still in the hands of the French, they succeeded in reaching the city.

In view of the disturbed state of the whole of southern Germany, the story was entirely plausible. The General accepted it and congratulated them on evading capture. He then told Colonel Orton to find suitable quarters for them, and invited them to dine with him in the Senior Officers' Mess.

The meal proved a by no means cheerful one. Those officers present were very conscious that, as in other pockets of territory on the right bank of the Rhine still held by the French, their enemies were rapidly closing in on them, and the prospect of being reinforced seemed extremely dubious. Moreover, the state of things in the city of Coblenz had become very different from what it had been when they had lorded it there. The German population had become openly hostile. The troops no longer dared go to the *beerhalles* in parties of fewer than a dozen, they were hissed at in the streets and had to walk warily to avoid the contents of a chamber pot thrown from an upper window on to their heads.

That evening Roger told the General that he naturally wished to rejoin the Emperor as soon as possible, and asked his assistance to get to Paris. The General willingly agreed, said that he still had the power to commandeer a coach and promised to provide a driver. By mid-morning next day a coach had been procured. As the driver was a soldier, an escort was provided to accompany the coach into the town, so that Roger and Charles could buy razors, soap, flannels, a change of underclothes, some bottles of wine and other things for their journey. They then crossed the river by the bridge of boats. On the far side the escort left them, and for the five days that followed they were able to enjoy relaxing in freedom until they reached Paris on December 23rd.

Roger directed the driver to Talleyrand's mansion. On alighting there they were informed that the statesman was dining out, but the *maître d'hôtel*, who knew Roger well, said he felt sure it would be His Highness's wish that they should partake of a meal while awaiting his return. Soon after eight o'clock Talleyrand came in, to find them still lingering over peaches and Château Yquem. As he limped into the room they both stood up. With a smile and a wave of his hand toward Charles, Roger said :

'Your Highness, permit me to present my friend, Count von Schweibacker-Erman.'

Returning the smile, Talleyrand replied, 'So you succeeded in your quest.' Then he extended his beruffled hand to Charles and said, 'I am delighted to welcome Lord St. Ermins to my house, and I hope that you will both remain here as my guests during your stay in Paris.'

They laughed and gratefully accepted. Some fine old brandy was produced and they sat round the table. Roger gave an account of all that had befallen him since he had left Paris toward the end of August, then Talleyrand gave them a résumé of the war situation.

Prince Metternich, anxious to keep France strong as a counterweight to Russia, had in mid-November offered peace on the terms that France must give up all that remained of her conquests in Spain, Italy and Germany and return to her natural frontiers : the Rhine, the Alps and

the Pyrenees. But Napoleon, then at Frankfurt, had shil-
lied and shallied until the offer had been withdrawn. This
had caused him, quite unjustly, to dismiss Maret, Duc de
Bassano, who had long been his Foreign Minister, and
replace him with Caulaincourt.

His efforts to re-open negotiations had been thwarted
by the Prussians. Determined to exact full vengeance from
the French, they now proclaimed both banks of the Rhine
to be German territory, and claimed Cologne, Treir,
Strasbourg and Metz. The Czar, moreover, was set on
dictating a peace in Paris. Ignoring a declaration of
neutrality by Switzerland, an Allied army was marching
through that country, and now menaced France from the
east. Von Bülow's Prussians, with the aid of a British
expeditionary force, had driven the French out of Holland, to the great rejoicing of the Dutch, and in the south
Wellington had crossed the Pyrenees.

At the end of this recital Roger said, 'Then it can now
be only a matter of weeks before the Emperor is forced
to give in.'

Talleyrand shook his head. 'I'd not gamble on that.
The man is as stubborn as a mule. Nothing will induce
him to give up the left bank of the Rhine, Belgium or his
Italian conquests. I fear there is yet much bloody fighting
to come.'

'But, my Prince, what has he left to fight with? After
the débâcle in Russia, he managed by a miracle to muster
another half-million men and he has since lost those in
Germany. One cannot make bricks without straw, and
there is no straw left.'

'You are wrong there, but it is a different kind of straw.
When he returned to Paris, he was openly cursed as the
destroyer of France's young manhood. For years the
people have become more and more sickened by his

foreign wars. But now they have changed their tune. The Allies are about to invade France—to tread the sacred soil won by the people's army, led by Moreau, Jourdan and Kellermann in the days of the Revolution. Men long since released from the Army, many even who were middle-aged in those days but can still march and fire a musket, are volunteering in their thousands to fight again.'

Roger sighed. 'How terrible that there must be yet another bloodbath.'

They talked on for another hour or so, then Talleyrand excused himself on account of having papers to go through, and had his guests shown up to bedrooms.

When Roger had left *La Belle Étoile* he had had his big trunk brought round to Talleyrand's mansion, and he recalled that he had an old uniform in it. It was one he had worn at the battle of the Nile, and had a big tear through the upper part of the left arm, made by a bullet that had narrowly missed him. Although the tear had been mended, he had been in half a mind to throw the garment away, but the providence he had inherited from his Scottish mother had led to his keeping it in case one day it came in useful. Now was just such a time, as going to the Ministry of War in uniform rather than in civilian clothes would save him from having to answer a lot of tiresome questions. Next morning, after the footman who was valeting him had given the coat a good brushing, he put it on and took a coach to the Ministry.

After the retreat from Moscow he had been listed as 'missing, believed killed', but while in Paris the previous August he had had his name restored to the pay roll and now had considerable arrears owing to him. Not expecting to be in Paris again until after a peace had been agreed, he drew the whole sum, partly in gold for current purposes, but the bulk in bills of exchange.

Having learned that the Emperor was not in the capital but making a tour of the principal provincial cities to encourage, by showing himself, more ex-soldiers to rejoin the colours, Roger was in no danger of again being caught up in his web, so he decided that as Charles had never before been in Paris, he would remain there for a few days, to show the young man something of the city.

During the past twenty-five years Roger had lived there for so many months that Charles could not have had a better guide; and, now that he and Roger had become boon companions, he immensely enjoyed going with him to the Louvre, to Notre Dame, the Sainte Chapel, the site where the guillotine had stood, and driving out to St. Cloud and Versailles.

It was on the evening of December 30th that Roger told Talleyrand that, greatly as they had enjoyed their stay, he and Charles must now make their way home, and that he proposed to set out on the following day.

The Prince expressed great surprise at this and exclaimed, 'Mais non! Cher ami, how can you even think of leaving Paris now? For many years happenings in France have been the great interest in your life. You witnessed the rise of Bonaparte; surely you do not mean to forgo being present at the tyrant's fall?'

Roger smiled. 'It will be a great day, Highness, and I'll regret to miss it. Indeed, I'd happily stay on here could it be anticipated in the course of the next few weeks. But that is more than we can hope for. It is your own opinion, and endorsed by many of the prominent men I have talked with while a guest here at your lavish table, that the new army, containing so many tough old soldiers, will put up a most desperate resistance when the Allies invade France. Unless the Emperor agrees to accept humiliating terms—which we both consider unlikely—it will be many months before he can be crushed by sheer weight of numbers.'

'That I admit. But even so you should remain. You are unique in being known and trusted by many men of importance in both camps; so, as a go-between for myself, you could be of immense help in bringing about a cessation of hostilities.'

'No, Highness. In such a way I could be of little use to you. When the Emperor returns to Paris, it is certain he will learn that I am here, so I could not avoid reporting to him. In this past year he has lost so many of his old intimates who knew his ways, that he will instantly seize upon me and require me to accompany him to the front. I've had more than my share of luck in having lived through so many dangers, and I'm determined not to risk death now in further battles.'

'You would have no need to do so. I am happy to know that you are now nearly recovered from your wound, and that it has left you with nothing worse than a limp. But Napoleon is not aware of that. An A.D.C. who cannot ride a horse is of little use in the field. You could easily excuse yourself from further service by pretending to be severely crippled, and your health seriously affected; then remain on here in Paris with me.'

Again Roger shook his head. 'The excuse you suggest might be accepted, but I'll not risk it. I could be useful to him in so many ways that the odds are he would insist on forcing me into some employment. Besides, I am anxious to get Charles home and so put an end to his dear mother's anxiety about his still being alive.'

The Prince shrugged. 'I'll say no more then. How do you propose to get back to England?'

'I hope, as I have done many times before, to find some smuggler along the coast who will run us over.'

'You'll not find that so easy as you did in the past. Now that the Allies are closing in about us it is feared that the English might attempt to land an army in Normandy or Brittany, so the coast is much more carefully guarded.'

'Sir,' Charles addressed Roger. 'I did not put on a uniform merely to strut about in it, but to play my part on active service. It was my intention when we reached England to sail again as soon as possible, in order to rejoin His Grace of Wellington's army. There is an alternative, though. Why should we not travel south direct to it? That would save me the voyage from England to Spain, and you would have no need to risk yourself with a smuggler. You could go home in safety and comfort in one of our ships sailing from a Spanish port.'

Roger considered for only a moment, then he smiled. 'Charles, you have something there. It is an excellent idea.'

So the matter was settled. Two days later, on New Year's Day 1814, they left Paris in a comfortable travelling coach, generously provided by Talleyrand who, when they took leave of him, handed Roger a letter which he asked him to deliver to Wellington.

They made the journey through France without incident, and on January 11th reached Bayonne, which was now actually in the battle zone. There they put up at a modest hostelry and next morning, having given Talleyrand's coachman a handsome *pourboire,* Roger sent him back to Paris with the coach. He then bought two good horses and, with their portmanteaux strapped to the backs of their saddles, they took the road east to Bidache.

From time to time Roger had heard news of the war in the south and, as he had expected, Marshal Soult had proved a much more redoubtable opponent than had King Joseph and Jourdan. During the late summer Wellington had driven the French back across the Pyrenees with a loss of ten thousand men, but his advance had then been badly held up by the fortresses of San Sebastian and Pamplona. It was not until the end of the first week in October that he had been able to plant the British flag on French soil, and he had then had to force the line of the river Bidassoa, which Soult had fortified with a chain of strong redoubts.

From there the French had fallen back on a still stronger line along the river Nivelle. It ran through very rugged country which greatly favoured the defence, and during the whole of November the weather had been appalling, which further hampered offensive operations; so it was not until the 10th that, after many desperate assaults, the enemy had been driven from it. Soult had then retired to the river Nive at the mouth of which lay the great fortress of Bayonne. This had placed Wellington at a strategic disadvantage because, further inland, his army was divided by the river into two parts. The able Soult had first concentrated his army on the west bank, hoping to defeat that half of the British force. Failing in that, he had transferred his troops to the east bank and endeavoured to overwhelm the one British and one Portuguese division there under the command of Sir Rowland Hill; but again he had been defeated. By December 13th the whole of Soult's army had been driven back and taken refuge among the ring of forts surrounding Bayonne.

On the evening of their arrival in the city and during the night, Roger and Charles frequently heard the sound of cannon as the British bombarded the forts to the south of Bayonne and the forts returning the fire. It was not until they had ridden several miles along the road inland that the sounds of battle faded in the distance. At an easy pace they covered the twenty miles to Bidache and Roger was greatly relieved to find that now, ten weeks after the last operation on his leg, riding did not pain or unduly tire him.

They had a meal at an inn in Bidache, and rested for a couple of hours. The little town lay on the fringe of the foothills of the Pyrenees, and that afternoon they took the road south toward the mountains. By making a big detour they had skirted right round the area in which there was fighting, so had seen only a few French troops escorting wagons. Evening found them in deserted, wooded country, some miles south of St. Palais. Noticing a small cave in a ridge of rocks a hundred yards or so off the track, they decided that it would be a good place to pass the night.

They had not yet reached the snowline, but it was bitterly cold, so they got a fire going as quickly as they could. On it they cooked some slices of ham they had bought in Bidache; then, having warmed themselves up with a bottle of Bordeaux and lavish rations of Armagnac, they wrapped themselves in their cloaks and did their best to get some sleep on shallow piles of fir sprigs that they had broken off from the branches they had collected for their fire.

In the morning, believing that they were now well outside French-held territory, Roger took off his old uniform coat, threw it away in the far end of the cave, and put on the grey cloth coat in which he had travelled from Germany. After watering their horses at a stream and giving them a feed, they ate some more of the ham, washed it down with another bottle of wine and resumed their journey.

Soon after leaving the cave they came upon cross-roads, so they turned west in the direction of the coast. The morning passed in a tiring ride up over spurs and down

across valleys, but early in the afternoon they saw ahead
of them a group of tents and some red coats in a clearing
by the trackside. A Lieutenant was in command of this
outpost, and when they made it known that they were
English he gave them a cheerful welcome.

By the time they had warmed themselves at a fire and
eaten a hot meal, the early winter dusk was already closing in, so they decided to remain there for the night. In
the morning the Lieutenant showed them on his map the
direction they should take to reach Wellington's headquarters. It meant a ride of another twenty-five miles, but
knowing they had succeeded in getting safely through the
dangerous area, they took the road in good heart.

After passing several other units of British troops they
reached the headquarters soon after midday. It was a
château with a beautiful view over the ridges of woodland
to the north. Dismounting outside it, Roger sent in his
name and that of Charles. Ten minutes later the Commander-in-Chief received them with his usual charm.

However, he told them that he was just about to hold
a conference of his senior officers, so must wait until later
to hear such news as they had brought him. He then said
they must join him for dinner and turned them over to
one of his A.D.C.s with orders to provide them with
accommodation. Having thanked him Roger, before leaving the room, handed him the letter he had brought from
Talleyrand.

Dinner that night proved a cheerful meal. Such brother
officers as Charles knew on the Duke's staff heartily welcomed him back among them. It emerged in conversation
that they were confident of soon taking Bayonne and
advancing on Bordeaux, where it was now known that a
great part of the population was secretly eager to welcome
the Allies. Intelligence had also been received that recently

Napoleon had ordered Soult to send ten thousand men to assist in defending the eastern frontier of France. The Spanish troops had inflicted such atrocities on the French in the towns and villages they had captured that the Duke, who was anxious to gain the good will of the French people, had sent the Spaniards back to their own country. But even without them, Wellington now had such superiority in numbers that Soult's final defeat could not be long delayed.

When the port circulated there was an eager audience to hear Charles's account of all that had befallen himself and Roger in Germany. The two of them then enjoyed a sound night's sleep in comfortable beds.

In the morning the Duke sent for Roger and said to him, 'Mr. Brook, are you aware of the contents of the letter you brought me from Talleyrand?'

'No, Your Grace,' Roger replied. 'He told me nothing of it.'

'I see. Well, to be brief, it is a most earnest appeal to me to use any influence I may have with you to persuade you to return to Paris.'

Roger shook his head. 'Your Grace must forgive me, but I am utterly sickened of war, and determined to go home to England.'

'One moment,' the Duke held up a finger. 'Talleyrand points out, and I know this to be true, that you are the only man in all Europe who has special qualifications for possibly hastening the end of hostilities. You are in his confidence and mine. You have long been an A.D.C. to Napoleon, who believes you to be devoted to him. You are known and trusted by the Czar. You know Prince Metternich, Lord Castlereagh and scores of influential persons in our camp and that of the enemy.

'You have served your country so long and so well that

you are trapped by the circumstances you have yourself created. How can you possibly now refuse to serve her for a few more months? You are not a soldier, so I am in no position to order you to return, neither am I accustomed to beg; but on this occasion I beg you to do so.'

Roger's face showed an agony of indecision. After a moment, he said, 'I . . . I don't really know. Your Grace must give me twenty-four hours to think it over.'

The Iron Duke's stern features relaxed into a faint smile. 'Mr. Brook, I will give you exactly two minutes.'

With a sigh Roger returned the smile. 'Your Grace leaves me no alternative. I will set out for Paris tomorrow.'

21

The Last Campaign

It was on January 20th that Roger again arrived in Paris. Having found that he could now ride considerable distances without affecting his leg, he made the journey on horseback, but by easy stages. In the cave a few miles from St. Palais, in which he and Charles had passed a night, he found his old uniform coat where he had left it, so he was able to wear it on his journey through France, and command all the facilities to which his rank entitled him.

Talleyrand, having been confident that the trick he had played on Roger would succeed, showed no surprise at his return, and only laughed when reproached for having trapped him.

On his way north Roger had picked up many rumours of the rapidly changing situation throughout Europe. The Prince confirmed many of them, and gave him a true account of what had been happening.

All Holland had now been liberated by von Bülow's Prussians, with the assistance of a British expeditionary force that had landed under General Graham. The Czar had marched his army right through Switzerland, invaded eastern France and was now threatening Lyons. Schwarzenberg's army had reached and crossed the Rhine in many places. Blücher, ever to the fore, had reached

Luxembourg. Davout was still holding out in Hamburg, but Bernadotte had overcome the Danes who, on the 14th, had signed a peace treaty surrendering Norway to him.

At that Roger commented with a laugh, 'So that sly rogue has secured the plum he was after all the time, and got it with very little serious fighting. How mad the Emperor must be.'

'He is, but the worst blow of all to him has been the defection of Murat.'

'What! Murat gone over to the enemy?'

'That is so, although 'tis not yet known to the public. I received private intelligence of it from Prince Metternich. On the 11th of this month Murat signed a treaty with Austria, that in exchange for his supplying a corps of thirty thousand men, he should keep his Kingdom of Naples and, in addition, be given a sizeable piece of the old Papal territories.'

'Such treachery is scarce believable. But Murat's head is solid wood. This is the work of his wife, that scheming whore, Caroline.'

'I judge you right. She was ever the most ambitious of Napoleon's sisters and, with the possible exception of himself, the cleverest of the whole Bonaparte family. Moreover, when Metternich was ambassador in Paris he had an affair with her; so his personal inclination would be to favour her continued aggrandisement!'

Roger raised his eyes to the ceiling. 'What a brood they are! Pauline alone among them is honest, and the only one who has shown any gratitude for the wealth and favours showered upon them.'

'You forget *Madame Mère.*'

'True, the old lady is a tower of rectitude, and at least conserved the great fortune she has been given, against a day when her wonder child should over-reach himself.'

'That day has come, and he had much of it off her to pay for the two hundred thousand new uniforms he ordered when he got back to Paris last November.'

After a moment Roger said, 'I take it that, now Murat has ratted, we can count Italy lost to France, as well as all Germany, Holland and Switzerland.'

'Not altogether. When the Emperor took over the command of the Elbe from Prince Eugène, he sent him back to his old post as Viceroy of Italy. The young Beauharnais at least is loyal, and an able General. Murat's Neapolitans are not distinguished for their love of battle, so Eugène has little to fear from them; and the Alps give him a strong line of defence to hold back the Austrians when they attempt to break through into the plain of Lombardy.

'But now we must think of yourself. The Emperor is in Paris, so you must report to him. He is holding a reception at the Tuileries three days hence, before leaving for the front. That will be time enough for you to make your service to him. In the meantime I suggest you give out that your wound re-opened again recently, and go about on crutches.'

Roger gave a wry smile. 'You Highness's advice is, as ever, sound. I'll do that, and pray to God it saves me from being forced into some unwelcome post. I cannot go to the Tuileries though in this stained and threadbare uniform. So, with your permission, I'll to my tailor without delay.'

At his tailors Roger demanded and received priority; so, on the 23rd, he was able to accompany Talleyrand to the Tuileries dressed with all his old elegance; but, owing to the ministrations of the Prince's valet, his appearance was very different from what it had been when he arrived in Paris.

The man was an artist in make-up, and had skilfully

transformed Roger's face. A liquid had made his cheeks pale, without appearing to be painted or powdered, there were deep shadows under his eyes and little lines radiating from the corners and from the sides of his mouth. The naturally grey wings of hair above his ears now merged into grey hair all over his head. In addition, not only did he walk with crutches, which he had used during the past two days whenever he went out, but his injured leg had been strapped up behind him on a peg leg with a sling.

As the Emperor was about to defend France from invasion he had again become a hero, and everyone who was anyone in Paris had come to cheer him on to victory; so the palace was a seething mass of senators, soldiers, officials and their ladies. Slowly Talleyrand and Roger made their way up the grand staircase and into the Throne Room. Napoleon was standing with the Empress on one side of him, and on the other, their fair-haired three-year-old son, the King of Rome, dressed in the uniform of the National Guard.

When Roger at last came opposite them and awkwardly made his bow, the Emperor exclaimed :

'Why, Breuc, what a pleasant surprise to see you. I thought you lost to us at Leipzig.'

'I thank you, Sire,' Roger replied in a feeble voice. 'I got away with my life, but that is about all. My only regret is that neither physically nor mentally am I any longer capable of serving you.'

Napoleon tweaked his ear, the old familiar gesture of good will. 'I am the loser, Breuc; but I take the will for the deed. And you should not be here in Paris, but in the sunshine at your little château near St. Maxime, where you used to winter on account of your weak chest.'

With a murmur of thanks Roger bowed awkwardly

again, and passed on, immensely relieved that his pretended inability to be of any use had been accepted.

When the last of those present had made their bows, the ushers rapped loudly on the parquet for silence. The Emperor then addressed the assembly in a loud, clear voice. He announced that he had appointed the Empress as Regent and his brother, King Joseph, Lieutenant General of France. Taking his small son by the hand he went on :

'Gentlemen, I am about to set out for the Army. I entrust to you what I hold dearest in the world—my wife and son. Let there be no political divisions.' He then lifted the boy on to his shoulder and carried him about among the great dignitaries of the Empire and the officers of the National Guard, to whom he had particularly addressed himself.

It was a most touching scene. He had not commanded, but appealed to their feelings as human beings. The great chamber rang for minutes on end with applause and fervid protestations of loyalty.

On leaving Paris the Emperor travelled swiftly eastward to Châlons. Blücher was to the south of him and, he learned, heading further south with the object of joining Schwarzenberg's Austrians. Napoleon, who throughout this campaign displayed a remarkable recovery in vitality, military genius and swiftness of decision, immediately marched south to prevent the two armies from combining against him. On January 29th, at Brienne—where, as a penniless youth of only the lowest stratum of nobility and speaking French with an atrocious Italian accent, he had been a cadet at the Military Academy—he fell upon the Prussians, driving them from the castle and the town. Blücher retreated toward Bar-sur-Aube and there had the support of Schwarzenberg. On February 1st the Allies attacked with greatly superior numbers. Although the French fought gallantly in a snow storm, endeavouring for eight hours to hold the village of La Rothière, they were outflanked and defeated with a loss of three thousand men and seventy-three cannon—a loss they could ill afford, in view of the hugely superior numbers of the Allies.

The immense wealth Talleyrand had acquired during his long association with the Emperor enabled him to maintain a small army of couriers. They not only brought him early news of these battles, but also kept him in communication with Prince Metternich, the Czar and Royalist agents of King Louis XVIII, who was living at Hartwell in England.

On February 3rd the Emperor entered Troyes and his distress at his defeat was much increased by his reception. Far from cheering him with their old ardour, the inhabitants, already half-starved themselves, sullenly refused to supply his troops with anything. The soldiers, too, were desperately hungry and so cast down that six thousand of them deserted.

The weather also inflicted the most terrible hardship on the combatants. It was the worst winter for many years, and so cold that oxen were being roasted on the ice that had formed over the rivers. Blizzards frequently hid opposing bodies of troops from one another, deep drifts of snow hampered their movements, wood for the camp fires was so difficult to obtain that they often went out long before dawn and the men were compelled to sleep in huddles to keep the life in their bodies.

The situation in Paris was also grim. The funds had dropped five points, and the rich, now fearing that the capital would be sacked by the ferocious Russians, were fleeing with their jewels to their châteaux in the country.

Up to the end of the year Lord Aberdeen had been Britain's ambassador to Austria, but early in January Lord Castlereagh, the Foreign Minister, had decided to take over negotiations himself, and travelled in great discomfort to join Metternich in Basle. They liked each other and found much common ground on how Europe should be reconstituted after Napoleon had been finally defeated.

Before leaving England Castlereagh, who dominated the Cabinet, had secured its approval of his own views. The most important of these were : no interference with Britain's 'Maritime Rights'; complete independence for Spain, Portugal and Holland, the latter to be given as a barrier Belgian lands which positively must exclude the French from the great port of Antwerp; that France should become a Limited Monarchy; no undue hardships to be inflicted on the French people, so that they might the sooner become reconciled to their late enemies; and that the Grand Alliance should be kept in being after the war to preserve the peace of Europe.

Metternich, both from fear of Russia and because his sovereign's daughter was Empress of the French, also wished France to remain strong and become a friendly Power. He was, too, willing to forgo Austria's claim to Belgium in exchange for a free hand in northern Italy. But the two statesmen knew that their wish to grant France a lenient Peace would meet with strong opposition from Prussia, as that country, so harshly treated by Napoleon, was determined to exact vengeance and intended to demand territorial expansion in several directions.

It was, however, the Czar's attitude that gave them most concern. The liberal principles of which he had long believed himself to be the champion, were in direct conflict with his ambitions. He talked with apparent sincerity of re-creating Poland as a Kingdom and restoring their liberty to the Poles; but the fact was that he meant to make the new Poland a satellite state subject to himself. Moreover this would have entailed Austria and Prussia giving up to him great areas of territory that they had acquired by the partitions of Poland.

To compensate Prussia he proposed to abolish the Kingdom of Saxony; which, to the end, had remained loyal to Napoleon. But these measures would have been of no benefit to Austria. On the contrary, they would give Russia a huge increase in manpower, bring her frontier many hundred miles closer to Central Europe and eliminate the buffer state of Saxony.

Having discussed these matters with mutual satisfaction, Castlereagh and Metternich took the icy road to Langres where the Czar had set up his headquarters with his principle advisers, Count Nesselrode and the Prussian statesman Stein who was Napoleon's most bitter enemy.

As Britain, alone among the Allies, had remained for twenty years in arms against Napoleon and again and again poured out her treasure to finance Coalitions against him, Castlereagh was in a very strong position and his influence did much to bring the disputants closer together. The prickly questions of Poland and Saxony were tactfully ignored, but Alexander agreed that France should be treated leniently and her people given the liberty of deciding for themselves on their future form of government. He also gave way to Castlereagh's insistence that France should be restricted to her 'ancient' as opposed to her 'natural' limits; that is to the territories she possessed in 1792 instead of her frontiers being the Rhine, the Alps and the Pyrenees. Thus she would be deprived of her Belgian lands and Antwerp. These understandings were set forth on January 29th in a document called 'The Langres Protocol'.

On the day following his victory at Brienne, Napoleon attempted to open negotiations with the Austrians, but while awaiting their reply he, in his turn, was caught napping.

The Allies had called a conference at Châtillon, which opened on February 5th. Napoleon sent Caulaincourt to it with instructions to accept the terms offered at Frankfurt the previous November, by which France would have retained her 'natural' frontiers. But the Allies had since advanced into the heart of France and were much more confident of victory. They now demanded the reduction of France to her 'ancient' boundaries, and that Napoleon should abdicate.

Caulaincourt fought hard for his master, to whom he was devoted, but on the 9th gave way and sent a despatch to the Emperor informing him that he had done so. On receiving it Napoleon erupted in ungovernable rage and vowed that he would yet destroy his enemies.

At their last Council of War it had been decided by the Allies that they should divide their forces. Blücher, with fifty thousand men, was to march direct on Paris, while the timid Schwarzenberg, who had three times that number, was to continue to engage Napoleon. Sound strategy would have dictated that the much larger army should have been that to advance against the capital; but the decision had been reached owing to dissension among the Allies.

By this time Blücher was well on his way to Paris but the Czar, determined not to be deprived of a personal triumph, sent him an order that he was not to enter the capital until the arrival of the Allied sovereigns.

His order proved unnecessary. Only a few hours after

receiving Caulaincourt's despatch Napoleon learned the whereabouts of Blücher's army. With his old energy and flair for assessing military situations, he ordered Marmont to occupy Sezanne and set off with Ney to support him. On the 10th at Champoutert the corps of both Marshals struck at a division of Russians about five thousand strong, and almost annihilated it. This attack on Blücher's army cut it in half. His leading corps, under Sacken, was west of Montmirail, while that of Yorck was far to the north. With the speed he had displayed in his best years, Napoleon followed up by hurling his troops against Sacken. In and about the village of Marchair there was the most appalling slaughter on both sides. Mortier with the Imperial Guard overcame their enemies and Sacken's corps was routed; its remnants being saved only by the tardy arrival of Yorck, whose men also gave way before the French.

Next day the Emperor drove the Russians from Château Thierry, to the surprise and joy of its inhabitants who believed him to have been defeated and awaiting the end at Troyes. On the 13th, leaving Mortier to continue the pursuit of Sacken and Yorck, Napoleon marched to reinforce Marmont, who was having to give ground before Blücher. The Emperor's arrival changed the tide of battle. Many Prussian and Russian formations were overwhelmed, but others fought with the greatest stubbornness, and only the veteran Blücher's courageous leadership enabled the greater part of his infantry to carry out an orderly retreat.

Never had Napoleon shown his mastery of the art of war to greater effect than in these battles. With thirty thousand hungry and ill-supplied men he had defeated fifty thousand, and eliminated the threat to Paris. His troops had again become jubilant, in the capital the fickle mobs were once more acclaiming him as a hero and predicting that he would drive the enemy from the soil of France.

Throughout this whirlwind campaign Napoleon found time to write to his Empress daily, and she sent him most affectionate replies. He seemed positively indefatigable and fought six battles in nine days.

But the odds were heavily against him. The Czar had browbeaten Schwarzenberg into taking the offensive. One of his columns defeated Oudinot in his attempts to hold the bridge over the Seine at Bray, the other advanced toward Fontainebleau. To his fury, Napoleon was forced to abandon his pursuit of Blücher and endeavour to halt these columns. By superhuman efforts he transported his troops by way of Meaux to support Victor and Macdonald and together they succeeded in checking the Austrian advance. On the 17th and 18th his activities were almost unbelievable. In addition to writing a dozen despatches and directing three battles, he laid and fired a number of cannon himself. When his artillerymen endeavoured to dissuade him from exposing his person, he inflamed their devotion to him by crying, 'Do not fear! The ball is not yet cast that will kill me.'

On the 21st he took advantage of his amazing succession of victories to attempt to detach Austria from her allies. From Nogent he wrote to his father-in-law, the Emperor Francis, asserting that Britain and Russia were using him as a cat's-paw, and that Austria had nothing to gain by continuing the war. They meant to grab all Poland and Saxony and give Austria's old Belgian lands to the Dutch.

The Austrians, more than ever alarmed by the highhanded attitude of the Czar, who had declared that when he reached Paris he intended to appoint a Russian Mili-

:ary Governor of the city, were inclined to listen favour-
ably to Napoleon. The Conference at Châtillon had been
suspended on the 10th. On the 18th it resumed its sittings
and, towards the end of the month, alarmed by Napoleon's
victories, was prepared to make concessions to Caulaincourt. But everything remained in the melting pot because
Napoleon would give no firm undertaking that he would
relinquish Belgium and the territories on the French side of
the Rhine.

On March 1st Castlereagh, greatly perturbed because
it now looked as though the Coalition might break up,
assembled another Conference at Chaumont. There on
the 9th it was definitely agreed that Britain, Russia, Prussia and Austria should bind themselves by a solemn treaty
not to negotiate separately with France for peace.

Meanwhile, Blücher, with nearly fifty thousand men,
had resumed the offensive. Napoleon, believing the army
of his most inveterate enemy to be broken, received this
news with consternation, but swiftly despatched Ney and
Victor to fall on the veteran's rear. Blücher wisely retired
northward, crossed the Marne and destroyed its bridges
behind him. Having delayed the enemy in this way probably saved him from defeat, as Marmont was hotly pursuing him, Napoleon preparing to turn his right flank and
his men were utterly exhausted by marching night and day
through snowstorms and on roads made slippery by ice.

On March 2nd, having got across the river to La Ferté,
the Emperor resumed his pursuit of Blücher, in the optimistic belief that he could drive his enemies back into
Lorraine, then rescue the garrisons that had been cut off
in Verdun, Toul and Metz, which would have greatly
added to his strength.

But by then Blücher had reached the neighbourhood of
Soissons and on the banks of the Aisne joined up with

Bülow, who was able to furnish supplies for the veteran's
famished men and add forty-two thousand troops to their
numbers. Next day Soissons surrendered.

The Emperor, still intent on relieving his beleagured
garrisons, pressed on across the Aisne and forced Blücher
to retire on Laon. There the veteran learned that Napoleon
was approaching Craonne. Near that town rises a long,
narrow plateau. Blücher ordered his Russian corps to
occupy it and, on March 7th, there ensued one of the
bloodiest battles of the war.

Five times the gallant Ney scaled the slope at the head
of his men, only to be driven back by the defenders. Napoleon then used his cavalry for a sixth assault. Blücher
meanwhile had attempted to outflank the French, but the
manoeuvre failed, upon which he ordered a general retreat
to Laon. The casualties on both sides were very heavy.
Grouchy, six other French Generals and Marshal Victor
were among the wounded.

In this campaign the Emperor was greatly handicapped
by the absence of many of his most able Marshals : St. Cyr
was a prisoner, Davout was shut up in Hamburg, Suchet
was grimly hanging on to Catalonia, Augereau was defending Lyons, and Soult, who had recently suffered
another severe defeat by Wellington at Orthez, was far
away in the south. Of those with Napoleon : Ney,
Oudinot, Mortier, Macdonald and Marmont, only the
latter had come off best when left to engage the enemy
without support, and even his corps was surprised and
badly cut up in a night attack shortly after the Emperor,
having on the 9th and 10th failed to dislodge Blücher
from the stronghold of Laon, was forced to withdraw by
the news that Schwarzenberg was advancing on Paris.

The Emperor's force had been reduced to twenty thousand men, while Schwarzenberg had one hundred thou-

sand. Yet such was Napoleon's prestige that, on learning that he had reached the Aube the Austrian, fearing an attack on his flank, hesitated to advance further or turn upon the wizard warrior. This delay gave Napoleon time to call up the corps of Macdonald and Oudinot. The fighting around Arcis-sur-Aube lasted two days and became ferocious. The Emperor rode about among his troops to urge them on. To the horror of those about him a shell burst just in front of his horse and, for a moment, he disappeared in a cloud of smoke. But he emerged unhurt, mounted another horse and continued to direct the battle.

But God was indeed 'on the side of the big battalions'. By the 20th he was forced to fall back northward toward Sezanne. Still convinced that he could relieve his garrisons in the east—where the French peasantry had raised armed bands of irregulars to help defend their beloved France by harassing the enemy's supply routes—he hurried his army toward Vitry; but on the 23rd Cossacks captured one of his couriers carrying a letter to Marie Louise. In it he said, 'I have decided to march toward the Marne in order to draw the enemy's army further from Paris and got nearer my fortresses. This evening I shall be at St. Dizier.'

Made aware of the Emperor's plans, Blücher marched south and joined up again with Schwarzenberg. At the Czar's insistence it was decided that, instead of following Napoleon, they should renew the advance on Paris. The greatly weakened corps of Marmont and Mortier were all that barred the way to the capital. They fought well with great gallantry, but were brushed aside and the advance on the capital continued.

When the ordinary citizens of Paris became aware that the enemy was within a few miles of the city they were amazed and horror-stricken. For over twenty years they had become accustomed to celebrating France's victories. Their armies had marched triumphantly into Milan, Vienna, Rome, Naples, Lisbon, Venice, Madrid, Berlin and even Moscow. It had been unthinkable to them that a day could come when barbarian Cossacks and jack-booted Prussians would shoulder them off the pavements in the streets of Paris. Yet all the woe that could be inflicted by an enemy army of occupation could be only days away.

The better informed, Talleyrand and Roger among them, far from being surprised by the Allies' break-through, found it difficult to understand how even the genius of Napoleon had prevented it from happening long before. It was nine weeks since he had left Paris and for the past six they had been waiting impatiently to hear that his army, less than a third the size of that of the Allies, had been completely defeated.

During these weeks of waiting the question upper-most in their minds had been what would happen in France after Napoleon had been vanquished. Through his secret sources Talleyrand knew the divergent views of the Allies. All of them were agreed that the Emperor must be deposed and France reduced to her old frontiers before the Revolution, but there their agreement ended.

Castlereagh was for giving the French liberal terms so that their good will would result in a treaty of commerce with Britain, similar to that which had been signed with King Louis XVI in 1787, and that they should be allowed to choose their own future form of government by a plebiscite.

The Czar also was not harshly inclined toward the French people. He was averse to a Republic, yet did not favour the return of the Bourbons. He would have preferred a limited monarchy under a new dynasty, and he had been heard to mention Bernadotte for that rôle.

Frederick William agreed with the Czar about a limited monarchy; but the Prussians generally were filled with hatred for the French and wished to impose upon them the harshest terms possible.

Austria wanted to leave France strong and, as Marie Louise was the Emperor Francis's daughter, he proposed that she be made Regent for her little son, the King of Rome.

Lastly, from January onward the Senate had at last thrown off its long subservience to Napoleon. A large majority in it wished to see the end of him, and many of the older members who had been Jacobins, eagerly hoped for the return of a Republic.

Talleyrand and Roger had discussed the question exhaustively. For many years they had agreed that the only hope of a lasting peace in Europe lay in a treaty of friendship between France and England. They therefore favoured a strong France. Both were for a limited monarchy as the most stable form of government, fore-seeing that a return to a Republic would lead to dissen-sion and, if the extremists got the upper hand, the possible repetition of '93, with another reign of terror. Talleyrand was confident that, given the power he hoped to have, he could restrain the hotheads in the Senate and he aimed to bring about the restoration of the Bourbons.

After Wellington's victory at Orthez Soult had skil-fully withdrawn his army to the east, knowing that the Duke, not daring to risk an attack on his flank by advanc-ing further up the coast, must follow him, and hoping to join up with Suchet. But this had necessitated his aban-doning Bayonne and Bordeaux. Wellington had detached General Beresford's division to occupy the latter city, and

M

on March 12th the Duc d'Angoulême had entered it with the British troops. This Prince, who had married Louis XVI's only daughter, the Princess Thérèse, having been welcomed by the Royalist Mayor, had proclaimed his Uncle, Louis XVIII, King of France; upon which the majority of the citizens had shown their delight and donned the White Cockade.

Soon afterwards the King's brother, the Comte d'Artois, had arrived in Nancy, and his emissary, the Baron de Vitrolles, had several times come in secret to Paris to confer with Talleyrand; but as long as Napoleon's Council of Regency remained in control of the capital, Talleyrand's hands were tied. Many senators were also strongly averse to the return of a monarchy. And, above all, each of the victorious Allies would have their say on what form the new government should take. So the future of France still lay on the knees of the gods.

22

Un Cri de Cœur

ON March 28th a meeting of the Imperial Council was called to debate the question of whether, now that the enemy was approaching the capital, the Empress, her son and King Joseph should or should not leave it. Six weeks earlier the Emperor had written from Nogent that if Paris was in danger they should retire via Rambouillet to Blois, taking with them the Great Dignitaries and Ministers. General Clarke, the Minister of War, stated that the garrison of Paris was incapable of resisting the enemy, so departure was decided upon.

The decision placed Talleyrand in a very awkward position. As a Great Dignitary he should leave with the rest, otherwise he would have defied the Emperor, and he was loath yet to come out into the open. On the other hand he was determined to remain in Paris, otherwise he would be deprived of all chance of influencing events in the way he wished them to go.

With his usual foresight he prepared a way out of this annoying dilemma. He drove in his coach to the *Porte de la Conference,* with the apparent intention of going to Rambouillet. But he was stopped at the gate by M. de Remusat, who was in command of the National Guard there, and refused permission to leave the city—a delightful little farce which had been arranged by these two friends the previous evening.

By this time the Russians had reached Montreuil where, with the remnants of their corps, Marmont and Moncey were putting up a last desperate resistance; but it was now plain to everyone that the entry of the enemy into the capital could not be long delayed.

That day, after his usual reception of a number of friends who were always to be found in the main hall of his mansion, Talleyrand drew Roger aside, into the small library, closed the door and said:

'Although I have not yet definitely committed myself to the Bourbons, you and I are agreed that the best hope of securing peace and prosperity for France lies in the restoration to the throne of the legitimate heir. But whether this can be achieved still remains far from certain. In my view, everything now hangs upon the Czar. Once he can be won over he will overrule his less powerful fellow Monarchs; but to influence him I must have ready access to him when he arrives in Paris. Now, at last, has come the moment when your help can immensely strengthen our chances of bringing about the situation we both desire. I wish you to take a letter to him.'

Roger nodded. 'There should be no great difficulty in doing so, if I approach the Allied troops under a flag of truce. What do you intend to say in your letter?'

Taking the letter from a drawer in the desk, the Prince handed it to him with a smile. 'I have had it from my friend, Count Nesselrode, his Minister of Foreign Affairs, that His Imperial Majesty intends to take up his quarters in the Elysée Palace. I have told him that this is also known to his enemies, and that they have mined the palace, with the intention of blowing him up. I have then said that my house is quite large enough to accommodate him and his personal entourage, and I humbly offer it to him as a residence in which I can guarantee his safety while in Paris.'

'I congratulate Your Highness upon this extraordinarily astute move,' Roger smiled back. 'And, I should have no difficulty in reaching the Czar through Count Nessel-rode's good offices. I knew him when he was Russian Ambassador here. Now I will be off.'

Before leaving he got from one of the footmen a white napkin and tied it to a malacca cane, to use as a flag of truce; then, in one of Talleyrand's carriages he drove toward Montmartre. From the heights there the smoke from the battle and formations of soldiers could clearly be seen, but in some sections there seemed to be little action. Roger directed his coachman toward one of those and when he showed his white flag he was allowed to pass through the lines. A Russian officer who spoke French gave him an escort to take him to the Czar's headquarters, which was only a few miles further on, and by early afternoon he reached them.

After waiting for a while he was taken to Count Nessel-rode, who greeted him politely as an old acquaintance. From the Count Roger learned that several of the French Generals had already capitulated, and it was hoped that Marshal Marmont could be persuaded to surrender the city, as that would save the inhabitants from the horrors of street fighting. Roger then disclosed the contents of Tal-leyrand's letter. At that Nesselrode's mouth twitched in a smile and he remarked :

'His Highness the Prince de Benevent is a monstrous clever fellow. Come with me and I will present you to His Imperial Majesty.'

When Roger had made his bow, the tall, handsome, curly-haired Alexander raised an eyebrow and said, 'It seems that you have a genius, Mr. Brook, for always popping up, as you English say of a bad penny, when least expected.'

'Perhaps, Sire, but I hope your Imperial Majesty does not liken me to one,' Roger replied with a smile.

'Nay.' The Czar extended his hand for Roger to kiss. 'There have been times when you have served us well. However, we had hoped that from Moscow you would return to St. Petersburg, bringing us intelligence of Napoleon's intentions.'

'Alas, Sire, I would I could have, and so been saved from starving near to death in your Russian snows. But the retreat was decided upon within hours of my rejoining the Emperor, and I became caught up in it.'

'And now, what brings you here? Surely not only to tell us that Paris is as good as ours?'

Nesselrode produced the letter. 'Mr. Brook brought this from the Prince de Benevent, Sire. Have I your permission to open it?'

'Do so, Count, and read the contents to us.'

When he had listened to the letter, Alexander asked, 'What is your opinion about this?'

'I would advise Your Imperial Majesty to accept the Prince's offer. His mansion is commodious and you could reside there in greater comfort than in many palaces. There is also the fact that, now King Joseph has fled, Talleyrand has become the most powerful man in Paris. He will have great influence with the Senate, and if you deign to accord him your friendship, he can do much to further your Imperial Majesty's designs.'

'So be it, then.' The handsome autocrat turned to Roger. 'We thank you, Mr. Brook, for bringing us the Prince's offer of his house. You may tell him that it is our pleasure to honour it by our acceptance.'

Roger bowed himself away, and by five o'clock was back in Paris. He found the mansion in the Rue St. Florentin crowded with people; not only Tallyrand's friends, such as the Duc de Dalberg who, although holding a post in Napoleon's government was secretly a Royalist and had brought about the meetings between the Prince and d'Artois's agent, the Baron de Vitrolles, but many important men who for a long time past had thought it dangerous to associate themselves with the crafty statesman. Immediately it had become known that the Council of Regency had fled from Paris, Talleyrand had become the man of the hour and everyone was eager to stand well with him.

Forcing his way through the crush toward him, Roger simply smiled and nodded. Returning the smile Talleyrand said in a low voice, 'France will owe you much, *mon ami*. The game is now as good as in our hands.'

Next morning the house was equally crowded and Roger learned from the Abbé du Pradt, another of Talleyrand's intimates, that a mansion in the Rue de Paradis was the scene of equal excitement, with cheering crowds outside in the street. It was that of Marshal Marmont. A few hours earlier he had received Count Nesselrode, Prince Orlof and Schwarzenberg's chief adjutant at one of the gates of Paris, and signed a surrender of the city. Instead of bewailing this humiliation, the fickle Parisians were acclaiming the Marshal as though he had won a great victory. They were to be spared the killings, the looting, the rape that had been the terrible lot of the inhabitants of the many great cities that the French troops had sacked without mercy. To render thanks to God was not enough, the population went delirious with joy.

Meanwhile, Napoleon was distraught by the ill news

that he was receiving from courier after courier. He had twice sent urgent despatches to Augereau requiring him to bring his army up from Lyon to aid in the defence of Paris, but the Marshal had ignored the order. Instead he had surrendered Lyon, and so betrayed his master. Napoleon's own contempt for Schwarzenberg had undone him and the Allies were within a league of Paris. Not only had his beloved wife and son fled, but his brother Joseph, who should have remained to hold Paris, had betrayed him and gone with them; although, under determined leadership the many thousand National Guards in the city could have held it, at least until he arrived to their relief.

Still refusing to consider himself beaten, he turned his army about. By incredible exertions, on the 29th it re-entered Troyes, next day it reached Fontainebleau. Late at night on the 30th he actually came in sight of the camp fires of Marmont's troops, only to be utterly stricken by the news that their Marshal, too, had turned traitor and surrendered.

At ten o'clock on the morning of the 31st the Czar Alexander, with Francis of Austria and Frederick William of Prussia on either side of him, rode triumphantly down the Champs Elysées into Paris. The bulk of the city's population had hastily donned the White Cockade and groups of Royalists shouted 'Long live the Bourbons'.

On the Czar's arrival in the Rue St. Florentin Talleyrand, according to protocol, handed his mansion and its contents over to His Imperial Majesty who thanked him graciously and proceeded to settle in with his entourage. When the rooms had been satisfactorily allocated Talleyrand had the opportunity that he had so skilfully schemed for of a private conversation with Alexander.

The Czar announced that he wished the French to

choose their own form of government by a plebiscite; but
Talleyrand pointed out that this would take many weeks,
and that they already had in the Senate a body representing the people.

Alexander expressed concern that the Senate might opt
for a return to a Republic; whereas he, his fellow
sovereigns and Lord Castlereagh all favoured France's
becoming a limited monarchy.

Talleyrand assured him that he could control the extremists, so the only question that remained was whose name
should be put forward to the Senate as the future King
of France.

'The Emperor Francis,' said Alexander, 'would naturally like his grandson to assume that title, with his daughter,
Marie Louise, as Regent.'

'Sire', Talleyrand replied. 'With a member of the
Bonaparte dynasty on the throne, Napoleon would remain, for all practical purposes the ruling power and,
wherever he might be, dictate the policy of France.'

'You are right, and on those grounds the rest of us
have already expressed our objections to Metternich.
What think you though of Prince Eugène?'

'As Napoleon's step-son and a man who had always
displayed great devotion to him, the same objection
applies, Sire.'

'Bernadotte, then. As Crown Prince of Sweden, he has
shown himself to be a most capable administrator as well
as a very able General.'

Talleyrand smiled. 'If we wanted a soldier to rule us,
Sire, we already have the greatest one in the world.'

'The only alternative with which we are left seems to be
the Bourbons,' the Czar remarked with obvious reluctance.
'But we do not like them, and neither do the French
people. The Duc d'Angoulême has been well received in

Bordeaux, but during the passage of our armies through eastern France we saw not a sign of anyone desiring a Restoration. And can one wonder at that? These stupid, arrogant Princes have learned nothing during their twenty years of exile. They and their émigré nobility would at once strive to secure their ancient privileges, batten on the people and again earn their hatred by the suppression of liberty.'

'Permit me to submit, Sire,' Talleyrand replied suavely, 'that while your description of the Princes well fits the frivolous Comte d'Artois, it cannot fairly be applied to his elder brother, who would become King Louis XVIII. In the old days at Versailles, when he was known as the Comte de Provence, although our tastes were somewhat divergent, I had ample evidence of his character. He is far from a fool. He was knowledgeable about scientific matters and a talented geographer. He is a man of peace and tact. He would, I am convinced, grant a liberal constitution fully protecting the people's liberties and make an excellent ruler.

'Moreover, I beg leave to differ from Your Imperial Majesty in your assessment of the French people. The French Army is more devoted to its own glory than to Napoleon. The whole nation longs for peace and can find it only under the old dynasty.

'Finally, Sire, surely anyone so well-versed in statescraft as yourself must agree that we should be guided by a principle, and in this case it is legitimacy. The legitimate King of France is Louis XVIII.'

The Czar nodded thoughtfully. 'There is much in what you say, Prince. We will think over the matter, and discuss it with our allies.'

That evening there gathered round a long table the Czar and Nesselrode, the King of Prussia and his First

Minister Hardenberg, the Princes Schwarzenberg and Lichenstein, representing the Emperor of Austria, and Talleyrand and Dalberg to speak for the Bourbons. At small side tables sat secretaries to take notes, the Marquis de Joucourt and Roger acting for Talleyrand.

Alexander opened the proceedings by declaring that they had a choice of three possible courses: they could make peace with Napoleon, make Marie Louise Regent for her son, or restore the Bourbons. The first, he said, they had already agreed to be unacceptable, the second might lead to Napoleon continuing to influence events but the third was a possibility to which he was prepared to agree, provided that it was the will of France. He then called on the Prince de Benevent to put the case for the Bourbons.

Talleyrand did so with all his persuasive powers, and his arguments were accepted without dispute.

Next day a proclamation, signed by Alexander on behalf of the Allied Powers, was issued, inviting the Senate to appoint a Provisional Government. Talleyrand, as Vice Grand Elector, summoned the Senate. Only sixty-four out of the one hundred and forty attended this momentous gathering, and the Prince had no difficulty in securing their agreement to his proposals. A Provisional Government of five was formed, with him as its leader. On April 2nd the Senate and the Corps Legislative passed motions that Napoleon was deposed. On the 3rd the Provisional Government published an 'Address to the French Armies', urging them to separate from 'a man who is not even French'.

But Napoleon was still far from finished. At Fontainebleau during the past week he had succeeded in amassing from many quarters an army of sixty thousand men. On the 4th, when the news arrived that he had been deposed, he had a furious scene with his Marshals. Led by Ney they argued heatedly with him, insisting that to continue the war was futile, and eventually persuaded him to sign a form of abdication with which Caulaincourt was sent off to the Czar. But while it contained his agreement to relinquish the throne and leave France, it stipulated that the Empress should remain as Regent for his son.

The decision already reached by the Allies made this unacceptable. Caulaincourt had to return and tell Napoleon so. This aroused in him a renewed burst of energy and fierce determination to fight to the bitter end. Orders were issued in all directions to prepare anew for a march on Paris.

Talleyrand received news of this in the middle of the night. The Provisional Government of five now held its sessions on the ground floor of the mansion; the first floor was occupied by the Czar and his entourage; so Roger had had to move up to an attic. Going up to it, the Prince woke Roger, told him what was about to happen and said :

'*Mon ami,* I ask one more service of you. Go to Napoleon. If you tell him what you have recently seen in Paris with your own eyes, he will believe you. Tell him that Schwarzenberg has one hundred and forty thousand troops surrounding the city. That Marmont's men are now fraternising with those of his enemies and will take up arms against him. That the National Guard here now wear the White Cockade. That if he carries out his insane plan to march on Paris it will mean civil war. In your dissuading him from entering on further hostilities lies our one hope now of saving many thousand lives.'

Reluctantly Roger consented. It was getting on for three months since he had seen Napoleon, so he no longer had to pretend to acute lameness, and had gradually given up aids to walking, using now only occasionally a stick for the sake of appearances. In the early hours of the morning he set off in a light barouche for Fontainebleau, and arrived there soon after seven o'clock.

Napoleon was still asleep in bed, so Roger breakfasted in the headquarters Mess, simply telling old acquaintances who were there that, having recovered his health, he had come to offer his services : a plausible lie of which he felt ashamed, but it was readily accepted by his sadly depressed companions.

It was half-past nine before he was at last shown in to the presence. Napoleon's pale face was drawn with worry, and his eyes red-rimmed from lack of sleep. He greeted Roger cordially and was eager to hear the latest news from Paris, but said that he was about to receive his Marshals, so that must wait until later.

A few minutes afterwards those of his paladins who remained with him were ushered in : Berthier, Ney, Oudinot, Lefebvre and Macdonald. With them were Caulaincourt, who had striven so desperately to secure an acceptable peace for him, and his ex-Foreign Minister, Marat, Duc de Bassano.

Once more animated by enthusiasm he spoke to them of the coming campaign. He would lead the way in person at the head of his devoted Imperial Guard, which still numbered nine thousand men. He had a new plan. They would strike south, by-pass Schwarzenberg's Austrians round Paris, march to the Loire, then join up with the armies of Suchet and Soult. His own sixty thousand together with their troops would again give him two hundred thousand men.

His audience heard him out in gloomy silence. Then they began to upbraid him for demanding further sacrifices in a cause now completely lost. Macdonald, who had just arrived with his weary corps, said, 'Our horses can go no further, we have not enough ammunition left for a single skirmish, and no means of obtaining more.'

Others declared that to continue the fight would result in civil war, and that now he had been deposed as Emperor he had no right to demand their allegiance.

At that he burst out furiously, 'You want repose! You are seeking peace for your own ease, but the army is still loyal and will obey me.'

'No,' retorted Ney bluntly. 'It will obey its com-manders.'

At that Napoleon gave way in despair. The Marshals trooped out of the room and Roger went with them. He had seen enough to know that anything he had meant to say was now redundant. The attitude of the Marshals made it clear that they would no longer lead their men into battle; so Napoleon was finished. With these welcome tidings he returned to Paris.

On that same day, April 6th, Talleyrand submitted to the Chamber a Constitutional Charter, which was duly adopted. It summoned to the throne Louis Stanislas Xavier, brother of the late King, on his swearing to adhere to the constitutional rights and liberties of the people, contained in the document.

After further negotiations with the Allies concerning conditions, Napoleon signed an abdication in accordance with their wishes. He was to keep the title of Emperor, but—at the insistence of the Czar, in preference to various other places suggested—exiled to the island of Elba with his own guard of four hundred—later increased to one thousand—troops. The Empress was to be given three Italian duchies, and her son would bear the title of Duke of Parma, that being the largest of the three. An annual income of two million francs was to be divided equally between Napoleon and Marie Louise and two and a half million francs allotted to the other Bonapartes between them.

Louis XVIII, then fifty-nine years of age, was immensely fat and severely afflicted with gout. Just at this time he was suffering so greatly from a bout that it was impossible for him to leave England. In consequence it was arranged that his brother, the Comte d'Artois, should enter Paris as his representative and Lieutenant General of the Kingdom on April 12th. The ratification of the Treaty of Fontainebleau, as Napoleon's abdication was termed, was fixed for the 11th.

Roger, relaxed and happy now that peace had at last been restored after all these years, was greatly looking forward to getting home and henceforth leading a life of carefree ease. But he decided to stay on for a week or so in Paris, to witness the entry of the Comte d'Artois and join in the celebrations of the Restoration.

He was not destined to do so. On the 9th Lord Castle-reagh arrived to sign the Treaty on behalf of Britain, on the 11th. That night he attended a reception given by the Czar at Talleyrand's. On seeing Roger he came up to him and said, 'Before I left London the Duchess of Kew came to see me. She had reason to believe that I should find you here, and asked me, if I did, to give you this letter.'

Having thanked the Foreign Minister, Roger tore the envelope open. It contained only a brief note :

'*Roger my Heart,*
'*I am distraught with worry. I have reason to believe both Susan and Charles have fallen into evil hands and*

are in great peril. I beg you, by your love for me, to hasten to my assistance without a moment's delay.

'Ever your Georgina.'

Half an hour later, in one of Talleyrand's coaches, drawn by six horses, Roger was on his way to Calais.

23

Lost, Stolen or Strayed

THE speed with which the coach covered the one hundred and fifty miles to Calais served no useful purpose, because when Roger reached the port a storm was raging. News of Napoleon's surrender had reached the city two days earlier and now that the war was over Roger had no need to seek out a smuggler; so had the weather been even moderate any skipper would have been willing to run him across the Straits for a few gold pieces. But a fierce wind, coupled with a Spring tide, rendered any attempt to cross the Channel suicidal.

Angry and intensely worried, he drove to the best inn, ate a belated breakfast; then, not having slept during his journey, went straight to bed. When he woke late in the afternoon his mind immediately resumed the futile speculations with which it had been plagued all through the night.

What could be the trouble that had caused Georgina to send for him so urgently? Into whose hands had Susan and Charles fallen? At first, the coupling of their names had puzzled him, because he had believed Charles to be with Wellington's army somewhere in south-western France. But only through Charles could Georgina have learned that from the Pyrenees he had returned to Paris at Talleyrand's request, and so might be found through him by Lord Castlereagh. Charles could have sent her that information in a letter, but it seemed more probable that, for some reason, he had gone to England. But why should the two young people be in peril? And from whom, or what?

In vain Roger racked his brains. The answer to this mystery could be found only across the Channel, and one glance through the window showed that while he slept there had been no improvement in the weather.

It was not until the afternoon of the following day, the 11th, that the sea subsided to an oily swell. Regardless of price, Roger had already arranged for a yacht, said to be the fastest in the harbour, to take him over, and the wind being favourable it arrived off Dover in the early hours of the morning. But the customs men at Dover having for so long had no dealings with French vessels, Roger's landing was delayed until, by threats of reporting this obstruction to the Admiralty, a senior official had been got out of bed and taken responsibility for his being allowed to come ashore. By the time he had roused an innkeeper, hired a coach and been driven to London it was well past midday.

Feeling certain that, having sent for him, Georgina would not be in the country but hopefully awaiting his arrival in London, he had himself driven straight to Kew House. He proved right in that, and was shown up to her. Dishevelled and unshaven as he was she gave a cry of joy when he entered her boudoir, ran forward, threw her arms about him and burst into tears.

'There, there, my sweet,' he soothed her, clasping her to him. 'I would have been here two days since, but for the accursed weather. Tell me now, what has occurred to cause you such distress?'

"Tis Susan and Charles,' she sobbed. 'They are bo*'
become Satanists.'

'Oh, come!' he expostulated. 'That is more th~
credit.'

"Tis so,' she insisted. 'There is no other ~ ,lanation for
their conduct.'

Putting an arm round her waist he led her to a
sofa, pulled her down beside him and said, 'I beg
you, my love, calm yourself and tell me all from the beginning.'

Dabbing at her eyes with a scrap of lace handkerchief,
Georgina drew a deep breath, then said more quietly, "Tis
all the fault of that little vixen, Jemima, Maureen Luggala's daughter. I could kill her. Soon after Charles went
to the war she and Susan became bosom friends. When we
were in London they went everywhere together. Scarce a
day passed without their seeing each other. The girl had
good manners, an amusing if somewhat bitter wit, and her
name had never been linked with any scandal, so I made
no objection to their friendship. Then in February Lady
Luggala decided to return to her home in Dublin for a
while, and invited Susan to go over on a visit. To pleasure
Susan I had had Jemima to stay both at Stillwaters and
Newmarket, so 'twas only a return of hospitality, and
Susan had never been to Ireland. I agreed to her going
with them.

'The visit was to have been for a fortnight, but early in
March Susan wrote to me that she was enjoying herself
so greatly in Dublin that she wished to stay on a while
longer. I replied that she could, but must be back by the
middle of the mouth, to choose stuffs and have her clothes
made for the coming season. She replied, again postpon-
ing her return. I wrote insisting that she should be back
by the 24th. Then, to my amazement, she defied me and

calmly stated that 'twas her intention to pass the summer in Ireland.

'On the day that I received her missive, Charles arrived unexpectedly from France. The Duke had sent him home with despatches describing d'Angoulême's enthusiastic reception in Bordeaux. Naturally he was upset by Susan's behaviour and wrote to her himself. A reply came four days later, but not from Susan. It was from Lady Luggala, and when we read it we were both amazed and horrified.

'She blamed herself bitterly for not having taken more serious notice of the way in which the two girls had been spending much of their time. They had become interested in mesmerism and were regularly attending meetings of a society to do with the occult. Susan had said nothing to her of my letters telling her she must come home, and she had been happy to have her stay on. Then, when she learned what the girls had been doing she had forbade them to go to further meetings. To her utter consternation they then revealed to her that they had both been initiated and had become witches themselves.'

'God's death!' Roger exclaimed. 'I no longer wonder at finding you in such a state.'

'But even that is not the worst,' Georgina began to sob again. 'There was a violent quarrel, the girls refused to listen to reason. They packed their things and, although Maureen Luggala did her best to prevent them, they left the house.'

'What, to go to this witch?'

'One can only suppose so. But that is not all. When we read Maureen's letter, Charles was distraught. He left immediately for Ireland, to go in search of Susan and bring her back.'

'That must have been three weeks ago. Surely by now

he would have traced the girls. What news has he sent you of his endeavours to do so?'

'None. And 'tis that which puts a crown upon my misery. After some days, hearing nothing from him, I wrote to Lady Luggala. Her reply reached me early this month. She said he had not been to her house, and she has heard nothing of his being in Dublin. He, as well as both the girls, has completely disappeared. In my extremity my thoughts naturally turned to you. Charles had told me that, when you left him at the Duke's headquarters, you were about to return to Paris and stay again with Talley-rand. It was common knowledge that Lord Castlereagh was crossing to France to sign the Treaty, so I asked him to take my note to you. From fear it might fall into wrong hands and so blacken Susan's reputation I dared not give particulars of this awful business, but I knew that my appeal to you would not be in vain.'

'I lost not a moment. In fact I left in the midst of a reception and, as I have said, would have been here early yesterday but for the weather.' Roger paused a moment, then went on with a frown, 'That two credulous young females should have allowed themselves to fall under the spell of some evil woman of strong personality is deplorable, but not remarkable. It is Charles's disappearance that is so inexplicable. Had he been a courier or servant and met his death in an accident, little notice would have been taken; but as an Earl his death could not fail to have been reported in the news sheets.'

Georgina sighed. 'Alas, there is a possible explanation, though the thought of it fills me with horror.'

'Whatever it may be, you must tell me of it.'

'When I showed him Maureen Luggala's letter about the two girls having become witches, he made a confession to me. The autumn before last a friend of his introduced him to an occult circle known as the New Hell Fire Club. He said that he took no particular interest in the ceremonies that were performed there, but joined the club for the excitement of participating afterwards in orgies in which partners were drawn by lots and both men and women remained masked. After midnight on last year's New Year's Eve he left a ball that I gave in Berkeley Square to attend a meeting of the club. Unknown to him Susan also left the ball with a Captain Hawksbury. She was under the impression that he meant to take her for an hour or two to a normal private party, but he took her to this club.'

'What!' Roger exclaimed, his blue eyes flashing with anger. 'By God, I'll kill him for this.'

'You are spared the trouble. He was killed last summer in a brawl. But fortunately Susan came to no harm. Before the orgy was due to start, the witch who ran the place stripped herself naked and began to perform some lecherous act with her high priest and a negro. In horrified disgust Susan demanded that Hawksbury should take her away. He refused. There was an altercation. She was masked, but Charles was near by and recognised her voice. After a fight, by a miracle he got her out of the house.'

'Praise be for that! But what you tell me explains your fear for Charles. He may have told you that he joined the Hell Fire Club only for the excitement of having masked women who neither needed elaborate courting nor were ordinary whores, out of reluctance to admit that he had actually become a Satanist.'

Georgina nodded. 'Yes. That is the thought that so appals me. He may have found the girls with the witch and been persuaded to join them.'

'Think you this Lady Luggala was telling the truth and

the whole truth, in the letters she wrote you? What sort
of woman is she?'

'I have no reason to doubt it. She is the widow of an
Irish baronet and, I should say, comes herself from a
reputable family. She is about my age and quite good-
looking, but self-centred, somewhat vain and not over-
burdened with brains.'

'It seems then reasonably plausible that she would not
have concerned herself greatly about the girls' doings, so
allowed them to go where they pleased, with no more
than an occasional question.'

'I am sure that is so from her attitude toward her
daughter. Jemima was much the stronger character, and
had quite a temper. Susan once told me Maureen often let
Jemima have her own way rather than risk a scene.'

'Then, apart from negligence, it would appear that no
blame in this awful affair attaches to Lady Luggala. But
I shall want her address, so that I may call on and question her as soon as I get to Dublin.'

From a casket on a nearby buhl table Georgina took a
packet of letters, and said, 'Here are those from Susan as
well as Maureen Luggala's. You had best read them all.'

Roger did so in the sequence of the dates on which they
had been written. As he handed them back, he remarked,
'There is something about Susan's last letter that strikes
me as a little queer. It is her usual scrawl, so they were all
penned by her without a doubt, but somehow the phrase-
ology strikes me as out of keeping with her character, and
she does not show the great affection we know her to have
for you.'

'That struck me, too,' Georgina nodded. 'In fact, when
I received the last one from her I re-read them all, and
I had a feeling that it might have been dictated.'

''Tis just possible. You say this girl Jemima has a very

strong character, and has great influence over her. If they have been monkeying with mesmerism she may have achieved control over Susan's mind. I'd not be surprised if that were not the root of the whole trouble.'

Changing the subject he went on, 'I'd be on the Bristol coach this evening had I not been away all these months from poor little Mary. As things are, I know you'll understand if I delay to spend tonight with her, and set out for Dublin tomorrow. How fares it with her, or have you not seen her recently?'

Georgina hesitated a moment. 'Until this present trouble arose I've not been in London since January. And I did not run across her during the little season. I gather she goes very seldom into society these days.'

'Ah, well, it will be a fine surprise for her that I am come home at last, and now the war is over soon be able to settle down with her for good. I've kept the coach I hired below, and if you'll forgive me, sweet, I'll now be on my way to Richmond.'

'If you must, dear heart, but you have travelled overnight from Dover, and will be travelling again tomorrow. 'Tis not for selfish reasons I suggest it, but would it not be best for you to dismiss your coach and take mine later? Meanwhile, lie down and nap in a bedroom here for an hour or so, then let me send you on your way fortified with a good meal.'

Although Roger had managed to prevent himself from being seasick during the crossing, he had felt far from well, and the hours of jolting in the hired coach had fatigued him, so he saw the sense in Georgina's proposal and smilingly agreed to it.

No sooner was he stretched out on a bed than he fell sound asleep, and would have slept on had not Georgina come to wake him at three o'clock. Over their early dinner

they agreed not to mention Susan or Charles, and he gave
an account of his last, hectic days in France before Napoleon's abdication. By four o'clock they had taken a fond
leave of each other, and he left Kew House in her
coach.

In a little under an hour the coach was within a hundred yards of Thatched House Lodge. Putting his head
out of the window, Roger called up to the coachman,
'Drive straight into the stable yard, then you can water
the horses and take a mug of ale with my man before you
drive back.'

At the sound of the horses' hooves on the cobbles of the
yard, old Dan Izzard came running down from his quarters over the coach-house, and as Roger alighted cried
happily :

'Why, bless me, 'tis the master! I been hopin' now the
war be over ye'd soon be home agin.'

Roger shook the smiling ex-smuggler warmly by the
hand. "Tis good to see you, Dan, and soon now you'll be
sick of the sight of me for ever lounging about the place.
How is Her Ladyship?'

The smile left Dan's wrinkled face, and his glance
shifted slightly as he replied, 'Oh, she be pretty well; but
I don't see much o' her these days. She don't ride no more
and scarce ever drives out. The horses be eatin' they's
heads off.'

During his drive from London Roger's mind had been
entirely occupied with worry about Susan and Charles,
so he had thought no more of Georgina's vague reply to
his enquiry about Mary. Now, with a frown, he turned
quickly away, strode across the yard and entered the house
by the back door.

A maid was sitting knitting in the kitchen. She came
quickly to her feet, and he acknowledged with a nod the

bob she made him, then walked through the dining room to the drawing room. There was no-one there. Crossing the hall, he looked into the small sitting room. There was no-one there, either. As he turned away, his housekeeper, Mrs. Muffet, came down the stairs. Her eyes widened on seeing him, then she forced a smile and greeted him pleasantly. He also forced a smile as he replied, then asked curtly :

'Where is Her Ladyship?'

'Up in her bedroom, Sir.'

'Is she ill?'

'No . . . No, Sir. But she . . . she spends a lot of her time in bed now.'

Instead of asking what the devil Mary was doing in bed at five o'clock in the afternoon if she was not ill, Roger took the stairs two at a time, strode down the corridor and, without knocking, flung open the door of the bedroom he shared with Mary.

She was half-lying in bed, propped up by three pillows. The dreamy look on her face was replaced by a startled stare as her eyes met Roger's. Jerking herself upright, she exclaimed :

'Why, bless my soul ! If it's not the man who calls himself my husband !'

Her words were slurred, and Roger's glance had taken in the fact that a decanter two-thirds full and a half-empty glass of port stood on a table beside the bed.

'What the hell's the meaning of this?' he snapped. 'You're drunk ! How can you so shame yourself with the knowledge of the servants?'

Mary lay back and smiled seraphically. 'Not . . . not drunk, darling. Jus' a little tipsy. Tha's all.'

'You're drunk !' he retorted angrily. 'And I gather this afternoon is no exception. You make a habit of it. God alive, Mary! What in the world has driven you to become a drunkard?'

'Nothin' else to do. Man I married leaves me after a . . . a few months, an' goes galli . . . gallivanting about on . . . on the Continent.'

'Oh, come now, Mary,' he said more gently. 'You know I had no option but to go in search of Charles.'

'Oh yes, you did. You . . . you pref . . . preferred to leave your wife rather than dis . . . displease that gilded whore the . . . the Duchess of Kew.'

'Mary! How dare you refer to Georgina as a whore.'

''Cause she's a whore. Every . . . everyone knows it. Besides yourself she's had a . . . a score of men in her bed. But . . . but, talking of bed, now you're home you . . . you might as well get your clothes off an' . . . an' come into mine.'

'For two people who care for each other to get gay on wine before making love is one thing,' Roger replied icily. 'To go to bed with a drunken woman is quite another, and a pastime I have never wished to experience.'

Stepping back he slammed the door and, white with rage, stamped downstairs.

In the library he poured himself a stiff brandy. His hand was shaking and his mind bemused. In his wildest dreams he had never imagined such a scene as had just taken place. What a homecoming! True, he had quarrelled with Mary before leaving for Spain, and he had been mainly to blame. But Georgina had brought them together as he was about to board the frigate, and they had made it up.

What should he do now? Best leave her to sleep it off and talk some sense into her in the morning. With him at home she would soon be cured of this habit of drinking.

But, no. Tomorrow he had to go to Dublin. When he told her that, there would be the most frightful scene. And he had counted on her this evening to take his mind off this terrible business of Susan and Charles. Now he would have to dine alone and brood about it half the night.

The thought was unbearable. To hell with it. He would return to London and sleep at Amesbury House. As the season had not started, it was unlikely that Droopy would be there, but he could sup at White's and, for once, distract his mind by gambling; then, with a bottle or two inside him, get some sleep.

Tossing off the brandy that remained in his glass, he marched out to the stables, shouted for Dan, had him saddle a horse, and ten minutes later was cantering off toward the park gate.

On reaching Amesbury House a pleasant surprise awaited him. The footman who answered the door told him that his Lordship was in London and at home. The reason for this emerged when Roger was shown into the library and the friends had exchanged greetings. Lord Amesbury had died in December, so Droopy was now the Earl, and had come up to take his seat in the House of Lords.

When they had settled down Roger began to pour out his woes to his old friend, first describing his most recent trouble of arriving home to find that Mary had taken to drink.

At that Droopy nodded his narrow head with its bird-like beak of a nose, and said unexpectedly, 'I am not greatly surprised. Until you brought her back from America she had not lived in England since she was married to that city merchant. It has ever been customary for persons of quality to look down upon anyone in trade; so, although she is daughter to an Earl, she could not be received without her husband. Naturally, she was not invited anywhere. By marrying her you restored her position in society, but between your return from America and your departure for Spain there was not time enough for her to make any intimate friends in our own circle. Georgina, I know, did her best to cultivate her, but for a reason you can well guess, Mary cold-shouldered the approaches of your lovely Duchess. I drove out to Richmond now and again to visit her until last November, but it was then that my father became ill, so I had to remain at Normanrood with him. Since his death I have been pestiferous busy on matters concerning his estate, so it is six months or more since I have seen her. Friendless, and neglected by you as she has been, what could you expect? What option had the poor girl but either to take a lover or take to the bottle? Now that you are home again and, praise be, for good, you'll soon have her sober and loving again.'

Roger nodded. 'There is much in what you say, Ned; and I'll confess I had not previously looked at the matter in that light. As soon as I can I'll put things right and make up to her for my long absence. But, alas, I cannot do so yet. Tomorrow I have to leave for Dublin.'

'Dublin!' Droopy leaned forward, peering with his short-sighted eyes at Roger. 'Why, in God's name, must you go there?'

With a heavy sigh Roger began to tell him all he had learned from Georgina about Susan and Charles. When he came to recount how, unknown to each other, they had gone to a New Year's Eve meeting of the New Hell Fire Club, Droopy interrupted :

'Wait one moment. This stirs a memory in my mind that may be of use to you.'

'You know of the place, then?'

'Yes, I am acquainted with several wealthy rakes who were members and, from their accounts of it, quite a number of titled dames participated in the Satanic revels. It was run by an Irish woman named Katie O'Brien and an unfrocked Catholic priest, one Father Damien. As they fled the country last autumn, it may well be that they went to Dublin and started another devil's circle there. Quite possibly 'tis she who has Susan and the young Luggala girl in her toils. That, too, could account for Charles's disappearance. Since he was in cahoots with her when she was here in London and may have found the girls with her in Dublin, maybe he decided to join the coven willingly, or perhaps she has some hold over him and used it to make him remain with them.'

'You may well be right about Charles,' Roger nodded. 'But why did the witch and her priest flee the country? I would have supposed that, having so many influential patrons, they would have had ample protection.'

'Against a charge of practising witchcraft, yes; but not for that which would have been brought against them. A great part of the Irish are loyal to the Crown, as witness the fine performance in battle of the Irish regiments under Wellington; but there are others who would have Ireland become a Republic and would have aided the French had they landed there. Katie O'Brien was such a one, and under cover of running her Hell Fire Club for bawdy decadents she was collecting information for our enemies. That emerged at the trial of a Dutchman named Cornelius Quelp, after he was arrested as a secret agent of the French. He had acted as her postman. But, as you would expect, all mention of what really went on at the Club was suppressed. Money talks and at the trial it was simply described as a gaming house.'

'I feel certain that Charles would never have given

such a woman information that might be damaging to his country; so, if she has a hold over him, it cannot be anything of that kind.'

Droopy shrugged. 'Who can say? He was then quite young and inexperienced. He may have done so in all innocence and only realised his folly later.'

After a moment Roger asked, 'What of this woman, Maureen Luggala. Did you know her?'

'Not well, but I met her on occasions at large gatherings.'

'What thought you of her?'

'She was passable good-looking and had a well-rounded figure. She was a somewhat vapid creature, and I imagine not difficult to persuade to let one share her bed, for she was always ogling the men—though in fairness I must say I never heard her name coupled with one.'

'You term her vapid, and Georgina described her as stupid, and self-centred; yet, however wrapped up in her own affairs she may be, I find it difficult to credit that during all those weeks she remained entirely oblivious of the fact that the two girls had begun to dabble in witchcraft.'

'They would naturally have taken every precaution to hide it from her, and it may be her shallow mind was entirely occupied by some other interest—a lover perhaps.'

Roger frowned. 'Your suggestion gives me food for thought. You have implied that she sought to attract our sex, yet she was clearly careful of her reputation. As a widow and only a little over forty who apparently craved satisfaction, does it not strike you that she was the type of woman who might have been a member of the Hell Fire Club. Masked she could have preserved her incognito, and her good figure would have made her acceptable.'

'If you are right, that would explain many things.'

'Indeed it would. The reason for her leaving England would have been to follow the O'Brien woman to Dublin, and there continue the association. She, not her daughter, may be at the root of the trouble. If she is a Satanist herself, she would have initiated the two girls, and her letter to Georgina be a pack of lies designed to keep Susan in Ireland by alleging that she has disappeared.'

'And when young Charles arrived, having been a previous member of the club he decided to throw in his lot with those people instead of bringing Susan home.'

'That could well be, since he has long been in love with Susan. Under this evil woman's influence she could have tempted him and, rather than lose her, he elected to remain.'

Over supper the two friends speculated further, but neither could produce any other theory, so they turned to Napoleon's defeat and abdication, while polishing off the best part of two bottles of Château Lafitte, followed by old port wine. These liberal potations ensured Roger a good night's sleep. But in the morning, instead of going to the Bristol coach station, he walked across St. James's Park to Birdcage Walk.

It was in a house there that, when he had first become a secret agent, he had made his reports to a Mr. Gilbert Maxwell. Later he had dealt direct with Mr. Pitt and a succession of Ministers of Foreign Affairs; but he had often had occasion to collect documents and money from a Mr. Desmond Knight, who had succeeded Maxwell, and he now sent up his name to him.

Mr. Knight was a tall, thin, greyhaired man. He received Roger courteously, then asked in what way he could be of service to him.

'It is a private matter,' Roger smiled, 'but, knowing you as well as I do, I feel sure you will not refuse me your help. I am anxious to learn all you can tell me about a man named Cornelius Quelp : a Dutchman who was tried and convicted some months ago as a secret agent in the pay of the French.'

Mr. Knight returned his smile. 'Mr. Brook, we have many secrets here, but none from a man so intimately acquainted with such affairs as yourself. Mynheer Quelp was sentenced to three years hard labour and is now quarrying stone on Dartmoor. What do you wish to know about him?'

'I understand that he acted as courier for a woman named Katie O'Brien, who collected information for our enemies. She lived in a house out at Islington. No doubt you know what went on there?'

'Yes; she was known as the Irish Witch, and ran a Satanic circle, called the New Hell Fire Club. Unfortunately, before her connection with Quelp emerged at his trial, she got away to Ireland.'

'So I gather. But why was she not arrested by our authorities there?'

'Because we could trace her only as far as Dublin. From there she disappeared.'

'I am told she is possibly there now, running another Satanic circle.'

'If she is it must be under another name, otherwise we should have learned of it.'

'Did you perchance secure a list of the members of the Hell Fire Club?'

'Yes, although by no means a complete one. The members went to considerable pains to conceal their identities. They put on masks before entering the house. But discreet enquiries among the coachmen of the nobility gave us the

N

names of some thirty-odd people who had been driven there at night and not returned until the early hours of the morning. Some, too, visited the house fairly frequently in daylight.'

'Was Lady Luggala among them?'

'Yes. She, I recall, was one of the regular visitors.'

Roger's guess had been right. He smiled grimly, then said, 'Mr. Knight, reverting to espionage. It will naturally have occurred to you that the woman O'Brien must have obtained much of the information she passed on to our enemies from the members of her club. Were many of them prosecuted on that account?'

The Secret Service chief shook his head. 'No, Mr. Brook. The majority of them, I am sure, were entirely ignorant of that side of the woman's activities, and anything she received from others would have been by word of mouth. There were a few that we suspected, but we had not a tittle of evidence against them.'

'Was Lady Luggala among those you suspected?'

'Yes, for a variety of reasons. She was one of the witch's most frequent visitors. They were both Irish and she was living beyond her means. Our undercover man at Coutt's traced several drafts on the O'Brien's account made payable to Lady Luggala.'

'She is now living in Dublin and I am about to proceed there. I have reason to believe that, given your help, I could secure the evidence needed to convict her and, perhaps, others.'

'Indeed! Well, the war, thank God, is over; but all the same if there are grounds for believing that she gave information to an enemy agent, she should certainly be brought to trial. What help do you need?'

'Authority to enter her house, to search it, to question

her servants and, if my suspicions are correct, to arrest her.'

Mr. Knight hesitated. 'Mr. Brook, as you are not an official agent of the Crown, you are asking a lot, particularly the right to take her into custody.'

'If, having got the evidence we need I am not empowered to do so, before I can get a warrant from a magistrate she will have the chance to disappear, as the other woman has done. You know enough about me to be sure that I should not abuse such powers as you may give me.'

'True, true, Mr. Brook. I am sure you would not. In the intimate circle in which we move, you are become almost a legendary figure. I recall that there have even been times when you have been given *Lettres de Marque* to speak on behalf of Prime Ministers. Unorthodox as your request is, it would be unreasonable in me not to grant it.'

As he spoke Mr. Knight tinkled a bell on his desk. A secretary came in and, a quarter of an hour later, Roger left the house with the papers he had asked for in his pocket.

He lunched at White's, wrote a brief, loving note to Georgina, just to let her know he had stumbled upon one lead that he hoped would facilitate his search for Susan and Charles; then, having said good-bye to Droopy, he took the night coach to Bristol.

Next morning, having booked himself a cabin at the ferry office, he had a clerk there produce the register of passengers who had taken tickets to cross during the last week in March and found that Charles had sailed on the 25th.

Satisfied that no accident had befallen Charles before leaving England, he went aboard and ordered champagne and dry biscuits; having found from long experience that sipping the one and nibbling the other gave the best hope that the queasiness from which he always suffered when at sea would not become actually sickness.

On landing in Dublin he hired a coach and told the driver to take him in turn to the best hostelries in the city. The second at which they halted was the Crown and Shamrock. His inquiry produced the information that the Earl of St. Ermins had arrived there on March 26th and stayed two nights, then departed leaving no address. He had not been seen there since.

Having taken a room, unpacked and had a meal, Roger went out and bought himself a cheap, ready-made trouser suit of brown cloth, a cloak of Irish homespun, a pair of heavy boots and a top hat made of shiny, black waterproof material. Taking his purchases back to the Crown and Shamrock, he changed into them, scruffed the boots and battered the hat a little, then slipped down the back stairs and into the stable yard.

By then it was growing dark. Out in the street, after enquiring of a passer-by, he soon found his way to Merrion Square, in which Lady Luggala had her house. On finding the number he was greatly relieved to see chinks of light coming from between the drawn curtains of a room on the first floor, which implied that she was at home, but no sounds suggesting that an entertainment was in progress. There were also lights in the basement.

From what Mr. Knight had told him, it was quite certain that Maureen Luggala was intimate with Katie O'Brien, and he felt convinced that she could tell him where to find the witch. With her, he had little doubt, were Susan and Charles. There was also good reason to believe that Maureen had furnished information to the spy Quelp; but he had no proof of that. He had a warrant for her arrest in his pocket, but he could not use it. By confronting her, as he meant to do, he was taking a great gamble. If she called his bluff, gone would be the only lead he had to tracing and rescuing from the devil's clutches the two young people he loved.

24

Blackmail

ROGER walked down the area steps and pulled the bell chain. A few minutes later the door was opened by a footman in a striped waistcoat and shirt sleeves.

In a gruff voice Roger said to him, 'I am one of the Viceroy's police agents from up at the castle. Are all the servants in?'

'Yes,' replied the man, with a scared look. 'It is having our bite of supper we are.'

Having judged the time of his call carefully, that was what Roger had hoped for, and he said, 'Good. Take me to them and I'll see you all together.'

The footman led him down a smelly passage, past the open door of a kitchen and into a room beyond it at the back of the house. Only one other man and three females were seated at a table, confirming Mr. Knight's statement that Lady Luggala was by no means well off, or she would have had a bigger staff. It transpired that the footman also acted as butler; the other man, an uncouth-looking lout, did the chores, the eldest woman was the cook, a pretty girl in her twenties combined the duties of lady's maid and housemaid, and a teenaged drab did the scubbing.

The three senior servants all had lilting Irish accents, the other two could speak only Erse. It was from the footman and the lady's maid that Roger got the information he wanted, and without their even asking to see his papers, as his manner of speaking told them that he was English, and his having said he came from the castle filled them with awe.

They confirmed that Lady Luggala and Jemima had arrived from England with Susan in mid-February. In mid-March all three had left Dublin in a hired coach, as her ladyship did not keep one of her own, but she had not said where they were going. Two days later Lady Luggala had returned alone. Then, one afternoon toward the end of March, a young English milord had called and spent over two hours with her ladyship. Two evenings later she had entertained both the young lord and a tall, lean priest to dinner. After the meal the priest and the young lord had driven off together in the priest's coach, but the servants had no idea where. Since then they had not seen either of the young ladies nor the English milord, and her ladyship had had no other guests to stay.

Roger then asked if any of them knew a woman named Katie O'Brien and, if so, when they had last seen her.

All of them shook their heads, with the exception of the middle-aged cook, who had been in Lady Luggala's service much longer than the others. She replied that in the old days, before her ladyship went to live in London, she had a friend of that name, who came frequently to see her; but since her return they had neither seen nor heard anything of Mrs. O'Brien.

Convinced that he could learn no more from them, Roger enquired if her ladyship was alone upstairs. When they said that she was, he bade the footman put on his jacket and take him up to her. But, before leaving the room, as a precaution against the cook having lied and perhaps leaving as soon as his back was turned, to warn the witch that Lady Luggala was being questioned by the police, he said sternly :

'All of you will remain here until I come downstairs. If any of you leave the house you will be charged with aiding and abetting a very serious crime.'

They could not know it to be an empty threat, and cowed into silence they resumed their supper of potatoes, bread and pickles.

Upstairs, outside the door of the drawing room, the footman asked whom he should announce, but Roger ignored him, pushed him aside, walked into the room and shut the door behind him.

Maureen Luggala was lying on a *chaise longue*, wearing a negligée and reading a French paper-back novel. At Roger's entrance she dropped the book, stared up in surprise and demanded :

'Who . . . who are you?'

Roger made a leg and replied with deceptive courtesy. 'May it please Your Ladyship, I am a government agent from London, and it is my duty to question you on a very serious matter.'

'I . . . I don't understand,' she faltered.

'The name Katie O'Brien will not be unknown to Your Ladyship?'

'I . . . yes. I knew her when I lived in Dublin some years ago.'

'And more recently when you both lived in London.'

Maureen Luggala came to her feet, pulled her negligée round her and said angrily, 'With whom I am acquainted has nothing to do with you, and I have committed no crime to be questioned in this manner.'

'My superiors are of a different opinion, milady,' Roger smiled a little grimly. 'A regular visitor to Mrs. O'Brien's house in Islington was a Dutchman, named Cornelius

Quelp. You, too, were a regular visitor, and you met him there.'

The blood drained from Maureen's face, so that the patches of rouge on her cheeks stood out and she pressed one hand over her wildly beating heart.

'Quelp was arrested as an enemy agent, tried, convicted and is now in prison,' Roger went on inexorably. 'We have recently come upon evidence, milady, that you supplied him with information to the detriment of the safety of the realm.'

'I . . . no,' she gasped. 'I told him nothing of importance. Perhaps I talked foolishly, but I had no idea that he was an enemy agent.'

Roger had no evidence, but his bluff had succeeded. 'Quelp will testify that you did know,' he declared harshly. 'And your assertion that the information was of no importance is untrue. Otherwise you would not have been paid for it, as you were through Coutts Bank by Mrs. O'Brien.'

His stricken victim collapsed on to the *chaise longue* and covered her face with her hands. Then after a moment she withdrew them and panted, ''Tis not true. The money was not for that. I am far from rich and was taking a daughter out in fashionable London society. Katie O'Brien is the girl's god-mother, and she helped to finance me.'

Drawing a paper from his pocket, Roger told her sternly, 'At your trial you will have the opportunity of trying to persuade the jury of your innocence, but I'd wager big odds on it that you will fail. And I have here a warrant for your arrest.'

'No!' Her voice quavered and tears began to run down her cheeks. 'No, please! I've done no real harm. I'm certain of it. And the war is over. I'd be ruined, ruined!'

'That would be only justice, since you have been responsible for the ruin of others,' Roger snapped. Then, abandoning his rôle of a government official, he sat down in an armchair, crossed his legs and went on in a quieter tone, 'And now we will talk of that. I am wearing these clothes only because they are better suited for questioning your servants than my usual attire, which might have made them doubt my being a police agent.'

She looked up quickly, with new hope in her pale blue eyes. 'Then you are not ... All this ...'

'Oh, yes I am,' he asserted quickly. 'I will show you the papers I carry if you wish. But I have assumed the rôle only temporarily. Although we have never met, my name is not unknown to you. It is Roger Brook.'

She stared at him aghast. 'Then ... then you are Susan's father.'

He nodded. 'And god-father to the Earl of St. Ermins. My primary purpose in coming here is to find out what has become of them. I am convinced that you know and could take me to them.'

'No!' she shook her head violently. 'I cannot. I've no idea where they are. The two girls left me against my wish. And I've not seen the young Earl since I left London.'

'You are lying, woman. That was the story you told the Duchess of Kew in your letter to her, but I know the truth. I had it out of your servants before I came up here. The girls left this house with you in mid-March in a hired coach, and St. Ermins also left here with, presumably, a friend of yours—a priest—on the 29th of that month.'

She shuddered. 'I know! I know! It was stupid of me not to realise that you would have found out. But I can't take you to them, I can't!'

'You can, and you will,' snarled Roger.

'I dare not. They are with the O'Brien woman, of course. You must have guessed that. If I betrayed the place where she is, she'd put a curse on me.'

'I'll take care of her. You have only to take me to the place where she has gone to earth, and leave the rest to me.'

'I won't! I'd rather die! She knows my weakness. She'd render me incapable of ever pleasuring a man again.'

Roger stood up, grasped her by the wrist, pulled her to her feet and shook her. 'I, too, have that power. If the witch remains in ignorance of who led me to her you'll have naught to fear from her, and I'll tear up this warrant I have for your arrest. Refuse, and I'll execute it. You'll sleep tonight in one of the dungeons below Dublin Castle. Then you'll be tried and condemned to penal servitude. When you have served a year or two with the female scum of the city, such looks as you have will have been replaced by lacklustre eyes, scrofolous grey hair and the wrinkled face of an old crone. Maybe you will catch typhus and die in prison. If you do come out alive, you'll have to haunt the lowest taverns to find even a drunken dock rat who'll be bemused enough to sleep with you.'

'You awful man,' she whimpered. 'How can you threaten a woman like me with such a terrible fate? Have you no pity?'

'None,' he retorted, shaking her again. 'None for lecherous bitches of your ilk who corrupt young people, and trade them to a priestess of the Devil in return for opportunities to gratify your lust. Come now! Make up your mind. Do you give me the information I require, or do I send you to live on skilly and stitch mail bags for a term of years? The choice is yours.'

Falling back on the couch, she sobbed, 'I . . . I'll do as

you demand. But it is already night, and the place is far from here—thirty miles at the least.'

'In that case we'll need a coach, and had best postpone our journey until tomorrow. But foster no illusion that you will succeed in playing me any tricks. I propose to hold you *incommunicado* for the night. Now show me the way to your bedroom.'

Stifling her sobs, she led the way from the room and upstairs to the second floor. Her bedroom was at the back of the house. Roger walked over to one of the windows and looked down. Below, in the semi-darkness, he could make out a small, paved garden. Satisfied that there was no way down to it and that the window was much too high for her to risk a drop, he recrossed the room to the door, removed the key from the inside and transferred it to the outside. Then he said to her :

'For tonight you must dispense with the services of your maid, as I have no intention of giving you the chance to smuggle out a letter or message. I am about to lock you in here, and I shall give the servants orders that if you ring your bell they are not to answer it. Moreover, I do not mean to leave the house. I'll doss down in one of your spare bedrooms. You are to be up and dressed in travelling clothes by eight o'clock. I will by then have made arrangements for our journey.'

As she stared at him in silent dismay, she was not a pretty sight. Her eyelash black had run and her cheeks looked raddled. She had clearly gone to pieces, and he felt confident that she would give him no trouble. But he was taking no chances; so, having locked her door behind him and put the key in his pocket, he went down to the basement to deal with the servants.

They were still sitting round the table talking in low voices in Erse. As he entered the room they fell silent and looked up at him apprehensively. He gave them a smile and said pleasantly :

'I have questioned her ladyship and I am now satisfied that none of you is involved in the serious crime of which she is accused. Providing that you obey my orders, you have nothing to fear.' Taking the paper from his pocket he handed it to the footman and went on, 'As proof of my authority, here is the warrant for her ladyship's arrest.'

The man took it, stared at it a moment, then murmuring, 'It's no great one at the readin' I am,' he passed it to the lady's maid, who slowly read it aloud before handing it back to Roger.

'Now,' he said. 'Had I arrived here earlier I should have taken her ladyship to the Castle for the night. As things are, it will be more convenient for her to remain here locked in her bedroom. If she rings her bell, none of you is to answer it. In the morning you,' he pointed to the cook, 'will prepare two breakfast trays by seven o'clock. You,' he pointed to the maid, 'will take one up and leave it outside her ladyship's door and put the other in the dining room for me. Tomorrow I have to take her ladyship some thirty miles into the country to confront a confederate. You,' he pointed at the footman, 'will go out and secure for me a two-horse coach from a livery stables, with a coachman prepared to drive that distance. It is to be here, in front of the house, at eight o'clock.'

He produced a guinea from his waistcoat pocket, gave it to the cook and said, 'In the depths of the country it may not be possible for us to get a decent midday meal, so when you have finished cooking breakfast I wish you to go out and get some things for me. At one of the better hostelries nearby you should be able to buy a ready-cooked chicken or duck, with some slices of ham and a cake or some pastries, also two bottles of red wine. We'll need butter and bread as well. Pack them all into a basket, with plates and cutlery, so that they are ready for me when we set off. There should be a few shillings change. You may keep them for your trouble.'

Delighted at such a windfall, she smilingly bobbed him her thanks as he added, 'You may now all stay up or go to bed as you wish. But none of you is to leave the house before tomorrow morning.'

From the beginning he had thought it most unlikely that any of this group of servants would have the temerity to challenge his authority; now, having shown them the warrant he felt confident that none of them would sneak out in the night to inform the police that a stranger had come to the house, browbeaten them and locked their mistress in her bedroom.

Going up to the second floor he found the room opposite Maureen Luggala's to be another bedroom. The bed was not made up, but folded blankets and sheets lay beneath the coverlet. Well satisfied with his evening's work, but still desperately worried about Susan and Charles, he partially undressed, made the bed and, still wearing his underclothes, settled down for the night.

In the morning he woke early, but remained in bed until his turnip watch told him that it was half-past six. That he was unable to shave or do his hair annoyed him, but he was able to wash as an ewer of water stood in a basin in one corner of the room. By the time he had dressed it was seven o'clock and, on going out onto the landing, he saw that a breakfast tray had been set down outside Maureen's door. Unlocking it, he pushed the tray inside and called out to her, 'Here is your breakfast. We start in an hour's time. Be ready by then. I dislike being kept waiting.'

Downstairs in the dining room the pretty maid served him, and he found that the cook had done him well : a fried herring with two poached eggs to follow, and the remains of a cold sirloin on the side-board in case he still felt hungry. But he scarcely noticed what he was eating, because his mind was so occupied by thoughts of his coming encounter with the witch.

A little before eight o'clock he went down to the basement, inspected the picnic basket and had it brought up to the hall, then he went upstairs to fetch Maureen Luggala. She was sitting waiting for him with, he was pleased to see, a cowed look on her face, for he had feared that during the night her terror of the witch could have caused her to change her mind and he might have considerable trouble in making her obey him.

'I have a coach below,' he said. 'Where shall I tell the man to take us?'

'Along the road through County Wicklow, that leads to Tullow,' she replied tonelessly.

'Good. You can tell the servants as we go through the hall that you expect to be back in a few days. In no circumstances are you to mention my name in front of them. Susan stayed here and I do not wish them to connect me with her. I gave them no name, and they know me only as a police agent.'

'How long shall I be away?' she asked anxiously. 'That . . . that is if Katie O'Brien does not keep me with her and enslave me.'

'You need not fear that; for I do not intend that you should even see her. Provided you behave yourself and do as I tell you, you should be home again before very long.'

With a sigh of relief she led the way out of the room. In the hall she spoke a few quick words to her maid. Roger told the coachman the road to take, then handed her into the coach. The footman put the basket on the opposite seat and closed the door. As they drove off Roger smiled to himself. His blackmail had succeeded.

The way lay almost due south and on leaving Dublin they passed through Donnybrook Fair. In view of their anything but friendly relations, for the two of them to have to travel together for a considerable distance created an awkward situation, and for the first few miles they sat side by side in silence. But as they passed Galloping Green, with its solitary inn and smithy, Roger found his speculations about what might have happened to Susan so worrying that, to divert his mind from them, he decided to break the strain, and asked Maureen if she had found life in Dublin dull after having lived for several years in London.

She readily responded that she missed the magnificent spectacles provided by the great entertainments given by London's wealthiest hostesses, but she had many old friends in Dublin and found the quieter social life there very pleasant.

From that point on they exchanged remarks intermittently, and she told him the names of the Anglo-Irish nobles whose mansions lay behind the long, stone walls they passed, and pointed out to him as they approached, features of interest such as Bray Head and the rushing Dargle river. There were stretches of beautiful, bright green grass, on which small flocks of sheep grazed, but no sign of cultivation.

About twelve miles from Dublin the narrow road became more winding as it entered the upward slopes to the Wicklow mountains, with the Sugar Loaf high above the ivy-covered trees on the right. A little further on a track to their left led toward the monastic settlement of Glendalough to which, Maureen said, the religious came from all over Ireland.

From that point onward the slopes became steeper, with deep, wooded valleys made very picturesque by granite boulders lying among the trees which were now showing their young spring leaves of tender green. Climbing all the time at walking pace, they eventually emerged from the trees on to high, flat moorland where heather grew between clumps of gorse. Then came more patches of woodland from which they came out on to another wide stretch of moorland, known as Featherbed Mountain. Maureen told him that Dublin drew a large part of its peat for fires from there.

As they crossed this area for a mile or so, they passed through low cloud, but came out of it to see on their left a deep valley in which lay the lochs Tay and Dan and a river where, here and there, white foam cascaded over clumps of rocks. Half a mile further on Roger noticed two stone pillars, evidently a gateway, but from which the gate had disappeared. The road veered off half right from them.

A moment later Maureen called to the coachman to pull up, then she turned to Roger and pointed to the gateway. 'It is here. There is a steep drive down for over a mile. At the bottom of the valley lies the loch, and near its edge, the castle.'

'What is this place called?' Roger asked.

'Luggala,' she replied. 'The castle was the ancestral home of my late husband's family. He took me to see over it once, shortly after we were married. It is little but a ruin now. Only a few rooms are habitable, but it seemed a good place for Katie to go into hiding, because she was in trouble.'

Roger nodded. 'Yes. I knew about that. And you are

right. In the past two miles we haven't passed even a cottage. I've rarely seen a more desolate piece of country.' Poking his head out of the window, he told the coachman to drive past the gate and on.

'Where are we going,' she asked anxiously.

'To find a suitable spot in which to have our meal. It is just on one o'clock, and we've been on the road for nearly five hours, so I am now hungry.'

Evidently glad that he had not decided to have their meal there in front of the gateway, she did not demur; and they drove on for the best part of two miles, until they came to another wood. There Roger halted the coach, picked up the basket and prepared to get out.

'What are you about to do?' she leaned forward quickly. 'Surely we can eat here in the coach?'

He shook his head. 'No. As it is a fine day I prefer the woods. There will probably be some wild flowers : dwarf daffodils, anemones and kingcups.'

Reluctantly she allowed him to hand her out, and accompanied him about thirty yards along a path into the wood. There, evidently fearing that he intended to avenge himself on her for having given his daughter into the power of the witch, and anxious to remain in sight of the coachman, she halted and said, 'This will serve. I do not wish to go any further.'

'You will do as I tell you,' he said sharply. 'I have promised that I will not harm you or prevent your returning to Dublin. Come now, or as an alternative I'll take you with me to visit Katie O'Brien.'

She shuddered, gasped, 'No! No!,' and hurried after him until he had led her deep into the wood, at least a quarter of a mile from the stony, rutted track which was termed a road.

Sitting down on a grassy bank at one side of a small

clearing, they ate their meal in silence, and shared one bottle of the wine. Roger then stood up, wrapped a chicken thigh and a large piece of cake in paper, put them in one of his capacious pockets and the second bottle of wine in the other. Smiling at her, he said :

'Here, my lady, we part. The odds are that you will have to walk a good part of the way back to Dublin before you can get a lift. Anyway it is as good as certain that you will have to spend tonight out on the moor.'

As she began to protest, he cut her short. 'For iniquities of which you have been guilty I am letting you off very lightly. And should I learn later that you lost your way in the darkness, fell in a ditch and broke your neck, it would not cause me one moment's loss of sleep.'

Turning his back on her he set off at a gentle run to ensure that, should she follow him, he would reach the coach well ahead of her. When he reached it, he said to the coachman :

'The lady who was with me is spending the night with friends who have a house on the far side of the wood. Take me back now to that gateway where the road bends, and set me down there.'

The man gave him a curious glance, but did as he was bade. On leaving the coach Roger told him that he was also staying the night with friends in the neighbourhood, then paid him off, gave him a lavish tip and sent him back to Dublin.

Roger had grudged the time he had given to getting rid of Maureen Luggala; but he had felt it a precaution he dared not neglect because, had he left her the use of the coach, it was possible that, to make her peace with Katie O'Brien, she might have driven to the castle by some other route and warned the witch that he was on his way there. But, as he stood for a moment in the stone gateway, he realised that he had lost nothing, because he had time on his hands. It was barely three o'clock, so there were several hours of daylight yet in which to reconnoitre the place and, impatient as he was to learn what had happened to Susan and whether Charles was there, it would have been stupidly rash to attempt to enter the castle until he had the full cover of night.

The grass-grown drive led steeply down, bordered on both sides by screens of trees : pines, beeches and laurels. Beyond them on the right the ground rose abruptly, but on the left it shelved down to a deep valley, on the far side of which, a mile or more away, rose another greenish hillside speckled with white stone boulders.

As he proceeded, his footfalls made no sound on the bright green grass. No bird was singing and the silence seemed uncanny. The drive snaked down, becoming still steeper after every curve, so that he doubted whether a coach, empty and drawn by fewer than four horses could ever have got up it. After descending for half a mile, between the trunks of the trees on his left he caught his first glimpse of the loch far below in the valley. His eyes alert for any sign of movement, he covered another half mile. That brought him to some thirty feet above the level of the lake, over the edge of which some outward sloping trees projected. Through a gap between their leafy branches he saw a part of the ruined castle. Another few hundred paces brought him to the end of the drive. It emerged into a small, flat, triangular area with trees here and there, bounded on three sides by steep hillsides. On the fourth side lay the long loch and the castle rose from its nearest end.

Keeping well under cover Roger stood looking at it for several minutes, taking in every detail. He decided that either it had been built on a small island, or hundreds of tons of rough stone had been dumped in the lake to form its foundations, for it appeared to be entirely surrounded by water, which served the purpose of a moat. From where he stood the nearest part of the castle was about forty yards from the shore, at the edge of which showed a rim, only about two feet in depth, of what looked liked sand, but might be silt. The main building was very old and the greater part of it had fallen into ruin. One tower still stood, but the much lower jagged edges of others showed where they had broken off. Gaping holes appeared here and there in the battlements, and a wall had collapsed revealing the empty interior of a lofty chamber.

The place showed no sign at all of being inhabited. No wind ruffled the surface of the lake or stirred the branches of the trees. Everything was so utterly still that it was vaguely sinister. As far as Roger could see along the valley there was no other habitation or evidence of life, and the castle could not be seen from the road on the high ground along which he had come in the coach. Surrounded as it was by desolate mountains and moorland, and not having been lived in for many years, even people who knew of its existence would be unlikely to suspect that it was being used as a hide-out; so it would have been next to impossible to find a better one.

Selecting a group of bushes among which he could sit concealed, yet continue to keep an eye on the castle, he settled down to his long wait. The hours dragged by while he remained there speculating fruitlessly on what might happen when he entered the castle. Would he find Susan sane, or driven mad through the hellish domination of the witch? And what of Charles? Would he be there, a willing participant of whatever went on, or was his disappearance due to his death in some unguessable mishap?

At last the shadows began to fall. When they were deep enough Roger made his way cautiously from tree to tree across the flat ground, until he could see the other side of the castle. There, an even greater part of the building had collapsed from age. A whole section had fallen outward, so that hundreds of slabs of the granite with which it had been built now formed a rocky causeway, slanting down from a height of about forty feet at the castle end until only odd corners of its last stones projected out of the shallow water about twenty feet from the shore.

At one side, the high pyramid of stones at the castle end ran down to partly cover a landing place, to which a rowing boat was moored. Beyond the boat rose a high, arched doorway, and the light was still good enough for Roger to see that it was iron-bound and solid, so there was little hope of his being able to force it.

Seeking some other means of entrance, he moved further along the shore. Just beyond the peak of the great pile of fallen stones, the building took a different form, due to a wing that had evidently been added many centuries later. The part that Roger could see consisted only of a single, flat-roofed storey about thirty-five feet above the water. There were two diamond-paned windows in it, suggesting the late seventeenth century. One of them was a little open. Although he could not see round the corner, he guessed that this new wing continued on there, as all the rooms would then have a lovely view right down the lake, and this must be the part of the castle still occupied. Yet, as with the derelict ruin, there was no sign of life, and the sinister silence remained unbroken.

Choosing another spot where he could watch without being seen, he again sat down, took out his leg of chicken and bottle of wine and slowly ate his supper. By the time he had finished full darkness had fallen, but he had no intention of attempting to enter the castle until the inmates could be expected to be asleep.

At about eight o'clock the two windows became dimly lit, and a form only vaguely seen through the diamond panes drew curtains across them. Chinks of faint light continued to show between the curtains; then, about an hour later, the windows became dark again. Judging by the time, Roger assumed the windows gave on to the dining room, and that the witch and her companions had just finished their evening meal, so would soon be going to bed. Nevertheless, to be on the safe side, he gave them another two hours before standing up, stretching himself and making sure that the pistol he had thrust into his belt was properly primed.

By then the moon had come up, but it was on the far side of the castle, so the side opposite him was still in deep shadow. Advancing toward the lake, he cautiously took a few steps into the water, in case what he had taken to be sand proved to be treacherous boggy mud, but the bottom was firm and the water shallow. He was barely knee deep in it when he reached the nearest stones of the rough causeway.

From there on he clambered up from block to block, on his hands and knees because many of the big stones were covered with moss and provided only a precarious foothold. It took him a quarter of an hour to get to the top; but once there, by leaning sideways he was near enough to the partly open window to get a grip on the sill.

Balancing carefully on his slippery perch, he stretched out a hand to the window, and pulled it back. Grasping the sill he gave a spring, dangled by both hands for a moment, then hauled himself up and landed on his chest with his head inside the room. Next moment he swore violently under his breath. The butt of the pistol had

struck the underledge of the stone sill, and been knocked
out of his belt. He heard it clatter as it bounced from rock
to rock below. Two-thirds of his body still hung dangerous-
ly out of the window. One false move and he would have
a very nasty fall, breaking some bones if not his neck.
First things first. He gave a swift wriggle and flung his
arms forward. It brought him half-way through the
window, and he was safe.

Only then did his mind turn fully to the seriousness of
his loss. Dare he go further, now that he was unarmed?
Could he retrieve his pistol? No, that was next to impossible. If he dropped back, he would almost certainly fail
to land safely and go rolling down the great heap of
rugged stones. Besides, even given the luck to escape that,
what hope would he have of finding the pistol in the dark?

Grimly he realised that he dared not risk a drop. He had
no option now but to go forward. Two thoughts swiftly
followed to console him a little. At least the pistol had
not roused the inmates of the castle by going off, and in old
castles skilfully arranged groups of weapons nearly always
decorated the walls. From one of them he might arm himself with a sword, mace or dagger.

Even when he pushed aside the curtain, no glimmer
of light penetrated the diamond panes of the window as
the moonlight did not shine on that side of the castle. The
room was in complete darkness, and he could not get any
idea of its size. Stretching out his hands, he felt the floor,
then pulled his legs through the window, squirmed round
and stood up. For a full minute he remained where he was.
No sound broke the stillness except that of his own
breathing. Cautiously he took two steps forward, his hands
stretched out before him. When he was well clear of the
curtains he fished out his tinder box and a piece of candle,
and struck a light. The flame had barely touched the wick

of the candle when there came a rustling sound and a voice said sharply :

'Who is that?'

The voice was that of a girl. As the candle flared, he saw her. Surrounded by dark hair her face was a white blob. She was sitting up in an iron bedstead and the light gleamed on the brass knobs at its foot. Again she cried, 'Who are you? What are you doing here?'

'Be quiet!' Roger said quickly. 'I mean you no harm. But if you rouse the house, I'll shoot you.'

As he spoke he walked forward so that he could see her better. At the same time he got an impression of the room. It was large and lofty and furnished only with a table on which was a mirror, a hanging cupboard, a round-lidded trunk and a single chair. Evidently it had not formerly been a bedroom, but had been turned into a temporary one.

Since he was holding the candle she could see him better than he could see her. Suddenly she exclaimed, 'I know you now! You are Susan's father, Mr. Brook.'

'I am,' he replied, 'and you are Miss Jemima Luggala.'

She nodded, gave a heavy sigh, then whispered, 'Thank God you've come! Susan and I were in despair. We'd given up all hope of being rescued from the witch.'

Roger looked at her in surprise, walked forward, lit another candle that stood beside her bed and said with a frown, 'I was under the impression that you and Susan had left your mother against her will, to come and live here with Katie O'Brien.'

'So that's what she told you?' Jemima's dark eyes flashed with anger. 'It is a lie. I've no reason to love my mother, Mr. Brook. She is mean, greedy and a nymphomaniac. Not being well off, she has always grudged the money for my keep and clothes, so she had no scruples about getting rid of me, and was glad of the chance to make a bargain with the witch. Have you ever heard of the New Hell Fire Club?'

'I have. Your mother used to frequent it when she lived in London and, I have reason to suppose, participated in the orgies that took place there.'

'She did. Katie O'Brien told me so. But when my mother left England she was deprived of that outlet for her lusts. That is why she followed the witch to Ireland. Katie had to go into hiding here, but that does not prevent her from still casting spells. They made a foul compact. By her magic arts Katie would provide my mother with a succession of lovers, and in return Susan and I were sold to the witch.'

'Oh, come!' Roger protested. 'You and Susan are not children, but fully grown women. You cannot expect me to believe that both of you allowed your mother to hand you over to anyone against your wills.'

Jemima stared angrily at him. 'Mr. Brook, I wonder that any man can be so dense. Naturally, we should have refused to go had we had the chance. My mother put a drug into the hot milk we always drink before going to bed at night. When we regained our senses, we were in bed in this castle and as it is surrounded by water we could not attempt to get away.'

'So that is the way it was,' said Roger thoughtfully. 'And what of Charles St. Ermins? Was he drugged and brought here, too?'

'My Lord St. Ermins!' Jemima looked surprised. 'No, why should he have been? What has he to do with this?'

'He came to Dublin some three weeks ago to search for Susan and take her home; but disappeared two days later.'

'I know naught of that. I thought him to be still in Spain.'

Roger was greatly puzzled. From all he had heard of Jemima, he had thought it probable that she was in part at least responsible for Susan's having fallen into Katie O'Brien's clutches. Georgina had said that the girl had both dominated her mother and achieved a great influence over Susan. Yet her account of her mother's bargain with the witch was highly plausible, because it was so in keeping with what he had learnt of Maureen Luggala's character. But what could have happened to Charles? That had become an even deeper mystery. Maureen had neither the brains nor the ability to put him out of the way; so, if he was not here, where could he possibly have got to? Another mystery was, if the girls had not become sister witches of the O'Brien's, why was she keeping them here? Of what value were they to her? After a moment he said :

'You maintain that your mother virtually sold you and Susan to Katie O'Brien, and that you are prisoners. What good can it do her to hold two young girls captive?'

Jemima gave him a slightly pitying look. 'It is evident, Mr. Brook, that you have little knowledge of Satanism. For the most important of all occult ceremonies by which great power can be obtained, the use of the body of a virgin is essential.' Suddenly, in a rush of words she burst out, 'It is this we are both dreading so terribly. That's why I was so overjoyed when I recognised you tonight and realised that you had come to rescue Susan. You'll take me with you too, won't you? Please! Please! I implore you to.'

The pleading look on the girl's face was so earnest that Roger felt much he had heard or assumed about her must be wrong. It was quite possible that she had been maligned and trapped. It dawned upon him then that there was a way in which he could put her to the test, and he asked :

'Where is Susan?'

'In another temporarily furnished room like this, also on this floor but on the other side of the castle.'

'Could you take me to her?'

'Yes. No-one will be about at this hour, and she is not locked in. Katie is confident that both of us are too frightened of the curse she would put upon us if we tried to escape.'

'Very well, then. Take me to Susan. If I can get her out, I'll take you too.'

'Oh, thanks be to God!' Jemima gasped. 'May He forever bless you!' Slipping out of bed she swiftly put on a chamber robe, picked up her candlestick and walked quickly to the door. Roger blew out the candle he was holding, nipped the wick and followed her out into a gloomy passage.

With Jemima leading, shielding the flame of her candle from the draught with one hand, they walked on tiptoe down a long corridor. Roger followed a few paces behind her, with every sense alert. The girl's plea for protection, and apparent anxiety to escape from the witch had impressed him. Yet he was worried by doubts about the wisdom of having accepted her as an ally, although she must be aware that if she led him into a trap she would be the first victim of it, for he had only to leap forward to strike her down. Again he felt bitter regret at having lost his pistol, but he now had no choice other than to trust her and, if she did betray him, he could at least fell her with a blow on the back of the neck from which she would not easily recover.

At the end of the corridor they entered a large, lofty hall. By the light of the single candle Roger could not see the walls, but he was aware that a gallery ran round it and in passing he glimpsed a few pieces of heavy furniture.

At the far end of the hall they entered another passage. On that side of the castle, shafts of full moonlight came through the tall windows, but they were so begrimed with the dirt of ages that it was impossible to see out of them. Nevertheless, Roger could see enough to realise that this part of the building was in almost total ruin. As they advanced, holes showed in the roof, a bat flitted by, the undrawn curtains hung beside the windows in moth-eaten rags. Here and there great festoons of cobwebs hung from the ceiling and swayed gently in the draught they made in passing.

They turned into another corridor and then another. No sound reached them but that of the sudden scuttling of a rat. Yet Roger remained uneasy, still fearful that Jemima might be leading him into a trap. Why, he wondered, should her bedroom be where it was, while Susan's was so far from it, in the ruined part of the castle? The silence was eerie, the whole atmosphere of the place fraught with evil.

Another bat sailed by. Roger started back. Jemima turned and smiled at him. About fifteen feet further on she suddenly took two quick paces forward, threw up her free hand and pressed it against an iron flambeau holder on the wall, then gave a sardonic laugh.

Without a second's warning, the floor beneath Roger gave way. His feet slid from under him. He fell backward on to a steep, sloping ramp. Instinctively he threw out both his hands sideways, to stop himself from sliding further. They met only flat, cold stone. There was nothing he could cling to. Smoothly, his weight carried him down, down, down, down into the stygian darkness.

25

Render unto Satan

TIME, it is said, is an illusion. Without doubt, as assessed by the human mind, it can differ immensely, according to circumstances. The last hour of an afternoon class at school, on a subject at which one is bad, under a master one hates, can seem endless; whereas a long evening spent together by two people who are in love flashes by so rapidly that it seems over almost before it has begun. As Roger slid down the shute on his back, his descent seemed interminable to him, and thoughts sped through his brain with the speed of lightning.

He must have been mad to trust Jemima. He had let her send him to his death. After all he had heard of her, how could he possibly have been such a fool as to be taken in by her clever acting? Never, never should he have followed her blindly, unless he had had a loaded pistol to hold against her back. Perhaps it would have been excusable to let her lead him fifty or sixty feet, but once they left the comparatively modern wing of the castle he should have been warned. If both girls had been prisoners of the witch, why should they not have been quartered together, or at least in rooms near each other? When walking down those long passages, inhabited by flitting bats and scurrying rats, where dim moonlight showed the webs of a thousand generations of spiders hanging from ceilings and

walls, even a schoolboy would have realised that his guide
was not taking him to Susan's room.

Frantically he thrust out his hands and elbows, endeavouring to check his swift descent, for he had no doubt at
all that death awaited him at the bottom of the slope.
During the years he had visited many ancient castles in
France, Spain, Russia, Sweden and other countries, and
in several of them he had been shown traps similar to this.
They were called *oubliettes*. In mediaeval times many an
unsuspecting guest had been led by a host, who had some
secret reason for wanting to get rid of him, along a dim
corridor until the host pressed a spring on the wall, and
a trapdoor in the floor flapped open. The wretched guest
fell through it, hurtled down a hundred feet or more and,
a few minutes later, was choking out his life in the blackness of an underground cistern fed with water from the
castle moat.

Roger heard the trapdoor above him slam, cutting
him off for ever from light and life. Even if he could have
checked his downward slide and turned over, the slope
was too steep for him to have crawled up it and attempted
to force open the trap. There was no escape. Except, yes.
It was just possible that the *oubliette* ended in a waterway
tunnel, large enough to swim through, to the lake. But if
that were so, how long was the tunnel? How deep was the
water in it? Would there be enough space between the
water and the ceiling for him to breathe while swimming?
If not, it was certain that he would drown.

These lightning flashes of thought and terror probably followed one another in less than a minute. Without
warning, the angle at which he was sliding suddenly
changed. The slope abruptly ceased, his feet shot forward
and he came to rest flat on his back on a solid floor. His
relief was instantaneous. It was not an *oubliette*. Yet it

might be. Perhaps only a foot or so ahead of him there was a perpendicular drop, and by luck he was now lying on a broad ledge, the speed of his descent not having been sufficient to carry him over the edge.

His speculation lasted only seconds. There came the sound of quick movement ahead of him, then a voice cried sharply:

'Who is that?'

Again relief flooded through him, acompanied by surprise, concern and the answer to one of the riddles he had been puzzling over for several days past.

'Charles!' he exclaimed. 'So they've made you a prisoner. And now I'm one, too.'

'Uncle Roger!' cried the voice out of the darkness. 'How in the world. . . . But stay still a moment while I make a light.'

There came the scraping of a tinder box, a sudden glow, then the rising flame from a candle wick enabled Roger to get an idea of his surroundings. They were in a circular dungeon about twenty feet in diameter. From some six feet up the walls tapered in a cone, but the light was not sufficient for Roger to see where they met the roof. Opposite the shute down which he had come there were ranged four low platforms, about six feet long by three feet wide, on short, square legs. On one of them was a straw-filled palliasse and some blankets, where Charles had been sleeping; on another a pile of books, three candlesticks and a number of loose candles. On a third were a tin basin, soap, towels and two wooden platters with fish bones and a cut cake on them. Beside the last stood a six-gallon stone jar and, between it and the place where he was now sitting up, there was a round hole in the floor which evidently served as a latrine.

As Roger was looking round, Charles said, 'I supposed

you to be still in France with Talleyrand. How come you to be here? And who led you into this trap?'

Roger's reply needed only a few quick sentences, then he asked, 'But you, Charles? What happened to you in Dublin? Did you trace Susan to this place and then got caught? Is she here? Is she all right?'

'Yes, she's here and, as far as I know, well. At least she was a little over a fortnight ago. I have not seen her, but we spoke together.'

'Is it true that the O'Brien woman persuaded her and Jemima to become witches? 'Twas that Lady Luggala wrote to your mother.'

'I know. But 'tis not true—at least as far as Susan is concerned. Jemima, I'd wager, has long been a witch, although Susan did not know it. She suspected nothing until she was brought face to face with Katie. She recognised her at once after having seen her at the New Hell Fire Club. She was taken there over a year ago by . . .'

'I am aware of that,' Roger interrupted. 'Your mother repeated to me all you had told her of it. Tell me what you know of the sequence of events in Dublin.'

'After I left for Spain, that bitch Jemima laid herself out to win Susan's confidence and affection. In February, for some reason of which I am in ignorance, Maureen Luggala left London for Dublin, taking Jemima with her. As Jemima and Susan were such close friends, she was also invited to come over for a fortnight's visit, and she accepted. She had a pleasurable time doing the social round, and her first letters to my mother, asking to be allowed to stay on for a while, were genuine. Then, when my mother insisted on her returning, she told Maureen that she must. The following night they put a drug in her drink and, while she was unconscious, brought her here. Soon after she came to, Katie came to the room in which

o

they had put her to bed, and mesmerised her. It must have been then, while under the occult influence of the witch, that she wrote the letter defying my mother and saying she intended to remain in Ireland with Jemima through the summer. When she came out of her trance Katie told her that if she made no trouble she would be well treated, but must remain locked in her room. Naturally, my poor beloved was distraught. But what could she do? Her clothes had been taken from her, and even had they not how could she escape from this place, surrounded as it is by water?'

'And what of yourself?' Roger asked. 'I traced you to the Crown and Shamrock and learned that you had been there for two nights, also that you had called on Maureen Luggala, although she swore she had not seen you. After that I could get no further, and could only suppose that, reverting to your membership of the Hell Fire Club, you had perhaps been persuaded by Susan to join their witches coven.'

'No! No!' Charles shook his head. 'As you discovered, I waited on Maureen the first day I was in Dublin. She pretended great distress and told me the same story she had written to my mother. But she said she had been endeavouring to trace the girls, and that did I give her another day or two, she had hopes of succeeding. Obviously she needed the time to let Katie know that I had arrived in Dublin and make arrangements for my reception here. The third day of my stay she sent a message, bidding me to dinner. On arriving at her home I found her there with a repulsive priest named Father Damien. It was he who acted as Abbot at the Hell Fire Club in London. He told me that Katie had done him an evil, and he had quarrelled with her; so he was agreeable to take me that night to the place where she had the girls. It was a trap to get me here.

We made the journey by coach, arriving in the early hours of the morning. The boat was moored by the lake shore. As we got into it he told me he had bribed one of the servants to let us into the castle. When we reached the great door, he rapped a special signal on it, and it was opened by a huge negro named Aboe, who was another of Katie's assistants when she ran the Hell Fire Club.

'At that moment Father Damien seized my arms from behind. As you see, I was in uniform, so was wearing a sword and I had come with a pistol in my sash. Aboe deprived me of them both, then the two of them hustled me up a stone staircase to the newer part of the building, along a corridor, pushed me into a bedroom and locked me in. As soon as they had gone, I attempted to break out, but the door was too stout. Then I tried the windows but found that they were thirty feet above a ledge of rock lapped by the water. Had I dropped down I would certainly have killed myself.'

'Why then, since they had you securely imprisoned, did they transfer you to this dungeon?'

'Because I attempted to rescue Susan. You must have realised how deadly quiet it is here. On my third night in the bedroom, just as I was about to fall asleep, I caught the sound of sobs behind my bedhead. From the beginning I had been convinced that Susan was no witch, and had been brought here against her will, so it flashed upon me that it was probably she who was crying, and that as I could hear the sobs the wall between the rooms must be quite thin.

'Pushing away the bed, I went to work on the wall at once with the stout prong in the buckle of my belt. The wall proved to be only lath and plaster. After an hour's strenuous work I'd made a hole the size of a crown piece. It was Susan on the other side. Having heard my scraping, she had pushed aside her bed and was listening there, so replied immediately I spoke. That was how I learned all that had befallen her, and now I had found her I at once started to plan a way in which we might both escape.

'In addition to Father Damien and the negro, Aboe, who I gather acts as cook, Katie has two Irish peasants here. They are burly, wild-looking creatures, with beards and great mops of red hair, who speak no English. I call them Gog and Magog. One or other of them brought my meals and, as Susan was also locked in, hers also. We planned that she should be dressed ready to leave at the hour when our supper was brought to us the following evening. I'd hoped to overcome the man, get his keys and release her and that both of us might escape before anyone else in the castle knew what was adoing.

'But fortune was against me. I lurked behind the door until Gog came with my supper, and as he walked in carrying the tray I brought a milking stool that was in the room down on his head. It felled him, but I opine the thickness of his hair saved him from being completely deprived of his wits. He was in bad shape, though, and having got my hands round his throat I could have choked him into insensibility.

'Alas, I had not counted on there being two supper trays. Magog had brought up Susan's. Hearing his fellow barbarian shout, he dropped his tray outside Susan's door, dashed into my room and hurled himself on top of me. Gog recovered sufficiently to roll from under us and I stood no chance against the two of them. In no time they had me lashed to the end of my bed, and locked in again. I was monstrous lucky to get off with no worse than a kick in the ribs and a black eye.'

Roger nodded. 'You were. And it was a gallant, even if

ill-fated, attempt. What happened then?'

'A quarter of an hour later the two brutes returned, accompanied by Father Damien. They untied me, hustled me along from that end of the castle to this, and pushed me down the shute by which you arrived.'

'And what has happened since?'

Charles pointed up to where the cone-shaped walls of the cell seemed to meet above in the shadows. 'The shute is not the only entrance to the dungeon. Up there, immediately above us, is a round manhole. From time to time one or other of them opens it. By a stout rope with a hook on the end, they lowered this palliasse for me to sleep on, the big jar that contains water, and the other things you see here. And every morning they let down in a bag enough cold food to keep me in provender for the day.'

'And even books,' Roger commented. 'That, at least, is considerate of them.'

'Jemima sent them down, and from time to time comes to talk with me.'

'That little she-devil fooled me completely, and I still cannot make her out, nor the witch's interest in the two girls. The story Jemima spun to me was that for the acquisition of supreme occult powers, the use of a virgin's body was necessary. She then begged me to rescue her as well as Susan from this horror, yet tricked and made a prisoner of me.'

'She did so because she is devoted to Katie, and has naught to fear. Of that I am convinced.'

'What, though, of Susan?' Roger asked anxiously. 'Clearly she is no disciple of the witch. Why should they have drugged and brought her here? Virgins are plentiful enough in this country, where the Church of Rome is dominant. They could, with ease, kidnap some peasant wench upon whom to perform their abominable ceremony.'

Charles shook his head sadly. 'Uncle Roger, I have been obtuse, and failed to make the situation clear to you. Doubtless these Satanists do, from time to time, perform a Black Mass; but 'twas not for that they invited my sweet Susan to Ireland, then drugged and imprisoned her. She was only the lure to get me here.'

'What the devil mean you?'

'Jemima is determined that I should take her for my wife.'

'This is news indeed!' Roger exclaimed with a frown. 'Have you been having an affair with her? But, no; how could you, seeing you have been so long abroad.'

'I was to some extent embroiled with her before I voyaged to Spain. During the summer and winter before last I saw much of her. She is attractive, witty and a passionate young creature. Susan and I had always had an understanding that we would marry in good time; but, until we were ready to do so, we should amuse ourselves by flirting with anyone who took our fancy. I've never loved anyone but Susan and never shall. To me Jemima was no more than a gay companion. I studiously refrained from giving her any reason to believe that my intentions toward her were serious. But she set herself to get me if she could, even to the point of endeavouring to seduce me —a trap into which I was not foolish enough to fall.

'When I sailed for Spain, I thought no more of her, but evidently she did of me and, with her mother and the witch, made her plans accordingly. That Katie has occult power I have no doubt. Foreseeing the fall of Napoleon and that shortly after that I should return, they all came to Ireland . . .'

'It was for quite a different reason that the O'Brien

woman left London,' Roger interrupted. 'But no matter. Continue.'

Charles shrugged. 'However that may be, it was on my account that Susan was invited to Dublin. In mid-March the witch must have learned from overlooking me that I was on my way back to England, so the time had come to spring their plot. When Susan had overstayed her visit, they forcibly detained her and brought her here. Meanwhile, Maureen Luggala had written her tissue of lies to my mother about the two girls having joined the witch's coven; knowing, of course, that directly I learned of it I would come over and attempt to get Susan back. I did, and fell into their clutches.'

Roger nodded. '"Twas a devilish clever scheme, and I'm not surprised that it succeeded. So this jade is now determined to keep you a prisoner until you agree to wed her. To have gone to such lengths, she must be nigh desperate with love for you.'

'Maybe she is. At least she finds me physically attractive. But that is not her only motive. She is also mightily ambitious and would fain be the Countess of St. Ermins. Still further, she wants money, and part of the price of my freedom would be a marriage settlement in which I make over to her my eighty thousand acre estate around White Knights Park.'

'The wench is no fool, then,' Roger gave a bitter laugh. 'She has the sense to realise that, having forced you into wedding her does not bind you to share your life with her. But for some such settlement you could have cast her off without even paying her a pittance. By these means she will net a great fortune.'

'Nay. She says she would keep the house and a sufficient income to maintain it. But 'tis her intent to sell by far the greater part of the estate and use the money to help the rebellious Irish who wish to free their country from British rule.'

'That fits with what I learned in London of her mother and the O'Brien woman. By rights, both of them should have been arrested, condemned as traitors and now be in prison. They were acting as French agents and collecting information of value to our enemies.'

'Indeed!' Charles exclaimed. 'I had no idea of that, but since my converse with Jemima this past week or so I'm not surprised to hear it. She makes it no secret that she is rabid on this question of freeing Ireland, and would stop at nothing to help achieve it.'

'Then let us hope she over-reaches herself and ends up in gaol. Fortunately, these fanatics are only a small minority, but they cause us a mint of trouble.'

'I judge you wrong there, Uncle Roger, in believing them to be only a small minority. I do not believe Jemima lied to me on that. The ordinary Irish are a backward people, and live greatly in the past. Although my Lord Essex's conquest dates back to Queen Elizabeth's time, and Cromwell's brutalities took place near two hundred years ago, the Irish think of them as having occurred only yesterday. Besides, as she argued, I think with justification, the Irish are just as much a different race from the English as are the Norwegians or Danes, and . . .'

'And so, for that matter, are the Scots, yet they have become willing subjects of the Crown.'

'Ah, but their case was very different. Our union with them came about by a Scottish king ascending the English throne. Here we occupy a land to which we have no right but conquest. To be fair, in this matter we must regard Jemima as a patriot.'

'There is much in what you say about Ireland,' Roger conceded. 'So one cannot hold it against Jemima that she wishes to have her countrymen rule themselves. But it has naught to do with the matter that immediately concerns us. Do you intend to give in to her?'

'I fear I'll have to in the end. So far I have hedged, hoping that some turn of fortune might occur which would enable me to escape, make my way to Dublin and swiftly return with troops to free Susan. Your sudden appearance here was the type of miracle I have been praying for; but, alas, it has proved abortive.'

'When your mother realises that I, too, have disappeared, I doubt not that she will come to Dublin, see the Viceroy and have him order the military to search for us. She will also have Maureen Luggala questioned. As the result of my talk with her she believes herself liable to be arrested and imprisoned, so it is most probable that, hoping to save herself, she will tell your mother where we are.'

Charles's eyes brightened for a moment, then he said dubiously, 'But is it likely she will arrive in time? Some days must yet elapse before she becomes sufficiently concerned about receiving no letter from you to decide to act, and then she'll have to make the journey from London to Dublin.'

'True. We can hardly expect her in less than ten days. But does that matter? You have been down here a fortnight, and if they had intended to starve you into submission they would have attempted that already. To have to remain cooped up here in this uncomfortable hole for two or three weeks is plaguey annoying, but we must be as patient as we can until Georgina comes to our rescue.'

'But you don't understand,' Charles burst out. 'Or perhaps I failed to tell you. There is a deadline, a time limit beyond which I dare not procrastinate. The hour Jemima would have me wed her has already been fixed by she.

'Tis midnight on the 30th—that is May Day Eve, or
Walpurgisnacht as some call it. 'Tis one of the four great
Satanic feasts of the year, and that is obviously why Katie
O'Brien chose it.'

'I see no reason why you should not refuse to marry her
that night more than on any other.'

'But, Uncle Roger, unless help does come I must! I
must, because of Susan.'

As Roger's mind grasped an awful possibility, he asked
in an appalled whisper. 'You don't mean ... ?'

'I do.' Charles nodded miserably. 'After I'd been in-
carcerated here a week, the witch came to the manhole up
there and, as I'd proved stubborn, gave me an ultimatum.
On the night of the 30th, whatever happens they mean
to celebrate a Black Mass. She would like it to form part
of my marriage ceremony, with me taking the priest's
place for the final act of copulating with Jemima on the
altar. But if I refuse, it will be Susan on the altar, being
deflowered by that filthy priest.'

'Oh, God, how frightful!' Roger groaned, burying his
face in his hands.

'It won't come to that,' Charles strove to reassure him.
'I made up my mind days ago that the chances of my
being rescued were almost non-existent, so I'd have to
marry Jemima when the time comes.'

Roger looked up. 'We still have a fortnight. Two of us
having now disappeared, there is a strong likelihood of
Georgina coming over and demanding the Viceroy's help
to find us before the end of the month.'

'That's true, and gives me a more realistic hope to
cling to than I had before your coming. But, Uncle Roger,
you're looking terribly fatigued. Had you not best now
try to get some sleep?'

'You're right,' Roger agreed. Firmly refusing Charles's

offer of the palliasse, he rolled up his cloak for a pillow and lay down on the fourth wooden platform, which had nothing on it, then Charles blew out the candle.

Both of them lay long awake, so when they did drop off they slept late, and were aroused by a shaft of light from the ceiling, penetrating the stygian blackness of the dungeon. In the manhole above, the negro Aboe's head appeared and, having called down to them, he lowered a rope with a hook on the end, to which a bag was attached.

Before going to sleep Roger had pondered the possibility of making a base of the four wooden sleeping platforms, standing on it then, if Charles stood on his shoulders, the manhole might be reached and lifted. But he now saw that the manhole was a good twenty-five feet from the floor, so could not possibly be got at in that way. To have seized the rope and climbed up it was equally impracticable for, as soon as his head came within striking distance, the negro would hit him. The shute he already knew to be too smooth and steep for them to wriggle up, so he now resigned himself to the fact that there was no way in which they could break out.

Charles lit the candle, removed the supply of fresh food from the bag and put his debris from the previous day in it. He also attached on the hook the six-gallon water jar. It was hauled up and a full jar let down, then a palliasse and blankets for Roger were lowered, after which the rope was withdrawn and the manhole closed.

They used part of the water to wash in, then poured it down the hole that served as a latrine; but they had no means of shaving. During the past fortnight Charles had grown an inch-long, dark beard and, not having shaved now for two days, Roger's chin was covered in stubble.

After eating, they passed the morning exchanging accounts of Napoleon's overthrow and Wellington's final triumphant campaign. In the afternoon the manhole was again lifted, and the witch's head appeared above it. She had come to take a look at her new captive, and to ask him how he had learned the whereabouts of her hiding place.

As Roger considered Maureen Luggala criminally responsible for having lured Susan to Ireland, then abducting her, he had no scruples in telling the witch how he had blackmailed Maureen into bringing him out there. Katie then urged him to persuade Charles to agree to marry Jemima without further argument and, as an inducement, promised to use her powers to ensure their marriage being a happy one.

When she withdrew her head, Jemima's took its place. She gaily twitted Roger on having outwitted him, and said she thought him a gallant fellow for having attempted singlehanded to rescue his daughter. She went on to say that she was genuinely fond of Susan, that Susan would soon get over losing Charles to her, and that when they were married and she had become mistress of White Knights Park, he and Susan would always be most welcome guests there.

The prisoners whiled away the rest of the day reading and chatting, then slept again. Charles had been so distraught about Susan when his attempt to get her away had failed that he was uncertain of the actual date upon which he had been thrown down into the dungeon. Roger, however, knew that he had arrived on April 16th, so they made a calendar on which to tick off the days.

Those that followed varied little from the first after Roger had joined Charles, except that the witch did not come to the manhole again, and Jemima only did so now and then, having found that Charles continued to be unresponsive to her blandishments. The food sent down to them was plain and consisted only of such items as could be procured locally, but it was reasonably good and Charles said that Jemima had apologised for there being only water to drink, but the cellars of the Castle were empty and they could not send anyone in to Dublin to buy wine. Rats, feasting on such food as they left, troubled them at times, but did not attack them. Their prison was ventilated only by the hole in the floor. Although chilly, it was not uncomfortably cold and, from time to time, they warmed themselves up by flailing their arms or doing exercises.

A simple calculation showed it to be most unlikely that Georgina would be sufficiently disturbed to come to Ireland before the 23rd. So, for their first week together Roger and Charles settled down philosophically to pass the time as well as they could.

But after the 23rd they both admitted that they had been subconsciously counting on Georgina arriving with troops to rescue them and, from then on, they found themselves constantly listening for sounds of strife above. As books could no longer hold their attention, Roger suggested that they should try to make a set of chessmen out of such oddments as they could gather together, and Charles promptly produced adequate, if unusual materials.

Reaching under one of the wooden forms, he pulled out a handful of bones, and said, 'Centuries ago captives for whom the Luggalas had no further use were not, I think, put down the shute but just dropped through the manhole and, poor wretches, left with broken bones to starve to death here. When I was first sent down candles to light this place, I found half a dozen bundles of rags scattered about, and each contained a skeleton. Not liking such company, I gathered them up and pushed them out of sight under these bed platforms, evidently furnished for prisoners of a later date, who were to be fed and kept alive.

It took them several hours to sort out from among the remains of the long-dead prisoners enough teeth, back-bone discs, knuckle, toe and other suitable bones to repre-sent the pieces of a chess set, and make the equivalent of a board. This they did, with alternate squares of printed and plain paper torn from some of the old books that Jemima had sent down. But when they had done, con-centrating on moves of these macabre relics of mediaeval brutality did take their minds off their anxieties for con-siderable periods.

Nevertheless, there were times, and particularly at night, while they were trying to get to sleep, when they could not rid themselves of their speculation about a future that looked black with menace. Inexorably the days wore on. With the passing of each there was a stronger possi-bility that Georgina, worried out of her wits by the dis-appearance of the two of them, would come to Ireland. As a Duchess and a famous society beauty, she would have no difficulty in obtaining the Viceroy's assistance in her search for them. Police agents would make enquiries at hostelries and livery stables, and troops be sent out to scour the country for many miles round. Maureen Lug-gala would be interrogated and, if at first she stubbornly refused to reveal the place where Charles and Roger were, although Georgina had no means of threatening her she was very rich and, as Maureen was very poorly off, Geor-gina should be able to buy the information.

Every morning the two prisoners woke, hoping that this would be the day when either the negro, with a musket at his back, would lead the rescuers to the manhole, or they would hear searchers of the ruin up in the corridor above shouting their names. Yet each night brought more bitter disappointment.

At length the long-dreaded last day of April came. Soon after their food for the day had been lowered to them the face of the witch appeared at the manhole and she called down to Charles:

'How does my young lordling feel upon his wedding morn? If need be I can have him dragged to the altar, but I hope that will not be necessary. What answer am I to take to Jemima?'

As Charles remained silent, she went on, 'Come now, be sensible. For this past month she has scarce been able to contain her itch for you, and as pretty a baggage as you could find in all Dublin she is. Ah, and well tutored in all lascivious arts by myself. Play your part willingly in to-night's ceremony and you will experience such pleasure in her arms as will drive from your mind all thought of that sulky wench, Susan. But do you continue to defy me I'll have to force you into marrying her by a red-hot iron applied to your arse. 'Tis dearly I'll make you suffer for it afterwards too. I'll have Aboe make a eunuch of you. I'll not stop either at inflicting only physical pain. Since this passion for Susan you have, you shall see her stripped, whipped, then violated in turn by Father Damien, Aboe and my two Irish morons.'

Roger closed his eyes and clenched his fists until his nails bit into the palms of his hands. Charles looked up and gulped out. 'If . . . if I agree, will you free Susan and Mr. Brook, without harming them?'

'It is me they would have harmed if they could,' replied the witch, 'but for Jemima's sake I'll forgo the punishment I intended to inflict on them. That you should put the past behind you and co-operate willingly, instead of being forced to it, means a great deal to her.'

'Do you swear to God that you will keep your promise?'

'Yes, I swear to God they shall remain unharmed and be freed.'

'Very well, then,' Charles sighed. 'Tonight I will do all that you require of me.'

The witch gave a pleased laugh and closed the manhole.

Charles and Roger sat down side by side and, for some minutes, remained silent, then the latter said, 'Participation in this Black Mass tonight will prove a revolting business for you. But try all the time to bear in mind that you have been forced to it in order to save Susan from appalling degradation and that, like a betrayal that has been extracted from you by torture, it will not be held against your spiritual integrity.'

'You are right in that,' Charles conceded miserably. 'But it means that I'll have lost Susan for ever.'

'Not necessarily. When this is over, no-one can force you to continue living with Jemima. And if Susan truly loves you, as I believe she does, she would agree to become your mistress.'

'I think she would, but I'd not ask it of her. Did we live together openly she would be ostracised by society, and a hole-in-the-corner affair would be a poor outlook for us both. She would not feel free to marry another, and we would be unable to share a home. But there are still many hours to go. My mother may yet arrive in time to save us. I intend to spend the day in prayer that may come about.'

'God grant, then, that your prayers may be answered,' Roger replied quietly. He refrained from adding that, although he believed that at times prayers are answered, they seldom were, as he well knew from the tens of thousands of men who had prayed that they might live through

Napoleon's battles, yet had died on the field or been frozen to death in the snows of Russia during the terrible retreat from Moscow.

Hour after hour crept by. Charles spent a great part of them on his knees. Roger sat silent, racking his wits for some means by which, when they were brought up from the dungeon, they might trick their enemies; but he thought in vain.

At last the long day was past. Charles refused to eat anything, but Roger, as had long been his habit when about to face a crisis, fortified himself with a good meal then lay down to doze during such time as remained to them.

He was roused by the sound of the manhole being opened, and Aboe lowering the rope from the hook of which now dangled a stout leather belt. The big negro then called down that one of them should buckle it round him, lest he lose his grip on the rope while climbing up.

Without consulting Charles Roger buckled on the belt and, hand over hand, hauled himself up the thick rope. His only hope now was that, as he come up through the hole, he would be able to get his hands round Aboe's throat. But he could not let go of the rope until he was through the hole, and the negro had taken a precaution against being attacked. The moment Roger's head emerged through the hole, Aboe slipped a noose of cord over it and jerked it tight round his neck. Half strangled, he was pulled out and immediately seized by Gog and Magog, who bound first his hands securely behind his back, then his ankles with the ends of a yard-long cord; so that he could walk, but could not kick out or run. Five minutes later Charles, having been rendered incapable of resistance in a similar manner, stood beside him.

Without a word their captors marched them through

the cobweb-hung passages to the great hall. It was now lit by a number of candles, and the witch was there with Father Damien. She was clad in a mauve robe on which the signs of the Zodiac were embroidered in gold thread. It was the first time Roger had seen her face to face, and he conceded that the account of her beauty, given him by Charles, had not been exaggerated. The priest was wearing his mitre and a gorgeously-coloured cope, which swung open as he moved, revealing his genitals.

Charles's hands were untied, and he was told to sit at a table upon which lay a parchment. As he took up the document and read it through, Aboe stood over him with a long, sharp knife.

The document declared his intention to receive instruction with a view to becoming a Roman Catholic, that he was about to be married to Miss Jemima Luggala by the ritual of that Church and that any children of the marriage should be brought up in the Roman faith. It continued to state that in no circumstances would he take any steps in an attempt to invalidate the marriage or live apart from his wife, unless it was her wish that he should do so. In a final clause, he made over to her his estate, White Knights Park, unreservedly, with the right to sell the whole or any part of it for her sole benefit.

It was a formidable commitment, but Charles knew that receiving instruction in the Roman faith did not commit him to changing his religion, and that if he chose he could make life so unpleasant for Jemima that she would be glad to leave him; so, without argument, he signed the undertaking.

The witch looked at Roger and said, 'Mr. Brook, it was as an uninvited guest that you came here but since you are with us I feel sure you would not object to witnessing Lord St. Ermins' signature; and, later, now that we are all friends, if you agreed to give the bride away a pleasant gesture it would be.'

Roger had read the document over Charles's shoulder and realised that, apart from marrying Jemima and making over White Knights Park to her, nothing in it could compel Charles to act towards her as an agreeable husband. He said therefore that he would both sign as a witness and give away the bride. His hands were untied, and he signed with a smile, as he had been quick to realise that the more complaisant he appeared to be towards these people, the better chance he would have of turning the tables on them should the opportunity arise.

The whole party then proceeded along further passages and down a flight of stone steps to a large and lofty chamber, the floor of which was only a few feet above the surface of the lake. The outer wall of the room had collapsed, and Roger realised that it must be the big room he had seen from the end of the drive when making his first reconnaissance of the castle. He now saw by the moonlight that it was a chapel, at one end of which, raised on two steps, there was an altar consisting of a low, rough-hewn, smooth-topped slab of stone.

Jemima was standing near it. She was wearing a dress reminiscent of those worn in ancient Egypt. Her skirt was of white lawn, only knee length and heavily pleated. Her legs were bare, and she had golden sandals on her feet. Fichus of lawn fell gracefully from her shoulders to her waist, but only partially covered her breasts; between them, on a necklace of turquoises set in gold, hung a *crux-ansata*. Framing her pale face her dark hair fell in ringlets to her shoulders; it was crowned by a circlet of gold, from the front of which rose a cat's head.

On seeing the diadem Charles recalled that Katie O'Brien was a priestess of the Egyptian cat-god Bast.

Roger, more cynically, thought how convenient the short skirt would be for the final act of the ceremony.

On the altar stood a blood-red, crooked cross. Father Damien genuflected before it, then turned round to face the others who had lined up in front of him. The hands of Charles and Roger were now free, but their ankles were still joined by cords that prevented them from moving swiftly. They also still had cords round their necks. Gog stood behind Charles and Magog behind Roger, ready to seize the ends of the cords at the first sign that the prisoners meant to make trouble.

Father Damien proceeded to intone the marriage service according to the Roman Church. Roger knew enough Latin to realise that, despite the bizarre surroundings, there was no deviation from it which could later enable Charles or himself to state on oath that the couple had not been properly married. At the right moment the witch, who was standing beside Jemima, reached behind the girl's back, touched Charles on the elbow and pressed a wedding ring into his hand. He put it on Jemima's finger and they both made the proper responses. Father Damien then gave them the orthodox blessing.

Even now Roger was still contemplating making a desperate effort to break up the ceremony, but the moment he took one short step sideways, Magog grabbed the cord round his neck and pulled it taut. He resigned himself then to witnessing the consummation of the marriage, which was to take place before them on the altar slab.

But that was not yet to be. The witch kissed Jemima, then drew her aside and said to the others, 'We have yet to celebrate a second Mass to propitiate the great Bast and the master of us all, Prince Lucifer, Son of the Morning.'

At a sign from her, Gog and Magog jerked down the

cords about Charles's and Roger's necks. As they put up their hands to prevent themselves from being throttled, the two peasants tied the ends of the cords to those attached to their captives' ankles. Both struggled wildly for a moment, but with their heads strained back, effective resistance was impossible. Their arms were seized and their hands once more bound behind them. They were then dragged a few feet from the altar and forced down on their knees. In that position the slackening of the cords down their backs enabled them to breathe freely again, but they could not come to their feet without choking themselves.

Footsteps at the far end of the chapel caught their attention and caused them to look in that direction. Three figures had emerged from a doorway down there, and could be clearly seen in the bright moonlight : a man, a girl and a lamb. The man was Aboe. With his right hand he held the girl by the elbow, in his left hand he held a lead attached to a collar round the neck of the lamb. The girl was sheathed in the long, white robe of a conventional bride and had a wreath of orange blossom on her head. Since she was veiled Roger and Charles could not see her features distinctly at that distance, but they knew she must be Susan.

As she approached she could not have helped seeing them, but she showed no sign of having done so. Her steps were even and her head held high. Roger concluded that she had been either drugged or mesmerised. Charles's face expressed shocked horror when he realised what was about to happen. Susan was about to be laid on the altar so that a Black Mass could be held upon her body. The priest would rape her. The lamb was to be sacrificed and, when it had been slaughtered, they would all be made to drink its blood. In agonised fury he shouted at the witch :

'You can't do this! You promised that no harm should be done to her! You swore it!'

Katie O'Brien's scarlet lips opened wide in an amused laugh, then she replied, 'You poor fool, you made me swear to God. I do not recognise your God. You should have made me swear to him you call Satan.'

'May you rot in hell!' Charles cried, and tried to get to his feet, but fell back again, choked by the rope around his neck.

Susan had not taken the least notice of the altercation. In front of the altar she halted. Aboe let go her arm and stepped back several paces from her. Father Damien began to recite the Lord's Prayer backwards in Latin. Roger's face was wet with sweat. Charles continued to hurl curses at the witch.

Suddenly Susan erupted from her trance-like stillness. Whipping a dagger from under her full robe, she turned and sprang with lightning swiftness at Jemima. Raising the dagger high, she screamed :

'False friend! Liar! Judas! Betrayer of trust! You've brought your death upon yourself.'

Jemima, her dark eyes starting from her head in sudden terror, was just in time to throw up her hand and grasp Susan's wrist. For a moment they struggled violently. The priest abruptly ceased his blasphemous prayer. Aboe leapt forward, but he had been standing a dozen paces away on the left side of the altar. Katie, to the right of it, was much closer. Springing toward Susan, she made a grab at the hair at the back of the girl's head, but her fingers closed only over the veil. The jerk upon it threw Susan off balance. The two girls fell in a writhing heap on the stone floor.

Aboe threw himself on Susan and dragged her off Jemima, who remained groaning where she lay, the hilt of the dagger protruding from her right breast.

The witch fell to her knees, threw her arms round her daughter, raised her head to her own lap and moaned, 'My darling! How could this have happened? The drug could not have taken effect. How did she get possession of that dagger?'

In a hoarse voice Jemima panted, 'I gave . . . gave it to her. And . . . and I didn't give her the drug.'

'But why, child? Why?' the witch asked in an agonised voice.

'Because . . . because . . .' came the gasping reply. 'That stinking beast, Father Damien. He . . . he has been pestering me for weeks. He came to my room . . . my room three nights ago. I . . . I was sound asleep. He ripped the bedclothes off and . . . and was on me . . . on me before I realised what . . . what was happening. To . . . to be avenged on him I . . . I gave Susan the knife. Told her what to do. Pretend . . . pretend to be drugged then . . . then kill him with it.'

Jemima's eyes closed, her head sagged and those about her realised that she was dead.

Sobbing, the witch came to her feet. For a moment she looked slowly round as though half dazed. Then her glance fell on Susan. Her beautiful face became distorted with rage, and she screamed :

'It is you that killed her! You've killed my beautiful daughter. After you'd been raped during the ceremony, I'd meant to let you go. To throw you out. But not now! Not now. Prince Lucifer would prefer human blood to that of a lamb representing Jesus. After we have offered up your virginity, your throat I'll cut myself.'

Turning her flashing eyes on Aboe, she yelled, 'Throw the bitch on the altar. We've said prayers enough. Hold her down for Father Damien.'

Aboe towered above Susan, holding her arms behind her back. Shifting his grip, he picked her up and threw her face upward on the altar. Father Damien grinned down at her. His mouth was working, and saliva ran from the corners. Screaming, Susan fought with tooth and nail. Her veil and the wreath of orange blossom had fallen off. Her auburn hair was in wild disorder as she jerked up her head and bit Aboe savagely in the arm. He let out a yelp of pain, then called Gog and Magog to his assistance. Gog grabbed her hands and pulled them up above her head. Aboe seized the hem of her skirt and wrenched it back, revealing her body naked up to the navel. Then he and the negro each seized an ankle and pulled her legs apart. Father Damien had moved round to the end of the altar, facing her. Opening wide his cope, he gave a gloating chuckle as he exposed himself to her. Held down though she was her eyes stared up at him, fixed in fear on his enormous genitals.

Charles had shut his eyes and was sobbing. Roger stared aghast at this bestial spectacle, overwhelmed with dismay that he was powerless to prevent its consummation.

Suddenly he became conscious of an unseen presence beside him. Silently, in his mind, the presence spoke and he knew it to be the voice of the Sagamore, Morning Star.

'It was because I foresaw this that I made you my brother.'

Instantly, with all the power of his lungs, Roger yelled, 'The Frog! The Frog! He who is of Water, Earth and Air. The Creator, the beginning of all things! To defeat this Evil I call upon the Power of the Frog.'

Susan ceased screaming. Everyone present became deadly still. They remained rigid, as though a tableau in a waxworks show. For a moment there was utter stillness, and it seemed as though the dust of ages was falling silently upon them. Then there came the sound of lapping water.

The cords that bound Roger and Charles had fallen from them. Roger came to his feet and saw in the moonlight that the waters of the lake were sweeping away from the castle. Gog and Magog saw that, too. Impelled by a primitive, animal instinct to save themselves, they bounded from the altar, leapt down the tumbled stones into the mud and, frantic with terror, raced neck to neck to the shore.

The witch, Father Damien and Aboe remained rooted where they stood. Susan rolled off the altar and, as Charles ran toward her, picked herself up. A moment later they were clasped in each other's arms.

Roger turned and stared out across the lake. A mist, partly obscuring the moonlit vista, had risen upon it. Out of the mist there loomed a gigantic figure. It was a huge frog, at least twenty feet in height, squatting in the water. The great eyes of this monstrous spirit of the frogs were focused on the castle. Its throat pulsated as though blown rhythmically by internal bellows. Its mouth opened wide once, then closed again.

Impelled by a silent signal, the witch and her two companions turned towards it. As though attracted by a magnet they could not resist, they walked with halting footsteps to the open side of the chapel, then staggered down the stones into the mud. Flailing their arms and dragging their legs, the three of them seemed to be fighting desperately against an invisible suction. They began to scream in terror and yell for mercy. But their appeals were of no avail. The last that Roger saw of them through the mist they were being drawn inexorably through knee-high water toward the again open mouth of the giant frog.

Afterwards Roger, Charles and Susan could never clearly remember what had happened to them. The floor of the chapel had begun to sink beneath their feet. Somehow they had got ashore. The crashing of falling stones made them look back, and they saw that the evil ruin was disintegrating. The waters of the lake were seeping back and, after a time they had no means of judging, the last remnants of the castle were submerged beneath them.

So weary that they could no longer think, they trudged for miles until they came upon a roadside bivouac, where a troop of soldiers sent out to search for them had made camp for the night.

Next day they were back in Dublin, and united with Georgina. A week earlier she had come over to find them. The Viceroy had given her all the help he could, but Maureen Luggala had proved useless. On enquiring at her house, it was learned that she had been taken away as a lunatic. Georgina had gone to Dublin's Bedlam, to find her, cursed by the witch, an old and crippled woman, white-haired, her cheeks sagging, and raving mad.

Epilogue

It was again high summer in Britain, the first for many years in which the people had known peace. During the past months soldiers and sailors, many of whom had not seen their families for a decade, had been coming back to homes rich and humble all over England, Scotland, Wales and Ireland.

In every city, town and village there had been rejoicing, and feasts in honour of the returned heroes. The victorious commanders had been handsomely rewarded. Wellington had received a dozen Grand Crosses in Orders of Chivalry, numerous bejewelled Field Marshals' batons, giving him that rank in the armies of the Allies, and had been dowered with many thousands of pounds-worth of presents from the allied sovereigns. Generals and Admirals were made Lords, Knights and Commanders of the Bath, in addition to receiving large sums of money voted them by Parliament.

Roger had received nothing, neither had he expected to; it was reward enough for him that the war was over and no-one would again appeal to him to risk his life on patriotic grounds.

Napoleon had attempted, but failed, to commit suicide; then on April 20th, in the horse-shoe court at Fontainebleau, he had kissed the tricolour and bidden farewell to

the weeping veterans of the Old Guard before setting
out on his journey south. There had been no shouts of
'*Vive l'Empereur*' and, as he approached the Mediterranean, the people openly displayed the hatred they bore
him for having robbed them of husbands, fathers, sons. At
Orange they stoned his coach while he cowered behind
Bertrand. Once out of the city, he changed into an Austrian coat, a Russian cloak and a round hat with a White
Cockade on it. Learning that a mob at Avignon was thirst-
ing for his blood, he made a detour to bypass that city.
Thus, disguised, humiliated and in fear of his life, the
once-mighty Emperor at last reached the coast and was
taken on board a British frigate to his minute kingdom
of Elba.

The Marshals, on the other hand, continued to be
popular heroes. Fat, gouty old Louis XVIII was no fool.
Once safely on the throne of France, he decorated them—
with a few exceptions including the brave Davout, who
had held out in Hamburg to the bitter end—with the
Grand Cross of the Order of St. Louis, confirmed them
in their titles and allowed them to retain their great
estates.

On Roger's return from Ireland, Droopy Ned had persuaded him to go out to Richmond and seek a reconciliation with his wife. He found Mary both sober and con-
trite. She confessed that she was still drinking, but had cut
it down and would give it up altogether if only he would
live permanently at home with her. Recognising that she
would never have given way to this weakness had it not
been for his long absence abroad, he said he would not
dream of depriving her of the joy of wine, but asked that
in future, even when he was away for a few days, as he
meant to be now and then, she should drink only in
moderation.

He had made his proviso about being free to come and go as he wished, because nothing would have induced him to give up an occasional night or two of paradise with Georgina at her studio. Nevertheless he was still very fond of Mary and determined to make her as happy as he could. So, after a few days they settled down to resume the tranquil life they had led for a short while after their return from America.

It was on a morning early in June that Roger mounted his horse to ride to London. He did so with a far from easy mind, as he had been summoned to wait upon the Prime Minister, Lord Liverpool, whom he had met on a number of occasions but did not know well. His disquiet was caused by the belief that the only reason His Lordship could have for sending for him was to ask him to under-take some mission. What it could be now that Europe was at peace he had no idea but, whatever it might be, he was determined to refuse.

When he was shown upstairs at 10 Downing Street, the Prime Minister greeted him pleasantly, waved him to a chair and said :

'Mr. Brook, I understand that your lovely daughter is to marry the young Earl of St. Ermins toward the end of the month.'

Roger smiled. "Tis so, my lord, and both I and St. Ermins's mother, Her Grace of Kew, are most happy about it, for we have been life-long friends and know the young people to have long loved each other dearly.'

Thoughtfully, the Prime Minister remarked, 'I feel it something of a pity, though, that one of the wealthiest nobles in England should be taking a commoner as his bride. 'Twould be so much more suitable if he were about to wed the daughter of an Earl.'

Puzzled and annoyed, Roger frowned. 'I fail to comprehend the point of Your Lordship's remark. Except that I am not descended from a king on the wrong side of the blanket, my mother's family do not take second place to that of St. Ermins. Their ancestry is longer.'

His Lordship laughed. 'You must forgive me my little jest, Mr. Brook. It was with regard to your ancestry that I requested you to call upon me. There are no secrets from one in my position. I am well acquainted with the many services you have rendered Britain over the past quarter of a century. Moreover, not only my Lord Castlereagh and His Grace of Wellington but also His Imperial Majesty the Czar and Talleyrand, have all brought to my attenion the invaluable part you played in helping to bring about a settlement in France which bids fair to ensure peace and prosperity to her people under a limited monarchy.

'As you know, it is a long established custom for secret services to go unrewarded, except for payments of cash. But I felt you were deserving of special consideration, and Talleyrand suggested, in his letter to me, a way in which we could acknowledge our debt to you. With the death of your cousin, the title of your mother's family went into abeyance. But titles can be revived for descendants of a noble family. I have spoken to the Prince Regent about it and His Royal Highness gave his willing consent. Be pleased to come here again, Mr. Brook, at the same hour this day week, suitably robed. Lord Castlereagh and I will then do ourselves the honour to present you in the House of Lords to your fellow Peers as the Right Honourable the Earl of Kildonan.'

If you would like a complete list of Arrow books please send a postcard to
P.O. Box 29, Douglas, Isle of Man, Great Britain.

*Below and on the following page are details of
Arrow Books that will be of interest:*

THE STRANGE STORY OF LINDA LEE

Dennis Wheatley

When Linda boarded the train that would take her to London
and freedom, she was penniless and alone. A polite offer to
help from the stranger in the seat opposite was the last thing
she expected.

Life with Rowley Frobisher was everything she had ever
dreamed of: fast, sophisticated – and expensive. In a few
months the rough country girl had changed beyond recognition.

But then Rowley has a fatal heart attack – and once again
Linda must take desperate action to survive . . .

CURTAIN OF FEAR

Dennis Wheatley

It is 1952 – the height of the Cold War. Political tension in Europe nears breaking point as the Superpowers double and redouble the nuclear stakes.

For Nicholas Novak, a left-wing professor at Birmingham University, the international situation seems a remote and vaguely exciting affair. His politics are born of ideals not harsh reality.

Then Nicholas's cousin, a top nuclear scientist, calmly tells him that he intends to defect. And within hours a quiet week-end dissolves into a nightmare adventure behind the Iron Curtain . . .